The

AUDACITY

of

GOATS

The
AUDACITY
of
GOATS

J. F. RIORDAN

NORTH OF THE TENSION LINE SERIES: BOOK TWO

Library of Congress Cataloging-in-Publication Data On File

Hardcover: 9780825308260
Ebook: 9780825307553
Paperback: 9780825308475

For inquiries about volume orders, please contact:
Beaufort Books
27 West 20th Street, Suite 1102
New York, NY 10011
sales@beaufortbooks.com

Published in the United States by Beaufort Books
www.beaufortbooks.com

Distributed by Midpoint Trade Books
www.midpointtrade.com

Printed in the United States of America

Interior design by Jane Perini
Cover Design by Michael Short

For Hugh and Ethel, who are always in my heart.

Wo zwanzig Teufel sind,
da sind auch hundert Engel.

Where there are twenty devils,
there are also a hundred angels.

—MARTIN LUTHER

PROLOGUE

It was just before dawn on Washington Island. On this fall morning the sudden drop in temperature after last night's cold front had made the air colder than the water. Towering mists enveloped the Island. Amand Ilstadt knew that as the sun rose it would burn away the heavy fog, but for the moment it was difficult to see beyond the edge of his pastures to the road.

Little things like this were of no concern to Amand. He had a farm to run and animals to care for. Amand had grown up on the Island, and this had been his parents' farm, and his grandparents' before that. The rhythms of farming life were deeply embedded. He was not one to bide his time with a second cup of coffee.

First on his list of things to do was to take a look at that wobbly gate on the eastern end of the paddock near the woods. His big Angus cattle had a talent for finding weaknesses in a fence line, and although the fence itself was electric, the gates were mere wood—too easy for his curious and wandering herd to push and break through.

Even though it was still dark, he made his way to the shed

for his tools and then headed out to the paddock wearing a headlamp, miner-style, to light his way. He sang to himself as he crossed the pasture, the rhythmic sound of a passing freighter's foghorn adding to the music.

Amand was a born singer. As a little boy he had sung while he milked the cows, sung as he walked to school, sung himself to sleep at night. Blessed with a rich baritone as an adult, the habit had remained with him, and he sang almost all day long on the farm. His wife always knew where he was by the sound of his voice, the music rising from the pastures, or the barn, or the work shed. Amand's singing had made him something of a local celebrity, and when, occasionally, a tourist commented on the seemingly random sound of singing out in the countryside, locals would just smile and say, with a certain amount of pride, "Oh that's just Amand. He sings all day."

The fog made everything seem alien and disconnected, and even though he knew every blade of grass on his place, Amand was finding it difficult to tell exactly where he was. He knew, though, if he just kept moving he would eventually reach the fence, and then he could make his way along it until he found the gate. Unconsciously, his voice rose as he walked, and soon he was singing lustily. He had just reached the second verse of "The Wreck of the Edmund Fitzgerald" when a sound came out of the fog that stopped his voice and froze his heart. It was the sound of a man screaming in abject terror.

"HEY!" yelled Amand. "Who's there? Where are you?" The scream came again, longer this time, filled with agony, and seemingly straight ahead of him. In a rapid sequence of thoughts, Amand considered what to do. How could he help this man? Should he run to him? Or go for help? No. This was too urgent to delay.

Dropping his tools, he called out, "I'm coming! Hold on! Try to let me know where you are!" As he ran toward the sound, Amand wished he had his gun. And his phone. There was one more bloodcurdling scream. And then there was silence.

Finding the gate, Amand opened it and headed into the woods. Desperately, he called out, searching where he thought the sound had come from, expecting that at any moment he would come upon the bleeding victim—or body. But as much as he called, he heard no answer, and he soon realized that he would have to give up and call for help. Heartsick, visualizing the suffering that could be going on only steps away, he called out words of encouragement, promising to return, and ran back through the fog toward the house.

By the time the emergency vehicles arrived, the sun was starting to rise, and although the fog was still thick, there was at least light. Amand had continued to comb through the woods, calling as he searched. Soon the rescuers were calling and searching, too. As the day broke and the fog lifted, the teams were methodically sectioning off the woods, and covering it foot by foot. The search went on until nearly six o'clock that evening. They never found anyone.

Bill Yahr, the Police Chief, had been briefly tempted to tease Amand that he'd been hearing things. But the look on Amand's face told him that whatever he had heard had not been his imagination.

There was almost no crime on Washington Island, and no animals dangerous to humans. If it had been someone seriously injured, no doubt they would hear about it, and sooner rather than later. No one could hide something like that for long on the Island. More likely, Bill supposed, it was one of the kids playing a joke. But he had to admit to himself, four-thirty in the morning was a strange time for a teenager to be out pulling pranks.

The

AUDACITY

of

GOATS

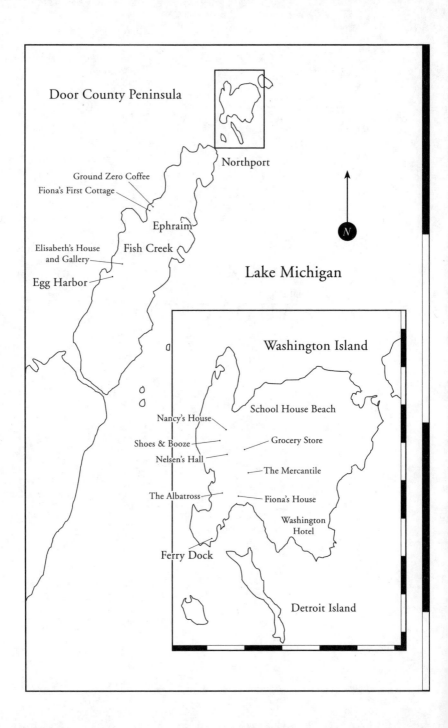

Door County Peninsula

Northport

Ground Zero Coffee
Fiona's First Cottage

Ephraim

Fish Creek

Elisabeth's House
and Gallery

Egg Harbor

Lake Michigan

Washington Island

School House Beach

Nancy's House

Shoes & Booze   Grocery Store

Nelsen's Hall

The Mercantile

The Albatross   Fiona's House

Washington
Hotel

Ferry Dock

Detroit Island

N

Chapter One ✤

A new picket fence and freshly painted wooden sign announced the presence of a new business on Washington Island. This was a rare enough occurrence in these days of ever-shrinking prosperity, but under any circumstances would be the cause of festivities, in which everyone, even skeptics, would join.

"Windsome Farm Goats," the sign said. "Makers of Artisanal Cheese."

The wind blew a series of jaunty blue flags that ranged along the dirt drive to the barn, and, accompanied by her neighbors and a few remaining late-season tourists, Nancy Iverssen followed the flags up the hill. She was not a fan of this kind of thing. She had a new calf to see to, a broken switch on a heat lamp in the barn, and a rooster—whose long history of bad behavior had at last made his presence on the farm dispensable— to butcher. But her loyalty to the island and its welfare overrode her natural impatience. And besides, she was curious.

The faint scent of goat drifted down the driveway. Nancy, accustomed to farm smells, found this, among all the others, the least appealing. It brought with it, however, the pang of recollection of Fiona's goat, Robert. "Water under the bridge," she told herself, brushing away sentiment. Nancy was not one to dwell on things, and she had not been one of Robert's admirers—if he had had any, which she doubted—but she was fond of Fiona, and didn't like to think of her unhappiness.

Standing behind a cloth-covered table near the barn was a woman with blonde curly hair. She was wearing an apron with "Windsome Farm Goats" printed on the front, and she chatted gaily with the small crowd of people standing near. Nancy found herself wondering whether the farm's name was a deliberate play on words or merely bad spelling. It was difficult to tell these days.

"Hi," said the blonde woman. "Hello, everyone, and welcome. I'm Emily. Would you like to try some of our cheese?"

On the table were trays attractively arranged with different varieties of goat cheeses, some crackers, and little pots of fruit preserves for tasting. A cluster of the inevitable fall yellow jackets circled the area, occasionally landing on the food—particularly the fruit preserves—and waiting to sting anyone who dared to challenge their territory.

Emily seemed to be continually speaking. Her voice was not exactly loud, but it had a carrying quality, and she had many opinions. "Oh, yes," she was saying, "we could have started the farm anywhere. Anywhere at all. But my husband and I thought it would be so perfect here, as a tourist attraction and all. We think the Island needs a little sprucing up, too, so we plan to be very active in the community."

She laughed at someone's comment. "Oh, don't worry. Don't worry at all. We have a lot of experience in local government. My husband used to be on the school board at home and he had everyone wrapped around his little finger. And me, well, I know it sounds like a brag, but I've been told so many times that I have natural leadership qualities, and people just like to listen to what I have to say. So, I know we'll be part of everything once we've settled in."

Nancy watched the faces of the people listening. The Islanders looked grim. The tourists were either rapt or indifferent. Someone said something about the cheese and the blonde woman launched into myriad details about butterfat, aging, and milking capacity. Everyone was served samples of cheese on little green paper napkins.

"Where are you from?" asked someone, in a tone of voice that made Nancy suspect he already knew the answer.

"Illinois," said Emily.

The islanders exchanged glances. Illinois tourists were both the bread and the bane of island life. Arrogant, brash, entitled, and always in a hurry, they did little, as a group, to endear themselves. Their wallets, however, generally made up for their other shortcomings. Now here was one come among them. No one from the Island expected anything good to come of it.

Nancy took a sample of cheese, eschewing the yellow-jacket-laden preserves, and, leaving the chatter behind her, walked toward the nearby pasture where three dozen or so goats were grazing. They were small animals with big puppy eyes and an engaging sweetness that, as far as Nancy could see, bore no resemblance to the surly, taciturn nature of Fiona's late animal. The sound of their owner's voice continued unabated, carried on the breeze, although Nancy could no longer distinguish the words. She stood gazing at the animals, a look of barely disguised skepticism on her face, and wondered what Fiona would think of this.

F iona Campbell was giving a party. She was not generally much for parties; they were uncomfortable reminders of an awkward childhood. She was not entirely convinced that her neighbors liked her, her house was really too small to hold a crowd, and the last time she had hosted a party, she had been given—as a sort of hostess gift—a goat whose presence had made her life a misery until a barn fire had terminated their acquaintance. Nevertheless, in a triumph of hope over experience, she sent invitations to everyone she could think of.

"Are you coming to my party?" she asked her friend, Pali, when she ran into him late one fall afternoon at Mann's Mercantile, the only general and hardware store on the Island. They had met at the cash register where Fiona was purchasing batteries and plant food. Pali had an assortment of nails.

"Of course. We wouldn't miss it. Nika is already pulling out recipes for cakes trying to decide what to bring."

"She doesn't have to do that. You don't have to bring anything."

Pali smiled a you're-not-from-around-here smile. "Just let me tell her whether you prefer yellow cake or chocolate. It will make everything a little easier."

Fiona smiled back. She had no illusions about her ability to blend into the culture. "Yellow, please."

"I will pass on that information," he said cheerfully.

They said good-bye, paid for their purchases, and went on about their business.

The reason for the party was an achievement of sorts. Despite all odds, Fiona had spent a year living alone on remote Washington Island—a place she had once described as being inhabited by hermits and crazy people—in an old, rather decrepit house already in the possession of various creatures who chewed and scurried. It had not been one of her better moments when she had accepted a casual dare from friends who had not expected to be taken seriously, but Fiona had set out to prove that she could do it. No one of her acquaintance had expected her to succeed, least of all Fiona herself.

The year had not been without incident, much—if not most—of which were distinctly goat-related. And yet, in a transformation that in other contexts might have been considered almost miraculous, Fiona had come to love the little house, to respect most of her neighbors, and even to have made some friends.

These friendships did not, however, include her immediate neighbor, Stella DesRosiers, whose capacity for malice was a new experience for Fiona. Stella had reappeared on the Island shortly after the barn fire with only the vaguest explanation for her disappearance, murmuring something about a family emergency. No one dared to ask her any questions.

The drive from Mann's to Fiona's house was about three minutes, and she was mentally planning her party to-do list as she pulled into her little driveway. The days were getting shorter, and everything glowed with the rose and gold light of sunset.

She looked at the house with pleasure. It was freshly painted and charming, its old-fashioned yard filled with peony bushes and hostas, hydrangea and lilies of the valley. There was a big maple, and an enormous fruit laden apple tree spreading its ancient branches. Fiona pulled on the hand brake of the car, gathered her purchases, and walked up the steps to the porch, carefully averting her eyes from the back yard.

She didn't want to see that the old barn, which she had so loved, was gone. It had burned to the ground last spring, and she felt struck with fresh grief whenever she saw what was left of its stone foundation. The gift goat, Robert, had been in the barn, and Fiona's grief was, perhaps, intensified by the complexity of her feelings for Robert. He had been a nuisance and a headache; she had resented every moment of time she had spent on his care. And yet she had felt responsible for his well-being, and the mysterious cause of the fire haunted her with guilt.

What had she overlooked? What should she have done differently? Why didn't she hear something in the night when the fire first started? Had she been too distracted by the joys of her new love in those first days? Fiona lay awake most nights with these questions circling her mind like bats. The image of the flames shooting high into the night sky returned to her in her dreams and in her waking. She knew that she should be grateful that the fire had not reached the house. But she could not shake the terrible sense of remorse which haunted her.

Fiona was forced out of her reflections by the exuberant welcome of Elisabeth's German shepherd, Rocco. Fiona's friend, Elisabeth, and her new husband, Roger, were honeymooning in Italy, and Fiona was the dog sitter. Rocco was more than good company. He loved Fiona with a shepherd's passionate devotion, loyalty, and single-minded purpose. Elisabeth was the first and foremost object of his dedication, but Fiona was a very close second.

Reheating herself a cup of coffee and giving Rocco a biscuit, Fiona resolutely turned from thoughts of the fire. Tonight she would not think of it. Tonight she would focus on the future.

Fiona sat at the kitchen table to drink her coffee, and Rocco settled under the table, resting his head on her feet with a deep sigh of satisfaction. With a feeling of pleasurable anticipation, Fiona got out her notebook and began to make a to-do list for the party. She looked forward eagerly to seeing Elisabeth and Roger, who would be returning shortly from their honeymoon. The party would not be complete without them.

L ars Olafsen had been Chairman of the Town of Washington for going on twenty years, and a member of the town board for five years before that. He was a dutiful man, and a public servant in the old-fashioned sense. He had earned the respect of his constituents through his fairness, his honesty, and his innate, steady, Scandinavian calm.

But Lars was beginning to feel the wear of so many years at the beck and call of his fellow islanders, and had begun to yearn for a reprieve. His children and grandchildren lived downstate in Milwaukee, and his wife was continually urging that they spend more time there. And Lars, though he was only in his early seventies, was beginning to feel his energy wane, and his enthusiasm for the job with it.

The major consideration, however, was one he would never admit to anyone, not even to his wife. Although his feelings were complicated, secretly Lars still glowed with a feeling of heady triumph after his out-maneuvering of Stella DesRosiers last spring in her mean-spirited attempt to drive her neighbor, Ms. Fiona Campbell, out of town. He had stooped to political blackmail, no doubt about it, and he had suffered many moments of doubt about what he'd done. Had it been a violation of the public trust that disqualified him for continuing in office, or a valiant stroke for the public good? Lars had struggled with this question, but he always returned to the conclusion that it had been no more than Stella deserved, and an act of natural justice. Stella had been bullying her fellow citizens for years without any repercussions other than her unpopularity. And while he continued to wonder whether it was wrong to feel proud of it, his career, Lars felt sure, could reach no greater achievement. "Might as well go out on a high note," he thought.

And so, one Wednesday night at Nelsen's Hall, when a quorum of his regular circle was in attendance, Lars Olafsen announced his retirement. He was immediately surrounded by a jovial, back-slapping throng, and shots were thrust into his hand in rapid succession.

"Lars," said Paul Miller, his childhood friend, "you can't retire. We're too young."

"You've been an asset to us, Lars," said another old friend.

"You run a tight ship, Lars. Those meetings will take twice as long without you."

But the real concern was the one voiced by Jake, who had a reputation for cutting to the heart of every discussion. "You can't leave. There's nobody who'll take your place."

This was true, as everyone at Nelsen's well knew. Being chairman was a thankless job, and few people wanted to be bothered with it. There was a slew of paperwork and arrogant state officials to be dealt with, not to mention the unceasing need to wrangle volunteers for committees and other public work, and the inevitable squabbles—both petty and potentially fatal. No, particularly in these days of escalating state bureaucracy, you'd have to be a fool to want the job. And the Island was remarkably short of fools, unless, of course, you counted that new woman, Fiona Campbell.

Fiona would have been shocked to know her reputation. Her intelligence, wit, street savvy, and seriousness of purpose were not things shown to good advantage in a small town. Add into the mix her city polish and lack of practical knowledge of rural life—not to mention the evil rumors that Stella DesRosiers had very particularly and intentionally spread—and an average observer might have an impression of a flighty young woman who wore impractical shoes, was oblivious to the first principles of survival and sensible living, and whose morals were, well, not what one would hope.

Fiona was, in fact, far from being a fool, but this didn't stop the locals from thinking her one. Many of them—particularly the men—had come to feel a mixture of pity and admiration for her, a circumstance that Stella's rumors had unwittingly created, and one which frequently worked in Fiona's favor. In this instance, however, Fiona was exactly as oblivious as her neighbors thought, and it may have been just as well. She went about her business utterly unaware of her many critics, observers, and secret admirers.

E mily and Jason Martin, the proprietors of Windsome Farm, were joiners. In a short period of time—and despite their frequent declarations that they were terribly, terribly busy—they had become members of just about every group on the Island. Their presence was met with varying degrees of acceptance. At church there was a certain amount of relief to have some new volunteers to take up the slack, and it was always helpful to have one more chaperone at a school event. But behind their backs the talk was decidedly unenthusiastic. The outspokenness of them both did little to endear them to their neighbors, and they quickly became known as "those new people who think they know everything."

Without hesitation Emily had informed the drama society that they could benefit from her college training in theater arts, and she offered to direct the next play. She told the Ladies Book Society that their reading list was shockingly old-fashioned and that she would help them to make a more modern one, which she proceeded to do, including a bestseller that sounded like a home decorating guide but turned out to be about something many of the ladies found shocking and secretly titillating, but otherwise hadn't much of a plot. Her husband notified the Lions Club that their bookkeeping methods were sure to draw the attention of the I.R.S., and took over the planning for next year's Little League without being asked. At the P.T.O. meetings they were quick to point out that their children's former school had a much better equipped gymnasium, and was further advanced in first grade mathematics.

In their brief few months on the Island their reputation for annoying people became so well known that attendance at various committees and club meetings sky-rocketed, as Islanders showed up just for the sheer fun of seeing what they'd say next.

When Lars Olafsen left Nelsen's Hall after the announcement of his retirement, he was thoroughly steeped in the warmth of his friends. He was also steeped in a good portion of beer, mixed with a fair portion of bitters, and just as fair a portion of Jaegermeister.

Lars had inherited the facility of his Swedish ancestors for turning an evening of drinking into a slow, steady glow, and although he had consumed a great deal, it would have been difficult for anyone to tell. His words were unslurred, his mind clear, his gait unfaltering, and his eyes bright, so he did not think it necessary to have anyone drive him home. Since Lars's friends' judgment was equally steeped in beer, bitters, and Jaegermeister, neither did anyone else. Island culture generally accepted this state of affairs, primarily because the odds of meeting anyone else on the road were rather small.

Lars reached home without incident, and parked his reliable

but elderly SUV on the driveway next to the woods. The Olafsen property was adjacent to Mountain Park, so named for the modest hill that lay, more or less, in the center of the Island. At its crest was a wooden tower that afforded a fine view of the Island to anyone with the stamina to climb. Lars had always thought that it was pleasant to have a park for a neighbor, since it created a buffer zone, almost as if his actual lot lines had been expanded to include the public land.

Accustomed to being alone in the dark in the remote countryside, Lars pocketed his keys and was headed toward the house when a peculiar sound froze him in his tracks. It was as if someone nearby were coughing. At first he felt a moment of fear, but Lars shook it off, laughing at himself. No one was anywhere near. The SUV was overdue for maintenance if the engine were making that kind of post-ignition noise.

It occurred to Lars that he had been taking the effects of overconsumption much too lightly. He shook his head at himself ruefully. He should never have driven home. Next time he would call Katherine. He resumed his path to the house. There it was again. That sound. Standing still, Lars was quite clear in his mind that it was not coming from the SUV. It was coming from the woods. A deer, maybe. Lars took a deep relaxing breath. There were many deer, and they made a chuffing sound, similar, a bit, to this. That's surely what it was.

There it was again, a coughing sound, and a snort, and a sort of chortle. This was no deer. No. He was quite certain: there was someone in the woods. And he was very close.

Lars Olafsen, a man whose Scandinavian calm was legendary on the Island, a man who rarely ran, and had rarely had any reason for doing so, made it into the house in record time. In his haste he slammed the side door and woke his sweet and patient wife from a lovely dream.

It was another thing for Lars to add to his ever-lengthening list of regrets.

Fall on Washington Island had an idyllic quality. The days were at the temperature where an afternoon nap in the hammock required a light blanket, and the nights required a bonfire. The number of tourists—small, in any season—was low, and many of the summer property owners had returned to their lives in The World, a world, presumably, that afforded them the means to own summer homes on a remote island. The roads were nearly deserted, allowing runners and bikers the blessing of solitude and safety among the rich colors of autumn leaves, deep blue sky, and the crisp, cool Island air.

During this quiet time, Tom, the manager of the Island hardware and general store, was away for a brief vacation, and he had left the store's management to one of his teenaged clerks, Gabe. Gabe was a perfectly competent and good-natured young man who took his responsibilities seriously, but occasionally his lack of experience had repercussions.

When a family of tourists stopped in to rent bicycles for the day, Gabe was pleased to see them. It had been a slow day at the store, and customers relieved the boredom. They were a young family: a pretty, brunette woman, her soft-spoken husband, and two round-cheeked boys aged about 5 and 7. They were from Milwaukee, they told Gabe, and had come to spend the day on the Island. Where did he recommend they go?

Gabe had the usual suggestions for them: Mountain Park, the sand dunes, School House Beach, the Stavkirke—a small, hand-built chapel at the end of a wooded path, in the tradition of medieval Nordic stave churches—and, of course, the Albatross. He remembered to fill out the forms correctly, carefully reviewing and checking off the insurance box. He rang up the sale, and he was warm, friendly, and helpful.

Because of Gabe's inexperience, however, it did not occur to him to mention a hazard everyone on the Island took for granted, and which had become so commonplace that the Mercantile had come to advise its customers to avoid a particular route. Gabe's customers, therefore began their ride blissfully unaware of the only peril likely to befall them in this rural paradise: Piggy.

Piggy was a small, ugly dog with a big, ugly temper, and his ability to inflict damage to flesh and property was out of all proportion to his size. Like so many small dogs, he had been cosseted, babied, and permitted to have his way, and this had given him his own sense of entitlement to world domination. His owner, Mrs. Shoesmith, was a nice enough woman, but she had a blind spot where he was concerned, and she remained convinced that her canine infant was misunderstood.

Piggy was legendary on the Island for his attacks on walkers, bikers, other dogs, and even, occasionally, cars. In one particularly memorable incident, he also took the blame for the destruction of the heirloom tablecloth belonging to the Island's other terror: Fiona's neighbor, Stella DesRosiers. In this case, at least, he was wholly innocent, but his reputation had made his guilt a foregone conclusion. Since Stella was generally disliked by Island residents, and Piggy, it was felt, deserved whatever he got, the resulting bitterness and recriminations between Stella and Mrs. Shoesmith had made for months of local entertainment, and promised to hold more in store for the future.

Fiona had been having a delightful day of procrastination. She had a deadline looming for an article on the security of the national energy grid, but the prospect of researching so depressing a topic was not appealing on a crisp, blue-skied autumn day. She had accepted an invitation to lunch with Nika, and they had spent some hours afterward sitting on Adirondack chairs in the autumn sun and talking. Fiona planned to buckle down to her work afterward, but nevertheless drove in the general direction of home in a dawdling fashion, grateful that there was no one else on the road for her to annoy with her slow crawl toward home.

Humming aimlessly to herself, she was thinking about which portion of her article to tackle as she came around a bend in the road. She had been going so slowly that she didn't have to slam on the brakes to avoid hitting the people in the road ahead. Two adults stood with their bikes before them and their children behind them, working to fend off an attack by Piggy, who, true to form, had been lying in wait for just such an adventure.

Fiona knew from experience what had to be done. With a curious sense of *déjà-vu*, she reenacted her own rescue by Nancy Iverssen almost exactly the year before.

Pulling her car in along the shoulder of the road behind the family, she rolled down her windows. "Quick! Jump in! Leave the bikes!" and obediently, the parents did as they were told, shoving their children into the car first, and then throwing down the bikes and jumping in themselves, she in the back with the children, and he practically vaulting over the hood of the car to get into the passenger seat.

Expecting anger, accusations, and possibly some tears from the occupants of the backseat, Fiona turned to the man in the seat beside her. "Are you okay?"

To her surprise, he immediately began to laugh.

"I think we are. You okay back there?" he asked gaily, looking around the headrest at his family. The two little boys were beginning to be a bit tremulous, but seeing their father's good spirits they, too, began to laugh. Their mother, who was shaking her head and smiling at her husband, said, "Well, boys, that was an adventure we will remember!"

"But what was that? A dog or an alligator?" asked the man, pulling off his baseball cap and running a hand through his hair. He gave the impression of having been invigorated by the experience.

"Alligator!" shouted the two boys in unison, now thoroughly enjoying themselves.

He turned to Fiona, who was now laughing, too. "That was some rescue, by the way. Don't know how to thank you. I'm Mark Hanley."

"And I'm Laura," added the woman from the backseat. "And these are James and Will."

"Fiona Campbell. And what you just experienced is an Island rite of passage. Now that you've met Piggy, you're honorary citizens."

"What about the bikes?"

"Oh, don't worry," said Fiona breezily. "We'll stop by the Mercantile and they'll take care of it."

Ver Palsson's son, Ben, was bored. His father, known by everyone as Pali, was a captain for the Island ferry line, and although the ferry had been properly moored and shut down for the night, Pali spent an extra hour going over the ship to ensure that it would be ready for morning. He was an honest man who took his responsibilities seriously. To Ben it seemed that they would never be finished. He had been sitting around all day, and there were only a few hours of light left. Ben wanted to go for a ramble in the woods before dinner.

"Dad, can we go?"

His father looked at him in a way that Ben knew was a substitute for a lecture.

"Sorry," said Ben, with just the proper amount of contrition in his tone. Without even a small sigh he went back to reading the book he had brought. His restlessness did not prevent him from enjoying it, mostly because he knew his father would not be budged until he was ready to be budged. But Ben had plans of his own, and he knew it was in his own interest to bide his time.

Ben Palsson was ten years old, and he had lived his entire life on Washington Island. He had attended the tiny school since kindergarten, and, if all went well, he would graduate from high school there. He knew pretty much everyone, and his parents had the anachronistic confidence in their surroundings that permitted him the freedom to wander that would have been both unheard of and unwise for a boy of his age living nearly anyplace else. There were six children in his fifth grade class, including Ben, and only two of them were boys. Ben spent a great deal of time on his own and was content to amuse himself, a skill lacking in many of his generation elsewhere.

A few minutes later, his father returned to find him engrossed in his book.

"Come on, Ben, what are you hanging around for? Let's go." Pali put his hand on his son's shoulder and squeezed playfully. "Always keeping me waiting."

They walked together to the truck. It had been a sunny afternoon, but as the sun got low, a brisk wind was rising, and the truck's heater felt good once it got going.

Pali looked sideways at his son as he drove. Ben's head was turned, looking out the window. He was blond like both his parents, and he had his mother's restless energy. In many ways he was still a little boy, but Pali was watching for the first signs of adolescent turmoil that was bound to come. "So far, so good," he thought.

Ben turned from the window to look at his father.

"Dad, would you mind letting me off near the beach? I can walk the rest of the way."

Pali had been expecting this request.

"It will be dark soon," he said.

"I know, Dad," said Ben patiently. "I'll be home before then. I just want to walk along the trail."

His father nodded and when they turned to head east along Jackson Harbor Road, Pali pulled into the drive of School House Beach and stopped.

Ben already had his hand on the door.

"Ben," said Pali. It was a tone that required attention, but a message that Ben had heard many times. He also knew that if he were rude his father would simply not allow him to get out of the truck.

"Yes, Dad," said Ben, politely.

"Stay away from the water when you're alone. Don't even go close enough to get your feet wet."

"I won't."

"And don't be late to dinner."

"I won't."

"Pay attention. Keep your mind on what you're doing."

"I will."

Pali broke into a grin at the restrained but dutiful tone in his son's voice. He was like a hunting dog desperate to give chase, but waiting for the command.

"I know you will. Okay, see you at home."

"See you," said Ben. And even as he said the words he was out of the truck and trotting toward the wooded trails that ran along the low bluffs above the lake shore. Pali watched until the boy disappeared into the woods, and then turned the truck back to the road and home.

Ben had the kind of boyhood that adults in the cities tend to romanticize, and with good reason. At ten, his solitary ramblings had developed in him knowledge, confidence, judgment, and a self-respect that would support him all his life. His parents gave him responsibilities, and had complete confidence that he would carry them out, probably because they had always invoked consequences if he did not. He had a gun, which his father had mother had taught him to use conscientiously, and a pocketknife, which, in a world far removed from the TSA, he carried everywhere and used frequently. Ben watched TV, used the Internet, and was acquainted with contemporary culture elsewhere in the world, but he had not yet reached the age where he had begun to chafe against this rural life. His parents, having also grown up on the island, watched for the first signs with trepidation. Their own adolescent restlessness had taken them both away from home at early ages. But, of course—and this comforted them—they had come back.

Pali was reflecting on all this as he pulled the truck into the garage. He was wrestling with a deeply felt problem, and had been distracted lately, and a bit distant from his family.

Pali spent his days as a ferry captain. It had always been his life's work, and his means of supporting his family. But Pali was also a poet. His work had been published for the first time only in the last year. This recognition had changed him profoundly, shifting his sense of self and purpose beyond the daily duties that he felt were a reflection of his personal honor.

But the success of Pali's poetry was also a source of anxiety and self-doubt. The strange experiences he and his crew had had on the ferry were closely held secrets, very difficult to keep quiet in a small community where talk was a way of life. Each man knew that their stories, if ever widely known, would make them a source of amusement and ridicule.

Pali knew what he had experienced. He knew the way the rhythms of the words had come to him. His crew knew what they had seen. Pali believed that the poetry was not entirely his own, but brought to him by the... spirit... ghost... presence... they had all witnessed on the ship. And now that he had had some success, when he was being pressed to write more by a publisher who valued his work, Pali found that he could not comply. He had no words, no phantom rhythms beating their music in his head, and no more ghostly encounters. His inspiration was gone. He was deeply troubled, embarrassed, and increasingly convinced that his glory as a poet had been a fraud. His muse—or, perhaps, his ghost—was silent, and Pali revisited daily a sense of loss and desolation in its absence.

Tonight, however, his problems seemed foolish, distant, and less important. He felt confidence and pride in his boy, and in the life he and Nika had made together. Walking into the house, he hung his coat on a peg near the door, and kissed his wife with a sense of gratitude.

After their encounter with Piggy, Fiona returned the family to the Mercantile shaken, but unhurt. She left them waving a cheerful goodbye. Abandoning bikes in the heat of Piggy battle was a scenario well-known to Mann's employees, and Gabe took it all in stride. The parents were remarkably philosophical about their ordeal, and their good humor extended even to their children's fright. "Things happen," the father had said. "It's all part of the adventure," his wife had added. Their geniality increased when they learned that their deposit would not be forfeited, despite the bikes not having been returned.

Gabe sighed with relief when they had gone. As an Island native he had learned at his mother's knee the rudeness and sense of entitlement of tourists, and this family had been a memorable exception. He was pleased that his only problem would be fitting all four bikes in the back of his mother's ancient hatchback when he went to retrieve them.

Gabe's day, however, did not go entirely as planned. He had meant to go to pick up the abandoned bicycles as soon as the store closed, planning to leave them in the car overnight and return to the store with them the next morning. But he met some friends in the parking lot as he was leaving the store, and they were going to someone's house to hang around and shoot pool. The prospect of seeing Lara Bjornstad there put all other things out of his head. By the time he remembered, it was dark and close to his curfew. A lifetime on Washington Island left Gabe with no doubt that the bikes would still be there. He would leave early and pick them up on his way to work in the morning.

It was dusk as Ben ambled across the fields, heading home. He still had a little time before he would be expected, and he was not yet ready to be inside for the night, so he was dawdling, despite his hunger. He had a new fossil in his pocket, picked up along the beach well away from the waves, and he had seen two bald eagles fishing in the blue-gray water of the lake.

Ben knew his home territory with the intimacy that only a restless boy can have. He knew the back trails along the edge of the beaches where the ruins of the cabins of 19th-century settlers were still decaying out of sight of the main road. He had investigated them thoroughly over the years, and had scavenged small bits of metal, glass, and rusted tools. He knew where the creek went under the road and disappeared into the woods, and where it emptied into the lake. He knew where foxes and raccoons and muskrats lived, and he spent hours sitting outside their dens watching without a boy's usual intent to harm. His affection for animals was unsentimental, and he was not offended or shocked by hunters. He recognized that killing and eating was part of life. He simply wasn't interested in hunting. He wanted to observe, to know.

As he walked he caught a movement along the place where the field met the woods. It was the time of night when deer congregate and move out into the open fields to browse, and Ben stood still to watch. Their movement, the woods, and the low light obscured their numbers. As he peered across the distance he could see the herd of about six animals. But even in the deepening evening light it was clear that there was something different.

Cautiously, Ben moved closer. One of the animals was moving strangely, not with the usual grace of a whitetail, and it was smaller than the others. In the growing darkness and against the black of the woods, it was difficult to see clearly, but its movements were wrong: different from the movement of the other deer. Instead of a deer's usual grace, it seemed to hobble. Was it injured? Ben peered at the distant creature. The herd seemed to notice him, and moved sharply into the depths of the woods. Ben watched, but could see nothing more. An injured deer wouldn't last long, Ben knew. It was sad, but he also knew that there was little likelihood of being able to help the animal. It would die before spring.

Suddenly he noticed that it was darker than he had realized. The warm orange glow of the trees had deceived him, and the sun was already down. Ben ran the rest of the way home and was just in time for dinner.

He lay awake for a long time that night after he should have been asleep, wondering about the animal he had seen and feeling troubled about its fate. Nature was merciless, Ben knew, and this animal's end would probably be a bad one.

Fiona watched the last red light of sunset from her porch steps with Rocco's warm body lying across her feet. The mild day had turned into a brisk evening, but she could not bring herself to go in. She knew that as soon as the door closed behind her, the loneliness would begin to close in, despite Rocco's affectionate companionship.

For most of the day she could distract herself with tasks, with only an occasional momentary longing. But at night, as the sun set and the world descended into stillness, her thoughts would drift, and with them her anxieties began their dance in her heart and head. No matter what music she played, book she read, or movie she watched, she could feel the emptiness of the house around her, and the full realization that Pete was so far away.

His presence on the Island had been so brief that it seemed as if she had imagined it. She wondered where he was, whether he could see the sky as she did now; tried to imagine what he might be doing. She knew well enough that with his job working for an international energy company, he could be literally anywhere, doing almost anything. And this made her extremely nervous. Would she see him again? Even if he wanted to, would he come back? Fiona spent a great deal of mental energy trying not to think about what could happen to Westerners in remote parts of the world.

Increasingly chilled, she sighed and stirred. She could not reasonably put off going inside any longer, she told herself, or they would find her body frozen to the steps. She stood for a moment watching the last flush of color in the autumn sky, Rocco leaning against her. Then she turned to go in, and standing aside to hold the door for Rocco, followed him into the empty house.

B en was looking out his bedroom window down at the meadows below. There were huge numbers of turkeys gathered together, and then he realized that there weren't just turkeys. There were... crows? Yes. Enormous crows walking on the ground. Crows ten times bigger than regular crows. As big as turkeys. And other *animals. Every kind of animal. Animals that did not belong on the island. They were flowing almost as one creature below the house, simply moving in the same direction in an eerie silence. They were not interacting with one another in any discernible way, just moving. In their midst was a river of water, and strange dream animals—along with those he knew—swam along with the flow of creatures.*

"Dad!" called Ben. "Come and look!" But his dad was away. He called his mom, but she was nowhere in the house. There was no one else to experience this mysterious, beautiful, and slightly alarming migration with him. No one to explain where these creatures had come from and where they were going. These creatures did not belong here. They should not be acting in this way. He had the uneasy feeling that something was wrong. No normal pattern would explain this behavior. He stood at the window and felt that something in the world was out of order, and he, Ben, had to make it right.

Ben awoke from his dream troubled and out of sorts. He moved slowly that morning, still feeling the after-effects of his dream, and had to be told three times to brush his teeth. He was almost late to school, and just made it into the building as the last bell rang.

When Gabe left the house the next morning, he went straight to Piggy corner, as the locals liked to call it. He knew from a lifetime's experience exactly where the bikes would be, and as he approached he could see the gleam of the sun on the bikes' chrome.

But when he pulled up close, it became obvious that all was not well. All four bikes were there, all right, but they were in tatters. Gabe stood by the side of the road trying to take it all in. The nylon packs that had been attached to the back of the two adult bikes had been ripped into shreds. The leather seats and the foam handle grips had been stripped away and were a complete loss.

Gabe's common sense told him that the bikes could be repaired. The seats and grips could be replaced. But what a mess. Normally when Piggy struck, the bikes remained mostly intact, maybe with a few broken spokes, and occasionally a ruined tire. Clearly this was an escalation, no doubt the result of allowing him to get away with his bad behavior. And what a thing to happen while Tom was away, and he, Gabe, was in charge. Gabe sighed. It was fortunate, he thought, that the only damage had been to the bikes, not to the customers, but still... .

"Damn Piggy," he thought.

Mrs. Shoesmith's neighbor up the road was also cursing Piggy. Bill Hanson had been coming to the Island for thirty-five years, and although it was not his official residence as far as the tax man was concerned, Bill's visits to the Island these days tended to be for twelve months of the year, more or less. He was, however, a new neighbor to the Shoesmiths, having built a house overlooking Detroit Harbor just last year. In that period of time Piggy had attacked Bill's wife, his dog, and more out-of-town visitors than Bill could count.

The stitches, tears shed, and family turmoil that had been

the result of previous Piggy encounters had been bad enough. But this. This was a bitter thing. Heartbroken, he looked upon the ruin of his baby orchard, lovingly planted young cherry and apple trees that he had nursed through the past summer's drought and the previous winter's vagaries. The tiny eighteen-inch saplings—representing the dreams of a lifetime—had been protected from deer by chicken wire. But chicken wire had clearly been inadequate to Piggy's rampage. Sadly, Bill stood in the sunlight and surveyed the damage.

It was remarkable, he thought, how much destruction one small, nasty dog could wreak.

Bill was a kind husband and father, a member of the church council, and as fine and upstanding a Christian as Washington Island had ever seen. He was teased by his friends and neighbors for his gentle, upright manner, and his mild way of speaking. But some things were more than a man could bear.

"Damn that Piggy," he said.

Chapter Two

Mike and Terry were deep in conversation one morning as they pushed open the door to Ground Zero and entered the shop, so they didn't notice immediately the change in personnel. Instead of the beatific calm of the man Terry had come to refer to as "The Angel Joshua," there was a singularly less angelic face scowling at them from behind the counter.

"Roger!" said Mike, suddenly looking up, possibly sensing the sharp eyes boring into his head. "You're back."

There was no audible response. Roger looked no different, neither tanned nor glowing with human warmth. Terry had privately expected Roger to be somehow different after his six-week honeymoon, to be changed by love. But Roger was as unsmiling as ever, his handsome face unanimated by ordinary responses, his hair sticking out at odd angles as if he had recently put both his hands in it and rubbed hard. The chill of his presence in the little shop was powerful enough to penetrate the warmth of the yellow walls, with its ambient lighting and gas fireplace surrounded by comfortable chairs.

The big Italian coffee contraption perched on the ledge behind the counter, its exotic, modern presence somehow perfectly in keeping with the bead board and rural photography on the shop walls.

"When'd you get back?" asked Terry, settling easily into the familiarity of the Roger chill. "Seems like you've been gone for a year."

Roger, with long experience of their preferences, was silent as he made their coffee.

"Day before yesterday," he said, after it had begun to seem he wouldn't answer. "We flew into Chicago and stayed over the first night, just to get some rest. Then we got up in the dark and drove up yesterday morning. Slept all afternoon and all night, and got up at three."

"How's Elisabeth?" asked Mike, his sweet, cherubic face filled with his innate warmth and kindness.

"Fine," said Roger abruptly, and he disappeared into the small kitchen in the back.

"Some things never change," said Terry, taking a long swallow of his coffee. His eyes sparkled and he put his cup down on the counter with a thunk. Terry had never gotten used to the bland calm of The Angel Joshua's personal atmosphere.

Joshua was, perhaps, not aware of Terry's name for him. Terry had never been completely comfortable around Joshua. He had found Joshua's unearthly good looks, long mane of hair, and unusual quality of benign grace a bit off-putting. The nickname, not meant in an altogether kindly fashion, had somehow struck a chord in the community. It was used by almost everyone, not as mockery, but as an expression of regard and general affection, and possibly a bit of awe. But only behind his back.

Joshua's tenure managing the coffee shop had been a relatively brief and—to Terry—unwelcome change. After many years. Terry was accustomed to Roger's rudeness and had come to prefer it.

"Feels good to be back to normal," said Terry, *sotto voce* to Mike.

"I wonder," said Mike quietly, looking down into his mug. Terry glanced sharply at him but said nothing as Roger emerged from the back.

"I could go for one of those egg sandwiches," said Terry. "And more coffee."

"The same," said Mike, his keen eyes crinkling as he smiled. "So tell us about Italy."

After he had started the eggs, Roger filled their cups as he spoke with unwonted animation. "We started out in Venice."

Ben Palsson had been thinking. Would it be possible, he wondered, to find that injured deer? He could take care of it for the winter; make sure it got enough food, and then, maybe it would have enough strength to survive until spring. He knew that injuries could be self-healing. The problem would be for the animal to survive long enough for the healing to happen.

But then a new thought struck him. Maybe, if he was clever and a little bit lucky, he could figure out a way to fix its leg. He stopped his after school wandering along a wooded path as he considered this. Gradually, the idea began to grow within him, and it wasn't long before Ben decided that he had to try. It would be fun to befriend a deer. And besides, he was worried about the little animal all alone and vulnerable, and maybe in pain.

But how, he wondered, should he start? After much thought, Ben decided that he should talk to his friend, Jim, the DNR ranger. He would have to watch what he said, because DNR people did not approve of rescuing sick animals. They always said that nature should take its course. But letting nature take its course in the death of his deer was exactly what Ben did not want. His plan was to thwart nature as thoroughly as possible, and he knew he would have to be careful not to give his plans away.

His mother had spoken often to him about sneakiness. It was something she despised. It was dishonest, she said, and showed a lack of integrity. Ben had never lied to his parents; never even felt a need to. He had an open life, and had always told them everything. But this wasn't sneakiness, he told himself. It was a secret. Like a birthday party or a Christmas present. Secrets were exciting. And this one would belong to him.

The news of Lars Olafsen's retirement was soon known everywhere on the Island. The usual morning conversation at the grocery store's meat counter was dominated by two topics: Amand's screamer and Lars's retirement. The screamer was the kind of story that gave everyone a frisson of excitement. Who could it have been? What was it about? Whose kids had been allowed out so late after a reasonable curfew? Lars's retirement, however—and its corollary: who would be his successor—were topics of far more importance.

The position of Chairman was elected by the citizens, not

by the board. Usually, though, the chairman would come from the board itself. Who else would be acquainted with the requirements of the job?

To the electorate, however, the field of prospects had the unprepossessing quality familiar to anyone who has pondered future candidates for any office: they were all lacking in some key qualification. The lack of grandeur or power of the office of Board Chairman were inconsequential details; the principles were the same: People are flawed, the needs of public office manifest, and the skills required daunting. No normal human being could possibly qualify. What is more, no normal human being would want to qualify.

And so, it should have been surprising to no one when a human being whose normality was earnestly discussed wherever islanders gathered, announced her candidacy for chairman.

The first yard sign of the campaign appeared less than a week after Lars Olafsen's announcement at Nelsen's. The speed with which it had happened—before papers had been filed, before, in fact, Lars had even officially given notice—was a strategy intended to seek the advantage of possession of the field and to deter opposition. Predictably enough, it was in the candidate's own front yard.

Fiona had awoken in a happy frame of mind, anticipating a visit from Elisabeth and Roger. They would be coming to take Rocco back with them, and although Fiona would be very sad to see him go, this was a relatively minor point compared to her delight at seeing them. She would take the day off from writing and make them a lovely dinner. It promised to be a good day.

Barefoot and sipping her coffee in the warm October sunshine, she padded down the driveway to her mailbox in search of a packet of leaflets for the upcoming charity book sale that the sale's chairman had promised to deliver. Participation in these community events was a necessity and a welcome opportunity for human contact. Rocco dawdled nearby, sniffing new and old smells under the bushes. It was another splendid autumn morning: brilliant blue sky, vibrant colors in the leaves that still clung to the trees, and a pleasant brisk quality to the air.

It was a rather gaudy sign, professionally printed in red and purple, but Fiona did not notice it until after she had retrieved the leaflets and the rest of her mail from her mailbox and pushed it closed. The bright colors first caught her eye, but its message engaged her entire being. She felt as if she had been slammed in the chest. Her heart raced, she felt herself flush, and her breathing became ragged. It was only an act of will that prevented her from sitting down right there in the road, where Stella could see and take perverse pleasure in her reaction.

"Stella DesRosiers for Town Board Chairman," the sign read. "Time for a change."

Emily Martin bustled into the grocery store that morning with a long list and little time. Their move to the Island had been delayed beyond the date they had hoped for, and as a result they were scurrying to get the new farm prepared for the winter. Her sweet-natured animals were adjusting to their new surroundings well, comforted, apparently, by familiar routines and interactions with people they knew well and trusted, but her children were less sanguine about the change.

Her youngest boy, a first grader, was happy wherever he went. But the older two—in the ninth and fifth grade—were most decidedly not. A new school and new friends were difficult to get used to, and the newcomers chafed against the Island's small town ways, tiny class sizes, and limited opportunities. Not having been raised to understand that the world did not revolve around them, they were extremely reluctant to adapt themselves to their new surroundings, and this, of course, made everything worse.

Only that morning Emily had received a phone call from the school asking her to come in for a conference, and this was the reason for her haste. She had just 20 minutes to gather up the items on her list before her meeting with the principal, and she didn't want to have to delay her return home afterward. She fully intended to spend 15 minutes at the school explaining to the principal exactly where he had gone wrong, and then head straight back to the farm.

It hadn't taken Emily long to acquaint herself with the layout of the little store, and she was coasting along nicely, flinging items into her cart as she mentally rehearsed her conversation at the school. Thus engrossed, she was rapidly exiting the canned goods section and turning the corner when she careened into a dumpy middle-aged woman standing—rather stupidly, Emily thought—in the middle of the aisle.

Emily sighed impatiently to herself and pasted on her pseudo-smile. "So sorry!" she said brightly but firmly. "I didn't see you there. Probably shouldn't be in the middle of the aisle, though. Blind spot, you know."

Her words swept on like rushing water, oblivious, at first, to the reaction of the other shopper. Her primary objective was simply to get the woman out of the way so she could finish her shopping.

The woman's eyes bored into her. "You should watch where you're going. You nearly broke my knees." She reached down and rubbed one leg more or less near where a knee might be, and appeared to search the fabric of her knit slacks for signs of damage.

"Really," thought Emily. "Did she expect to find blood?"

Slowly the woman raised her eyes to Emily's.

"You are a menace with that cart. Don't you have any sense?"

For once, speechless, Emily merely stared for a moment before she recollected herself.

"Well, I am sorry, but there's no need for you to be rude. I don't have time for this. Excuse me."

Emily attempted to maneuver her cart past the woman, but she stood, deliberately, Emily thought, in her way.

"Are you going to let me pass?" asked Emily frostily. "I am in a hurry."

"Go around," was the response.

"Fine," said Emily. "I will."

And spinning her cart around she retraced her path up the canned goods aisle and took a different route to the counter. She shook her head to herself over the bad manners and general stupidity of these people. No wonder her children were having trouble at school. Well, she would resolve that little problem in short order. She reached the meat counter and quickly scanned its contents.

"So you've met Stella," was the laconic comment of a man standing next to her, a package of ground beef in his hand. "Sooner or later, it's got to happen. May as well be sooner."

He strolled off as Emily, fuming, threw a slice of ham and some chicken breasts into her cart and pivoted toward the cashier.

She was late to the principal's office, which made her, really, quite cross, and not, she thought to herself, in her usual cheerful mood. She would deal with this Stella. But not today. Mentally shelving this for future consideration, with effort she focused her mind on the principal's bland colloquy.

"Really," thought Emily. "How these people do go on." After a few minutes of impatient listening, Emily stepped in and took a firm hold of the conversation. Without brooking any interruption, she explained to the principal, in minute detail, precisely what he should do.

As she left the school, satisfied, it was clear to Emily that the Island was in need of her guidance and instruction. Well, she would take care of that. All in due time.

As the day progressed, Fiona had to admit that the impending departure of Rocco made her feelings about seeing Elisabeth and Roger increasingly mixed. The big shepherd's steady affection had been a great comfort, and the house would feel empty without him. Resolutely, she turned her thoughts to her preparations for her friends' arrival, and consoled both herself and Rocco with more than the usual number of snacks. This enhanced Rocco's interest in her kitchen activities, and he lingered hopefully nearby. She had spent the day preparing a welcome-home dinner with hors d'oeuvres, a homemade dessert, and two particularly lovely bottles of South African wine, specially ordered from Shoes and Booze in anticipation of the occasion. With the reduction of the ferry schedules for the fall, they would have to stay the night, and for this Fiona had prepared her guest room with fresh linens and flowers.

She reached an acceptable level of dinner preparation and went upstairs to put on lipstick and do what she could with her hair. Rocco patiently followed, temperamentally unable to permit his people to leave his protective care. He was lying nearby when suddenly his head shot up in alert, his big shepherd ears fully upright like antennae. In a flash he was down the stairs and barking at the door, not a threatening bark, but one of joy. Not until then did Fiona hear a car pull up, and voices. Elisabeth and Roger had arrived.

"Sorry we're so early," said Elisabeth after Rocco had danced and trilled with ecstasy, jumping to reach their faces with his, lovingly nibbling at Elisabeth's fingers and lips, and pushing his body against Roger like an enormous cat. Fiona's effusive greeting seemed weak by comparison, but her reaction was heartfelt. Even Roger was giving hugs, apparently, albeit rather stiff-armed ones. In her mind Fiona struggled a bit with this new phenomenon. It was vaguely disquieting, like hearing a favorite song played on an elevator, or watching that Star Wars sequel in which Darth Vader started smiling and being avuncular. She didn't like social hugging in the first place, but hugging Roger was an experience she thought she'd prefer to avoid in the future.

"I couldn't wait any longer," said Elisabeth. "I had to see Rocco."

The big dog stared adoringly into her eyes. She was here. He didn't know where She had been, or for how long, but She was the core of his heart and all that mattered. He was filled with joy. He curled himself against Her, drinking in Her scent and the scent of all the places She had been, and of what She had been feeling. He didn't recognize them all, but he recognized some as the Away Smells, the ones he always found on Her when She had been gone.

"That's all right," said Fiona. "I'm delighted to have you here. Help yourselves to some wine, and I'll be back in a moment. Rocco will host." She ran upstairs, put on her favorite earrings—a recent gift from Pete—her newest pair of Italian sandals, and a dab of perfume at her throat and wrists. She smiled at herself in the mirror, shrugged at her slapdash toilette, smiled again to herself, and ran back downstairs to her friends. As she went, she had a flash of emotion about Stella's plans, but quickly dismissed it. Let Stella ruin someone else's night.

Roger and Elisabeth were sitting in her living room side by side on the couch. Rocco lay at Elisabeth's feet, his head pressed against her, sound asleep in a picture of canine bliss. Fiona poured herself a drink and sat down happily. "So how was it? Where did you go?"

Fiona studied them as they spoke looking for indicators of change. Surely married life—life with Roger—would have made some alteration. But Elisabeth sat on the couch, radiating her usual serenity. If there were any change, it was, perhaps, in Roger.

The hugs had been one indication, surely. Perhaps the scowl had lessened? Fiona mentally shook herself and turned her attention back to the conversation. She had no idea what anyone had said.

They spent the evening in the rambling conversation of old friends, laughing and drinking wine. Or at least Elisabeth and Fiona did. Roger mostly sat and scratched Rocco behind the ears, but seemed not to mind being there, which was, Fiona thought, something of a change in itself. Occasionally he would add a word or two, but mostly not, and he seemed to enjoy the wine. Fiona saw Elisabeth turn a besotted gaze to him from time to time, and was relieved and surprised to see him return it. He did not sparkle or emote. Neither was Roger's style. But Fiona thought she could detect some silent communication between the two, and this reassured her as to her friend's happiness.

They stayed all the next day. Fiona and Elisabeth had much to talk about, and Roger seemed sanguine about walks with Rocco and reading in the living room while they laughed and chatted.

At the end of the day, as the sun was setting, they said their good byes and left to catch the ferry, Rocco joyously bounding into the car with them without a backward glance.

Fiona walked slowly up the steps to the porch. It was suddenly very quiet. Rocco was not a dog who barked much or made a lot of noise, but he had made his comfortable presence felt. She had heard German Shepherds described by someone as "Velcro dogs", and this was perfectly true. He had followed her wherever she went, and even when she stayed in the same room, he followed her with his eyes. On the rare occasions when she went anywhere without him, as soon as she pulled into the driveway she could see the two ears, pointing up like antennae, silhouetted against the glass in the top of the door, waiting for her return. Fiona would miss him, and her eyes filled with tears at thought of being without him. She shook it off. She was not normally weepy.

Glad that it was nearly dark and no one was there to see her, she poured herself a glass of wine, grabbed a crocheted blanket from the couch, and went out to the porch to breathe in the cool air. She sat on the steps, the blanket around her shoulders, listening to the sounds of the descending night and feeling just the tiniest bit sorry for herself. It was dark when a familiar truck passed by, slowed, and then turned around to park in front of the porch.

Jim Freeberg got out of the truck and came up the walk. Jim was an island native, one of those young people who leave the Island to find their paths and find themselves drawn inexorably homeward. He was a park ranger who worked for the Wisconsin Department of Natural Resources.

In a commentary on the agency's bureaucratic dictatorship, locals liked to say that DNR stood for Damn Near Russia. But Jim was an easygoing man with a kind heart and a deep affection for animals of all kinds. For a time after she had arrived on the Island, Fiona had been aware that he was interested in more than friendship, but she had turned down his tentative questions, and since he had done nothing more, she had been under the impression that his feelings had faded.

"I thought I saw you sitting here in the dark. Don't you know enough to go inside? There will be frost tonight."

His tone was light, and but he didn't smile as he said it.

"I've been sitting here long enough not to have really noticed. How are you, Jim? Want to join me?"

"Only if you give me a drink."

"I can do that," said Fiona. "But this is the last of the wine. Scotch okay?"

"Sure," said Jim.

Fiona went into the house to get him one. When she returned, Jim was sitting on the same step where she had been, leaning against the porch column, his legs stretched out in front of him. She handed him a glass and a blanket.

Jim laughed. "I'm not going to sit here with a blanket on my lap like some old geezer. Keep that for yourself, if you're cold."

"Are you calling me a geezer?"

"Geezers are men, I think."

Fiona looked at him doubtfully. "I suppose so, but I still don't like the implication."

Smiling, Jim took a drink of scotch and sighed.

"Hits the spot."

Fiona watched him with an intensity she wasn't conscious of.

"What are you so serious about?" asked Jim.

She shook off her mood and smiled.

"Rocco's gone, and I'm feeling a little blue." She smiled again. "I'm glad you stopped by."

Jim eyed her speculatively.

"When's your boyfriend coming back?"

Fiona felt suddenly wary. "I'm not sure, really. His job takes him all over and it's difficult for him to get away."

Jim nodded slightly, took another drink of his scotch, and changed the subject.

"So Stella's running for Chairman, I see," he said.

"Ugh," said Fiona. "Don't remind me. I've been trying not to think about it." She looked seriously at him. "What are people saying? Do you know who's going to run against her?"

"Well, since, technically, Lars hasn't officially resigned yet, it's too early to tell. But so far, nobody." He shook his head and looked down at his drink.

"Heads will roll if she gets into office. What a disaster." For the second time he looked thoughtfully over at Fiona. "Have you thought about what this could mean for you?"

Fiona laughed. "Do you mean have I considered that she'll make my life a living Hell? Oh, yes. I've thought about it. I have until the election in April, I suppose. I'll have to sell the house and get out of here." The thought made her stomach clench. She paused, struck by a sudden idea.

"You could run, Jim. You'd be good at it. You're an Islander. People like you and trust you. You'd be great." She looked at him hopefully.

Jim chuckled. "Not one chance of that, I can guarantee it. Political life is not for me. Not even on the Island."

"Not even to save the Island from the likes of Stella DesRosiers?"

"Not even for that," he answered comfortably. "I prefer problems that I can trap or shoot."

"Now there's an idea."

They laughed.

After another half an hour of casual talk Jim emptied his glass and stood up to go. He put his hand out and hauled Fiona to her feet.

"It's too cold to sit out here any longer. You should go in."

Fiona nodded, feeling slightly uneasy about what would come next, but Jim was all casual and light.

"Thanks for the drink and the conversation. See you around."

And with that he bounded off the porch steps, got into his truck and was gone.

Fiona stood for a moment on the steps and watched him go. It was cold. She gathered up the blankets and the glasses, and went inside to the warmth and silence of the little house.

The ugly truth that Stella would be unopposed began to dawn on the Island residents, and as the realization spread, its implications became increasingly clear. With her temper, her obsession with detail, and her ruthlessness, life on the Island was likely to become very different.

"Too bad we don't have any trains," commented Eddie one night. "We'd never have to worry about whether they were on schedule." He was leaning gloomily over the bar at Nelsen's, chatting with Lars Olafsen and a few of the regulars.

"Might be handy for pushing her in front of," said Jake, staring into the bottom of his nearly empty beer glass. No one smiled, but Jake drifted off into a happy reverie as he envisioned Stella's look of shock and outrage just before the train hit. His imagination stopped short of graphic detail. He didn't need revenge. Only salvation.

When Roger returned home from Ground Zero late the next afternoon, Elisabeth was already sitting on the porch waiting for him, eager to begin married life in the real world. Two glasses of wine and a dish of olives sat on the table beside her.

The gallery lights were still on, and an unfamiliar car was in the drive—evidence that Christine, Elisabeth's assistant, was still with a customer. She would close up when she was through. It was unusual for Elisabeth to relinquish this role, but she was jet-lagged after six weeks in Italy. There was no reason, she mused, not to allow Christine to take on these kinds of small routines on a daily basis. She did them anyway when Elisabeth was away. It might even make things more efficient to have a single hand on the rudder.

Elisabeth liked her work, although, as she would be the first to admit, this was easy when you worked for yourself. Her small, highly respected gallery was in the barn adjacent to her simple, comfortable house, and she could keep whatever hours she chose. Elisabeth's family had left her with rather substantial resources, and the gallery was her passion, not a means of existence.

As soon as Roger's car could be heard coming up the driveway, Rocco flung himself off the porch and made a mad dash to the car, dancing perilously in its path in his excitement.

As Roger emerged, Rocco leapt with joy, eager to touch the face of his hero. Roger returned Rocco's greeting with a warmth that was missing from his usual interactions with people.

After six weeks of honeymoon and a series of nights of reestablishment that had involved returning from the airport, going to Fiona's to get Rocco, and the flurry of unpacking and retrieving Roger's few belongings from his house, this was the first night of their real life. No errands, no upheaval, no obligations, just finishing a day of work and coming home to one another. Elisabeth wanted to run to him and to throw her arms around him in a passionate embrace, but she was enjoying watching this reunion with Rocco, so she smiled from her rocking chair and waited, her calm exterior belying the depth of her feelings.

She was beautiful, Roger thought, as he walked toward the house, an exuberant Rocco bouncing beside him. Even from a distance he could admire her ivory skin and curling lashes. Her long, wavy, auburn hair cascaded over her shoulders, and was colored now by the rose light of the late sun. He had noticed in Italy how frequently passers by had turned to look at her—both men and women. She looked exactly like a Renaissance painting, warm and voluptuous. A sharp emotion ran through him as he stepped onto the porch, and he was filled with joy. Elisabeth smiled up at him, her love pouring from her gaze as she held out a glass to him, on this, the first real night of their married life.

"Welcome home, Roger."

"Thanks," said Roger. Unceremoniously he took the glass from her and sat.

Elisabeth kept her disappointment and hurt feelings to herself.

Ver Palsson was early to the evening meeting of the Boy Scouts. The Scoutmaster was in bed with a particularly virulent form of flu, and Pali had been asked to step in. He knew all the boys, and occasionally joined events to help out, but he was tired tonight. He planned a quiet evening of knot tying to keep them busy. Knots, after all, were something Pali, as a ferryman, knew well.

One by one the boys trailed into the church basement where they met. Their Scoutmaster was strict about punctuality, so by 7:01 Pali had them lined up for the ceremony of the colors that began every meeting. The boys knew their parts, and they fell easily into place. They were about to say the Pledge of Allegiance when a noise on the stairs alerted them to a new arrival. All eyes turned to the door. It was unusual for anyone to be late, and even more unusual for anyone to enter so noisily. In a moment the door opened, and Jason Martin of Windsome Farms entered the room with his small son, a first grader named Noah. Noah looked embarrassed to be interrupting so solemn a ceremony, but his father took no notice.

"Hey there!" he said jovially, crossing the room to Pali with his hand extended, walking between the troop and the flag bearers who stood in a respectful line at the front. Interrupting the trooping of the colors was an enormous breach of protocol, and one known to even the youngest Scouts. Pali, aware of the many eyes on him, said nothing, but with a sweep of his arm politely indicated a place for the newcomers to stand.

Noah, who knew instantly what to do, stood where he was and removed his cap. His father, winking at Pali to show that he was in on the joke, did the same. With an inward sigh, Pali nodded to the eldest Scout to begin the Pledge again. It was going to be a long night and he looked forward to a brandy in front of his own fire.

Once the boys were started on their knot tying, Jason Martin took Pali aside. "So, Pali," he said, "I have an idea I'd like to try out on you."

Pali, after a meaning glance at a pair of giggling cub Scouts, gave his respectful attention.

"I have an idea that we could get the whole troop involved in the Animal Science merit badge" continued Jason. "We could do the Dairying option, and time spent at Windsome Farm would help the boys to qualify. With my expertise, I, personally, can guide them through the process," he added hastily. "Science shows that goats milk is far superior to cows milk, and the boys would have a great advantage in learning this."

Pali listened patiently. "I'm just filling in tonight, and don't have the authority to make any decisions. Why don't you wait 'til John gets back and talk it over with him? I'm sure he'll appreciate the offer."

"Maybe I should call him tonight," suggested Jason eagerly. "Get things rolling right away."

"Well, I don't know about that," said Pali slowly. "He's pretty sick or he'd be here himself. If I were you, I'd wait."

Reluctantly, Jason Martin agreed.

One morning when she went to get the mail, Fiona was surprised to find an envelope from the insurance company. She was even more surprised when she opened it. Fiona was not particularly good with life's details, and frequently handled them in a state of inattention. Apparently—more by luck than by intelligent planning—she had insured the barn for replacement value, and the amount was substantial. Thinking, she walked slowly back to the house.

She entered the kitchen, poured herself a cup of coffee, and stood at the window, looking back at where the barn had been. Did she want to replace it? For what? She had no animal any longer. She looked down at the check on the kitchen table. With that amount of money she wouldn't have to worry for quite a while. She could buy a new furnace. She could take a trip... her mind turned to Pete and his visits to many of the world's most beautiful cities.

On the other hand, she recalled with a pang the first moment she had seen the barn, and the spell it had cast on her. She remembered climbing the steep, ladder-like steps to the loft, leaning her chin on the floor at the top and seeing the play of sunlight across the wooden floor. But hadn't the beauty of the barn been mostly in its history? In the smells of ancient hay, of animals, and of the gasoline from the lawn mower? Could a new building have the same essence?

She thought about the old stone foundation still standing, and the smell of new lumber, of freshly laid planks and new windows. She could see it all in her mind's eye.

At the same time, it struck her that the issuance of the check must indicate some resolution on the part of the company. Did this mean that they had ruled out arson? Did they have a continuing investigation, or did they consider the matter closed? She didn't know.

Fiona herself wasn't entirely sure what she thought had happened, but this check seemed to indicate that no one else thought it mattered. It mattered to her, not knowing whether she lived next door to someone who would stoop to arson. And it mattered, too, whether the new barn would be a target.

Fiona knew that whatever she decided, if she spent the money, or if she built a new barn, nothing would be as it had been before. And it grieved her. She drank the rest of her coffee and went upstairs to work on her article.

Chapter Three ❖

After school, Ben headed straight to Jim's house, a small cottage near Washington Harbor. Jim frequently invited Ben to walk some trails with him, and Ben knew he would be welcome. He liked Jim and always learned something interesting from him. And being out in the woods together would give Ben a chance to ask questions about caring for the injured deer in a way that wouldn't make Jim suspicious. To his delight, Ben saw Jim's truck parked beside the cottage, and he went up to the porch and knocked. Through the window he could see Jim sitting at his kitchen table, working at his computer. Jim looked up and waved Ben in.

Jim's cottage had been built in the 19th century, and sat on a bluff above the rocky shore of Washington Harbor, near an old neighborhood known to residents by the rather unappealing name of Gasoline Town. The house had a porch that wrapped around two sides, with a small screened-in section to keep away the mosquitoes. There was a panoramic view of the harbor, and of the western horizon. Inside was small and snug, with a little kitchen, bathroom, and sitting room on the first floor and two bedrooms and a bathroom upstairs. The back bedroom, the one Jim occupied, had broad views of the harbor, and Jim had put in a big window that made it possible to see the water while lying in bed.

Jim had restored the place himself, painstakingly saving what he could of the original beams, stone fireplaces, and wood floors, and updating the kitchen and bathrooms with simplicity and good taste. The place had the feel of a carefully maintained boat, with everything crisply painted, compact, and efficient. Ben liked Jim's house, and imagined that someday, when he was grown up, he would live in a house exactly like it.

"Ben," said Jim in greeting, as he rose from his work. "What are you up to today?"

Ben noted the papers on the table, and recalling his father's mood when doing paperwork, began with the kind of apology that would have been appropriate in his own house.

"I'm sorry to bother you."

"That's okay," said Jim, glancing over his shoulder at his table. "I'm in a good place to take a break. Besides, I hate paperwork."

Ben nodded seriously. "My dad does, too. He always says he'd rather have a root canal." Ben did not actually know what root canal was, but his father made it sound like a primitive form of torture.

Jim laughed. "I completely sympathize with that point of view." Jim leaned back on the edge of the table and folded his arms.

"So, what's on your mind, Ben?"

"I wondered if we could do some trails today. You said I could stop by."

Jim thought a moment, nodding to himself. "Your timing is perfect, actually. I need to cover some trails I haven't been on for a while, and my head could use some clearing." He went to a kitchen cupboard and pulled out two protein bars and two bottles of water.

"Here," he said, tossing one of each in Ben's direction. "May as well go well-supplied."

He took his jacket off the wall rack, and held the door open for Ben.

"After you, Mr. Palsson. Let's go see what's happening out there."

He followed Ben out onto the porch, and together they set off down the road, toward the woods.

As they walked, Ben peppered Jim with questions about wildlife, injuries, and the hard realities of nature. Jim listened seriously and answered, sometimes explaining in simple terms the philosophy of land and animal management. Ben listened and absorbed everything with a child's vigorous capacity for memory. As Ben asked, he couldn't help worrying whether Jim would guess the purpose of his questions. If he had been more experienced, Ben might have realized that he had the guilty man's sense that everyone knows what he is thinking. Jim, used to the boy's intelligent curiosity, and good-naturedly determined to encourage it, didn't notice anything out of the ordinary. They passed the afternoon in good spirits, both happy to be doing what they loved.

When at last they emerged from the woods, it was getting late. It was easy, out in the woods, for your eyes to adjust to low light so you lost track of time.

Jim noted guiltily how close to dark it was.

"Come on, Ben. I'd better give you a ride home. Your mom will be wondering where you are."

"Thanks," said Ben. "She worries a lot."

"That's what moms do," said Jim. "My mom still worries about me."

Ben tried not to stare. "Really?" he asked, aghast. Jim was old. Probably over thirty.

"Yessir." He glanced at Ben sideways and grinned. "It has its upsides and its downsides. But it's good to be loved, Ben, and worry is just a kind of love. Remember that."

Ben nodded silently. He was still slightly shocked about Jim's mother. Somehow, he had always hoped to put that kind of thing behind him. But if Jim could be so cheerful about it, then, he thought, probably he could, too. Doggedly, he returned to his primary objective.

"Do you think a deer with a broken leg could survive very long?" he asked as they turned onto Jacksonport Harbor Road.

On this topic their conversation continued until Jim pulled up to the Palsson house a few minutes later. Thanking his friend politely, Ben jumped out and trotted up the driveway. Jim watched until he was safely inside the house, then drove on, feeling the sudden silence after an afternoon spent with a chatty ten year old. The solitude of his house did not appeal to him at the moment, he realized. He would head down to Nelsen's and see if there was any news. Eddie always knew the Island's business.

After a full day of writing, Fiona was chatting on the phone with Elisabeth. It got lonely in the little house, and she needed a little conversation. She told Elisabeth about the insurance check.

"Well, in one way, anyway, your new barn would be safe."

Fiona was puzzled. "How so?"

"Think about it. If Stella did burn the barn down—and I'm not saying that she did—the fact that she wants to buy your place now ought to mean that she wouldn't want to reduce the value of the property."

"If that were the case, she wouldn't have burned it down in the first place."

"But that was when she thought you were there for good. Now that she's running for chairman, she has to assume that you'll be leaving. She has to think that your place is coming up for sale."

"Even if that were true—and I'm not saying that it is—I don't think Stella much cares about the barn."

Elisabeth was quiet for moment considering this. "I suppose not."

"I'm not even sure that I do. Care, I mean."

This was patently untrue, and even as she said it, she knew she didn't mean it. Fiona fiddled with the pen in her hand. She had been drawing little buildings with flames rising from their roofs.

"So what are you going to do?" asked Elisabeth. "With the money, I mean."

"I haven't decided yet."

"You could visit Pete."

"Mmm," said Fiona.

"Don't you want to?"

"I want to see him. But I don't want to show up on his doorstep. Besides, I don't even know where he is." Fiona sighed heavily, completely unaware that she was doing so.

Elisabeth, always a thoughtful friend, decided that it might be best to leave this topic alone, and deftly moved the conversation on to other matters.

When Jim walked into Nelsen's, all eyes were glued to the local television news. Eddie was on the far end of the bar, but as soon as he saw Jim he moved up to talk. "Did you hear the news?"

Jim shook his head. "I've been doing paperwork and walking the trails all day."

"State turned down the harbor dredging project. Transportation Department says there's no money in the budget for it."

"There's money to build those damned roundabouts all over the state," commented Jake, coming to sit next to Jim. "Can't drive 100 yards without running into one of them things."

Jim frowned. "So now what?"

"Nobody knows. It's a big deal. Coast Guard says the water levels are getting so low it won't be safe to run the ferry." Eddie pulled a beer for Jim and put it down on the bar.

"And they're all out in the middle of nowhere, where a stop sign'd do just fine. Waste of taxpayer dollars," continued Jake. He was in a grumpy mood, a rare thing for him.

"Guess we'll all have to move," said Jim.

"Or go back to the old days and drive across."

"Hard to do in July."

They were all silent, thinking their own thoughts.

"Want a menu?" asked Eddie.

"Sure," said Jim. "No, on second thought, I'll just have a burger. With fries."

A side from a sense of horror nearly as intense as Fiona's, the Town Board's incumbents were offended by Stella's slogan and its implications of incompetence, or worse. A change from what? A change from the steady integrity and patience of Lars Olafsen? A change from the fiscal responsibility and good stewardship of the Board over the past 30 years or more? A change from the peace and goodwill among islanders that had been regnant—more or less, and not counting the factions that formed and shifted over every issue large and small—for generations?

Lars, too, pondered these questions. He didn't flatter himself that he had any particular insight beyond that of a thoughtful observer, but he thought he had a pretty good idea of what change Stella was hoping for. It wasn't a specific policy or a project, it wasn't hope for advancing favorable legislation at the State level, and it had nothing to do with fiscal responsibility. No matter what smoke screen she might throw up in order to be elected, Stella DesRosiers wanted two things: control and revenge. And if she were elected, he had no doubt whatsoever that she would get both. What she would do, or how she would do it, now, that was another matter altogether, but he was pretty sure that whatever it was, it would start with Ms. Fiona Campbell.

One of the things Fiona loved about owning a house was that it always required some kind of tweaking. What others considered an annoyance for Fiona was a delight. Each repair, each small improvement created a fresh feeling of accomplishment and renewal. And so, her regular trips to the Mercantile were pleasure jaunts, and also lovely distractions from whatever writing deadline loomed ahead. Today there were several, all past due.

She was happily foraging in the fasteners aisle, looking for something with which to hang the mirror she had acquired recently at a rummage sale, when she sensed that someone else was nearby. She looked up, smiling. It was Stella.

Fiona's smile faded and there was a chilly silence. She imagined that Stella was as surprised to see her as she was surprised herself. Stella merely looked without speaking, her face wooden.

"Hello, Stella," said Fiona steadily. This, she felt, was sufficient interaction, and she turned back to her perusal of picture hooks and fasteners, feeling pleased with herself for managing to be civil, even as she felt Stella's eyes boring into the back of her neck.

Under her mask of feigned calm as she picked absently through drawers of wood screws which would serve no purpose in hanging a mirror, Fiona recalled the day that the goat, Robert, had chased Stella into her house, and how, to Fiona's astonishment, Stella had been wearing pink fuzzy slippers. They seemed, even now, so utterly incongruous with Stella's personality that Fiona felt they must be important, somehow. Pondering fuzzy slippers, she realized that she could no longer maintain this odd hardware stalemate. No matter how cold or how rude Stella was, Fiona would not be goaded this time. No. She, Fiona, would keep a stoic calm. Stella was a force of nature. Like a tornado. There was no point in fighting. Fiona decided that she would move on, and do so with dignity. "Resistance," she thought, with a faint gleam of silent amusement, "is futile."

With what she hoped was an infuriating smile, she inclined her head slightly and walked past Stella, who was standing intimidatingly in the middle of the aisle. Fiona's basket of hardware store sundries swung lightly on her arm.

She was pleased when she heard Stella's angry huff behind her. "Point won. Advantage Team Fiona," Fiona thought as she made her way down the aisle to the checkout counter.

The fasteners aisle was filled with small plastic bins filled with screws and nails of every conceivable size and purpose. They were stacked on metal shelves that stretched the length of the aisle. As Fiona turned the corner into the main path of the store, she didn't notice when her big, loose-knit cardigan sweater caught the corner of a tall, metal mesh shelf that had a display of light bulbs on the top level, and cans of on-special spray paint underneath. Fiona felt the small tug on her sweater, and thinking it was some new indignity from Stella, she turned swiftly. In one moment, as if watching a movie in slow motion, Fiona saw the teetering movement of the shelf of light bulbs. She tried to reach out her hands to hold it in place, but her movement caused the sweater to pull the shelf harder, and the entire display wobbled in one last moment of final dignity before collapsing spectacularly to the floor. The movement of the display threw Fiona off balance, and she grabbed wildly for something to catch herself. Her hands grasped the only solid thing nearby, the shelving that held the nails and screws.

As she went down, Fiona watched in a detached way the easy movement of the fastener shelves, swaying gracefully like the Hindenberg on its tether. Then, in a long and fluid arc, they gave way, and with the same grace fell to the floor, carrying their cargo of an entire aisle of plastic bins filled with nails and screws. There was a crash, and then the aftershocks of several cases of spray paint rolling with force along the aisle, as tens of thousands of little metal pieces came cascading from their bins and spinning along the uneven surface of the floor.

It seemed a long time before there was silence. Helplessly tangled in sweater and metal mesh, her face next to the old linoleum floor, Fiona found herself noticing the little black dents on the floor that had been made by older displays. A dead fly and some old gum that would have been invisible from normal heights were precisely at her eye level. She heard the clerks calling out and running toward the disaster, just as Stella's sneaker and striped socks stepped without care over Fiona's carrier basket, crunching broken light bulbs as she went. Mentally noting the striped socks for future consideration, Fiona lay back and closed her eyes, imagining the pleasures of death. Her advantage, she felt, had been extremely short-lived.

It was not in their family nature for Emily or Jason Martin to allow any opportunity to improve their community to pass them by. They were agreed that teaching Boy Scouts about goats would be a great opportunity for the boys to learn about farming, that it would be good for the Scouts' long-term health—since goats milk, they felt, was so much healthier than cows—and, between themselves, they privately anticipated a debt of gratitude from the community that might be turned to their advantage. So it wasn't long before Jason followed up with the Scoutmaster on his idea for a goat farming merit badge.

Ben's Boy Scout troop was a particularly active one, led by a man whose experience in the woods was extensive. He was a native Islander, and had spent his life relying on his own wit and skill to take care of himself and his family. When his own expertise did not apply, he happily sought out someone else to teach his Scouts, and the result was a broad exposure for the boys in the traditional arts of outdoorsmanship, survival, and citizenship.

Since the Scoutmaster had no real objection to Jason's proposal, at least nothing he could say aloud, he gave way to the Martins with, if not enthusiasm, then, at least, resignation.

One chilly Saturday afternoon, the Scouts met for the first time at Windsome Farm. Jason and Emily greeted them with gusto, and led them to the goat pens. Their young son, Noah, joined his troop with the earnest sweetness that was his natural disposition, and hung back so the others could see what was so completely familiar to him.

Boys and goats regarded one another with curiosity as the adults spoke about the care of goats and goat personalities. Some of the herd came toward the fence hoping to be fed, and Jason distributed a handful of pellets to each boy. The boys hung over the fence laughing and exclaiming as the animals pushed against one another greedily to get closest to the fence and the eagerly proffered snacks. Inevitably, there was an attempt to mimic the goats' voices. The boys' calls seemed to inspire the goats', and soon the air with filled with the voices of both species, to the evident enjoyment of both.

After a graphic discussion of the necessity for farm hygiene and a vigorous hand washing for all, Emily served hot chocolate and sloppy joes in the kitchen. Everyone left feeling that it had been a most successful beginning for the Animal Science Merit Badge.

At her next trip to Mann's it was immediately evident to Fiona that the news of her hardware store disaster had traveled quickly. She noticed some sly smiles and the quick, stolen looks of her fellow shoppers just before they innocently looked away. With a deep sense of humility she made her way through the small store, stopping, when conversation seemed inevitable, to immerse herself in reading without comprehension the labels of random items on the shelves.

Just as she was approaching the checkout, she ran into her friends Jake and Charlotte in the dairy section. Charlotte was extremely solicitous about her well-being.

"We heard about your fall at the Mercantile," she said kind-ly. "I hope you weren't hurt."

Jake's eyes sparkled as he looked Fiona up and down. "Hope there aren't any bruises in inconvenient places. These digital cameras pick up every flaw these days, don't they?" He leaned closer and spoke confidentially. "But I'll bet you have a few spe-cial tricks of the trade to cover up things like that." He looked at her expectantly, filled with curiosity. Charlotte nudged him hard with her elbow and changed the subject.

It occurred to Fiona that this remark indicated a shift, and possibly an escalation, in the illicit rumors about her. Hadn't her activities been said to have been limited only to writing pornog-raphy? Was she now supposed to be making videos? Had Stella upped the ante?

But this was not a topic Fiona felt equal to discussing with Jake, or, in fact, with anyone. With what dignity she could mus-ter, she extricated herself hastily and moved toward the checkout line before the topic of harbor dredging could even arise.

Emily had not forgotten her encounter with Stella at the gro-cery store, and it was with shock that she realized one after-noon, that all those purple signs for Town Chairman had Stella's name on them. Surely the Islanders would not want that woman to run the place? It was unthinkable. Emily acknowledged to her-self that she did not have time for such a job. But someone needed to run in opposition. If only she knew the area better, she was certain she could have found someone suitable. Someone who could hold the office and run it with reasonable competence until she, Emily, or, in a pinch, her husband, Jason, could take over. "Oh, well," she thought to herself. "I can't do everything."

It was this reflection that reminded her that the Scouts would require poster board for tonight's planned activity. Each boy was expected to produce a chart showing the components of goats' milk. She shifted her thoughts to determining when she would have time to run into town to purchase the necessary supplies.

The day of Fiona's party was cool, crisp, and sparkling, and she was hoping for a cold evening so she could use her newly repaired fireplaces.

Not normally a superstitious person, Fiona had waited until the year had been completed before celebrating, lest she somehow jinx herself. But once the date had come and gone, she felt it was time to acknowledge this small milestone.

Her other key reason for delay was that she couldn't imagine a party without Elisabeth and Roger, and she wanted to give them a chance to breathe after their return from their honeymoon. As for Pete, well, Fiona had already learned that she could not postpone events waiting for his availability. This, she felt, was a flaw in the relationship, but one for which she had no solution.

Pete's work travels were unpredictable, remote, and prolonged. Sometimes she heard from him every day, but then he would go off the grid for weeks at a time, and although he tried to give her warning, it was still difficult to be always wondering where he was and how he was. Today, however, she had a distraction.

Fiona approached the preparations for the party with the sense of both accomplishment and nostalgia. She could not help feeling that circumstances were not propitious for her future on the Island.

"But when," she thought wryly, "had they ever been?"

It was not as if the whole sojourn had been a festival of joy. She considered Stella, the terrible rumors she had spread, and which—as she recalled Jake's recent remarks—seemed to have taken root, even among people who should have known better. She thought of the winter, the demon goat Robert, and the *fire*. And yet, when she thought about her life in Chicago, of the crimes she had reported on and the ugliness she had witnessed, the stress of daily deadlines, and the pace of city life, she couldn't help appreciating the contrasts. Fiona looked at herself and saw a fundamental change, and it was one she wasn't willing to let go.

In preparation for the evening, she had made dozens of stuffed mushrooms and tiny cheese turnovers, and arranged—if she said so herself—some spectacular trays of canapés, none of which included mango salsa or cilantro—two food fads whose tenacity Fiona felt, had defied explanation.

She had noted, on a recent trip to Chicago, a new culinary fascination among the fashionable: that toast had been elevated from mundane to the forward edge of chic. This, she felt, was an unfortunate development. Toast would now be following in the culinary footsteps of meatloaf, macaroni and cheese, cupcakes, sliders, and grilled cheese sandwiches—all fine in their way—but all of which had been snatched from delicious domestic routine and ruined by fame.

They had had their turns passed on elegant trays at parties, and tinkered with on the menus of celebrity chefs with additions of goat cheese, fennel, shaved coconut, fresh sea salt, avocado, chipotle, or heirloom tomatoes, and occasionally all of the above—even with the cupcakes. Fiona supposed that this series of comfort food elevations was the price of modern cuisine's obsession with weirdness; its peculiar flavor combinations, and the same mad hunt for the new that despoiled modern art.

But food trendsetters quickly abandoned their stars and moved on seeking another innovation, leaving some perfectly respectable food forgotten in fashion's dust, as unloved and purposeless as bustles or spats. It wasn't that grilled cheese was any less delicious than before—although Fiona preferred hers without truffle oil—it was simply that it was no longer beloved of the in-crowds.

Toast, she knew, was fated now to a future worse than obscurity: it would become a shameful relic, one of popular culture's has-beens, as forgotten and unbeloved as a fading Hollywood idol. Fiona felt sorry in anticipation. She was fond of toast.

Shaking off this rumination, Fiona continued with her preparations.

She had invited more people than the little house could hold, and ordered candles and vast quantities of wine and beer. If she had learned one thing over the past year, it was her neighbors' capacity for alcohol. She had noticed more than once that she rarely saw any of them drunk, but she had concluded that it was related more to tolerance than abstemiousness.

She could imagine the smooth voices of her Chicago friends making comments about there being nothing else to do on the Island, and in this imaginary conversation she rebuffed them. "In the first place, there's more to do here than you could handle in a day, and in the second, you drink just as much."

She caught herself muttering irritably as she unwrapped cellophane from candles—an exceptionally frustrating task— and then, laughing at herself, shook it off. Had she gotten to the point where she had to invent annoyances? Remembering Stella's gaudy sign, she recognized the lack of necessity here. But—and this was more pertinent—why was she feeling defensive about the Island and its ways? And to whom was she actually defending it? Having caught herself in this little exercise in self-awareness, she fell again into her quandary.

Fiona had never belonged anywhere, but at least in the city, no one else really belonged either. To settle here would be to cast herself forever into outsider status. She recalled a recent conversation at an Island event in which a thirty year resident had been referred to, though affectionately, as a newcomer. Was this how she wanted to live? Never fitting in? Never feeling at home?

And then there was the house. A money pit, she fully acknowledged, but one beloved. She looked with pleasure around the cozy little rooms as she placed dishes of nuts and olives at strategic points and set up the bar. The house was charming, mostly untouched by the hazards of bad remodeling.

Charm, however, was not a substitute for structural integrity, as Fiona had quickly learned. The bills for the repair of the

porches, the roof, the foundation, and fireplaces had been stag-
gering, and had stretched Fiona's meager finances to the limit.
The floors needed to be refinished; the upstairs bathroom's ugly
laminate vanity and, dreadful peel-and-stick floor needed to be
replaced; and the refrigerator was doddering. She still had frequent visits from the nighttime crunching animal, doing God
Knows What to the infrastructure of the attics. There were
clearly many more expenses to come. And then there was the
question of whether to rebuild the barn.

Beginning to feel overwhelmed, Fiona chose to set these
thoughts aside. "Just for tonight," she told herself, knowing full
well her propensity for midnight angst.

By the time the first guests began arriving, Fiona had shifted the focus of her thoughts to more pleasant things. Everyone
she knew, no matter how remotely, had been invited. Terry and
Mike and their wives had come from the mainland, along, of
course, with Elisabeth and Roger, and, separately, The Angel
Joshua. Nancy, Jim, Pali and Nika, and their circle had come,
along with Jake and Charlotte, Young Joe and many of the ferry
crew. Even Eddie the bartender, who normally felt that he had
had sufficient professional encounters with Island society, had
promised to stop by after closing.

Lars Olafsen and his wife, Katherine, were the first to arrive.
Fiona heard their steps on the porch, and hastened to receive
the beautiful iced cake they carried. It was a homemade carda-
mom cake, a Swedish tradition, and one of Fiona's favorites. She
set it carefully on the side table, and offered them both a drink.
Before long, the other guests began to arrive, and soon the little
house was filled and overflowing onto the porch. Fiona's favorite

Billie Holiday songs were mostly inaudible amid the din.

Stella had not been invited to the party, but she was an invisible presence. Her yard signs had been noticed by almost everyone almost immediately, and the first question out of nearly every guest's mouth to Fiona and one another was: "Have you seen them?"

The resulting conversations were by turns hilarious and grim. It was too early to take Stella's candidacy very seriously, but for those who had thought it out, like Nancy and Pali, the prospects were unpleasant indeed.

Fiona had chosen to take the high road. She would not think of Stella tonight; it was her celebration. She laughed off the questions about her plans to stay or go, deflecting the need for any serious response. But she knew that tomorrow she would have to come to grips with some decisions about her future. A future, she fondly hoped, unmarred by the activities of Stella. Unfortunately, as Fiona was well aware, this would also mean a future off the Island.

Circulating among her guests, Fiona was having a good time. The party had reached a pitch of enthusiasm that generated a fair amount of noise, and there were a number of people there she could not remember having seen before. She was silently and, she hoped, subtly checking out a group by the fireplace and trying to identify them before approaching when Young Joe came rollicking into the kitchen from the back porch.

"We have Northern Lights tonight!" he called out in a voice accustomed to shouting over ferry engines. "Best I've seen in a while."

The Islanders, while no strangers to this phenomenon, were

blessed with a genuine appreciation for their surroundings, and almost everyone flowed out into the back yard, drinks in hand, to observe.

Fiona followed her guests outside. She had been too busy even to have poured herself a glass of wine. Her new high-heeled Italian short boots had proven unequal to an evening of standing and moving, so she was now barefoot. The dew on the grass was cold, but the autumn air was still balmy. She looked up at the sheets of green and blue and deep red lights that shifted in the night sky as if they were raining onto the earth without touching it. The red became purple and deep rose, and the green gleamed at the edges closest to the earth and to the sky. The universe seemed to hum with color.

The crowd became respectfully silent, awed by what fell before them. Fiona felt that the glory of it was almost terrifying, as if the earth had come to an end and some new universe had come into being. They watched, together, unified by this phenomenon before them.

It was at this moment that Fiona became aware of a different source of red light, and she realized that it was the circling strobe of a police car pulled up at the side of the house. She moved toward it and found her old friend, Sergeant Johnsson, approaching the house.

He nodded politely to her. "Good evening," he said.

"Good evening," said Fiona, and checked herself before she could ask: Is there a problem? Instead she said: "It's spectacular, isn't it?"

"Sure is," he said. And then, "I'm afraid we've had a complaint."

Fiona was genuinely puzzled. "About what?"

"Well, noise for one thing."

Fiona gestured toward her somber and wondering guests. "There's your noise."

The Sergeant almost smiled, but he responded in a dead-pan. "We have to investigate."

"I can imagine who called."

"It's a matter of public record, ma'am."

"It was my neighbor."

"Yes, ma'am."

"Well, thank you for doing your job, Sergeant," said Fiona, about to go.

"But there's another thing," he said. "It's the parking."

Fiona waited respectfully, restraining her sigh.

"You can't have this many cars parked after midnight. It's against town ordinance."

Fiona looked at him steadily.

"You can't be serious."

"I'm afraid I am."

"Are you giving everyone a ticket?"

"I'm afraid so. And you."

"Me?" asked Fiona. "For what?"

"Constituting a public nuisance."

"A nuisance?"

"Yes, ma'am."

"What nuisance?"

"The party and parking, ma'am."

"Please stop calling me ma'am," said Fiona. She knew she shouldn't make things worse for herself, but ma'am was a word she detested.

The Sergeant looked at her steadily.

A thought came to her, inspired by her experience as a reporter in Chicago.

"I suppose I ought to know this by now, but what constitutes the designation of a nuisance property here on the Island?"

"Three citations, ma—" he broke off. "Three citations."

Fiona nodded slowly. "I see." She was silent for a moment. "Do my guests all have to move their cars?"

"They already have tickets."

"You have had a very busy night, Sergeant."

He shrugged philosophically.

"Okay, Sergeant. Carry on." Resigned to her fate, Fiona turned to go announce the news to her guests.

"Uh, Ma'am?"

Her back to him, Fiona rolled her eyes and turned toward him politely. "Yes?"

"I need to write out your ticket."

It was Fiona's turn to deadpan. "Write away, Sergeant." She stood stoically as he wrote on his clipboard.

He started to write her name, which, by now, he knew very well, but he paused and looked up.

"I've forgotten your middle initial."

"A," said Fiona.

"Oh, yes. For… ?" He looked up curiously. "It's something unusual."

"Ainsley."

"Oh, right!" he said, delighted.

She stood with him, contemplating the juxtaposition of the

spectacle above them and the mundane before them. When he was finished, he gave her a copy of the citation and explained about a court appearance.

As he was leaving, he broke, for just a moment, his official demeanor and leaned forward confidingly.

"Maybe next time you should invite her."

Fiona did not feel like laughing, but she made a brief noise. "You do know her, right?"

This time the Sergeant smiled. "Yes, ma'am."

The Northern Lights swirled above their heads as they each parted to their separate duties. Fiona found herself looking forward to the new book of essays that lay on her bedside table, William Hazlitt's *On the Pleasure of Hating*.

F iona was wandering the streets of a foreign city with a group of friends, but no one whose names she knew. Everyone was urgently going somewhere, but they were all cautioned to be careful of the snakes, which were extremely poisonous. Looking down at the sidewalk, Fiona realized that the snakes were everywhere: on the streets, hanging from trees, slithering out of sewer grates. They were an iridescent blue and their yellow eyes glittered.

Cautiously, she made her way toward a distant hill outside of the city, but as she was stepping from a bus onto the curb, she looked down into the gutter, and there was a snake, moving toward her, about to strike. In a quick movement, she grabbed the snake behind its head, holding tightly, so that it could not turn its *head to bite her. The rest of its muscular body writhed furiously and she used her other hand to grab it. The snake was terrifyingly powerful, and she knew that if she loosed her grip, it would turn and bite and she would die. Desperately, she squeezed the neck of the snake, hoping to kill it, but it fought hard. The snake's tail thrashed with so much power that she could barely hold it, even as it struggled to turn its head to bite her arms. Her hands were aching from the struggle, and she did not know if she could hold on long enough. She squeezed harder and the snake's eyes began to pop, but it did not lessen its strength in the fight. Harder and harder she squeezed with both her hands, knowing that her only hope of saving herself was to strangle the snake. It was horrifying and it disgusted her, but she did not have any choice.*

Fiona felt her strength failing, and even as it strangled, the snake renewed its battle to kill her. Finally, just as Fiona began to doubt that she could hold on, the snake went limp.

Unsure that it was dead, and afraid to let go, she continued to strangle the snake with both hands, looking for a safe way to release it and get away quickly. At last, in a clear space on the sidewalk, with no one else near, Fiona flung the limp snake away from her, and as she had feared, it began again to move. Suddenly, a hole opened in the sidewalk, and in one moment the snake slithered down it, disappearing into the dark. The hole disappeared in a small bright flash, and the sidewalk was clear.

Fiona woke with aching hands. In her sleep she had been acting out her dreams and her hands were stiff from clenching the dream snake. Feeling slightly sick in her heart, she looked at the clock. 3:17. Sighing, she turned on the light and reached for the book at her bedside. It was unlikely that she would sleep anymore tonight. Even with the light on, she couldn't help imagining snakes coiled in her slippers next to the bed, or hidden under the covers. Chiding herself, and with great effort, she turned her mind away from the dream and concentrated on her book, *On The Pleasure of Hating*. Hating, she found, was becoming increasingly easy.

"So how's married life, Roger?" asked Terry one morning. Roger looked clean, and rumpled as usual, but he also had dark circles under his eyes.

"Fine," he said.

His friends had not expected a paean to wedded bliss from Roger, but there was something defensive in his manner that made them both suspicious.

Mike took in the expression on Roger's face and put some things together.

"Women can be hard to understand," he said in his quiet way. Roger glanced at Mike with a look of recognition.

"First year is rough," added Terry. "You need to learn to work together as a team, not to keep pulling your own way." He looked with sympathy at Roger. He had doubted all along that Roger was capable of the kind of personal interaction required for a successful marriage, but, of course, it had not been his place to say so. He felt sorry, too, for Elisabeth, who surely deserved more.

Roger burst out unexpectedly, "I want her to be happy. I

don't think I make her happy."

There was an astonished silence after this, and everyone felt a bit embarrassed at this unwonted intimacy.

The Angel Joshua, who had not been invited to participate in the discussion, looked up from polishing the Italian coffee machine, and turned a beatific gaze of peace and beauty at Roger. "You need to get in touch with your feminine side to help you communicate. You should come to yoga with me."

"Now, that's something I'd like to see," said Terry. "Let me know, so I can clear my schedule." Mike smiled, and watched the expressions on his friends' faces without speaking.

Roger turned his back on all of them and stalked into the back room. Terry and Mike stood up to go, taking out their wallets and putting bills next to their empty plates.

"Got to get down to Sturgeon Bay to the lumber yard," said Terry. "Anybody need anything while I'm there?"

Mike and Joshua shook their heads and expressed their thanks, but from the back room came a kind of bellow.

"Paper towels!"

"Got it," called Terry, and the door closed behind them as Terry and Mike headed out to their trucks and their separate ways.

Roger returned from the back, picked up a rag, and began wiping the counter. Soft jazz played tunelessly in the background.

"When is this class?" he asked, casually.

"There's one at two o'clock today," said Josh. "St. Anatole's community room. Wear loose clothing. You know, like sweats."

Roger nodded. The two men worked in silence until the next customers arrived.

"So is that it? You're leaving us?"

Nancy Iverssen's frank blue eyes bored into Fiona with such intensity that Fiona looked down in embarrassment. She felt like a schoolgirl caught in some underhanded endeavor.

It was the morning after Fiona's party, and the house was in a reasonable state of post-party restoration. The only signs remaining were the random placement of chairs in the living room, the peculiar tilt of one of the lampshades, the prodigious array of empty bottles on the back porch, and the long row of newly washed glasses and dishes, neatly arranged along the kitchen counter waiting to be put away.

Nancy had stopped by on one of her random and unsolicited social calls, which Fiona generally enjoyed. They were sitting in Fiona's kitchen drinking coffee. Fiona, who had been too busy at the party for even one drink, felt nevertheless as if she were nursing a hangover. If anything, she thought, the hangover came from her dream.

On top of that, the prospect of Stella DesRosiers running the Island crouched like an ugly toad in the corner of Fiona's consciousness, making her head feel even worse. Stella would be capricious, petty, vindictive, and mercilessly efficient. She would seek out those whom she considered her enemies—chief among these would be Fiona herself—and find every means possible to make their lives a misery. The prospects for Fiona's future happiness on the Island, she felt, were small indeed.

"Well," began Fiona, weakly. "It was only supposed to be for the winter. I just felt that if I made it a year, no one would be able to quibble."

Nancy harrumphed impatiently. "Damn fool idea. Moving to the island on a dare. But now you're here, you might as well stay." She paused, frowned, and pursed her lips as if considering some very serious proposition. "We're kind of used to you."

Fiona got up and stood at the window. This, she knew, was high praise coming from Nancy. She looked out at the autumn leaves falling from the big, old maple tree in the yard. There was a blank space beyond, where the barn used to be, and Fiona instinctively averted her gaze.

From the beginning, Fiona had had no intention of staying on the island for another winter. She had won her dare—with nothing but her own self-respect to show for it—and had been prepared to pack up and go back to the relative comforts of Ephraim on the mainland of Wisconsin's Door County Peninsula. For a few brief and wild moments, she had even considered returning to Chicago where she had worked for some years as a reporter for a major newspaper.

But now that the time had come to make the move away, Fiona wasn't sure that she could do it.

Moving back to the mainland felt like some form of disloyalty or betrayal, even though she wasn't quite sure of what or of whom. But the trump card was Stella's candidacy. That would change everything. Life here would be most unpleasant. Fiona shrugged her shoulders in a gesture of helplessness and turned back to her guest.

"The truth is, I don't know if I can sell. The real estate market is pretty soft everywhere, but especially on the island." She picked up an apple from the basket on the table and turned it idly in her hand. "I really can't afford to leave if I don't sell the place."

Nancy grunted. "No doubt Stella would buy it," she commented shrewdly.

Fiona nodded. She had thought of Stella buying her house, and she hated the idea, as Nancy had known she would. Stella desperately wanted Fiona's property, and had schemed ruthlessly to acquire it. So ruthlessly, in fact, that Fiona couldn't help suspecting that she had been involved in the barn fire. Would Stella have been capable even of that? It was no secret that she had feared and despised Robert, Fiona's unwanted but oddly beguiling goat, who had been lost in the fire. And Stella no doubt blamed Fiona for the public victory she had won last June in front of the town board. But arson? "Surely not," thought Fiona for the thousandth time. No, even Stella could not have done such a thing. Surely not.

Why, Fiona asked herself, should she even care whether Stella bought the place? Why should she care what Stella did or didn't do? Let Stella find whatever warped victory she wanted. Let her run the Island. Why give Stella control of her life by letting her determine Fiona's path?

Fiona recalled one of her favorite lines from Marcus Aurelius: *You have power over your mind, not outside events. Realize this, and you will find strength.*

She turned from the window, smiled at Nancy, and shrugged. "More coffee?" she asked.

Nancy was not to be deterred. "Maybe you're planning to follow Pete to wherever he is." She smiled wickedly. "He's one probably worth following." She nodded to herself in recollection.

"I liked him. Capable, direct, and just a bit wily." She looked at Fiona over the tops of her glasses. "Definitely a keeper, I'd say."

Nancy paused for a moment, seeming to catch herself in a reverie, then shook her head as if shaking a strand of hair from her eyes, and smiled a bit regretfully.

"Well, time I was off. Those apples won't pick themselves." And with a nod of thanks, she was out of her chair, out the door, and down the path to her truck in her usual blaze of energy.

Rather dazedly, Fiona watched her go, and went slowly back to the kitchen to wash the coffee cups. She smiled to herself, remembering Nancy's description of Pete. "A bit wily, indeed," she thought.

Finishing in the kitchen, Fiona sat down at her desk to work on an article she had due, but her mind was preoccupied.

Despite what Nancy and Island gossip seemed to presume, Pete Landry—though ever charming—had not invited her to follow him anywhere. Even if he had, Fiona was not at all certain whether she would want to. To be fair, they had only really known one another a few months. He led a busy life, travelling all over the world for the energy company he worked for, often to remote and unfriendly places, and for months at a time. If she went to London, where he was based, she'd be alone most of the time anyway. Fiona had drastically uprooted herself twice recently: once when she moved to Ephraim from Chicago, and again last year when she had accepted the dare. Pete's absence had left a hole in her life, but she was tired of upheaval. She wanted routine and normalcy and calm.

She sighed and turned her attention to her work. So far,

nothing of her life on the Island—or anywhere else for that matter—had included any of those things.

At one-forty-five, Roger walked down the steps into St. Anatole's basement community room to discover that he was the only one there. The light in the stairway was sufficient for him to find the wall switch, and he flipped it on. The room still smelled of the coffee and cake that had been served there for Bible study that morning. Folding chairs and tables had been stored neatly against the wall; and a series of posters announcing day care, rummage sales, and Alcoholics Anonymous meetings covered the wall near the big double doors that led upstairs to the church.

He was just in the process of deciding whether to sit somewhere or flee when he heard the voices in the stairwell, and two women clad in form-fitting clothing came in, followed closely by The Angel Joshua. The newcomers all knew one another, and Joshua introduced Roger to them. Roger gave a curt nod, but said nothing.

"I brought an extra mat for you," Joshua told Roger. Roger accepted the mat, and following Joshua's example, spread it out on the floor.

"I like to be toward the back," said Joshua, "so I can follow the movements if I get lost."

Still silent, Roger sat on his mat, and watched the others go through a series of similar, but, to Roger, impossible stretching and swaying movements. The room was beginning to fill, and the sound of women's voices began to reverberate in the cinder block walls of the room.

Then, in a rush of energy, the instructor swept into the room, carrying a big tote bag and apologizing fluently for being late. She was a lithe, blonde woman, about forty. She was not beautiful, but she had an animal grace and vivacity that made her striking. Her wild blonde hair seemed to surround her face and shoulders like an aura.

She shed her boots and set up her mat quickly, then turned her attention to fidgeting with a small portable speaker that was wirelessly connected to her phone. This whirlwind of activity completed, she sat on her mat facing the class and began a little monologue of greeting.

"I'm so sorry for being late, everybody, but I had to take my car in for service down in Sturgeon Bay, and they didn't have the right part, and it was just barely completed in time, and then I still needed to grab a couple of essentials down there, and, well, you know how it is. Time just got away from me, and I missed the ferry."

All of this was delivered as she sat cross-legged on her mat, making a circle with her slim, perfect body as if she were hypnotizing a cobra. Roger, too, was mesmerized.

"I see we have a new class member. You're a friend of Joshua's?"

Roger nodded, but she barely paused before continuing.

"Just take it easy, if this is your first time, and I'll come around and help you through. I'm Shay."

She seemed to be expecting a response.

"Roger," said Roger.

"Okay, Roger, great. Nice to have you here. Okay, everybody. Everybody nice and warmed up?"

A chorus of responses came from the group, and the class began.

Self-consciousness had never been a problem for Roger, since, in order to feel self-conscious, one needed to be aware of other people's feelings. Thus unencumbered, Roger endeavored to follow the class as best he could. A series of movements Shay called "Sun Salutations" provided one challenge after another to Roger. Shay may have appeared scattered, but she was a gifted teacher, and she quickly realized that Roger was out of his depth. Only a few moments after the class began, she began to move to the back of the room, and talking non-stop to the class, directing and cajoling, she was simultaneously standing near Roger, pulling on his leg here, nudging his shoulders back and his arms higher, gently pushing his head further toward the floor.

Roger did what he was told, to the extent that he was capable, but he wasn't very flexible, he discovered. The rest of the class seemed to easily bend themselves into the requisite shapes, and the strange sound of their rhythmic breathing filled the room. Roger couldn't touch his toes, his downward dog was spread too far apart, and his sun salutation was clumsy. His arms and legs seemed to have minds of their own. Shay came around to him again, offering instructions to the class as she moved to the back of the room. She told them to lift their legs to the sky, and Roger thought he was doing so until she tugged it into a place that did not feel natural. His leg did not go that way, he was quite certain. He tried rotating his shoulder back during downward dog, as instructed, but he didn't know what it meant to rotate his shoulders, and he succeeded only in appearing to writhe in some kind of yogic agony. He tried to concentrate on breathing as Shay instructed, but this added a level of complication he had not imagined possible. After what seemed an hour of the deepest concentration and pain, he caught a glimpse of the clock and saw that seven minutes had passed.

Sun salutations, Roger discovered, were nearly endless, and endlessly difficult. He had no difficulty in raising himself from the floor in a plank pose, which Shay called "Phalankasana," on the way to Cobra, but for all practical purposes, this was the extent of his abilities. With relief, he heard Shay announce that they were moving on to Warrior pose. Warriors, Roger felt sure, were something he could understand. But when the warrior pose morphed into inverted triangles and other geometric eccentricities, Roger, his head pointing to the floor, began to realize that there would be no refuge.

At last it was over. The class sat cross-legged facing the front of the room, and Roger, whose legs didn't exactly cross, copied the others as they put their palms together in front of their hearts and bowed to their teacher. "Namaste," they said in unison. Roger had heard this word, but did not know its meaning. Perhaps it was Sanskrit for "gratitude after pain."

There began a bustle as the students began rolling up their mats, gathering belongings, and putting on jackets and sweaters. Shay came up to Roger and put her hand on his arm.

"What did you think, Roger? Will we be seeing you again?"

"Yes," said Roger in his economical fashion. "When?"

"On Thursday, same time. Be sure to practice. And Roger,"

she put her both her hands on each of his arms as if she were about to shake him, "I sense a deep well of spirituality in you. Nice work."

Roger watched her go, and then turned to hand Joshua's mat to him.

"Hang onto it 'til you get your own, man. I don't need it."

And with a wave, The Angel Joshua departed, leaving Roger to find his own way out, his borrowed mat rolled carefully under his arm.

Emily and Jason Martin were quite pleased at the way their Scouting project was going. The visits from the boys inevitably led to visits from their parents, coming to pick them up, or to chaperone the small, boisterous, but essentially well-mannered group. This growing familiarity with their new neighbors would help to ensure the Martins' entrée into the community, and this was all according to plan.

Today they were working on the presentations each boy would have to make about what he had learned. This, on the Island—where finding entertainment in small things was something of an art form—would be an opportunity for a well-publicized community event. The presence of an audience would place additional pressure on the boys, but would nevertheless provide support and enthusiasm as well. Making the posters for the presentations would come later. There was a visit to the barn to make first.

The Martins felt strongly that it was important for the boys to spend as much time as possible with the animals, and therefore every session for the animal husbandry badge began with the boys heading out to the barn to participate in the many aspects of goat care and feeding. The Scouts grew increasingly confident around the animals, calling them by name, leading them in and out of their enclosures, and knowing the farm's routines and the locations of various necessary equipment. In encouraging these encounters, the Martins proved to be thoughtful and effective teachers.

Among the vital lessons taught was the necessity of keeping the bucks and does separated. On a farm, there could be no unplanned co-minglings, and Emily and Jason were clear and firm in explaining these common sense facts of life. The boys listened with only a few secret, gleaming glances at one another. They were duly impressed by the responsibilities being shared with them, and by the unexpected revelation of this adult knowledge. Their usual chatter somewhat diminished by self-consciousness, they returned to the house and their posters afterward, and set to work with a seriousness of purpose. It wasn't long before their animation returned, however, and fueled in part by the appearance of cookies, the house was soon filled with boyish exuberance.

Chapter Four ✦

Once Lars had officially given notice of his retirement, the gaudy red and purple signs began popping up around the Island with the same kind of welcome as tent caterpillars might receive, and for more or less the same kind of reason: nobody particularly wanted them, but it was impossible to stop them without poison. It was the rare Islander who felt safe enough to say no to Stella. Her tantrums and vindictiveness had continued without hindrance since her childhood, and anyone who had ever crossed her regretted it. She had a cadre of friends who, for reasons of their own, were able to overlook or share in her flaws, but this was a small group. For the rest, it was simply easier to let her post a sign. After all, the thinking went, it didn't mean you had to vote for her.

Stella's campaign was beginning the way her time in office would inevitably continue: by intimidation and fear. The general opinion expressed in whispered voices or behind closed doors was that it was a damned good thing there was a secret ballot. But, of course, this would only be helpful if someone actually ran against her, and as the deadline for candidates' submission of papers came near, a new sense of urgency began to dawn on the Island's electorate. Somebody had to run against Stella.

"You should do it, Pali," said Fiona as they sat one evening at Nelsen's. The Scoutmaster had recovered, and Ben had his regular troop meeting. His parents were taking advantage of the opportunity.

"Oh no, he shouldn't," said Nika quickly. "We see him little enough as it is without adding more to his obligations." Her husband smiled and patted her knee affectionately.

"Have no fear," he said. "Political life holds no appeal for me."

"You, then," said Fiona brightly, turning to Nika with a wicked smile.

"Ha ha!" said Nika nervously. "No thank you."

Eddie, the bartender, had been listening to this conversation. It was one which had been repeated countless times at Nelsen's in recent weeks. He leaned over the bar to speak.

"You know, it's funny. Everybody's trying to get everyone else to run, and no one is willing to do it." He paused to pour a couple of beers for the guys at the end of the bar and returned. "It's actually pretty unusual. Normally it becomes clear that there's some likely candidate, someone everybody thinks should do it. This time...." Eddie shook his head. "People are starting to get worried."

Fiona took a deep breath and sighed. "I have to admit that I am. If Stella becomes chairman, I don't know if I could stay on the Island."

"Maybe you should do it, Fiona," said Nika, happy to be able to turn the question back.

"Good God, no. It will be a cold day in Hell. Public office? Against Stella? Never!" Fiona punctuated this speech by putting her glass on the bar with an emphatic thump. "I need to go. I have a Skype date with Pete." She gathered her things and headed for the door. "Keep thinking. You'll come up with some-one. Bye. Thanks, Eddie."

"Bye," said Nika.

"See you around," said Pali.

Pali and Eddie watched Fiona leave.

"Hmmm," said Pali.

Eddie kept his thoughts to himself, but he and Pali shared a long speculative look.

Sitting at her desk staring at her computer, Fiona wanted to dive into the screen at Pete's image on Skype. He seemed so illusory, so distant.

"Do you think it's possible that Stella burned down the barn?" he asked.

Fiona was silent as she thought about this.

"I've wondered about it," she said at last. But I can't accept that anyone I know could do such a thing."

"People do ugly things." His voice echoed strangely across ocean and continents.

"Yes. Yes, I know. I used to be a reporter in Chicago, remem-ber." She fell silent again, remembering with grim specificity the details of some of the things she had witnessed one human being do to another. "It's possible, I suppose."

"Be careful, Fiona."

"I feel safe here."

"I know. But maybe you shouldn't."

After they hung up, Fiona felt bereft. She had always worried about Stella, but did not fear that she threatened physical harm. Stella was anxiety-provoking and infuriating, but not actually dangerous. At least, that was how Fiona had always perceived the situation. Pete was very far away. And now, entertaining these new thoughts, Fiona felt more alone than she had felt in a very long time.

And she found, much to her annoyance, that on top of everything else, she was starting to miss Robert.

She closed her laptop and meandered downstairs for a drink. It was late, and she had done enough for today. She poured herself a scotch in one of the hand-blown glasses that had been Elisabeth's gift from Italy, and slowly wandered around the house, turning off lights before heading upstairs. She had a new book that she was looking forward to.

In one of those interesting and occasionally odd paths that one takes from one book to another, Fiona had found herself interested in the writings of Martin Luther. There were some glaring inconsistencies—and rather appalling hypocrisy—in the thinking of the Reformation's first voice, and instances of his brutal anti-Semitism had driven her to abandon Luther several times. But Fiona was not one to run from ideas that offended her, and she ultimately picked up the book again. Her interest was fueled, in part, by the contradictions. She was fascinated by the mixture of an almost romantic theology with a sort of native German crudeness. She had found this particular book at a rummage sale, drawn at first by its green leather binding and gilt letters, and then delightedly discovering what it was. She had come to think of it as Martin's Little Green Book—her private joke.

Fiona's German being somewhere between rusty and non-existent, she was spending an inordinate amount of time with a German-English dictionary, but she found this oddly restful and satisfying, like solving a puzzle, and since it also had the fringe benefit of engaging her busy mind, it had become her bedtime ritual.

She settled into her pillows, warm beneath her comforter, with the cool autumn air coming in through the open window. She took a sip of scotch and sighed. She missed Pete. She missed Rocco. She steadfastly refused to miss Robert. The house felt very silent. Very empty.

Just as this feeling moved over her like a wave, she heard a scrabbling sound in the wall behind her head, and then, as if by invitation, the intensive crunching of her unknown tenant and frequent nighttime companion began with particular vigor.

Fiona pondered the change in her approach to life that was indicated by her present reaction to the chewing animal, whatever it was. What before had seemed an alarming intrusion, she now welcomed as an act of companionship. Was this, she wondered, a sign of resignation to lower standards—the harbinger of personal deterioration that would increase and intensify the longer she lived alone on the Island? Was she now on the path to becoming one of those old ladies who live in filth with twenty-seven cats and stacks of ancient newspapers—or, perhaps, books of Reformation theology—everywhere? Was this her signal that it was time to get out while the getting was good? To move back to civilization and get on with her life?

Or was it simple, almost agonizing loneliness?

It occurred to her that knowing that Pete was in the world

somewhere made the loneliness actually worse than when she hadn't loved him. She longed for him, and her longing sometimes made everything an exercise in discipline: forcing herself to go through the motions of her days rather than moving through them with joy. "No, this will not do," she told herself. Shaking off the mood, she returned her attention to her book.

"*Du kannst nicht verhindern, dass ein Vogelschwarm über deinen Kopf Hinwegfliegt. Aber du kannst verhindern, dass er in deinen Haaren nistet.*" Fiona flipped rapidly through her dictionary. "Ah," she said aloud, with satisfaction, finding the missing word in her vocabulary.

She read aloud as she translated, "You cannot keep a flock of birds from flying over your head, but you can keep them from nesting in your hair."

"At least," she thought, "I don't have that problem." She took a sip of scotch and then corrected herself.

"Yet."

She settled more deeply into her pillows, basking in the stalwart and companionable crunching of her fellow creature. She turned the page of the Little Green Book, and took another sip of scotch.

I t did not occur to Ben that his plans to help an injured deer might, in fact, be dangerous to the animal. His Scout leader, or Jim, or his father, for that matter—had they been able to advise—would have pointed out the difficulties of getting close enough to help in the first place; and then the dangers of having a makeshift splint in the wild, of the need to supervise the animal in a protected location, of the prospect of infection, and of the foolishness of trying to practice medicine—even veterinary medicine—without training or a license; and even how an animal rehabilitator might help.

But Ben had not confided in his Scoutmaster, in Jim, nor in anyone else, and he'd never heard of an animal rehabilitator. This project to save the little animal, he was certain, would be frowned upon by the adults who would see it as foolishness. To them, he was convinced, it was just a deer, a disposable animal, and the adults would have found ways to prevent his attempting to save it. But to Ben, the deer was more than that: it was an irreplaceable living thing deserving of his compassion, and the disapproval of adults meant simple bossiness, not the possibility of some very good reasons. Ben wanted to save the deer. Saving it would not be looked upon with favor. Ben, therefore, would not tell anyone about it. It was that simple.

In order to accomplish his goal, Ben needed to assemble some equipment. Leaping over any other difficulties, he had given this part of his plan a great deal of thought. His Boy Scout troop had given him extensive training in First Aid—considered an essential skill on the Island—and armed with this knowledge he had a reasonable sense—for a ten year old—of what he didn't know. In a remarkably short period of time, he had found the information he needed on the Internet, along with how-to videos and lists of the necessary items.

Most of these things he needed would be simple for him to acquire on his own: garbage bags, rags, rope, and antibiotic ointment. Among the methods recommended for splinting an injured leg, however, the one he thought made the most sense involved the use of PVC pipe. He would need to split it lengthwise, and this meant he would need some help. But how to engage the adults around him without alerting their suspicions? Carefully, Ben devised a little plan, and made himself a list.

One afternoon after school, Ben presented himself at the Mercantile. The store was empty, just as Ben had hoped. He was greeted by Tom as he entered and walked past the candy section without pausing.

"Hey, Ben," said Tom. "What can I help you find?"

Ben had thought this out very carefully. He would have to be deceptive, yes, but he would not tell a lie.

Without being fully conscious of it, Ben had two powerful value systems that had been instilled in him: the steady integrity of his family and the morality of fairy tales. And while they were mostly complementary, there were certain ways in which they were, perhaps, a bit contradictory. His Boy Scout training—not to mention his parents and his church—had embedded the need for truth. The fairy tales, in which honest men and women usually triumphed, had ingrained the virtues of wit and trickery to overcome evil. He had argued with himself about this quite extensively, and he had come to the conclusion that if he did not actually lie, then he could defend his actions as in protection of a life. He had practiced his response in the privacy of his room, and delivered it now in an offhand manner.

"I'm working on a project and need some PVC pipe, but"— and here Ben paused—"Christmas is coming," (this carefully worded sentence was perfectly true, if unrelated: the trickery), "and I don't want my parents to know." (Also perfectly true on every level). "Could you help me cut it here so I don't have to ask my dad?"

Tom did not hesitate for one moment. "Sure. I'd be happy to." And then came the inevitable question that Ben had anticipated.

"What are you making?"

"A birdfeeder," said Ben. This was also perfectly true. But it had nothing to do with his reason for buying PVC pipe.

Chapter Five ✤

"So what's the worst she could do?"

Elisabeth and Fiona were sitting on Elisabeth's porch discussing the Stella situation. It was still warm for late October, and they were taking advantage of the sun. There was a pot of tea on the small metal table between them, and the remains of very fashionable—though still delicious—buttered toast and cherry jam on their plates.

"I've been trying to figure that out," said Fiona, absentmindedly folding and re-folding the paper napkin on her lap.

"She could change the zoning laws, I suppose."

"But she can't do that unilaterally," said Elisabeth sensibly.

"Well, no, but everybody's intimidated by her. They'll do what she tells them."

"Are they really all that spineless?"

"I'm not sure that it's spinelessness. It's an island. People need to get along. I'd say it's more an aversion to conflict."

"That's how Hitler came to power. And anyway, what if they do change the zoning?" Elisabeth hesitated briefly before completing her thought. "After all, the main point of contention was Robert. Without him, what difference does it make?"

Fiona nodded solemnly. "I wish I knew. The thing is, she's up to something. I can tell by the way she's been taunting me."

"Taunting you? You make it sound like an elementary school

playground."

"It feels like that," admitted Fiona. "But a really high-stakes playground. One where she can destroy you."

Elisabeth looked over the tops of her sunglasses at Fiona.

"Destroy you? Be serious, Fiona. You give her too much power."

Fiona shrugged and gave a rueful smile. "It's how it is. Ask anyone on the Island."

Elisabeth decided to let this go. "Okay, so let's get back to the original question. What can she do to you?"

"I think I have to start with what she wants."

"Okay," said Elisabeth again. "What does she want?"

"She wants my property. I know that, but after what happened last spring, I doubt that's her main objective. It's certainly safe to say she wants me off the Island. At least, that's the best-case scenario. I think it's entirely possible that she really just wants me dead." Fiona grinned at the look of schoolmarm-ish disapproval on Elisabeth's face, and shrugged again. She was beginning to enjoy herself. "Maybe her campaign goal is to establish village stocks so she can publicly humiliate me."

"Actually, humiliation probably would be on the top of her list, don't you think?"

Fiona's smile changed. "Yes. Without a doubt. Humiliation would be a good goal." She paused, remembering the hardware store. "Better than death, actually."

They looked at each other for a moment, and silence fell over them as they each considered this possibility.

Rocco lay nearby, his head carefully positioned to be exactly equidistant from each of them, so as to maximize his ability to love and protect. Fiona's Italian sandals were under her chair, and she reached out her bare foot to run it along Rocco's soft fur. Pleased, he made a low, rumbling, cooing sound. A crow called from the woods nearby, and was answered in the same rough pattern by its fellow. A soft breeze had begun, and there was beginning to be a chill in the air. Elisabeth was staring off into the distance. Fiona pulled her sweater tighter and wrapped her arms around herself for a moment in a gesture of comfort before reaching for her mug of tea.

At last she spoke, a look of grim determination on her face. "I can't run away from this. I started it by moving to the Island, and now I have to deal with it directly. I can't believe I'm saying this, but there's no other way."

She put down her mug and looked at Elisabeth.

"I'm going to have to run against Stella."

Chapter Six

H eading home on the ferry, as they crossed Death's Door, Fiona couldn't tell whether the light on the water was the reflection of the moon, or mist rising in the warm autumn air.

The lighthouse of Plum Island was immediately before her as the ferry took the western route, the shorter, summer route less sheltered from the wind and waves, toward Washington Island. Fiona contemplated the view. Elisabeth had once told her that the Island seemed desolate and depressing to her, as if she'd fallen off the edge of the earth. But that feeling was exactly what had always made Fiona feel so completely and utterly safe.

Washington Islanders liked to say that they were "north of the tension line," and Fiona had always felt that this was true. There was something about the remoteness that made her feel that nothing could be wrong. Bad things happened on the island, of course. People got sick, they died, there were accidents; all the myriad tragedies of human existence played themselves out here as they did anywhere. But the world and its troubles seemed like something apart, something alien to the golden trees on the shore, the cranes at the dock, the big American flag that flew over the harbor, the warm lights of the houses dotted along the shore. There was no war, no pestilence, no danger of attack. There were no tsunami, no sharks. People left their houses unlocked, their engines running. They walked alone without a second thought, despite the rural isolation. Everyone knew everyone else. And any criminal would have to take the ferry, fly in rather conspicuously at the tiny grass-field airport, or dock at the marina, making stealth impossible.

For the ten-thousandth time, Fiona contemplated the observation her father had once made: "People are what you should fear most in life, my dear," he had said. Her life in Chicago had taught Fiona that this was true.

On the island—Stella notwithstanding—Fiona had always felt safe among these people, and she felt that there was a gulf of distance and of security between her and the world. She was, in every way "north of the tension line," as the islanders liked to say, far away from the pressures and stresses of modern city life.

The ferry's pilot house was half-way between the 2nd and the top decks, and its occupants were visible as if on a stage in the deepening darkness. Lit by a red lamp and the screens of the guidance systems, it had the coziness of a fire-lit hearth. She watched, a trifle enviously, the warm comfort of the men who sat there, talking, perhaps of philosophy, perhaps of the Packers, engaged in the ordinary comforts of human interaction.

No matter how warmly welcomed by the island community—and the warmth was not universal, to be sure—Fiona felt alone, an outsider. She pondered whether her alien stature was something the islanders truly felt, or merely her own projection, a perpetual feeling of not-belonging she carried with her wherever she went. She'd felt it at school, awkward as she had been in the gay social interactions of the other girls; she'd felt it at the newspaper in Chicago, even after she had been recognized for her reporting; she had felt it in Ephraim, among Elisabeth and Terry and Mike, all of whom had belonged there for much of their lives. Only Roger shared her isolation and differentness, and Fiona wasn't sure that this particular club was one of which she wanted to be a member.

For the first time, in the dusk of an autumn evening, Fiona could genuinely understand the crews' whispered stories of the haunted ferry. The sea smoke, the rising mist from the cold air against the still warm water, the moon, the last rim of light along the horizon, and the sense of isolation made it seem that a ghost was in the natural order of things. A wave sent a faint spray of water across the deck, and Fiona shivered a little as it hit her. She drew herself deeper into her jacket, and huddled into a niche against the inner cabin, away from the wind. She was cold, but it felt good to be out in the air. Leaning against a corner, Fiona gave herself up to the rocking of the ferry, and felt herself slide into some deep place of the soul.

After a while, the engines shifted, and the ferry began its pivot toward the dock. The captain—one of Pali's colleagues, and one she knew—came down to open the piloting box. As she stood in the shadows unseen, Fiona, in her loneliness, was drawn to him for company and conversation. But he was busy. Not wanting to be a bother, she watched for a moment as he guided the ferry home, intent on his work. Then she quietly slipped away so that he wouldn't think she had been spying on him.

She started her car up, gave a polite wave to the crewman who directed her off the ramp, and turned her car along the dark and wooded road toward home. She would make herself something good for dinner, she thought. Comfort and warmth and light were what she needed. But her greatest source of comfort would not be there. And he was probably in greater need of it than she.

It was nearly 3:00 in the morning. Eddie had closed up the bar and was heading home to his little cottage on the harbor. It was a calm starry night, and he was glad to be alive. Eddie lived alone, and on nights like this it was his habit to make himself something to drink and sit on the porch watching the water. It was calming after the fuss and clatter of the bar and the chatter of his clientele. Sometimes he would forget himself and sit there until dawn, listening to the sound of the waves, of the fish jumping, sometimes watching the moon, sometimes the northern lights. Usually he had a book waiting by his bedside, but he had the luxury of being able to pick it up in the morning for a while if he didn't get to it before he slept.

Eddie was a methodical reader, and was now working his way through Russian literature. He was reading his second Dostoevsky—*The Idiot*—and finding it dreary. He smiled to himself as he thought about this. He had not yet discovered Russian art that was anything else.

As he seated himself, his mug of tea in his hand, two great

horned owls were somewhere near, calling to one another, and it was still warm enough that a few tree frogs still sang. Eddie sighed a deep relaxing sigh and leaned back in his rocking chair. There was a slight mist just near the water that gave everything a blurred softness. The stars seemed very near.

Eddie was going over in his mind a conversation he had had with Jim that evening. Jim was a good guy, and Eddie sympathized with his passion for Fiona Campbell. Jim might still have a chance with her if that boyfriend continued to be so elusive, but Eddie knew from sad experience the pain of unreturned love. Things were rough for Jim right now.

The sound that ripped through the darkness shocked him so thoroughly that Eddie leapt to his feet and threw his cup of tea into the air, heart pounding. It was the sound of a woman screaming as if she were in desperate fear for her life. Without a pause, Eddie was off the porch and running in the direction of the screams, dialing his phone as he ran. He saw the lights come on in the cottages nearby, and doors slamming as his two neighbors joined him, clad variously in sweat pants and pajamas.

"Where is it coming from?" asked John, who lived two houses up, as he dashed into the street.

"It sounds like the marina," said Kevin.

Together they sprinted toward the sound, which continued unceasingly. The marina was about a half mile off. Kevin was a heavy man, and began to breathe hard, but he bravely pushed on. Eddie was a runner, and he led the way, John was somewhere in the middle. They heard the siren of the police car approaching, and they moved off to the side of the road to let it pass.

As the Island police officer slowed the car and rolled down

the window, Eddie shouted to him,

"We think it's the marina!" and the officer sped off.

"Listen!" said Kevin suddenly. "It's stopped."

Not knowing whether this was good news or bad, they continued to run, reaching the marina only a few minutes after the patrol car.

Sergeant Johnsson had disappeared around the building, and there was the sound of more sirens approaching. In the ensuing chaos of fire, police, and rescue vehicles, of volunteers arriving in their trucks and SUV's, no one heard another scream. Every inch of land from the marina to Eddie's, and in a mile radius beyond, was searched for some sign of the woman whose scream had been so terrifying to hear. By the end of the second day, the searchers were forced to give up.

Chief Bill Yahr stood on the marina dock with some of his team, shaking his head. "So we have two screamers: a man and a woman. Multiple witnesses. All reliable. No sign of anyone injured or of any struggles. We have searched every field, every tree, looked under every rock, and in every house." He paused and rubbed his forehead wearily. "My best theory is that it's a prankster."

"Several pranksters," pointed out Sergeant Johnsson. "A man and a woman."

"Or a boy and a girl. It's got to be some kids enjoying making us jump."

"Or some summer people gone nuts," added one of the volunteers helpfully.

Chief Yahr shook his head again. "I don't know." He turned to Young Joe, who had been among the hardest-working of the volunteers, and at twenty years old, the one, presumably, with the closest connections to the underworld that was adolescence.

"Joe, what do you think?"

Joe looked embarrassed and fumbled with something in his pocket.

"I don't know anyone who'd think it was funny. Nobody's that bored."

The Chief stared at him for a moment, sizing up his truthfulness, then shrugged slightly. "Hard to say."

Suddenly brisk, he looked up at the people gathered around him. Their expressions were serious, each following his own thoughts and theories, each wondering if evil had suddenly come to the Island and whether they should be afraid.

"Well, I guess we'd all better get back to business. If any of you see anything or hear anything, make sure you let me know."

With a murmur of assents and farewells, the group dispersed, and Chief Yahr walked slowly to his car. He had no better theories than anyone else. And he was beginning to feel uneasy. Most pranks didn't go this far.

Roger had no illusions about himself. He knew he was not good with other people. But his awareness of this basic fact was not sufficient information to assist him in understanding exactly why it was so. In evaluating the ways and means of human emotion, he was like a visitor to unknown lands. He could follow a map if one were provided, but once on the path, he could not recognize the meanings of the signs along the way. He could, however, see that there was something different about the way Elisabeth was behaving, and this he took as a sign that something was wrong. Since Elisabeth, in his view, was perfection itself, this could only mean that he, Roger, was doing something wrong. What this could be he could not imagine.

When Joshua suggested that yoga would be a means of achieving his feminine side, Roger had no idea of what this could mean, or why it would be useful. Nevertheless, with his usual dogged persistence—and in the absence of any other guidance—Roger had determined that he would do this thing. It did not occur to him that Joshua had never been married and might not know anything about marriage. But he had observed that Joshua had a comfort with other people—like, for example, women, who were also people—which gave him an air of authority on the subject.

His backpack loaded with his deer-saving equipment—several garbage bags, PVC pipe, and all the rest, Ben was ready to launch his rescue attempt.

He chose a path that led to a place he knew where deer liked to come for water. It was sheltered in the woods from the worst of the wind, and he had often found the tracks of deer, raccoons, and foxes criss-crossing the mud or snow. Ben was excited to be ready to execute the plan that had consumed him now for so long. He hoped he would not be too late. He had tried to get everything together quickly, knowing that the animal must already be suffering; but it hadn't been easy, hampered, as he was, by adult observation and restrictions.

Suddenly a thought struck Ben that caused him to stop in the middle of the path. What if the animal didn't have a broken leg? He had been assuming this without ever actually knowing for sure. What if the problem were something else? Ben considered what else might have caused the deer's irregular gait. An injured hoof, maybe, or a bad cut. One thing for sure: his opportunities to get close to the deer would be extremely limited. He had to get this right the first time. What an idiot he had been! Still, at this point, he might as well keep going. His plan today was just to put out the bait. He wasn't likely to meet the animal just along the trail anyway.

As he went along, his plan seemed more and more stupid. How was he expecting a wild animal to hold still while he applied the splint—or whatever it needed? He had been imagining befriending the animal and waiting until it learned to trust him. But every day with that bad leg lengthened the odds that the deer would not survive. Ben realized now that he might not have that kind of time.

He was mad at himself for his poor planning. His father always told him that he jumped into things without thinking, and here was another example. Ben felt ashamed. He needed to think about this the way his father had taught him: consider the situation, list the obstacles, and try to find solutions.

His father's steady voice in his head, Ben began to reason his way through his problem. The only real predators on the Island were the coyotes. Foxes weren't likely to bother a deer. Even an injured one. He'd seen that the deer was getting around pretty well for now. It could find food and eat. So unless it had an infection—in which case there was nothing Ben could do—the animal would probably be okay for a while. Taking the time to make friends would probably not be a factor in survival. The only significant problem they faced was another one Ben could not control: a human being. Ben knew that if an adult found an injured animal, there would be no hesitation over shooting it. Maybe if he kept the food supply steady and in a remote place, no one else would see the animal before he could befriend it.

Now he thought of a new problem: what if someone saw the splint? He had heard his father and his father's friends talking about how strict the DNR was. Would he be breaking the law? Would he go to jail? A shiver of fear ran through Ben. But then he remembered the sight of the injured animal in the distance; how it had hobbled; how shy it had been; how alone it was, probably unable to keep up with the herd, and Ben was filled with compassion and a sense of duty. Ben Palsson had been raised to do the right thing at all costs. If relieving the suffering of an animal meant going to jail, then he would go to jail. Ben imagined himself standing bravely before the court in handcuffs, his mother weeping as he was led away.

His resolve strengthened, Ben went on to the place he had chosen as the most likely spot: a small pool where the creek spread out for a bit before hurrying on to the lake. He looked for signs of deer as he approached, but he could find no tracks. He knew, though, that this was a favorite spot, and anyway, he had no better ideas. Ben put down his backpack and began to get out the food he had brought to lure the deer.

A cold front came through that night, and the temperature dropped thirty degrees in an hour. The rain that came with it dragged the last leaves from the trees, stripping the color from the landscape. The gray bleakness of the world penetrated more deeply than the chill. Islanders pulled their shades and lit their fires. It would be five months before warmth came again to the Island.

Chapter Seven ❋

F iona was spending a lot of time at Elisabeth and Roger's, coming for dinner and staying in their comfortable guest room. The reason was simple loneliness, but the election was her excuse. She and Elisabeth had discussed many of the related details, but the first question was how Fiona should announce her candidacy. There was no doubt that news of it would spread like a brush fire, but it would be wise, they thought, to whisper in a few ears, lest someone be offended at not having been trusted with the secret. Together they composed a list of local worthies whose support and wisdom they would seek, and a few friends who would feel wounded at being excluded.

Roger sat nearby for these conversations without comment. The intricacies of social interaction were phenomena he neither understood nor cared about. These were concerns for other people to consider. He was willing to be helpful, but he had doubts about how he could be.

Tonight, as Elisabeth and Fiona talked on, making lists and planning their next moves, he was thinking that Shay's advice to roll his shoulder blades down had improved his downward dog. Today had been a good class, and Shay's enthusiasm about his progress had been most satisfactory.

Fiona and Elisabeth were engrossed in conversation when

Roger suddenly rose from his chair and bent to the floor, evenly distributing his weight onto his hands and feet in the downward-facing dog pose.

Rocco, instantly intrigued, got up from his place near the hearth. This was something new. Wanting to be helpful, he put his nose on Roger's upside down face, and licked thoughtfully.

Fiona paused in mid-sentence for only the briefest moment, then, with her eyes on Roger, continued to speak, and with an exercise in self-control that she considered heroic, she returned her eyes to Elisabeth. Elisabeth, with only a glance at Roger, acted as if there were nothing out of the ordinary. It occurred to Fiona that life with Roger must be full of the unexpected. Elisabeth, perhaps, had already grown used to it.

Despite the change in the weather, Ben remained undaunted. His first day of searching had yielded no results, but he was excited to see whether his bait had been discovered. He knew perfectly well that there would be no way to ensure that the animal he was searching for would be the only one to find the food, but he hoped to see tracks or scat, or other signs that would indicate who had been there. There was nothing. After waiting as long as he dared, Ben headed home.

The cold and rain that had come with the shift in weather made visits to the barn more onerous, but it was a part of farm life that could not be shirked. Emily liked to make her first trip out before the children were awake, before the bustle and chaos of school mornings.

On most farms, the children themselves were responsible for these early morning chores, but Emily did not like to delegate what she could do perfectly well herself. In this way, she unwittingly deprived herself of the pleasures of industrious, responsible children, and, instead, had a family who believed that it was perfectly normal to lie on the couch watching television while others worked around them, expected that what they wanted would be given to them, and disdained the kinds of work that might smell bad or make them dirty. All except Noah, the youngest, whose sweet disposition seemed to come from some distant part of the family tree.

On this morning, Emily woke earlier than usual. She had not slept well, in part because the goats had been restless during the night. She had heard their voices several times, and this was unusual, as they were sweet-natured, docile creatures, who generally settled down well for the night.

As she made her way to the barn, it was still dark. She was surprised to find that the barn door was open. She was usually meticulous in these kinds of things. Still, she had to admit, it was increasingly easy to make a mistake these days. There was so much to think about, what with the new farm, settling into a new community, and establishing relationships with the locals.

Her does greeted her with gentle calls, but the bucks

stomped their feet impatiently and displayed some agitation. Emily let them out into their pens, and turned her attention to the barn itself, dismissing the open door from her mind.

The goats must have been particularly hungry and thirsty overnight. Every last bit of food and water had been consumed. Emily noticed this, but in the midst of her morning routine she did not think much about it. She was really very busy, after all, too busy to mind trifling details.

Chapter Eight

The challenge of bending himself into yoga poses interested Roger. He saw it as an experiment in the capacities of the human form. If other people could do it, he thought, it must be possible for him to do it, at least within certain limits of his athletic capabilities. But Roger did not have a clear sense of what would be required over the long term, nor how much time he should allot for his progress.

During his classes, he analyzed the various stages and sequences of stretching that seemed to be the basis for the fundamental movements, and he had requested from Shay a list of daily poses that would help him to progress most efficiently.

Flexibility, balance, and strength were the goals, Shay had told Roger. These seemed to Roger reasonable measures of fitness, and he might as well strive for these through yoga as anything else. But his main inspiration was this other thing, suggested by The Angel Joshua: the notion that yoga would somehow make things right with Elisabeth. Roger was uncertain about how this would work, but he was willing to test the theory. Clearly, only two classes a week wouldn't be sufficient.

Fiona was sitting at her desk one evening when the peculiar ringtone of a Skype call came through. Eagerly, she clicked on the icon. It was Pete.

"Hey," he said.

"Hey." There was a pause as they each took in the sight of the other's face. Fiona sighed.

"I miss you."

"I miss you, too. Why don't you come see me? I'm back in London. I'll send you the tickets."

Fiona sighed. "I can't right now."

"Why not? The city is particularly vibrant at this time of year. Covent Garden's season is beginning soon, and The Royal Shakespeare, and you can work from anywhere. It's the beauty of being a writer."

Fiona hesitated.

"I have something here I have to take care of."

"What do you have to take care of?" asked Pete patiently.

"Well," said Fiona. "I seem to be running for office."

"You seem to be? You sound uncertain."

"Well… ." Fiona was starting to laugh in spite of herself.

"So, you haven't even been elected and you're already absolving yourself of responsibility? In politics that's usually a sign of guilt."

"I don't think I'm guilty of anything yet," said Fiona.

"What office are you running for?"

"Chairman of the Town Board."

"I see," said Pete. "And this has, in some fashion, come as a surprise to you?"

"It has," said Fiona. "No one could be more surprised about

this than I am."

"Put the dog on. He'll make more sense."

"Possibly. But nevertheless." Her voice trailed away. "Besides," she added, rather sadly, "Rocco's gone back to Elisabeth and Roger."

Pete smiled his most engaging and sympathetic smile, and Fiona sighed again at how far away he was. Her loneliness was intensified by the sight of him.

"Well, I hope you win. What is your slogan?"

"I don't actually have a slogan yet. But if I did, I think my philosophy could be summarized as 'Anyone But Stella.'"

"I like it. It has a ring of authenticity."

"I have to win, Pete, because she has to lose."

"Hmmm," said Pete. "Whatever happened with that soil remediation?"

"She has a nephew in the legislature. He whispered in somebody's ear. Or something. It's never come up."

"Hmmm," said Pete again.

"Have I told you that I want an asteroid named after me?" asked Fiona. "I saw an advertisement saying that for a fee you could name an asteroid after anyone you choose."

"I shall bear it in mind," said Pete, with a turn of phrase that suggested how much of his life had been spent around British speakers of English. "And may I say that it seems increasingly appropriate."

Chapter Nine

Fiona's announcement of her candidacy had an electrifying effect on the community. There was both relief that Stella would not be unopposed, and the delighted anticipation that accompanies a street fight. No one had anything but the most dire predictions for the campaign, but everyone—or nearly so—felt confident in the result of the spring election. While Fiona's competence was not particularly highly regarded, nevertheless, the opportunity to avoid Stella's competent malignity was widely viewed as a sign of a beneficent God. Washington Island, it was widely held, had dodged a bullet. Or would.

Fiona had accumulated a small group of advisors: Pali, Nika, Nancy, and Elisabeth were the core group, with Lars Olafsen offering advice from the phone so as not to excite the notice of Stella. You couldn't be too careful, he told himself. It would be better for everyone if Stella didn't know.

Their first task was to raise a little money. Fiona was in her usual state of virtual penury, having exhausted her minor resources last year with the purchase of the house and its various repairs, and had tucked away her insurance check for future purposes, whatever those might turn out to be.

They would need to buy signs and, perhaps, an ad or two in the local newspaper. But by and large the campaign would consist of door-to-door contact with voters. In a community of

400 or so, this was still a major job. Fiona was also advised to make herself visible at every possible public event between now and the April election. This was not difficult since life on the island made every event an important occasion, there were very few of these that she missed anyway, and everyone on the Island knew within hours who had attended, what had been worn, and what had been discussed. This would be useful in developing the campaign.

The hopes of the election centered on one irrefutable reality: just about no one wanted Stella to be in charge of anything, much less all of the Island's political life. To win, all Fiona had to do was not be Stella. This, she felt, would be fairly easy.

Nevertheless, the stakes were high for Fiona. If, by some chance Stella were to win, Fiona had no doubt that her life would become significantly more difficult. Stella's pettiness and vengeful nature made that a certainty.

Fiona dreamed that she was dreaming. She was looking down from her bedroom into the yard below, and she could see herself sleeping. As she slept, peacefully, a tree was growing rapidly out of her forehead. She was charmed, rather than frightened by it. It wasn't disfiguring, but seemed a completely normal process. She could see the spreading canopy of branches opening above her sleeping self, and it seemed to her as she watched, how peaceful it was to have a tree always over her head, to always be engulfed by the twittering of birds and the soft play of breezes. She wondered

that this had not happened to her sooner, and how she had man-
aged to live so long without it. But then, as she watched, the peace
turned to panic. The tree was rooted beneath her, its weight fully
on her head. How would she move? How would she live? It must
crush her skull, breaking through her body with its roots. Terrified
now, she watched herself helplessly as the tree continued to grow,
reaching magnificently through the earth and toward the sky.

M ike and Terry arrived one morning at Ground Zero at
about the same time, just as they did on most mornings.
Their daily routine was a pleasant way for them to begin their
solitary workdays.

Terry ran a carpentry and cabinetry business and Mike was
an artist—a painter—with an increasingly international reputation. Each had genuine talent and each worked happily alone,
but these morning conversations set them up for their day of
solitude, and both men had come to depend on their friendship. The period last winter when Roger had disappeared and
Ground Zero closed had been hugely disruptive to each man's
work and sense of well-being. It was with a profound sense of
relief that they had welcomed Roger's return and the continua-
tion of their ritual.

Roger, too, expected to see them every week day morning,
and most Saturdays, and while emotional connections were not
his habit, he did prefer predictability.

On this morning, by coincidence, Mike and Terry were

both a little early, and they each pulled up at the same time. Mike stood waiting in the parking lot for a few moments while Terry fumbled with something in his truck. It was still dark, and there was not even a lightening of the horizon in the east. There had been frost that night, and the air was cold, but Mike breathed deeply. He loved the late fall with its clean lines and rich, somber colors. It was always a time of great productivity for him, and he looked forward to his day's work.

At last, Terry climbed out of his truck, apologizing for the delay and exclaiming over the cold. The lights were on inside and outside the shop, as always, and the bright yellow awning with the words "Ground Zero" and the image of a mushroom cloud rising from a cup created a glow, if not exactly a welcoming one.

Already talking boisterously, as the two men approached the shop they were stopped in their tracks by what they saw through the glass door: Roger lying, eyes closed and apparently unconscious, on the floor in front of the counter.

Terry pulled the door open, thanking God that it was unlocked, and they both rushed inside. Roger, hearing them, opened his eyes without moving and looked up. He said nothing.

"Roger!" said Terry. "What happened? Are you all right?"

Mike squatted next to him and reached for Roger's wrist to take his pulse.

Roger pulled his wrist away and sat up.

"I'm okay. I was doing yoga."

Mike and Terry exchanged a look, and then looked back at Roger.

"I thought yoga was bending and things. You were just lying on the floor," said Terry.

"It's Dead Man's pose," Roger told them seriously. "It is the culmination of the daily practice."

"Death is the culmination of the daily practice?" asked Terry.

"Not death," Roger answered, with a pedant's lack of humor. "Dead Man's pose. It's a pose of complete relaxation."

"I suppose that complete relaxation would be one definition of death," remarked Mike dryly.

Terry grinned. "Do dead men make coffee?" he asked.

"They can't drink it," said Roger, glowering.

Message received, Terry and Mike took their places at the counter and changed the subject.

"My morning macchiato," said Terry. "And an egg sandwich."

"The same," said Mike. "But make my coffee regular."

The morning continued in its usual way, and when The Angel Joshua arrived a short while later, bathed in his usual beatific aura, no reference was made to what had gone on before.

Fiona's group of advisors had gathered around Fiona's tiny kitchen table to discuss the campaign. There were more people than was comfortable, but they needed a writing surface and Fiona still didn't have a dining room table, so they all crowded in, their chairs—pulled randomly from the house and porch—arranged haphazardly around the table.

It was a cold, rainy afternoon, and the glowing warmth of the house did not suffice to eliminate the chill around Fiona's heart. What on earth had she gotten herself into? How did she always manage to create these ridiculous situations for herself? She tried, on the now inevitable sleepless nights, to think of ways to extricate herself from running for office. She hadn't been on the Island long. Perhaps she didn't qualify for citizenship. She was in the midst of pondering this unlikely possibility when Pali's voice called her back.

The group consisted of Pali and Nika, Elisabeth and Roger, Jake and Charlotte, Mike, Terry, and Nancy. Elisabeth and Roger were there primarily for moral support, and Mike and Terry had been invited because even though they weren't Islanders, they had the perspective of two lifetimes of service in small town politics. Their experience would be helpful.

"So," said Pali, whose role had morphed into unofficial campaign manager. "I think we already have a pretty good plan of action that should take us right up to April. Fiona is going to focus on door-to-door campaign work, and will make herself as visible as possible at all public events."

"Visible, but not conspicuous," commented Elisabeth, unthinkingly. Fiona looked at her sideways.

"It seems to me that the next order of business should be to choose a slogan," continued Pali. "Stella's is "Time for a Change.""

"And we all know how irritated people are by that," said Nika.

"Just a harbinger of things to come," commented Elisabeth. "The irritation, I mean."

"Well, yes," agreed Nika.

There was a silence.

"I suppose 'Anyone But Stella' wouldn't work?" asked Terry. They laughed.

"God knows it's what everyone's thinking."

Everyone doodled on their notepads.

"I have an idea," said Nika. "What if at the bottom of the signs we just put the letters "A. B. S.?"

"But people will ask what it means," protested Fiona. "And then what will I say?"

"Everyone will know," said Nancy.

"True," said Mike. "But you should have something prepared, just in case. It's never good to appear arrogant in politics."

"Since when?" asked Terry, taking a drink of his coffee.

"Okay," said Pali, "so what does A.B.S. stand for? In public, I mean."

There was a silence as they contemplated the problem.

"Alien," said Roger, and then in response to the turned heads he added, "Well, she is. She's not from here."

"Alluring," suggested Jake. Charlotte kicked him under the table as the conversation moved on.

"Active?"

"Adequate."

"Adequate is good. I like adequate."

"Damning with faint praise," murmured Fiona.

"Bawdy." This was Jake.

"Befuddled?" suggested Roger. Fiona shot him a look that was lost on him.

"Beige," said Nika.

Pali looked at his wife.

"I'm just brainstorming."

"I'm so glad you all have such a high opinion of me," interrupted Fiona.

"Believable," said Elisabeth.

"Benign?" suggested Mike.

"Bighearted!"

"Bland."

"Fiona is not bland."

"No, but compared to Stella...."

"Sage."

"Savior," said Jake. "The Island's salvation, God knows."

"Swell. It has a double-meaning, see what I mean?" asked Charlotte earnestly. "'Swell,' as in, well, 'She's swell', and 'Swell' as in 'a big city swell.'"

"No one uses swell in that way anymore," said Nancy bluntly. "Probably not since 1940."

Charlotte looked chastened, and Fiona smiled encouragingly at her across the table.

"Adequate Bland Service," said Roger suddenly, in the flat intonation that was his normal means of expression.

Everyone stopped talking and considered this.

"That about sums up small town requirements," said Mike.

"It's a bit... unimpressive," ventured Fiona.

"That's what we want," Pali assured her. "It will put the electorate at ease."

Fiona looked doubtful.

"Look," said Terry. "I think he's right. You say everyone's worried about the upheaval that Stella would bring. This is exactly the opposite message. It's perfect." He leaned back in his chair looking satisfied. "Perfect," he repeated.

Mike nodded slowly. "I think that's probably true," he said. "You don't want people thinking you're going to try to change things. As a newcomer—an outsider, people will say—you need to make it comfortable for them to vote for you."

"Besides," added Nika, "as someone already pointed out, everyone will know what it really means."

"Does it have to be 'bland?'" asked Fiona. "What about believable? That doesn't sound so bad." She turned to Elisabeth. "What do you think?"

Elisabeth nodded slowly and a bit apologetically. "Adequate Bland Service makes sense to me."

Fiona could not help thinking that Elisabeth was reluctant to contradict her husband in his rare contribution to the public discourse.

"Everyone agree?" asked Pali, looking around the table. Everyone nodded except Fiona. "Then we have a slogan."

"Both an official and an unofficial one," added Elisabeth. "And I think the signs should be in soothing colors. Nothing garish. A contrast to Stella's."

"How about blue and white?" asked Nika.

"Perfect," said Terry again. He had checked his watch and it was approaching time for the last ferry. Now that they had determined the main point he was not particularly interested in the color of the signs.

"Okay," said Pali. "We have a plan. I'll order the signs and a couple of posters. We'll probably need about $700."

Fiona was aghast. "Really? So much?"

Pali nodded ruefully. "These things are expensive."

Nancy spoke up. "I'll put in a couple hundred. It's worth it to me to keep Stella out of office."

"Here's fifty," said Jake, pulling money out of his pocket.

Fiona felt embarrassed. She didn't think Jake and Charlotte had much to spare, and that seemed like a lot.

"I'll handle the rest," said Elisabeth quietly.

"Hold on, now," said Pali. I need to write all this down. There are laws about campaign contributions, and we need to make sure we do everything by the book."

It was in the exchange of checks and information, and the bustle of finding coats and saying good-byes that the meeting ended. Fiona went into the living room and poured herself a generous scotch. Even that, she knew, would not be sufficient to help her sleep tonight. Outside, the rain came down without any sign of stopping.

Fiona was walking along the beach near the sand dunes. The waves were high, and the harbor had white caps. The wind blew hard, and she knew that turning back and walking into it would be heavy going. She had a baseball cap that she was fighting to keep on her head. Suddenly she realized that Rocco was in the waves, romping and leaping, but getting too far out for safety. She called and whistled to him, but she could see quickly that he was struggling in the water. At that moment, an enormous white bird swept down on her and began pecking violently at her head. She fought against the attack, trying desperately to see Rocco, and knowing that she would have to go in to save him. Her anxi-

ety rose to terror that Rocco would drown. The waves were rising, and threatening the beach. The bird called raucously, and Fiona, ignoring its dives and beating wings, flung herself into the water toward Rocco. No longer certain where he was, she swam desperately toward where she had last seen him, her mouth and nose filling with water.

Fiona awoke herself with the thrashing of her own arms. Outside the rain lashed against the windows, and the wind found the loose places of the old house and made them sing eerily. The clock said 2:07. She lay awake in the dark for a long time, waiting for her heart to slow. She knew that no more sleep would come that night. Switching on the lamp, she reached for Martin's Little Green Book, and the dictionary.

The crunching animal, who appeared to have been stationed at her ear waiting for the sound of the light switch, began its nighttime mastications. Fiona was beginning to wonder whether there was anything much left of the house's attic infrastructure. She made a mental note to have someone check, and returned to her book, vaguely reassured by the presence of another living thing.

"*Lieber Ratten im Keller als Verwandte im Haus,*" she read. With a little surge of pride, she realized that she didn't require the dictionary for this one. "Better to have rats in the cellar, than relatives in the house," she translated aloud. She wondered briefly what Martin Luther would have thought about chewing creatures in the attic, then turned her attention back to her book. She had made deep inroads into her translation of Martin Luther before she fell back to sleep, with the sound of crunching deep within the wall continuing throughout the night.

Chapter Ten

F iona was scheduled for her first public appearance as
a candidate. Pali had brought her all the legally required documents to sign, everything had been sub-
mitted, and the campaign was official. She had felt
grateful to him for navigating these bureaucratic exigencies, but
at the moment she felt merely appalled by it all.

After her dream she had finally drifted off to sleep just before dawn. Her body clock woke her at the usual time nevertheless and she now dragged herself from bed, stiff and exhausted,
and in no mood for the day's events. But then, she reminded herself, when would she ever have been in the mood for this kind
of thing? She was quite certain she had planned her entire life
specifically in order to avoid them. She sighed, and took herself
down to the kitchen for coffee. Then she would have to dress for
a luncheon with the League of Women Voters.

The dream had left her in a state of anxiety for Rocco, which
she knew was not entirely rational, but given the intensity and
realism of the experience, it was hardly surprising. Her coffee
in her hand, she called Elisabeth. Even though it was early, she
knew her friend would already be up. It wouldn't hurt just to
check in, and she was in need of some consolation.

Terry pulled into the parking lot of Ground Zero that morning, and found Mike already there, sitting in his truck with the engine running. The lights of the shop were on, so he got out and walked over to Mike. "What's up?" he asked, as Mike rolled down his window.

"Door's locked. Roger must be in the back or something."

"Huh," said Terry. "Did you check the floor?"

Mike grinned. "Yup. Nobody there. Come on and wait in the truck. It's nippy this morning."

He unlocked the door as Terry walked around to the passenger side. They sat and talked for a few minutes, their eyes on the shop door.

"Look, there's Roger," said Terry suddenly. "He just stood up from behind the counter."

Mike turned off the engine. "He's a little late this morning. Must have forgotten to unlock the door."

They got out and walked toward the shop. Roger, seeing them, came forward and let them in.

"We thought maybe you forgot to open up this morning," said Mike.

"No," said Roger.

"Seemed like you were rising from the depths there behind the counter," said Terry. "What were you doing down there? Spill something?"

"I was practicing *Anuvittasana*, the 'heart opener,' " replied Roger with dignity.

"What's that consist of?" persisted Terry.

"Well," began Roger, "you start in Tadasana, or 'Mountain Pose.' Your feet should be together, toes touching, and your weight evenly distributed. Then you inhale, moving your arms up, relax your shoulders away from your ears, engage by squeezing your thighs and buttocks. You push your hips forward and start to gently bend back from the torso until your hands reach the floor; you keep your gaze up, and then, after a few breaths, you slowly return to neutral position."

Mike's eyes twinkled, but he only pursed his lips. He was quite sure that this was the longest he had ever heard Roger speak at one time.

"Ah," said Terry, looking interested. "That sounds hard."

"It is, so far. But daily practice brings progress, I'm discovering," said Roger seriously. "I will practice with the wall."

"What does it do for you?"

"It stretches the shoulders and opens the body. It requires a certain amount of strength, too."

"Show me what you mean by—what did you call it?" asked Terry.

"*Anuvittasana.*"

Obligingly, Roger put down the coffee pot and the spotless white cloth he always had nearby, and walked to the middle of the floor. While Terry and Mike watched, Roger assumed the beginning pose, and then, looking genuinely graceful, he reached his arms over his head and sank into a backbend arched powerfully to the floor.

Terry watched intently as Roger held the pose. "Do you think I could do that?" he asked.

"No doubt with practice," said Roger from the floor. "Everyone has different physical capacities, but most people can develop flexibility over time." He reversed the position, and rose to a standing pose.

"Hunh," said Terry, whether in response to the pose or to Roger's unusual garrulousness, was unclear.

"Usual?" asked Roger, returning to his place behind the counter.

"Yeah," said Terry, distracted by his thoughts.

"Yes, please," said Mike.

Fiona had managed to find a suit in the back of her closet and debated whether to put it on. No, she decided, it was too much formality. She wasn't running for Congress, which was, come to think of it, a small mercy. No, a dark pencil skirt and sweater would do. She stood looking at herself in the mirror. "Pearls?" she asked herself. But no. It was bad enough she had put herself in this position in the first place. She was not going to wear a costume.

As she entered the main room of the community building Fiona felt, rather than heard, the censorious mood of the room. They had all heard the rumors, so cunningly spread by Stella, that Fiona's source of livelihood was writing pornography rather than the dry public policy articles that actually paid her mortgage.

Some of the ladies were more inclined to believe the rumors than others, and even some of her friends, like Charlotte, felt secretly proud of her for living such a free and exciting life. If a show of hands had been taken, Fiona would have been horrified by how many of these respectable women believed her to be, in the words of the League's secretary, "a trollop."

The substance of the rumors had a life of their own, in part because those who believed them rarely spoke of them above a whisper, and then only to those who were likely to believe them, too. Non-believers—either by faith or by knowledge—tended to be Fiona's friends, and were either indignant or amused if the story reached their ears, and this tended to spoil the fun of the believers. The exchange of information between the two groups was therefore virtually non-existent, and the rumors were able to continue along their own path, unchallenged, and gathering fresh details along the way.

Fortunately for Fiona—although she would have, perhaps, been unlikely to see it that way—Stella's reputation was such that even Fiona's alleged moral slips paled in comparison to Stella's well-established malevolence. As any observer of politics will recognize, voters tend to see sexual escapades as less serious than wholesale meanness. Fiona's support in running for office was therefore reasonably assured.

Perhaps a primary reason for the mood in the room was that Stella was there, having arrived well before, and had been busily promoting her misinformation. Fiona saw her in the center of a group of women—an unusual event in Stella's life—dressed in an odd shade of green with an orange scarf around her neck, and making the grimace she used for a smile.

The outfit was a departure from her usual purple. "She looks like a pimento olive," thought Fiona, wonderingly. Was this a look she intended? It seemed unlikely. Fiona had never had much success in trying to imagine the works of Stella's mind, and today dismissed the effort instantly. She had enough to think about, and the combination of the circumstances and the thought of olives made her wish for a martini.

Fiona's need for a drink would have been greater had she known the substance of many of the conversations around the room. Today, it was becoming clear that Fiona was the center of a ring, which, Stella hinted carefully, might involve the co-ordination and provision of services to highly placed executives. This was delivered each time with a knowing nod to a circle of horrified and delighted listeners.

"You've seen that man who comes to visit her," pointed out Stella. "You can tell that he's one of them. Obviously rich."

They all considered this. They had, indeed, seen him. And to Island eyes he certainly had the air of a rich man about him.

"But we don't see anyone else," pointed out one of the bravest. "It can't be a ring if there's only one."

"It can't be done on the Island. Use your brain," said Stella, rudely. "He's her partner, and they have services in big cities all over the world."

This last was, even for Stella, stretching credulity just a bit. She waited to see if the crowd were with her.

"I heard he's from London," offered one woman, wonderingly.

There was a brief silence as they all considered what this might mean.

Unconsciously they all turned their heads slowly to observe Fiona across the room. She looked so... normal. Contemplating this new information, they each drifted off to carry this morsel to other parts of the room.

Fiona found her conversations that morning both difficult and puzzling.

"So you say you're a writer," ventured one lady with what Fiona thought was a peculiar emphasis.

"I am," smiled Fiona.

The woman looked back at her coldly. "I suppose it's one way to make a living."

"I suppose so, but it's only just barely a living, really. Hardly anyone gets rich doing what I do," laughed Fiona.

"Then, perhaps, you're not doing it right," responded the woman tartly, and walked away.

Fiona watched her go with the feeling that something had just happened that she didn't understand. She was about to go more deeply into this question when a voice interrupted her thoughts, urging everyone to take her seat.

The president bustled importantly up to Fiona, putting her hand on her arm. She was a handsome woman in her sixties with the aura of having been in authority. She had been the principal of the Island school for forty years.

"We will ask you to say a few words. Nothing much. Just a word or two about yourself and why you're running."

Fiona nodded dumbly, a false smile on her face. Fiona's appearance had been intended merely for the sake of visibility, so she was, perhaps naively, unprepared to speak.

"Of course."

The president looked pityingly on her. "You'll sit with me. And I promise, I won't let anyone talk about anything upsetting." She patted Fiona's arm, smiled encouragingly, and hurried off to her other duties.

Fiona felt relieved. She had half-expected that the local love of drama would have placed her at the same table with Stella. But the comment about not upsetting her made her realize that she had better up her game. She couldn't, she thought, have the gossip be about how intimidated she had been by Stella.

At lunch, Fiona pushed her food around her plate with a false smile she had never used before and which even she hated. The conversation around the table seemed stilted and pointedly about unrelated things. Would this luncheon never end? Fiona thought with longing of her jeans and sweatshirt and a long walk in the woods. The martini recurred in her thoughts like a distant dream of rescue to a shipwreck survivor. Had one been offered she would have downed it. It occurred to her suddenly that she could go stay with Elisabeth and Roger tonight. Anything to get away. Rocco would be there, safe and affectionate. And Roger. He would not be such a consolation, actually, but he was, at least, familiar. But Elisabeth always had good scotch. Better than any martini.

Fiona was escaping into this reverie when she was interrupted by the movement of the president, who was rising to go to the front of the room.

"I'll just make a brief introduction," she whispered as she departed.

Secure in her power, the president smiled benignly on the crowd and simply waited. The chatter of women's voices ceased almost instantly. The president smiled approvingly.

"We are fortunate this afternoon to have our two candidates for Chairman of the Town Board. Of course we all know one another, but can you each say a few words about yourselves?"

Stella stood immediately and thrust herself to the front of the room without further invitation. Fiona, aware that she was being observed, fixed a look of polite disinterest on her face, and stilled her fidgeting.

Stella spoke well, and, perhaps not as briefly as the President would have wished. Her topics were the Island economy, state aid, and the falling water levels in Lake Michigan. Fiona couldn't help wondering what Stella thought she could do about that, but she noticed there were heads nodding, and she made a mental note.

As Stella finished, Fiona walked to the front of the room. They passed one another, and Fiona fixed her new smile firmly on her face, and in a moment of inspiration put her hand out for Stella to shake. Stella looked at her as if she were being handed a snake before gingerly shaking hands, and that split-second of reaction in front of the entire room gave Fiona exactly what she needed. Feeling gleeful, she made her way forward, smiled a genuine smile at the room, and introduced herself.

At last it was over. Feeling, if not triumphant, at least satisfied, Fiona was thankfully preparing to leave when she felt a hand on her arm. A plump, grandmotherly woman with gray hair and rosy cheeks was looking at her with a friendly expression. Fiona felt pathetically grateful at the kindness on her face.

"So," began the woman, her eyes sparkling with interest and delight. "You must travel a great deal."

And they had what seemed to Fiona a very odd conversation about how often she found herself in the world's big cities. It was some time before she could extricate herself gracefully, and Fiona returned to her plans for a trip to Elisabeth's. "And, of course," she reminded herself hastily, "Roger's."

The encounters with Roger's yoga practice had gotten Terry thinking. He had been struggling with his blood pressure for a while now, and a recent significant birthday had made an impression on him. He did not have the same margin for error he had once had. There was that little roll around his waist that hadn't been there before, and he had to admit that his work did not include much physical exercise. It was clear that he had to do something, but when it came right down to it, the whole thing was a bit humiliating. The idea of going to a gym and showing his incompetence to the world at large made him reluctant to try. He needed to find something that was not so off-putting; something that would make it easier for him to make exercise a part of his life.

Unlike most people, Terry felt a deep comfort around Roger. He liked Roger's silence, respected his intellect, and didn't worry one bit about Roger's opinion of him, primarily because he was convinced that Roger didn't think about him at all. It seemed to him that he was faced with an opportunity that he really ought to take.

Fiona could not fully understand why the luncheon had been such an ordeal. It was particularly vexing when she considered that until today, she had begun to feel as if she belonged on the Island. Now she had felt again that she was an outsider, and something more that she couldn't quite pinpoint.

As she was leaving, the goat woman, as she had come to be generally known—a soubriquet that Fiona was only too happy to relinquish—approached.

"Oh, Fiona! Fiona! Wait a minute. I want to talk to you."

The Islanders, though openly friendly, did not welcome the participation of newcomers in their affairs, as Fiona well knew. But Emily's outspoken approach to nearly every topic made Fiona seem, by contrast, unassuming. For this reason alone, Fiona felt a certain sense of obligation toward Emily, and she was prepared to give her a great deal of latitude.

Emily bustled up and put her hand on Fiona's arm in a proprietary way.

"Listen," she said, without preamble. "Jason and I want to help you. You know, if things weren't so terribly, terribly busy at the farm right now, one of us would have run, and of course, that would have been ideal. But we just couldn't this time. Maybe next year things will be more settled and we'll be able to jump in. But we wanted you to know that we are on your side. We newcomers have to stick together. If there's anything you need—anything—we are here to help. We have a lot of experience in these things. Jason was on the school board back home, you know. So if you need any advice, you just call on us, okay? I just wanted you to know that."

Fiona suddenly realized that Emily had stopped talking and

she was expected to respond.

"Thank you, I—"

"Anything at all. You know—" and here she looked around to see if anyone was close enough to hear and dropped her voice— "these people aren't very sophisticated. So it will be important to try to speak on their level. We can help you with that, too."

Fiona smiled weakly. "I'm sure you can."

"Well, I'd better run. Talk to you soon!" Emily bustled off to her sleek German SUV and left Fiona gazing after her, still smiling. She recalled a line from William Hazlitt's *On the Pleasure of Hating*: "Public nuisances are in the nature of public benefits." This, she suddenly realized, was going to be fun.

Reflecting on the universality of human experience, she went to her car and headed home.

After the second, and then the third time that Emily found her barn door swinging loose in the morning, she determined she should do something about it. She had many things on her mind, but she was not so busy that she could have been routinely forgetting such a basic act of daily routine.

Whoever was leaving the door open was spilling feed around, too. And there had been things missing: little things, like rags and bits of rope. She needed to speak with the family about putting things back after using them, and she would mention it to Jason, too. Probably, the children were being careless. She shook her head to herself and sighed.

Chapter Eleven

"So how was the luncheon?" asked Elisabeth. They were settled in Elisabeth's living room after dinner. A fire was burning before them, and Rocco was lying with his head on Fiona's foot. Roger's steady gaze turned on her inquiringly, but he was silent, and so far, still seated in his usual place.

"I've had better times at coroner's inquests."

"It can't have been that bad," said Elisabeth with a faint note of scorn.

"You weren't there." Fiona picked up a crystal tumbler of scotch. Tell me again why I'm doing this."

"Because you don't want Stella to ruin your life."

"Too late for that."

Elisabeth rolled her eyes. "You'd better buck up if you're serious about the election. You'll never win if you let little things like this bother you. And you'll never sleep, either." She eyed Fiona. "Are you sleeping?"

"Not much."

Elisabeth continued to gaze at Fiona as if evaluating her condition.

"You don't have to do this, you know," she said, with an abrupt change in tone. "You could just drop out."

Fiona sighed.

"No, I can't. It's not my style." She paused and gazed into her glass. "As you well know," she added. Looking up, she caught Elisabeth's worried expression and laughed. "I'll be all right," she said. "But I may need to borrow Rocco. He might be good protection against the screamers."

Elisabeth looked confused. "Screamers?"

"We seem to have a new phenomenon on the Island." Fiona told them the stories she had heard. Elisabeth listened, first with skepticism, and then with growing concern. Roger scowled in his usual way, his thoughts inscrutable.

"What do people think is going on?" asked Elisabeth, remembering her grandmother's lifelong belief in banshees.

Fiona, affecting indifference, shook her head and shrugged. "No one seems to know. The most likely theory is bored teenagers." She put down her glass. "We have a lot of them up there."

"I wouldn't imagine that boredom is limited to Island teenagers," said Elisabeth dryly. She looked seriously at Fiona. "But this is not a joke. Is anyone doing anything about these... screamers?" She looked as if she were personally prepared to head up to the Island and begin an investigation.

Fiona shrugged again. "They called out the entire rescue system twice and searched the areas thoroughly. Nobody found anything. Not one thing."

Fiona, her thoughts drifting on waves of scotch, was remembering her own strange experience last fall in Elisabeth's woods. She slipped down to the floor and took Rocco's big head into her lap. He sighed as she rubbed his head, gently stroking the big sensitive ears. As his body began to vibrate in a purr of contentment, Fiona felt the circumstances of the day melt away. She would like to have Rocco back. She had been missing him.

A silence descended on the room, only the crackling of the fire and Rocco's deep purr were audible. Fiona did not particularly need conversation, but she basked in the companionship. She realized once again how deeply lonely she had been.

Elisabeth, who had been studying Fiona for signs of madness, sighed. "Would you like another scotch?" she asked, rising.

"Yes, please," said Fiona.

*B*en dreamed that he was in a small boat on Washington Harbor. The autumn sea smoke was around him, and land was invisible, but he was not afraid. The little boat drifted comfortingly on the waves, and Ben began idly to look down into the water. There were schools of fish below him, which he recognized variously as salmon and pike, sturgeon and northerns, all the varieties that he knew so well from his fishing trips with his father. He was leaning over the edge of the boat in a way that wasn't possible outside of dreams, when a flicker of color caught his eye. Turning his gaze, he saw one small fish, brilliantly colored in blue and green and orange, flitting in and out of the larger, more somberly colored fish that Ben knew so well. Leaning over more deeply to see it better he wobbled for a moment on the edge of the boat, and fell into the water among the fish. He was not afraid. The lake was warm and beautiful, and Ben found that he could breathe underwater. He swam through the schools of common fish toward the bright flash of color he had seen, but the little fish was elusive. Soon

Ben knew he had strayed a long way from the boat, and began to worry about where he was.

He woke feeling grateful to be safe in his bed, his mother calling his name to get up. But he kept thinking about that one fish that didn't belong.

Having survived the League of Women Voters, Fiona still felt in need of some respite when she returned to the Island, and accordingly took herself out for some more congenial companionship than she could expect from Martin Luther and the Midnight Cruncher.

It was spaghetti night at Nelsen's, and there was the usual crowd. Fiona was there with Pali and Nika, and they were sitting together at the bar waiting for a table. Eddie wiped the surface in front of them and took their orders.

Fiona had fielded the expected questions about the campaign, and now turned the conversation to more interesting topics.

"So what do you think of this screaming business?" she asked as he set their drinks before them. Her eyes met his. "I hear you were caught up in the middle of it all."

Eddie nodded seriously. "I about jumped out of my skin when I heard it. I'd have sworn someone was being ripped to pieces." He took on a distant look as he recalled the experience. "I'm still not sure that she wasn't."

Fiona frowned with concern. "It was you and John?"

"Right. And Kevin. We all heard it and took off running for

the marina while the screaming was still going on, but by the time we got there it had stopped." He shook his head briefly as if to shake off the image in his mind. "I don't know. Can't stop thinking about it."

"Hey, Eddie," called someone from down the bar, "How about another one?" Eddie went to pour another beer.

"I know it's probably all a joke, but still, it's disturbing, don't you think?" Nika asked, pushing a strand of blonde hair away from her face.

Fiona nodded. "Is that still the consensus? It's a joke? Just some bored teenagers?"

Nika shrugged helplessly. Fiona knew she was worrying about Ben and his solitary rambles.

"Seems like it," said Eddie returning to his post, leaning against the bar and wiping away imaginary spots. "What else could it be? I can't imagine any normal adult thinking that creating that kind of fear was even funny. But kids have a different sensibility, I guess." He smiled suddenly. "I know I did."

Fiona smiled back. "Me, too. But I don't know if I'd have gone this far. Especially since it's hard to imagine that you wouldn't get caught. I mean, here on the Island, the chances of being found out are pretty high."

Nika and Eddie nodded.

Nika was thinking about the things that had been so intoxicating during her youth on the Island. They had done some naughty things, certainly. She glanced at her husband seated next to her at the bar. But nothing like this. They had never been malicious. She reached over and put her hand on Pali's knee. She remembered the first time she had known that she loved him, this man who was like her other self. They had been very young. She looked at him. Pali was silent, staring at the bottles along the back of the bar. Something was troubling him, she knew. But she also knew that whatever it was, he would not talk about it here. Absently, he patted her hand. She gave his knee a squeeze and retreated.

It occurred to Fiona that this conjecture was all within the bounds of a reality on the Island that was utterly different from reality almost anywhere else. However alarming the screaming incidents had been, everyone now assumed that there could not possibly be any actual foul play. Terrifying things were for other places. It was a refreshing change from her life in Chicago. Feeling grateful, she pushed her glass toward Eddie, and he refilled it with his usual competence and flair.

There was one of those random silences that happen in a group of people, and a snippet of a conversation from down the bar drifted toward them.

"Gotta be one of the kids, I guess."

"Hate to be the parents once we find out who it is."

Lars Olafsen had been sitting at the far end with some of his friends. He had been thinking about the situation for some time now, and was considering the fact that he didn't have to watch what he said as carefully as usual. As an office holder, he would have simply nodded and murmured reassuring noises, but now, he thought to himself, he was a free man, and he could finally say out loud what he had been thinking for some weeks. What he said would be taken seriously, he knew, but he wouldn't have to think and double-think and worry. He could say what he wanted without trying to figure out what was responsible public behavior.

"I can't help wondering," he said aloud, in a voice that carried down the bar. There was a stillness in the room as conversations stopped to hear what this respected public servant had to say. Lars noticed the faces turned toward him and with the instincts of many years in the public eye, he unconsciously waited a moment for the full effect. All eyes were on him.

"I can't help wondering about something that happened to me. It was the strangest thing." He stopped and took a sip from his brandy old-fashioned.

Lars took a moment to savor his drink and put his glass down on the bar. The room waited respectfully.

"I was coming home a few months ago, and I heard something in the woods that really knocked me back on my heels. I didn't say anything to anybody because, to be honest, I felt kind of foolish. But now...." He stopped and looked into his glass. "Well, now I'm kind of wondering if I should've said something." He looked up at the faces around him, his frank blue eyes and open face serious and troubled.

The silence that followed was long enough that one of the men in his group felt the need to prompt him to continue. "So what was it, Lars? Are you gonna tell us or make us sit here and wait?" There was uneasy laughter, but Lars still looked serious.

Fiona looked around the room at the faces of her fellow Islanders. They were country faces, most of them, unused to shaping their responses to the expectations of others—faces of integrity. These were men and women she had come to know well and to respect over the past year, and there was a feeling in the room she had not experienced here before. This was a subject that mattered to them all, and for good or for evil, it was forming a common bond among them.

"Well, it was something I heard," continued Lars. "At night. I was coming home and it was kind of late." He took another drink and looked around at his audience. "You all know the woods next to my place, part of Mountain Park."

Heads around the bar nodded, but no one spoke.

"Well, to be honest, I was coming from Nelsen's and I'd had a couple," here there were some chuckles of recognition, "but I wasn't imagining things."

Fiona began to feel vaguely annoyed. Couldn't he just get on with it? But if she had learned anything this past year, it was to check her need to rush through everything. "Unless," she reminded herself, "when making outrageous political commitments." She took a deep breath and waited, but apparently she wasn't alone in her impatience.

"Come on, Lars. Out with it. Tell us what it was."

"Well, that's just it, Ray," said Lars turning calmly toward the speaker. "I don't know what it was. I was heading toward the house and I heard something—stopped me cold. I thought at first maybe there were some deer in the woods, there, but it wasn't the sound of a deer really. Not at all, in fact. No."

He paused again and looked into his drink before continuing.

"It was a human sound. Not a sound I've ever heard an animal make." He looked around the room at the people whose attention he held. "It sounded like someone was in the woods. And I can't help wondering—" he stopped. "I can't help wondering whether we have someone we don't know on the Island. Someone, maybe, living in the woods."

Pali was silent all through dinner that night, and spent most of the meal pushing his spaghetti around his plate. Normally he was charming and, if not effusive, then easy and lighthearted. But tonight he seemed distant and preoccupied. Fiona pretended not to notice, and did her best with Nika to keep up the conversation. Friends stopped by the table to comment on Lars's story and offer their own theories about the mystery, and through it all Pali remained somewhat removed and distant. Fiona was vaguely disturbed. She had never seen him like this.

Fiona waited for a moment when the others at the table were engaged and turned to Pali.

"You seem a million miles away," she said. "Everything okay?"

Pali compressed his lips and nodded unconvincingly. Fiona was the only real writer he knew, and she had always understood his poetry.

"Going through a bit of a dry spell with my work. Can't seem to come up with anything."

Fiona nodded. "Writer's block. It happens." She could see that he was troubled, and was surprised that it should affect him so deeply.

Pali lowered his voice and leaned in. "It's not that, exactly. It's... my..." he took a deep breath, "... friend. I haven't felt his presence in a long time. He seems to have abandoned me."

Fiona looked at him sympathetically, but said nothing.

"I keep wondering what's different," said Pali, turning his

empty glass in his hands. "Is it me? Am I different? Or has he—whatever he is—moved on?"

And now Pali spoke so quietly that Fiona could barely make out his words.

"Or worse... is that the source of the screaming?"

Fiona looked startled. Pali seemed to be in a strange new place. Believing what he'd seen was a ghost was one thing. But this... .

Pali seemed to sense her reaction. "You're right, of course. I guess it is just writer's block."

"Or in your case, ghost block," said Fiona, pleased with herself at her little *bon mot*. Her mood changed when she saw his face. "I'm sorry. I didn't mean to mock. I was just trying to cheer you up."

Pali smiled and shook it off. "It's okay. I'm not offended. It's just a hard thing for me to laugh about."

Fiona nodded. "The writer's block will pass. It always does."

Pali smiled again, grimly. "No doubt."

But he did have doubts. Many doubts. And he wondered seriously if he would ever write again.

Toward the end of the evening, Jim appeared unexpectedly, and responding to the general invitation, sat down at their table.

"Did you eat, Jim?" asked Nika.

"Yes. Hours ago. Just thought I'd stop by for a drink."

Fiona eyed him skeptically. She recalled that he had told her about some qualification exam he was studying for and that he wouldn't be around for a while. She had no illusions about the Island grapevine. Someone, she felt sure, had told Jim she was here.

"I'll buy," she said.

He started to argue, then smiled. "Thanks. I'll have a tapper." Fiona rose to get it.

As soon as she left he turned to Nika and Pali. "What's going on?" he asked. "Young Joe called me and said I should come down. Some story about a guy in the woods."

They filled him in and he was silent until Fiona returned.

"Thanks," he said, as she handed him his beer.

"Jim, what brings you here?"

He shrugged. "Just felt like it."

Fiona held his glance.

"Did someone tell you about Lars' story?"

Jim looked sheepish, but he was incapable of deception. "I heard you were here and I didn't want you to go home alone."

Fiona could not restrain herself from expressing her irritation. "Good grief, Jim. This is Washington Island. I don't need a babysitter. What do you think is going to happen?"

Jim looked at her unperturbed. "I don't know. But as long as we don't know, I'm going to make sure you're safe."

"I'm not ready to go."

"Fine," he said, easily. "I'll wait."

"I drove myself."

"I'll just follow you home and make sure you get in okay."

Fiona, not pleased, could see no graceful way to change his mind. She caught herself just before asking him whether he was planning to come in to check under the bed. No point in giving him any ideas. Resignedly, she said no more.

When she had postponed her departure as long as possible, Fiona said her goodnights and left, Jim faithfully at her heels. He waited until she was in her car before going to his truck. As she pulled out of the parking lot, she saw him back out and pull in neatly behind her on the road. "What," she wondered, "will happen now?" Jim's feelings for her were now fully on display. Would he be content to stay in his truck, or would he follow her into the house? Her head abuzz with these thoughts, she pulled into her driveway, hoping that Jim would stay in his truck. But he turned off the ignition, and walked up the path with her in silence.

She opened the door, and turned reluctantly to say good night, but he was already running lightly down the steps, and calling his good bye. She heard the sound of the engine as he started his truck and drove away. In the silence of the little house, her loneliness rose within her and curled itself tightly around her heart.

She tried calling Pete, the unbroken sound of the ringtone underscoring her solitude. There was no answer.

Nika and Pali stopped to pick up Ben, and he chattered all the way home about the Scouts' animal sciences badge and what they were learning about goats and goat milking from Mr. Martin. Nika asked questions and feigned enthusiasm, but Pali was silent.

After Ben was in bed, Nika made a pot of tea, brought it into the living room on a tray, and sat down with Pali next to the fire.

He sat with his head down, his eyes troubled.

"What is it, Ver?" she asked. "Something's bothering you."

He shook his head.

They sat in silence as Nika's thoughts ran through the possibilities. Suddenly she felt a spark of insight.

"It's the screaming, isn't it?"

Pali looked at her and nodded once.

"But why? Why is that upsetting you?" Then she had a terrible thought. "Do you know something?"

Pali took a deep breath. "I don't know. I don't think I know."

Nika frowned.

"But I'm wondering."

Nika sat waiting. She would let him tell it his own way, whatever it was.

Pali got up and began to walk around the room, then sat down again and ran his hands through his hair.

"What if my experiences on the water aren't benign? What if I have been consorting with... something? What if I have brought evil here?"

Nika stared at her husband. "You can't be serious. You can't honestly believe that the screaming is something supernatural. That's crazy!" She stood up and went over to him, putting her hands on his shoulders. "This isn't like you, Pali. You're not a superstitious man."

"I know what I've seen Nika. I know what I experienced. Or at least, I know that I experienced it, and so do the crew. We don't actually know what. That's the problem."

Nika went over to the sideboard, poured him a brandy and put it in his hand.

"Ver Palsson, you need to get a grip on yourself. In the first place, there is a logical explanation for this screaming. It's either some kids pranking or it's some crazy in the woods. But it's NOT a ghost, or the devil, or whatever you're thinking. In the second place, you are the best man I know, and you have not brought evil to anyone. It's not even possible. Now drink that and come to bed."

Pali shot back the brandy, stood up and put his arms around her, crushing her against his chest. They stood that way for a long time before they went up to bed in silence. Just before he turned out the light, Pali turned to look at her.

"What bothers me most is that I don't care what it is. I just want it to speak to me again."

He turned out the light. Nika moved close to him and put her face against his neck. Soon she could hear his measured breathing, and he slept soundly all night.

Nika, however, did not.

It was before dawn when Terry pulled up in front of Ground Zero. The lights were not yet on inside, so he knew that neither Roger nor The Angel Joshua had arrived.

There was no definite pattern as to which of the two would open the shop, but generally speaking, it was Roger who opened and The Angel Joshua who stayed later in the day. The habit of early rising was one long established with Roger, and he was not usually interested in changing his habits. At least, thought Terry, when he did make changes, they were big ones, not minor ones like opening times.

He waited in his truck for a few moments before he saw the headlights of Roger's truck.

Terry got out and waited for Roger on the walk. Roger did not loiter in the driver's seat gathering belongings. As soon as the truck stopped, the door was open and he was out.

"Morning," said Terry cheerfully. "I'm a little early today."

Roger made a noise that might have been a greeting and unlocked the door. Carrying a small black duffle bag, Terry followed him in. He was already regretting this idea. He should have stayed home and gotten an extra hour of sleep. He waited while Roger turned on the lights, flicked the switches of some gadgets, and started the brewing. Terry noticed that the big coffee machine was already on, ready to be put to use. Without further preliminaries, Roger took a mug from the shelf.

"Macchiato?"

"No. Well, yes. Well—" Terry paused.

Roger gazed at him with what might pass for patience.

"The thing is, umm, yes. Yes, I would like a macchiato."

Somewhat discomfited by Roger's glare, Terry settled himself at the counter.

Without comment, Roger turned to the machine and began the process of making the coffee. The unpronounceable Italian name announced itself across the top of the gleaming copper apparatus, and Terry, who admired good design of all kinds, watched with interest as his macchiato was being prepared.

After a few moments, Roger turned and put the mug in front of Terry with a thunk. Terry gazed blankly at the design in the froth at the top. It was, he always thought, an incongruous touch from Roger, these delicate pieces of coffee froth art. Today it was an autumn leaf—an oak leaf—with stem, and veins, and rounded lobes, filling almost half of the top of the cup.

"Thanks," said Terry to Roger's back. "So, uh, Roger," he continued. "I suppose you're wondering why I'm here so early."

"No," said Roger, without looking back.

Terry paused a moment. He was used to Roger under ordinary circumstances, but this morning he certainly wasn't making things any easier. Obliquely he wondered whether Roger ever made anything easier. He rather doubted it.

"Well, um, there um, there is a reason." Terry took out his reading glasses and began polishing them with his handkerchief.

Roger remained silent, wiping off the stainless steel counter with a pristine white cloth he had just taken out.

Terry looked at Roger's back and took a deep breath. "Out with it," he thought to himself.

"I was wondering if you could show me some of those yoga poses. I've been thinking I need to do something to get myself in shape, and I just thought, well, you could help me get started." He pressed his lips together in a hard line and nodded once, briefly to himself. There. He had said it.

In the ensuing silence, the stereo seemed particularly loud. Music at Ground Zero was something Terry had difficulty getting used to. He had grown accustomed to the various changes at the shop over the course of the past year, and he had almost completely succeeded in not referring to it any longer as "Coffee." But he never could get used to having jazz playing in the background. It was unsettling somehow. So different from the way things had been before.

Beginning to think Roger had not heard the question, Terry asked again.

"So what do you think? About the yoga?"

"No," said Roger.

"No?" This was the response Terry had been expecting.

"No."

"Uh... why not?"

"I'm not a teacher. I can't tell you how to do it."

"You don't have to. I'll just watch you."

"No."

Terry was silent for a few minutes. He sat down at the counter and watched Roger begin to set up his yoga mat.

"Are you going to throw me out?"

Roger stopped and looked at him, puzzled. "No."

Terry picked up his duffle bag and disappeared into the men's room.

In a few minutes he reappeared wearing sweats, a t-shirt, and white socks.

Roger was just beginning his sun salutation. He ignored Terry and went on with his routine.

Without a word, Terry took up a position a few feet away and began to copy Roger's movements.

His head facing the ground in downward dog, Roger's voice was a bit muffled.

"Take off your socks."

Obediently, Terry removed his socks, and barefooted, they continued in silence.

After Lars Olafsen's story, there was a rush on ground beef at the grocery store meat section, the traditional location for local gossip. Islanders clustered around the refrigerator case as if they hadn't eaten meat in weeks, the smell of fresh-baked bread wafting enticingly around them.

"Did you hear about what happened to Lars?"

They had.

"Don't you think it makes sense after what's been happening?"

They did.

"Is it possible that there's someone we don't know living somewhere in the woods?"

It was.

"But even if there's someone there, we still haven't found anyone hurt or... "

There was a silence as this mystery was considered.

"There's no body," ventured someone, timidly.

"Maybe not. Or maybe we just haven't found it yet."

Glances were exchanged as this idea, not new to any of them, was spoken out loud.

"Balderdash," said Nancy Iverssen in her inimitable fashion. "There's no body. "We'd have found it by now if there was."

"Or the coyotes would have."

There was general relief as everyone agreed that this was

probably true.

"But it's still damned worrying to have all this going on."

Everyone agreed that it was.

The grocery store had record sales that week.

Chapter Twelve

F iona's announcement of her candidacy immediately raised the question of a most delightful prospect: a debate. A political event of any kind was always greeted with interest on the Island, but this one promised to be particularly enticing. It would have required the soul of a saint and the disposition of a hermit not to look forward to a confrontation between Stella and her despised neighbor, that new woman who was running for Lars's seat. No one particularly expected Fiona to win an argument with Stella—who could?—but they all figured they'd vote for her anyway, so the debate itself could hold no peril, only pure enjoyment. "Anybody But Stella" was the phrase on everyone's lips, but they murmured it privately, just in case Stella overheard.

Knowing this, Fiona found herself in a quandary. Having declared her intention to run, and what's more, having further declared her intention to leave everything pretty much as it was, she really didn't have much of anything to say. She did some desultory research on the responsibilities of the chairman, and had a long conversation with Lars at Nelsen's one evening, but beyond that, she really didn't have much to prepare.

"Well, for one thing," said Elisabeth impatiently, "you'd better know what Stella's running on."

"Something about dredging the harbor."

"Well, what about it?"

"I'm not quite sure."

"Fiona, do you want to win or don't you?" Elisabeth was exasperated. "There's no point in going to all this trouble if you won't do anything to help yourself."

Fiona looked apologetic. "I'm sorry. You're right. I'm just a little distracted. I haven't heard from Pete in a while, and every time one of those hostage videos comes up, I'm afraid to look."

Elisabeth frowned. She had been worrying too, but hadn't wanted to say anything. "Do you have any idea where he is?"

"None. And when he doesn't tell me I get suspicious." They were silent for a while.

"Worrying doesn't help," pointed out Elisabeth.

"No."

"So let's talk about harbor dredging to take your mind off it."

Fiona smiled suddenly and rather fiercely. "It's hardly a gripping topic. But since you're so interested, the lake levels are at historic lows, and the harbor is about four feet too shallow for the new ferries and increased traffic. So the harbor needs dredging. Only problem is that it will cost nearly $8 million and the state has refused to pay for it. It's a potential disaster for the Island, and somebody has to do something."

"I thought you said you didn't know anything about it."

"I didn't actually say that."

Elisabeth gave Fiona the kind of look that, if she'd been wearing pince-nez, would have been over the top of them.

Fiona smiled serenely back. "The question isn't about the

dredging itself. It's about how to find the money to pay for it. And that, my friend, is the problem I don't know how to solve."

"Does Stella know how to solve it?"

"I hope to Hell not."

"Do you have anyone you can ask?"

"I've asked."

"And what did they say?"

"Federal money."

"And?"

"That it's highly unlikely."

"Well, they can't just shut down the Island."

"You wouldn't think so."

They were silent again. Fiona got up suddenly and went into the living room. Elisabeth could hear the clinking of glass. "What are you doing?"

Fiona reappeared with two glasses. "Getting some scotch."

"I thought you were giving up scotch."

"I keep thinking I will. But it helps me think." She handed one glass to Elisabeth, and they both took a drink.

"Ugh," said Elisabeth. "Nasty stuff."

Fiona shrugged. "Lots of nasty stuff in politics. Guess we'd better get used to it."

❖

When Roger arrived at Ground Zero, he found Terry waiting for him, and so began a new pattern for their mornings. By the time Mike arrived, Terry would be sitting at the counter drinking his macchiato, with no indication of anything unusual other than a certain color in his cheeks and a new and uncharacteristic preference for sweat pants. Mike, who was an observant man, made no comment about these changes, but he privately began to develop a theory.

Pali and certain members of the ferry crew had a secret that they had been keeping for some time. They were a group of some half dozen men who had seen or experienced someone— or something—on the ferry. Some had seen the shadowy figure standing behind Pali in the pilot house one stormy night. Some had seen things inexplicably moved or out of place. But only Pali had felt some kind of communication with… it—whatever it was.

Those who had known about the ferry's ghost were a small, silent club within a small gossipy community. The reason they did not speak of it was simple: none of them wanted to be ridiculed. They each knew what they had seen; each privately questioned the experience; each re-lived the moments again and again searching for an explanation that would not uproot a lifetime's philosophy. For some of them, there had been just one experience. For others, it was an irregularly recurring and unwelcome event. For Pali, it was something else.

His—and he never knew what to call them: Visitations? Manifestations? Hauntings?—had been more than merely benign. They had been lifesaving. In the first case, literally, and then, as the contact grew and deepened, in a more metaphysical sense. On that stormy night when the wave had hit the ferry, when an invisible hand had taken the pilot wheel and steered the little ship to safety, Pali had been struggling with the meaning and purpose of his life. His poetry—what he had thought of as dabblings—had been all along an attempt to come to grips with his mortality. The shock of the first contact with—whatever it was—had shifted the focus of his life. As the contacts increased, and he began to feel a communication with It, the ghost had become his muse, even, he sometimes thought, his co-author.

Now Pali was a published poet, selling first one poem, then another, then another. It had not been gradual. It had happened as rapidly as spring buds popping. Poetry was not, as any writer knows, a source of a living income, but nevertheless, out in the world there were these tiny things, a dozen, then two, then thirty poems that were proof that Ver Palsson had lived on this earth. For Pali, it was everything.

But just as he had begun to feel that he had moved to a new place in his creativity, the music had died within him. The experience of a cadence awakening him in the night was gone. He no longer felt the spin of new words whirling into place like birds settling on a line. It had been months since he had reached for his notebook to write something down before it passed from his memory. At the same time, he had not seen, nor heard, nor sensed the presence of his friend.

The visits were at an end.

Pali could not explain the depths of his loss even to himself, and as the weeks, then months went by, his depression grew. It was more than writer's block. It was a feeling of abandonment, as if a door to mystery and wonder had been closed to him, and he stood on the outside of it, unable to gain entrance to the place where he had once been welcomed. He felt a failure.

From the beginning, the subject had been one Pali rarely discussed. Although he had told his story to Nika, and although she seemed to believe him, for reasons he could not explain, it was Fiona who always seemed to genuinely understand his experiences. After her initial skepticism she had come to trust him. She did not say much, but she listened well, and as a writer, she understood the vagaries of creation. And although she liked to laugh, so far, at least, she had not laughed at this.

But this last part, this loss, he had been struggling through on his own. He did not know how to explain any of it, and he did not know how to understand it. He knew instinctively that there were those in his own church who would consider him to be consorting with evil. But Pali knew there had been no menace and there had been no bargain. There had simply been a presence. A presence that seemed to understand poetry.

"Maybe it's an angel," said Nika one night, as they sat together after dinner.

"Maybe," said Pali listlessly. "But if it's an angel, it has passed me by."

"You should feel blessed. Angels don't appear to everyone."

"I know," said Pali. But he did not feel blessed. He felt abandoned.

Pali thought of the accounts he had read of angel appearances. Angels were creatures of awe, and according to his readings, the most common reaction they inspired was fear. Pali's experiences had not been frightening. They had been intensely quiet, accompanied by a deep internal roar as of some spiritual wind, and a feeling of companionship. And always, a poem had come into his mind, full, complete, and intact, like Athena springing from her father's forehead. These were not his only poems, but they were his best ones. And they were the ones that had been published.

Did this mean, Pali wondered, that he wasn't a poet after all? That he was merely the secretary, the recorder of a greater mind than his? That his achievement, his proofs of his worth, did not actually belong to him? Pali went through his life as before. He loved his wife. He raised his son. He went to church. He piloted his ferry and directed his crew. But through everything, in the dust of his aspiration, these unrelenting questions dogged Pali's thoughts and unsettled his dreams.

Chapter Thirteen

Sitting at her desk, Fiona was looking at Pete's face for the first time in a long while.

"Pete? What was that? What was that sound?"

Pete looked briefly over his left shoulder, then turned back and smiled into the camera. "Nothing serious. Some gunfire."

"Gunfire?"

Even in the distorted lens of the computer camera, Pete's characteristic expression of rueful good humor was captured and transmitted across half the world.

"It's nothing serious," he said again. "Just a bit of exuberance."

Fiona took a deep breath. "Exuberance." She paused before asking, "Where are you, exactly?"

It was Pete's turn to breathe deeply. "I'm in the Middle East."

He held up his hand before she could say anything. "It's okay. It really is. The men like to celebrate by firing their guns in the air. They're happy. It's fine. We had a good day." He smiled into the camera. "I'm fine."

"But if it's fine, why do they have guns?"

Pete smiled again. "It's traditional. Sort of." And then his tone changed and he became brisk.

"It's a beautiful country. Beautiful. And the troubles are

limited, really, to only a few specific regions. I'm nowhere near anything dangerous. I promise."

"If that were true, they wouldn't have guns."

"Everyone has guns, Fiona. Absolutely everyone. It's a Second Amendment paradise." He grinned.

"I don't like it."

"Well, no. I didn't imagine you would. But I didn't want to hide it from you, either." This was only sort of true, but it was his best approach at the moment. He couldn't have her thinking he would be deliberately keeping her in ignorance of his whereabouts, or her anxiety would be permanent and unrelenting. But there was no way he was telling her where he was headed next.

"Where are you, exactly?"

"It's okay. I'm leaving here tomorrow. I'll be fine. And then maybe I can come help you with the campaign."

The conversation deteriorated into exchanges of affection.

After they hung up, it occurred to Fiona that he hadn't told her exactly where in the Middle East he was.

Wily, indeed.

It was on a routine trip to Sturgeon Bay for supplies that Roger saw a flyer posted that got him thinking: a group trip to Utah for a week-long yoga workshop. "Suitable for every level, from beginner to advanced," it said. "Come and develop your practice in the serene beauty of the Utah mountains." Color photos of mountain scenery were enhanced by silhouetted figures in warrior pose. "Take your skills to the next level."

The need to improve things with Elisabeth continued to loom large for Roger, and with growing urgency. He wanted to make more progress, and faster. Despite his usually impenetrable nature, Roger knew things were not going well at home. Getting better at yoga was therefore imperative.

Frowning and nodding to himself as he studied the poster, Roger took one of the entry cards, stuffed it in his shirt pocket, and went on about his business.

Chapter Fourteen

Elisabeth was surprised one afternoon to find that Ground Zero was closed. Roger's car wasn't there, so she knew he wasn't working in the back room, but she knocked on the door, thinking that The Angel Joshua—who had no car—might be. No one came. She looked at her phone. 2:15. What a very odd time for Ground Zero to be closed. Frowning slightly in puzzlement, but unconcerned, she shrugged to herself and went on with her day.

His backpack loaded with his deer-saving equipment—several garbage bags, PVC pipe, and all the rest, Ben was ready to launch his rescue attempt. He was finding that his schedule was getting rather full, with his rescue planning, birdfeeder making, the increasing burden of fifth-grade homework assignments, and, on top of everything else, his mother starting to ask questions.

He chose a path that led to a place he knew that deer like to come for water. It was sheltered in the woods from the worst of the wind, and he had often found the tracks of deer, raccoons, and foxes criss-crossing the mud or snow. Ben was excited to execute the plan that had consumed him now for weeks. He hoped he would not be too late. He had tried to get everything together quickly, knowing that the animal must already be suffering, but it hadn't been easy, hampered, as he was, by adult observation.

It was about this time that the story of the ferry line's ghost began to be whispered on the Island, and with it, the notion that perhaps the ghost had something to do with the screamer. In retrospect, it was surprising to Fiona that the story had been kept quiet as long as it had been, but she felt a deep regret that it was now a public topic of conversation. Her biggest concern was for Pali. He was not the kind of man who liked being the center of attention under any circumstances. But to be the center of a story like this would be excruciating for him.

Fiona felt thankful that she had practiced her reporter's instincts in not sharing his tale of ghostly inspiration with anyone. Pali had trusted her, and she had proven herself worthy of his trust. Whatever pain he might feel at the public discussion of the ghost, at least it would not encompass this deeply felt and personal experience. Not, of course, unless he had told it to someone else.

But once the story had somehow surfaced, it flashed through town like a hot fire. It was all anybody talked about, and Pali, the reluctant center of the tale, was questioned incessantly wherever he went. By tacit agreement, neither he nor Fiona mentioned the poetry. This was too personal, too private a detail.

One of the most keenly interesting questions pursued was

who the ghost had been. Was it a European who had gone down with his ship? The victim of some long-forgotten crime of passion? Or could it be an even more ancient spirit, perhaps a member of the Potawatomi or Ho-chunk tribes? Could the screaming somehow be related to this spirit's personal story? To its undoubtedly tragic demise?

The more practical residents rolled their eyes at this silliness. The occurrences were mysterious, no doubt, but there was always an ordinary explanation for these things. Some bored kid's prank was the obvious cause. At the most extreme, maybe there really was some summer person who had lost his mind. Everyone needed to just take a deep breath and get serious. Ghosts indeed! But even these sober and steady souls were enjoying the excitement. Everyone, at least, could agree that life on the Island wasn't going to be dull this winter. And besides, if it wasn't a ghost, then what—or who—the Hell was it?

Mike had an artist's eye. Small details in color or texture registered automatically in his awareness, and perhaps because his eyes were so intimately involved in his work, he was an acute observer of human behavior. So it was with growing interest that he noticed that Terry had been beating him to Ground Zero every morning, and that he had been carrying a small duffle bag.

The first time the duffle bag had made its appearance, Terry had tried to push it out of sight—a difficult thing to do at a counter—and the next morning it was not there. But Mike couldn't help noticing as he passed Terry's truck each morning that the duffle bag was on the seat. Struck by an idea, he touched the hood of the truck as he passed one morning on his way in. It was cold.

Mike thought about the duffle bag, about Terry's many questions to Roger about his yoga practice, and about the conversation he and Terry had had about his growing concern with his blood pressure. These things added up to a remarkable possibility in Mike's mind, a possibility so unlikely—and yet so clearly in evidence—that he was finding it difficult to resist the temptation to see it for himself. "Who could?" he asked himself.

Observant though he may be, however, Mike was not nosy, and he assumed that his friend would tell him what he wanted when he wanted to. Since Terry had not chosen to confide in him, that meant he would be embarrassed. Mike had an impish nature, and Terry's secretiveness about what he was doing in the mornings deeply amused him. Wisely, discreetly, and patiently, however, Mike decided to leave it alone. Chuckling about it in his truck on his way to a day's work, he had to admit to himself that it wasn't easy.

Ben had had another disappointing day. There had been no sign of any particular animal at the creek, but the corn had been gone, and there were lots of turkey tracks in the mud. He had lingered on a boulder nearby, trying to be patient and quiet in hope that the deer would come while he was there. But besides the company of birds and squirrels he had seen no other creature.

At last he bestirred himself. It was getting dark, and he was expected home. Heading across the field on his usual route, a movement near the woods caught his eye, and Ben looked up to see a herd of deer. There was no way he could know whether it was the same herd, but although there were several smaller animals—yearlings, probably—there were none with a hurt leg or peculiar gait. Maybe it was a different herd. Or maybe his little friend had already succumbed to natural selection. Discouraged, Ben made his way slowly home.

Fiona's campaign plan, developed with the advice of her friends, was a simple one. In a bigger environment, there would have been consultants and media managers waiting in the wings to fatten themselves with promises of perfectly useless robo-calls, door hangers, and television advertising. On the Island, however, the pickings were too slim for these professional vultures, so the soundest principle was the one most easily followed: talk to your voters.

Terry, an old hand at local campaigns, had given Fiona advice that she intended to follow. She had come to the mainland to run some errands and stopped by to drop off a tool he had forgotten at her house. Terry was building new cabinet doors for an enormous summer house being built to overlook the harbor. "Listen," he said, talking over his shoulder as he adjusted the table saw. "Around here people don't like that big city stuff. They don't really care what party you're in. They want to know whether they can trust you. People will vote for you because you told them you liked their dog. They'll remember you for that. Don't waste your money on all that other stuff. Knock on doors. It's the fundamental requirement of politics."

And so, dutifully—if a bit resignedly—Fiona embarked upon a methodical plan to knock on every door on the Island. It was not as simple as it might have been in a bigger community— even one the size of Sturgeon Bay—because the houses were generally too far apart to walk. Instead, it meant driving from house to house, usually on Saturday and Sunday when people might actually be home. She had gone to the Town Clerk's office, retrieved a list of registered voters, and carried a clipboard so she could keep track of where she had been and to whom she had spoken.

The weather was not cooperative. Every weekend now, it seemed, was damp, windy, and raw. More than once Fiona found herself questioning why she was doing this. But the thought of Stella running the Island, of being bullied by her; the thought of having to sell her little house to Stella, of being driven off the Island by Stella's vengeful power plays, was sufficient incentive. Figuratively and literally, Fiona put her head down and got on with the business of running for office.

Without planning to, Mike drove up to Ground Zero one morning a bit earlier than usual, and saw Roger's and Terry's trucks already in the lot. The lights were on inside the shop, and in the darkness, the interior was revealed as if it were a stage. There they both were, standing side by side, facing the counter. Their left legs were bent with their bare feet resting against the insides of their knees, and their arms were raised above their heads each with the palms of his hands touching as if in prayer.

Mike nodded to himself in confirmation of his theory and, unobserved, waited until his usual time to go in. He hadn't meant to snoop, so out of respect for their privacy he tried not to watch. But despite his resolution, he found his gaze irresistibly pulled back to the activity going on inside. He had to admit that, surprising as it all was, they looked as if they knew what they were doing.

If Island news had a recurring theme, it was the continually dropping lake levels. No one knew exactly why, but there was controversy as to the cause of the change. One theory was that the army corps of engineers had dredged the St. Clair/ Detroit river system three times in the early 20th century, leading to water level drops in Lakes Huron and Michigan.

Another was that it was the result of last year's drought, and the mild winter, which had, in turn led to increased evaporation. There were other theories, too, ranging in their degrees of seriousness, and all discussed earnestly.

The bottom line, however, was simple: Unless Detroit Harbor were dredged the ferry would no longer be able to operate. Without its lifeline, Washington Island would die. This fundamental problem was the only public policy that mattered. The resulting morass of confusion, complexity, and anxiety was the perfect mix for political opportunity. Stella had a plan.

It was after four on a Saturday afternoon, and Fiona was tired and cold. She had spent the entire day knocking on doors, pausing only to put in an appearance at the public library's used book sale and raffle. "A meet and greet," as Emily Martin had called it when they met there by chance. Fiona had felt this a bit grandiose for the casual event, but had kept this thought to herself.

Leaving the warmth of her car, Fiona walked up the long stone path of a farmhouse, a curious mixture of wood smoke and scented dryer sheets wafting in the air around it. She did not recognize the name on her list, but she was beyond caring. Her reticence was long gone, and her little speech was now smooth and unvarying. She had actually woken herself that week reciting it in her sleep. Reaching the porch, she pushed the doorbell. People on the Island weren't much used to unexpected visitors, and she was never quite sure how she would be received.

The ring was answered with the sound of a dog barking. Fiona waited a minute or so before she heard the latch turning. The door opened and an elderly man stood before her, an impatient grimace on his face, a white-faced black lab standing beside him. There was the smell in the hallway of something that had been fried last night. The dog wagged its tail as it continued to bark.

"I hope I'm not disturbing you," said Fiona. "I'm here to discuss the election for chairman of the Town Board."

The man rolled his eyes irritably.

"Well, get on with it," he said.

"I'm Fiona Campbell, and I'm running for the office. I have a great deal of respect for Lars Olafsen, and I want to continue his policies of quiet, efficient service."

The old man's face was stony. "You know Lars?"

"Yes I do. And his legacy of good government has worked well here for many years."

"How do you know? You been here, what? A few months? What do you know about it? Shut up!" He said this last to the dog, who sat down promptly and was quiet, still looking hopefully up at the stranger who might possibly have a ball, or at least a kind word.

With an utterly false calm and the new equally false smile, Fiona looked down at cloudy eyes of the dog and reached her hand out for him to sniff. "That's a nice dog you've got there. I used to have a Lab when I was a girl. How old is he?"

The old man looked steadily at her without softening.

"Old enough," he said, and slammed the door.

Nika watched her son without seeming to, trying to glean some clue about his preoccupation. He had always confided in her, and their conversations had been open and easy. Now he was different: closed away and silent. He had suddenly gone from being her boy to being a mysterious stranger. He ran out the door in the mornings without his usual childish hug, and no longer wanted to talk to her when he came home. Nika watched him one morning as he jogged down the road toward school.

This was what she had expected, and what she had feared. The long process of his drawing away would culminate in him leaving the island. He wouldn't belong anywhere else—she knew from her own experience—and nowhere else would be enough. It would all be bright and shining and new and exhilarating, but it would be missing the mysterious essence of life on the Island.

Would he care? Would that matter to him? She thought it did now, but as he grew, he could change a great deal. She knew that it was part of the process of growing up; that he would have to go through it all himself. But she dreaded the rejection, and the angst, and the teenage scorn of their beautiful life that was bound to come. Watching his figure disappearing down the road, she wished he could be a little boy for just a bit longer.

Her heart hurt.

Dean Hillard, Door County's representative to the Wisconsin Assembly had been in office for five years, and although he had been re-elected twice, his popularity was sometimes difficult to fathom. He was a preening, officious little man who liked feeling important and telling people what to do. He wore his hair too long, and he had a habit of continually brushing it back from his face as he spoke. In his youth, he had been arrested for shoplifting; as an adult he drank too much, and his drinking made him nasty. He bullied the people who worked for him. He was smug, rude, arrogant, and under the impression that he was much smarter than he actually was. He had contempt for the people who elected him, and did not hesitate to show it to his colleagues. And yet, standing on the platforms erected before the crowds at county fairs, VFW chicken dinners, and public library open meetings, he was charming, self-deprecating, and, when necessary, just the tiniest bit flirtatious.

He was, in short, the perfect politician, and, it just so happened, he was also the nephew of Stella DesRosiers.

Ben had been going to the creek every day and had not had one tiny bit of luck. Even though he was beginning to realize that his plan wasn't going to work, Ben still felt a sense of obligation to try to save the deer. He had looked in other places, but this was the water source closest to where he had seen the herd the first time, and it just made the most sense to him.

Every day the corn was gone, and every day he carefully laid out more, took his position on the nearby rock, and waited as long as he dared. He was beginning to think that he should change his bait to one less appealing to turkeys. He had been using up a lot of the cracked corn that his mother kept for birds, but so far she hadn't said anything. If he had one thing going for him, he thought, it was that she was used to his feeding all kinds of animals.

One day after school he dutifully made his way to the creek. There had been snow flurries this morning and more snow was predicted tonight. It was cold, even for Ben, who was used to spending hours out of doors. He was losing hope that he could ever find the little animal.

He was walking as softly as he could, but as the certainty of his mission faded, his mind had wandered, and he was thinking about a book he had read last night about World War II. Ben had acquired his father's love of history, and he was encouraged to read at night rather than to use the Internet. He had been reading about the London Blitz, and was trying to imagine what it would have been like to hide with so many people in the Underground when a flash of movement caught his eye. He froze and looked through the woods. There it was again. He could just make it out through the trees about twenty yards away. Not a herd of animals, just one, and it didn't seem to have a deer's normal graceful gait. Holding his breath, Ben waited to see if the animal would move again.

It seemed like an hour that Ben stood frozen in the woods, hoping not to startle the little deer. He couldn't see it fully, but he could see its brown hide and hear its movement. He was fairly certain it was making its way toward the creek. Now if he could manage to get there, too, without startling it....

With infinite care Ben took a step forward on the path, watching to see if there was any sign of recognition from his quarry.

It didn't move. Ben took another step. Still nothing. Gradually gaining confidence, Ben made his way, slow step by slow step, toward the creek. Suddenly a movement told him that the animal had sensed his presence. Quietly reciting some of the curse words he had heard his father use in private, Ben froze. The animal froze with him, and Ben guessed that it was sniffing the air.

All at once, to Ben's astonishment, there was a flurry of movement, and the animal began to move in his direction. Ben stayed frozen, and in a moment the object of his long days of preparation and searching stood in front of him. They regarded one another with astonishment, and Ben chided himself for how stupid he had been. The animal took another step. Slowly, incredulously, Ben reached out his hand, and without hesitation, the animal came toward him, sniffing his hand for food.

Terry was showing up at Ground Zero every morning to practice yoga with Roger. At first Roger sighed and rolled his eyes, but never having had many friends, Roger secretly came to look forward to their sessions, and stopped voicing his objections quite so frequently.

For his part, Terry had acquired a yoga mat and stopped having to be told to remove his socks. His technique, however, which Roger had done nothing whatsoever to correct, left something to be desired.

They were in the midst of their practice one morning when they were interrupted by the sudden appearance of The Angel

Joshua. He usually arrived after the first burst of the earliest customers, but he had forgotten his phone the day before and was
eager to retrieve it.

Roger and Terry had completed their sun salutations and
were addressing the challenges of Warrior when the door
opened, and The Angel Joshua walked in, bringing with him a
blast of cold air.

"Whoa, dudes," was his first remark. He stood regarding
them for a few moments, as they continued unfazed, and then
he disappeared back out the door. When he returned, he was
carrying his own mat. Without further comment he removed
his shoes, spread out his mat, and joined in.

Afterward he and Terry sat on the floor, putting their shoes
on while Roger prepared to open the shop.

"That is the worst down dog I have ever seen, man. Seriously," Joshua said to Terry. "You should come to class."

Terry nodded solemnly, took his calendar out from his jacket pocket, and looked up. "When did you say it was?" he asked,
pencil poised.

The date for the debate was to be one week before the April
election, close enough to encompass whatever topics might
arise during the campaign.

Fiona had no qualms about speaking in public, but the prospect of a debate with Stella filled her with dread. In her mind's
eye she could see Stella's sneer, she could hear the voice, drip-

ping with scorn and sarcasm, and feel herself dwindling into a small, ineffectual shadow of herself. This mental approach, she knew, was exactly the opposite of correct preparation, but she found it difficult to focus her mind on anything else. Reluctantly, she sought the help of her advisors.

"You need to anticipate the questions, and practice answering them," said Elisabeth. "I've made a list of everything I could think of, but maybe somebody who actually lives on the Island can come up with better ones."

"Thank you," said Fiona. "This is great."

Terry advised her to speak with Lars Olafsen. "He can tell you what kinds of things have come up in the past, and help you get a sense of the room. That kind of experience will be invaluable."

It was Emily Martin, however, who, unsolicited—as always—offered advice on presentation style. She stopped Fiona one afternoon at the grocery store. "I had a debate coach in college," she said, "who advised holding a pen while you speak. It gives you something to do with your hands, looks professional—as if you're just about to write down something important—and it's very helpful to gesture with."

For once, Fiona felt, Emily's advice was both welcome and useful.

The Angel Joshua had not waited for an invitation to join the morning yoga practice at Ground Zero, he simply started showing up. This was a great help to Terry. Unlike Roger, who, in his usual way, was oblivious to Terry's efforts, Joshua—who had many years of yoga experience—gave advice, made minor corrections, and demonstrated poses. Terry was not gifted, but he was in earnest, and his desire to improve was rooted in a desire to be healthy.

Roger continued his own practice without comment, only occasionally shooting a poisonous glance at the others when they talked too much. Even Joshua—who was as immune to Roger's criticism as Roger was immune to everyone else—did not dare to offer corrections to him.

Through observation in class, Roger had picked up on the need for music during yoga, and he implemented this in idiosyncratic ways. Subtlety not being his strong suit, the detail that Roger missed was that the music for yoga generally tended to be quiet, soothing, and somewhat monotonous. Not being quiet, soothing, or monotonous himself, it was hardly surprising that Roger should not have noticed this particular detail.

One of Roger's frequent choices was a Beethoven piano sonata, which, though quiet in places, had a pattern of sudden crescendos and abrupt changes in tempo or volume, which tended to be jarring. Roger appeared to be oblivious to this, but his companions—particularly Terry—were occasionally shocked into losing their balance. The frequency of these events made it necessary for Joshua to begin to issue warnings about a coming change in the music.

"Incoming!" he would hiss at Terry, and Terry would accordingly steady himself in preparation for a shock.

The system only worked occasionally.

"OOPS! Damn!" said Terry under his breath as he toppled

into The Angel Joshua for the third time one morning and they both went down.

"Sorry," he muttered to Joshua as he scrambled back onto his mat and tried to reassemble himself.

"No worries," said Joshua in a low voice. "But maybe you should move your mat a little further over there."

Roger said nothing, but glared at them from under his right leg. The music began a crashing phase that made Terry think of horses galloping to battle. He wasn't convinced that the choice of music was ideal. He had nothing against Beethoven *per se*, but it wasn't soothing.

Ben, whose conscience was increasingly complicated, had reluctantly determined from the beginning that if he were to say he was making a birdfeeder, he would have to actually make one. Ideally, it should be one made from PVC, but this shouldn't be hard. There were hundreds of projects of this kind online. The birdfeeder's construction would be something he would have to accomplish away from home, and this, in turn, would provide him with an excuse to be away without too many questions from his mom.

Jim was the obvious person to ask. He wouldn't mind, he would be helpful in the construction of the birdfeeder, and since they were old friends, his parents wouldn't object to Ben being at Jim's house. Besides, he would be good company.

Ben wasted no time in presenting himself at Jim's house after school. As predicted, Jim was more than happy to help with the birdfeeder, and cleared a space on a table in the sitting room where the project could remain during its construction.

"Let's see your plans, Ben, so we can figure out what tools you'll need."

Ben pulled the crumpled printouts from the pocket of his backpack, and they spread them out on the table.

On Tuesday, Shay was pleased to see a new pupil in her class at St. Anatole's basement.

"Hey, everyone. Meet Terry. He's going to be joining us from now on."

Her wild blonde hair swirled around her as she sat, cross-legged and swaying before the class in her traditional warm-up. After the class began, Shay walked the room making corrections to her students' form, gently pushing a head down here, pulling a leg straight there. She spent a great deal of time at the back of the room where her male students gathered. It may not have been equitable, but it was clearly necessary. At least for the two newest. "Wow, Roger, great plank! You are making amazing progress!"

"Terry, you need to keep that foot straight, not turned in. No, the other way. There you go! Good job!"

"Oh, Joshua, you're such an old pro! I can tell you're from California!"

The class slowly progressed to the traditional ending, the Dead Man's Pose. As the students lay on their backs with their eyes closed, Shay went around to each of them and massaged their temples with the lavender oil she kept in a tiny brown bottle in her bag. Sometimes her hair brushed their faces as she bent over them.

When she had finished, they were invited to sit up, cross-legged on their mats, touch their fingertips together and bow to the teacher, to the student, and to the light within. "*Namaste*," Shay told them.

"*Namaste*," said the class, dutifully, without having any idea of its meaning.

In the shuffle of rolling up mats, putting on socks and shoes, and gathering up coats, there was a little quiet conversation. It was a shock to the system to come back to the world after the intensity and calm of the class.

Only Shay remained as always, bright, light, and cheerful.

"Bye everybody! See you next time, and don't forget to practice!"

She put her hand on Terry's arm as he passed. "You stick with it. Look at how fast Roger's made progress!" She smiled her beachy smile at him and watched him go.

"Wow," said Terry, remembering, as they climbed the stairs from St. Anatole's Church basement, the way her hair had brushed his face. "Shay's a dish."

Roger looked at him with his usual scowl—which could have meant anything from disapproval to agreement—and stalked off to Ground Zero to meet the afternoon crowd, trailing the scent of lavender as he went.

P ali stood at the window of the small room he used as an office and looked out over the adjacent fields. He had a rare
day off, and, in an occasion just as rare, was alone in the house.

Behind him on his desk was his computer, its idle screen
now dark.

There was nothing to see outside, and, he thought, bitterly,
nothing much on the inside, either. He had been sitting at his
desk all day, waiting for inspiration. So far, it hadn't come.

Circumstances had been a bit trying these past weeks with
the ghost story circulating around the Island, and Pali had been
embarrassed. He and his crewmen, who had shared the experiences of the ferry's ghost, knew what they had seen. But until
very recently, they had all agreed not to discuss it in public for
all the reasons that had now been made apparent.

It is difficult enough to believe if you have seen a ghost—
even with witnesses—but if you haven't, and you hear someone
tell a story, you are inclined to think that the person who tells
it is either a fool or a liar. Pali, who was neither, found this extremely difficult. He took pride in his reputation for honesty and
straight shooting, and he felt that his neighbors would never take
him seriously again.

Pali couldn't know that it was only his reputation that had
lent any credence whatsoever to the story. Even if he had known,
he would have found no consolation there.

The rest of his feelings, however, were more complex. What
was the thing they had seen? Was it good or evil? It had saved

his life, and the lives of his crew, but, he thought, even Satan could appear to do good in order to achieve evil. If only they knew what this screaming was. If only they could find some explanation for it, then Pali could at least feel more confident that he had not been collaborating with some demon spirit. That somehow he, Pali, had not brought evil to the Island.

And here he was—selfishly, he told himself—longing for its return. Whatever it was. Wherever it came from. "This," he thought to himself, "is the definition of sin." He had thought of discussing the situation with his pastor, but he wasn't sure he wanted to hear the response. The truth of the matter was that Pali did not want to turn his back on this spiritual contact. He did not want his muse to leave him; he was far more troubled by the loss of communication than by its potential for evil. And this, Pali firmly believed, was unforgivable.

Nils Gunlaugssen had spent the evening at his friend Arn's house with a group of men who had known each other all their lives. They were celebrating the birth of Arn's first grandchild. By the end of the evening, Nils—like all the others—had had a few too many. He was generally a responsible man, a grandfather himself, and although he knew he probably shouldn't drive, his house was only up the road a bit, and anyway, there was unlikely to be any traffic. He'd made this gamble many times before, and always without incident. There was no reason to believe that anything would be different this time.

210 The Audacity of Goats

It was a chilly night in early November. The last of the leaves were long gone from the trees, and a premature blast of winter air had brought the first snowflakes just that morning. This was January weather, not usual for late fall, but Nils rather liked the cold, and particularly loved the snow, so he had pulled out his winter parka without grumbling, and departed for Arn's after dinner in great good humor.

He had been surprised, but undismayed when he emerged from the warmth and cheer of Arn's into a changed world. The snow had been falling heavily for several hours, and there was already a good four inches on the roads.

Stepping out into the wind, he had hurled his last joke over his shoulder, pulled up the hood of his parka, and hurried to his truck. The island habit of warming up a vehicle in cold weather had not yet kicked in for the season, and Nils was regretting that he hadn't thought of this as the cold sank in around his feet and ears. He never felt comfortable driving with his hood up, and he pushed it back from his head reluctantly, feeling the instant shift in his body temperature. Damn, it was cold. There hadn't been any time yet to get used to it, he thought to himself. This was a fast start to winter.

The brand new truck leaped easily to life, and Nils flipped on the seat warmers. They wouldn't really even have a chance to work before he got home, but this was the first time Nils had had this feature, and he was thoroughly enjoying the luxury. With caution born of care for his new truck and a little extra brandy, Nils pulled out of Arn's yard and into the road, and began the short drive home. Bed would feel good tonight, that was for sure.

He was rounding the last curve of the twisting wooded road

that led to the house he shared with his wife of thirty years, Paula. She would be sitting up for him with the television on, fast asleep in her favorite chair, her crocheting on her lap and Og, their big old black lab, sound asleep, too, with his head on her feet. Nils smiled to himself imagining this scene. He was lucky to have a happy home life. Not all of the fellows he'd spent the evening with could say the same. Poor Danny had a devil of a time with his sharp-tongued, critical wife, and although they had been married for nearly as long as Nils and Paula, their time together had not been bliss. Of course, thought Nils, Danny was no prize himself, truth be told.

Nils was almost dreaming at the wheel when he caught himself with a start. Was that something in the road? Without thinking he slammed on the brakes. The still warm asphalt had melted the fresh snow next to the surface of the road and re-frozen into a thin layer of ice coated with more snow, and Nils's reactions were blurred with brandy. The rear wheels drifted side-ways, and before Nils could catch it, the truck was spinning al-most in slow motion toward the side of the road, where a boulder and a clump of birch trees stood waiting to reshape the pristine black paint of the beautiful new truck. There was a sickening thud and a grinding noise as it came to a halt, and then just the sound of the engine running and the windshield wipers.

Unhurt, Nils sat for a moment and lay his head on the steer-ing wheel in exasperation and disgust. Sighing, he shook his head, sat up, and got out to survey the damage. Cold and adrena-line had sobered him up, and he stood resignedly in the snow, playing out the inevitable "if only"s. If only he had let Jake drive him home. If only he had taken Paula's old Jeep, as she had suggested. If only he hadn't had that last brandy old-fashioned. If only... Nils paused in his self-recrimination and frowned. An image of what had just happened flashed across his mind. He saw again the image of something in the road. A deer, probably. He frowned again. The movement had been kind of... jerky... awkward, even. And then... He tilted his head and stared blindly off into the falling snow, thinking hard. There had been something else, too. Something really strange. He struggled to gather the flash of images in that moment of crisis. Slowly, his head came up and his eyes moved from side to side as he pursued an elusive memory. And then in his mind's eye, the memory came again: an animal in the road, leaping clumsily across his path, and then turning to look back, a sharp gleam of eyes caught in the headlights just as the truck began to spin.

Turning quickly, Nils shivered uneasily, zipped up the pocket of his jacket where he kept the keys, and quick-marched up the road toward home. He would call for a tow truck in the morning.

Ben burst in through the back door one night, smelling of fresh air and snow. He was late again, and it was nearly dark, and he came in without his usual exuberant greeting. Nika looked at him, trying to read his face.

"Come and kiss your mother." She sounded old to herself as she said this. Matronly, dull, and disapproving. She smiled warmly at her son, unconsciously counteracting this self-image.

Dutifully, Ben gave her a kiss. He had always been a cuddly boy and didn't seem to mind his mother's caresses. Tonight, though, his mind was elsewhere again, and Nika didn't probe.

"You're just in time to set the table," she said cheerfully. "You were about to owe me a dollar." This was their system. Setting the table was Ben's job, and if he forgot or was late, he had to pay for his mother to do it.

"Sorry," said Ben without conveying any actual remorse. He began to get dishes from the hutch.

"Wash your hands, first," said Nika in the singsong way that comes from thousands of repetitions.

Ben went to do as he had been told, Pali arrived a few minutes later, and the household went on in its usual routine.

Later that evening, after Ben had gone to bed, Nika sat in her rocking chair, thinking. Ben had always been a good boy, easy to be around, easy to please. She had listened over the years to her friends' stories about raising their children and considered herself lucky. Ben was no trouble. He was generally affectionate and respectful, healthy, did well in school, ate what was put before him, and seemed to be happy.

It was true that he didn't have any particularly close friends, but there were so few opportunities on the Island to meet new people, and there weren't many boys his age. Maybe he just hadn't clicked with anyone. Or maybe he was like his father, content with his own company, content with others', and perfectly happy to roll with whatever came his way.

But he had been coming home from school later and later. Nika gave Ben a lot of freedom; there was no reason not to. He was a good boy with good sense, and the Island was a pretty safe place. But this change in his routine meant something beyond the mere approach of adolescence, and she was wondering what it was. There was no real reason to worry, she told herself, but still, it was important to know his mind, to stay in touch with him now, before he moved out of reach.

She would talk to him, she decided, and gently probe to see if he would tell her what was going on. She would watch for the right moment. And maybe, she thought, it wouldn't be a bad idea to bake some cookies tomorrow. She smiled to herself. "Catch a bear with honey," her mother used to always say.

Fiona sat in her warm kitchen, a hot mug of tea in her hands, listening to the calls of two great horned owls. They must be very near the house, she thought. She would not have expected them to be so active in this weather. The snow was falling heavily now, clinging to the limbs of the trees, and outlining each detail. This was a big storm for November, and there were still leaves clinging here and there to branches, and a few neglected piles of them lingered in corners of the yard.

Fiona loved to walk in the snow, but a walk alone this afternoon was not appealing. It would be too lonely. Pete had been gone for months, tending to an ill-defined petroleum crisis somewhere in the world—his vagueness made Fiona nervous for his safety. And Elisabeth's big dog, Rocco, was, even at this moment, snugly curled on the rug before Elisabeth's and Roger's big stone fireplace, many miles away on the mainland. The ticking of the antique walnut clock that Pete had given her as a goodbye gift made the room feel emptier. Without even the questionable companionship of the demon goat, Robert, Fiona felt utterly alone and unloved. This, she knew, was not true, but it was a feeling of old habit, and one she fell into easily, without resistance.

Perhaps because of the storm, Fiona's mind drifted to Robert, to the unexplained barn fire in which he had perished. It was still a recent enough event that she felt the grip of anxiety and fear at the memory. And yet, she was not quite sure how to articulate, even to herself, what she felt about it. Not grief, really, because Robert had made her feel throughout the duration of his presence as if she were merely an unappreciated goat servant. Regret, surely, for the terrible way he had died, that was true.

But there was something else: The feeling that, in his odd, saturnine fashion, Robert had understood her. And it was this connection, or rather, its absence, that affected her more than she could allow herself to admit.

Suddenly, tea seemed inadequate for the cold, and she bestirred herself to find some scotch on the living room sideboard. Also, she thought, some music. Schubert or Haydn, or something, in contrast to the weather, exceptionally civilized. Maybe, she mused, flipping through her collection, some chamber music. At last she settled on a Robert Schumann piano quartet. It went well with loneliness, nostalgia, and scotch. And not just any nostalgia, she reminded herself: goat nostalgia.

She sighed. Even Martin Luther would not be sufficient companionship this evening.

P ali had a sincere and deeply held faith that occasionally side-stepped the specifics of his church's teachings. His conversations with God were personal, and he felt buoyed by his belief. But there were occasions when, in the privacy of his own mind, he weighed the teachings of the church, and set them aside. He was a man who trusted his own judgment, and there were some elements of orthodox theology that did not meet his standards. The institution of the church, he was acutely aware, was a creation of man, and subject to man's fallibility. This, he had no doubt, bore no reflection on God.

His objections were closely held. For the most part, he did not discuss them, even with Nika. He had no intention of worrying her, or of disturbing her natural and deeply held faith. His ideas were his own, and although he believed they were true, he was not interested in prolonged theological arguments. If he were, he knew of a few people on the Island who would have credibly engaged with him, but he saw no point in offending or outraging anyone else.

His unorthodox theology notwithstanding, however, Pali did accept an idea that, though a fundamental tenet of Christianity, was mostly ignored or dismissed in contemporary society, even by Christians. He believed that there was evil in the world, and that its power challenged the faith of men.

After the first meeting in the woods, Ben's relationship with his new friend was firmly established. To Ben's relief, his peculiar walk was unrelated to injury, but he was skinny and very hungry. Every day after school Ben hurried to the creek to find the animal. If nothing was there, Ben would wait for a while and leave food. But on most days he was there, and Ben began to realize that his friend was waiting for him. Sometimes he came alone, but gradually he began to come with the small herd of deer that Ben had seen that first night, and although the other animals were less bold, they, too, began to treat Ben, if not with enthusiasm, then, at least, with indifference.

This was the realization of Ben's dreams. He reveled in the trust of an animal, and was thrilled as its confidence in him grew. But along with the trust, Ben also felt the weight of obligation, and he worried about the cold, the increasing snow cover, and coyotes. Most of all, Ben worried what would happen if, in a world of hunters and rule-following grownups, someone else came across a little creature who trusted human beings.

Meanwhile, Christmas was coming, and he had not yet completed the birdfeeder that he planned to give his mother. It was mostly finished, but there remained a few final touches.

It had not occurred to Ben that his project would incite so much friendly interest.

"So how's the birdfeeder coming?" asked Tom one afternoon when Ben came into the store after school to buy a candy bar.

"It's okay," said Ben with a shrug. "Kind of ugly, though." The white plastic PVC piping, while sturdy, offended Ben's sense of a birdfeeder's proper appearance.

Tom nodded thoughtfully. "You could paint it. Since it's

mostly white anyway, maybe you could make it look like a piece of birch wood."

Ben's face brightened. "That's a good idea." Since he was now committed to making his project a gift, he wanted it to look right.

"I'll show you the right kind of paint to use," said Tom, coming out from behind the counter and leading the way to the paint aisle. "It will be easy."

Roger, now properly trained, had learned that he should kiss his wife when he came in the door. Elisabeth had been home for an hour or more and was standing over the stove cooking some kind of sauce. The kitchen was filled with the rich smell of red wine, shallots, and butter. As he kissed her, she gave him a peculiar look. "You smell like lavender."

Roger shrugged, and picked up the ball Rocco had dropped at his feet.

"I'll take him out for a run."

"Dinner's in half an hour," said Elisabeth casually. But she watched him as he left the house, with the big shepherd gamboling around his feet.

Chapter Fifteen

Roger had been having mechanical trouble. He owned an ancient vehicle that had been nursed through many failures of mechanics and will, but he knew that its useful life was coming to an end. Determined to push on for as long as possible, he ignored the warning signs of a cracked head gasket, slipping clutch, and eccentric electrical system.

One snowy December morning, however, the old beast gave up the ghost, and before he could admit the truth and borrow Elisabeth's little Japanese station wagon, he had spent half an hour tinkering with various possible fixes, alternately praying and cursing, hoping for a vehicular miracle. It was not to be.

Roger pulled up to Ground Zero nearly forty-five minutes late. Terry and The Angel Joshua were sitting together, waiting. When they saw Roger they met him at the door to the shop.

"It's pretty late. Do you want to skip this morning?" asked Terry.

"No," said Roger. "People can wait."

Terry looked at the ground and took a deep breath. He wasn't crazy about being seen in public wearing his yoga clothes and doing awkward yoga things. But it was winter, and there were no crowds. Besides, he was no coward.

"Okay," he said.

They all went inside and began their daily routine. In his haste, Roger forgot to lock the door behind them.

St. Johann's Lutheran Church Men's Prayer Group had been in continuous existence for almost 100 years. The men came from all backgrounds, and were highly respected for their commitment to Christian principle, their families, their country, and service to their community. Membership consisted of both retired and working men, so their schedule was designed to allow members to head off to work after the meeting. With the coming Christmas season, the group decided to celebrate with a special post-meeting breakfast.

The yoga practice had progressed to the later phase of the morning ritual—*Ustrasana*, the Camel—accompanied by Richard Strauss's "Also Sprach Zarathustra." The choice of music may have been an expression of Roger's mood, but it was difficult to be sure. The pose was well beyond Terry's level. He was finding it more difficult than usual to keep from tipping over, and The Angel Joshua had moved his mat well away. The musical jolts were so frequent that the usual warnings of "Incoming!" were ineffectual, and Terry resigned himself to a few more bruises than usual.

They were moving from *Ustrasana* to *Vrksasana*. Known as the tree, and deceptively simple in appearance, it was a pose Terry found particularly challenging even without Richard Strauss. He bobbled continually, frequently having to put his foot down before he went over. The music was in one of its more vigorous moments, accelerating quickly and creating a mood that reminded Terry of snowballs gathering speed as they rolled down a mountainside.

He had just gained sufficient balance to attempt to raise

his foot into the penultimate step of achieving the pose when the door to Ground Zero opened abruptly and the St. Johann's Lutheran Church Men's Prayer Group, accompanied by hearty voices, laughter, and vigorous foot stomping, entered the shop.

Terry fell over.

There was an awkward silence as the Men's Prayer Group gleaned that all was not usual at Ground Zero.

Roger merely continued his routine without acknowledging their entrance. The Angel Joshua, serene in his manly beauty and holding his Vrksasana, turned his gaze upon them, bathing them in its light. He spoke.

"We're almost done. Have a seat and we'll be with you in a few." And turning to Terry, "Terry, man. You okay?"

Without replying Terry scrambled to his feet, and drawing inspiration from his comrades, resumed his pose with new success.

The practice took its course, and for ten more minutes Roger, Joshua, and Terry focused on their poses and their breathing, while the St. Johann's Lutheran Church Men's Prayer Group looked on, bemused.

With the passage of time, a greater sense of comfort emerged, and some of the men began a quiet murmur of conversation. Those who caught Roger's glance fell silent instantly, but the others continued in blissful unawareness.

As they reached the last pose, The Angel Joshua spoke again, this time to Roger and Terry. "You guys go ahead and practice *Shavasana.* I'll start taking orders."

He moved with angelic grace through the Lutherans, his radiance shining from him.

As coffee was being served, Roger and Terry lay on their

mats, face up, and completed their practice with *Shavasana*, the dead man's pose.

Rejuvenated by *Shavasana* after his brush with humiliation, Terry arose from his mat and took a seat at the counter as Roger resumed his position behind it and began serving coffee and egg sandwiches. The men in the prayer group were well acquainted with Roger, and their familiarity with him made teasing out of the question. Terry, an old friend to them all, was a different story. But he took it with good grace, and got in a few shots of his own.

They were all getting ready to leave when one of the Lutherans took Terry aside. "So… that looks really hard."

"Well, it is for me," said Terry, with easy candor. "But I needed to do something about my blood pressure, so I figured I'd try it."

"Really? My blood pressure isn't so good, either." He looked thoughtful. "How'd you get started?"

"I just bought a mat and showed up here."

"Every morning?"

"Yessir," said Terry. "It's pretty early."

"Think I could come?"

Terry looked doubtful. "Well… it's not my place." He paused and looked at his friend, a man he'd known since second grade, and emboldened by the morning's experience decided to take the leap. "But why not? Tomorrow morning at five." He leaned in and whispered, "But I don't recommend telling Roger. Just show up."

Terry was in the parking lot checking his pockets for his keys when another member of the men's group came up.

"So," he said without preamble. "That yoga looks pretty hard."

Stuffing envelopes with the candidate's brochures is among the many requirements in running an election, and this tedious chore was one Fiona had been dreading. In an act of friendship Fiona felt was beyond repayment, Elisabeth and Nika had offered to come and help on a weekday afternoon in order to free Fiona up for her weekend door-knocking.

Nika arrived just after lunch as planned, at just about the time the ferry—with Elisabeth aboard—was expected. Fiona heard her knock, and came to the door. As Nika was unwrapping herself from her down coat and removing her boots, she handed a canvas tote bag to Fiona and gave her a sly smile. Inside, tucked in among some personal items and a box of business envelopes, was a full bottle of Door County's local gin. She laughed as Fiona's eyes widened.

"I got the idea just as I was leaving the house. My grandma always said that gin was the only way to get through Christmas. She used to add it to her tea. So I thought, given the time of year, envelope stuffing was a close enough parallel. It's sort of a tribute to her memory."

She laughed again. "I don't think she liked my grandpa's mother very much."

"Well, I think I would have liked your grandma. Come on into the kitchen. Elisabeth should be here any minute."

Elisabeth arrived shortly afterward, and after taking inventory of their materials, they set to work. They quickly developed an assembly line of folding, stuffing, and sealing, and for a while there was nothing but the sounds of moving paper in the kitchen.

"All this must have made a dent in the campaign funds," commented Nika, scrutinizing one of the color brochures with Fiona's photograph.

"Not as much as you would think. It was the signs that killed me."

"I think you need to have more fundraisers, Fiona," said Elisabeth. Even if you don't really need the money, you need people's commitment to support you."

"I know. But what do you do if the person who most wants to fundraise for you is busily alienating the entire populace?"

"It can't be as bad as that." Elisabeth was in her bossy mode.

"Oh really? My chief fan—for reasons I haven't quite figured out, but which involve a deep and wholly understandable animosity toward our friend Stella—is Emily Martin. Emily, however, isn't exactly popular around here."

Nika smiled in agreement as Fiona continued.

"Last week she told the owner of the ferry line that his captains' uniforms weren't dignified enough. She told the newspaper editor that as soon as she had time she would come over and show her how to lay out the ads properly, and she told the Lutheran minister's wife that the coffee hour needed 'a little jazzing up.'"

"Oh," said Elisabeth. "I see your point."

"On her last trip over, she told Pali that he was swinging the helm too far when he docks," said Nika.

Elisabeth and Fiona stopped what they were doing and stared at her. They responded at the same time.

"Seriously?"

"You are joking."

"God's honest truth." Nika began to laugh. "She tried to come into the wheel house last week, and Pali told her that there were new regulations about who could ride up there. He didn't say that the regulations were his."

"I'm sure he was very polite," said Fiona, laughing.

"Oh, you know Pali. He's always polite."

"At least you can understand that woman's feelings toward Stella," said Elisabeth returning doggedly to her subject. "At least you know she's a sincere supporter."

"Well, yes," said Fiona. "There is that."

They were silent for a moment as Nika went to the next room to retrieve a new batch of envelopes. Elisabeth brought another stack of brochures to the table.

"Did you hear that Charlotte is going to have to have a knee replacement?" asked Nika, returning.

Fiona grimaced. "Fortunately, we have no doctor on the Island, or Emily would be scrubbing up to assist with the surgery. She really is a plague upon the landscape. The question is, if we actually allowed her to host, who would come?"

Nika was carefully folding brochures into neat thirds. "Why don't you tell her that I've already agreed to host, and you don't want to saturate the territory?"

"Really?" asked Fiona. "You'd do that?"

"Sure," said Nika. "No problem."

"You'd have to invite her."

"I know."

"She'll try to take over."

"I know."

"She'll want to redecorate your entire house and make Pali get a haircut."

Nika laughed. "I know. It's okay. I can take it."

"Wow," said Fiona, who wasn't usually given to saying wow. "Thanks."

"Those are the last two stacks," said Elisabeth, returning from the next room. "We should be finished in record time."

"What shall we do with the rest of the afternoon?" asked Fiona. "It's newly free."

Elisabeth sighed and looked weary. "I should be baking Christmas cookies for the church bazaar. Why do I always volunteer for these things? I hate baking cookies."

"I think it's time for tea," said Nika, pulling the bottle of gin from her tote bag.

"Absolutely." Fiona rose from the table.

"You know, it's funny," she said over her shoulder as she filled the teakettle. "It's Christmas time, and somehow I never get around to cookie baking. But given Nika's family traditions, I'm beginning to think that I've been missing something."

Roger drove up to Ground Zero one morning, and frowned. There were half a dozen trucks in the parking lot, all with their lights off and engines running. He pulled into his own space around the back and walked around to the door. Behind him he heard engines being turned off and doors slamming.

Eight men joined him at the door, all carrying rolled- up yoga mats under their arms. Roger turned and looked at them with his habitual look of cold fury. Knowing Roger, none of them took it as anything other than Roger's normal expression. Some of the men looked sheepish, and some were grinning.

"What?" he said, in what seemed to him an acceptable morning greeting. "We're closed."

Terry, unwilling to be the spokesman for the group, remained silent.

"Thought maybe we could join your yoga class," ventured Stef, the unofficial leader of the St. Johann's Lutheran Church Men's Prayer Group.

"There's no class," said Roger.

"Well, what do you call it then?" asked another of the Lutherans.

"This is practice," said Roger. "Private practice."

"Well, can we join?"

"No."

"Can we watch?" asked one of the other men, to laughter. "It's kind of fun when Terry falls down." More laughter.

"No." Turning his back on the group, Roger unlocked the door of the shop and went in, followed by The Angel Joshua. Terry looked back, apologetically, and went in, too.

The orderly, obedient, God-fearing, and dutiful Lutherans stood for a moment watching, uncertain of what to do. And then one by one, they followed Roger into the shop.

Chapter Sixteen ✤

The approach of Christmas brought with it all the annual excitement. The school and church concerts, the festive teas and luncheons, the charity drives, and all the rest. Fiona, newly conscious of the need for a candidate's visibility, joined in, with, if not enthusiasm, then at least, good grace, and found that she was rather enjoying herself. If nothing else, it was a distraction from her increasingly painful longing for Pete. It was already clear that he would not be able to get away for long enough to come, and she was resigned to spending the holidays alone.

The Christmas decorations had been installed. This consisted of live trees perched at the tops of the light poles in what could optimistically be called Downtown Washington Island. It was a tradition Fiona had never seen anywhere else, and one she kept forgetting to inquire about. She assumed that there was some ancient Druidic or Norse tree spirit connection, one that had been assimilated along with all the other Christmas traditions.

Meanwhile, she was finding it difficult to decide whether it would be better to put up a Christmas tree at home and celebrate alone, or whether it would be less lonesome to do nothing. Neither approach was particularly desirable, but in the end she decided to honor the observance. "Life goes on," she told herself, with more spirit than she actually felt.

In contemplating his dilemma, Pali could find no guidance because there was no one he felt he could ask. He did not want to worry Nika, and the only other person he confided in, Fiona, seemed already to be carrying a burden with the impending election. He had rejected discussing it with his pastor, who was a good man, but intellectually one-dimensional. This left Pali on his own.

On two points, at least, Pali was clear: He must do the right thing—at least as right as he could surmise; and he must honor his primary obligation to his family. Their trust was his honor.

And so, sadly, Pali determined what he had to do. He did not believe in bitterness. He was arriving at this decision freely, and he would not bend to regret. Life was filled with hard choices. He told himself that he was fortunate that this one involved only his own relatively small sacrifice.

Ben was coming to understand that the best part of secrets was having someone to share them with. His treks to the creek were beginning to feel lonely and a little bit burdensome. He would have liked to have had someone to come with him, or to go in his place from time to time. He would have liked to ask for advice about what he should be doing, what kind of food he should be bringing, or even how often he should go. But there wasn't anyone in his class he felt he could trust not to blurt it out, and he remained convinced that all the adults in his life would disapprove. Even Jim—especially Jim—he feared, would not approve, or might even try to stop him. Ben needed someone who wasn't like everyone else, and unfortunately, on the Island, he didn't have a lot of choices. Doggedly, he carried on his daily routine, hoping that he was doing the right thing.

It was remarkable, Fiona thought to herself, in the face of her move to the Island, her attempts to escape from the stress of her life in Chicago, and the somewhat ironic local slogan that life here was "north of the tension line," that she was nevertheless continually finding herself faced with some task that filled her with dread.

In this particular instance, she was trying to work herself up to a phone conversation with Emily. Emily's offer of a fundraiser, though it should have been a kindness, felt, instead, like a criticism of the Island, its citizens, Fiona's campaign, and Fiona herself. Emily and her husband's eager insertion of themselves into every aspect of Island life seemed less like community spiritedness than it did a conviction of personal superiority. Nothing, it seemed, was as good as it could be if they, the Martins, could only take charge.

After much procrastination, Fiona steeled herself to make the call. She hoped she would be able to withstand what she had come to think of as The Onslaught from Emily.

The phone rang and Emily answered.

"Windsome Farm," she said. "Emily Martin speaking."

"Hello, Emily. This is Fiona…" Before she could finish the sentence she planned, Emily was off.

"Fiona! I was just thinking about you. You know, I saw some of your yard signs today, and I couldn't help wishing you'd chosen different colors. Something brighter, something that stood out more. I'm so afraid that they look like advertisements for replacement windows, if you know what I mean. It's too bad I wasn't there to advise you. But, I suppose it can't be helped now. What's done is done. Now, I suppose you're calling about the fundraiser. I've chosen the perfect date, one when we can be sure that the maximum number of the right people will be in town, and there are no local conflicts. You know how people around here love their church suppers and community events. We don't want to get between an Islander and his pancake supper around here, that's for sure!"

Emily paused in The Onslaught as she laughed at her own joke. Fiona tried to jump in, but she wasn't quick enough.

"We'll schedule it after the holidays, when everyone will be looking for something to relieve the boredom. Winter around here can get the best of you if you don't have a plan."

"But…" said Fiona, wondering, since Emily had only just moved to the Island, how she could speak with so much authority about winter.

"Now don't you worry about a thing. I'll take care of everything. I know exactly who we should invite, and I've already figured out the perfect menu. Some good wine, some beer, some simple hors d'oeuvres. With goat cheese, of course." She laughed. "You won't have to do anything but show up."

"But Nika—" persisted Fiona.

"Don't you worry about Nika. I'll just tell her that we'll let her do a little coffee morning. Just some coffee cake or something for people who don't have to punch a clock. It's perfect for her, and of course, she won't be able to have a lot of people because their house is so small. Don't you worry, Fiona. I'll take care of Nika. She's a nice girl. She won't be any trouble."

Fiona, although she'd said barely a word, was feeling a bit breathless. As if Nika would be the one who would be trouble. She opened her mouth to respond, but Emily was already speaking.

"Oh gosh! Look at the time! I need to get out to the barn and make sure everyone's all set for the night. Now, remember what I said. Don't you worry about a thing. Bye!!"

And there was a click.

Fiona hung up the phone, walked into the living room, and poured herself half a tumbler of neat scotch. She was beginning to understand the clichés about politicians and drinking. It was a wonder more of them weren't dying of cirrhosis.

She would have to call Nika in the morning, and she'd have to get up very early if she wanted to talk to Nika before Emily did. She took a drink and sighed. She would go to bed early. She felt that she deserved it.

As she settled into her bed, the tumbler of scotch and the little green book on the table beside her, she felt herself relax. She picked up the book and opened it to the last place she had marked. Determinedly, she picked out the German words she didn't know and cobbled together a translation. "War," she read, "is the greatest plague that can afflict humanity; it destroys religion, it destroys states, it destroys families. Any scourge is preferable to it."

Clearly, thought Fiona, Martin Luther had not met Emily Martin.

Roger had not said anything to Elisabeth about the yoga. It wasn't that he was hiding anything from her; it was that sharing things was not in his nature. Roger had never read a marriage manual, and so far the only advice he had received had come from the two very brief conversations with Terry and Mike and The Angel Joshua at Ground Zero. It did not occur to him that married people shared details about their lives. He was not averse to it, he simply didn't know that he should.

"I stopped by the shop this afternoon," said Elisabeth one evening as they sat by the fire. They had decorated their Christmas tree—their first one together—and were celebrating with a glass of champagne. Rocco was lying at their feet noisily chewing a big squeaky ball that Roger had brought from his trip to Sturgeon Bay that afternoon, and conversation was a bit difficult.

Roger looked at her attentively but said nothing. The ball squeaked ear-piercingly, and Rocco shook it vigorously back and forth.

Elisabeth began again. "It was the second time recently that it was closed. I didn't know you closed the shop in the afternoons," she said.

"Just Tuesdays and Thursdays between 1:45 and 3:15. During yoga."

The ball squeaking shrilly in the background, Elisabeth looked at him blankly, wondering whether she had heard correctly.

"Did you say 'yoga?'"

"Yes. I'm taking a yoga class. With Joshua."

"Oh." There was a particularly loud and prolonged squeak, as of a dying animal, then silence.

"We'd better take that away from him," said Roger. "He's got it in pieces."

Elisabeth bent to pick up the latex smithereens. Rocco seemed puzzled that he was being prevented from this pleasure.

Rocco had become a reason for Roger to speak more than was his usual habit. Normally, Elisabeth would have viewed this as an opportunity to reach out to Roger and coax him into speaking more with her. But lately, she was feeling brittle and out of sorts, not her usual self, and in her preoccupation, she did not see the opportunity when it occurred.

"Come on, Rocco," said Roger. "Let's go into the kitchen and get a treat."

Happily, Rocco followed, leaving Elisabeth in the living room to think. A few moments later, she followed them into the kitchen to throw away the remnants of the murdered toy.

"I think it's great that you're doing yoga," she said, washing her hands at the kitchen sink and drying them on a paper towel.

Roger simply looked at her. "You do?"

"Well, yes." She looked at him over her shoulder. "Why wouldn't I?"

Roger had no answer for this. "It's only twice a week," he said. "But it doesn't really seem like enough to make progress."

He paused, contemplating a new detail. "I'm thinking about going down to Sturgeon Bay on Saturdays for an extra class."

Elisabeth was silent, trying to evaluate this newfound yoga passion. Roger's interest in it was, to her, inexplicable, on the one hand. On the other, it did explain the increasingly frequent and abrupt interruptions of their evenings with toe touches and peculiar stretches.

"Well, that's a big commitment of time. You must really like it."

"Shay says I have a deep well of spirituality. It's a gift."

Elisabeth's eyes changed just the smallest fraction and for just the smallest instant. She turned around to face her husband.

"Who is Shay?" she asked, calmly.

It was a bitter December morning, still dark, when Pali arrived at the ferry dock to begin his day. He liked to arrive before the crew and go over the boat alone. This was as much a spiritual occasion as a work obligation. He liked being there on the water when the first light brightened the horizon. On most days he would stop what he was doing and watch the slow turn of the earth, his mug of coffee warm in his hands.

The wind was hard and cold, and carried the promise of snow. Pali liked winter. He welcomed the clarifying quality of the cold and the beauty of the snow, and he relished the long nights. Winter was his season. But today, Pali did not feel the joy he usually felt at sunrise.

Normally, when he had made a decision, he felt his mind

and body relax, and this was a signal to him that he had done the right thing. This time the hard, tight places in his chest and stomach were harder and tighter. Maybe, he told himself, he would relax after he had done what he planned to do.

The voices of his crew arriving sent him to his tasks, and he greeted them with his usual steady demeanor. The snow clouds were to the north and west, but there would still be plenty of sun for a while. The lake had the heavy, gelatinous quality that came before the ice. It looked thick and dark, and moved with a languor that belied its deadly nature. In these temperatures, hypothermia was a greater danger than drowning.

The first cars began to arrive, and Pali, with long experience and an expert eye, arranged them on the deck in order to properly distribute their weight on the ferry. He knew almost everyone, and engaged in the easy chat of casual interactions. In a short time, the passengers and cargo were boarded. The engines started, and the ferry began its slow pivot away from the dock.

Although it was late in the year, they were still taking the route west of Plum Island, out of the shelter of land, directly across Death's Door. Pali knew exactly the right place for his plan, and he waited until they were nearly there. At the chosen moment he turned to Greg, and asked him to take over the helm. He didn't need a reason. He was the captain.

Greg agreed without hesitation, and Pali made his way to middle deck at the stern of the ferry, where he knew he would not be seen.

The wind was blowing and it bit hard, and Pali braced himself as he stood at the rail. He had done many hard things. He had uprooted himself from the Island to go away. He had been

in the military, enduring first, its training, and then its cold realities. He had dedicated himself to a life of quiet responsibility
and duty. But this, he was quite certain, was the hardest thing,
and it was a thing he was asking—no, demanding—of himself.

Slowly, Pali withdrew the battered spiral notebook that had
been lying against his chest inside his jacket. All his notes: his
nascent poems, lines that were waiting for the right context; they
were all in this one place. As much as his wife and his son, this
notebook was the repository of his dreams—and of whatever
strange spirit haunted him. Resolutely turning from the temptation to change his mind, Pali held the notebook with both hands
as he raised his voice.

"Whatever you are, by all that's Holy, I renounce you."

If someone else had been standing near, the wind and the
waves would have made it impossible to do anymore than see
his lips move.

Pali stood for a moment, looking off at the horizon, as if
watching a dream float away, and then, in one movement, he
flung the battered treasure that was his notebook into the lake.
He did not stop to watch it fall. His shoulders squared, his head
up, Pali turned away. He was the captain of his ship. He went on
about his duties, his chest leaden.

Chapter Seventeen

Fiona looked out her kitchen window one morning and saw an unfamiliar car parked in Stella's driveway. Instead of the battered station wagon without a muffler, there was a sleek, red vintage convertible, which seemed to Fiona utterly out of character, even though its gleaming chrome grill had a sneering quality that was reminiscent of Stella's personality.

"Perhaps," thought Fiona, "it belongs to someone else." She marveled momentarily about the possibility of anyone enjoying Stella's company.

But later that day, Fiona was at the Mercantile when she saw the car go by with Stella in the driver's seat, and a red and purple magnetic sign on the door that said "Stella DesRosiers for Town Chairman" in big, ugly letters. A convertible—particularly a vintage one—was, perhaps, not the most practical car for the Island's unsalted winter roads, ferry passages, and rutted dirt byways, but no one could tell Stella anything. Fiona wondered, briefly, where the money for such a car could have come from, but only briefly. Stella and Stella's affairs were topics Fiona generally preferred not to think about.

After practice, Terry was seated at Ground Zero's counter, drinking his macchiato. Mike was in Santa Fe at an art show that was featuring his work.

The shop was quiet, well past the morning rush. Roger was silently polishing the Italian coffee machine's brass and copper fittings. They gleamed in the warm light of the shop. As far as Terry could see, they did not need polishing. He was used to Roger's silence, and didn't actually mind it. Most people chattered on, even with nothing to say. Not Roger, and Terry respected that. He also found it restful.

Terry had just completed his big job. It was a very large shingle-style house, perched on the bluffs overlooking Green Bay. All of the wood work and cabinetry had been custom-built by Terry. He was enjoying the feeling of having this project behind him, and of the unusually healthy state of his finances. This house represented nearly half of what Terry would normally expect to earn in a year.

"Guess I'll have another," he said, pushing his cup across the counter.

"You know," said Roger, looking up from his work, "If you want to lose a few pounds, you probably should cut out the macchiatos. There must be 500 calories in those things."

"Got it," said Terry. "Good idea. Just a regular coffee, then. I'm celebrating."

Roger filled the cup and set it on the counter with a thunk, and went back to his polishing.

Terry drank his regular coffee, relishing the silence.

He was startled when Roger spoke suddenly.

"How do people stay married?" he asked.

Terry shifted uncomfortably on the counter stool. He was pretty sure where this conversation was going.

"Not everybody does, I guess."

Roger did not respond to this, and there was a long silence, not so comfortable as the one before. Terry drank his coffee. Roger refilled it automatically, and without speaking.

Then just as suddenly as before, Roger spoke again. "I need to understand this."

At first, Terry thought Roger was talking about some mechanical thing gone wrong with the coffee equipment, but Roger was standing at the counter looking off into the distance. Eye contact during conversation was not something that Roger recognized as important. His face reflected no particular emotion. He was simply staring. Since his normal expression resembled cold fury, Terry guessed that its absence indicated some shift in mood.

He looked at Roger with a mixture of admiration and pity. The admiration was for his determination. The pity was for everything else. He had never thought of Roger as helpless, but that was how he now seemed.

"Listen, Roger," he said. "Marriage is hard. No one is good at it right away." He stopped, considering. "Maybe ever. But that's not the point. The point is that marriage doesn't just happen. You need to work at it."

Roger now looked at him with the curiosity of a scientist regarding a lab experiment. He understood work, at least. He could do work. "How?"

Terry was struggling with how to simplify this complex question. Roger was an MIT physicist. He was brilliant. But, thought

Terry, in some things he was flat ignorant, and this was clearly one of those things.

"Well," said Terry at last, settling on some universal truths. "You need to talk to her. Tell her things. Women like that."

"What things?" Roger was frowning with concentration.

Terry sighed inwardly, wondering how he was going to get out of this, but he continued patiently. "You need to tell her what you did that day. Tell her about what you will do tomorrow. Talk to her about your plans for the future. Things like that."

Roger nodded seriously, as if making a mental checklist.

Terry suddenly saw this as an opportunity. It was for Elisabeth, he thought, that he needed to say these things. He felt deep sympathy for her, sweet woman that she was. He needed to help her. "Who else would?" he asked himself.

"But most of all," and here Terry cleared his throat, "you need to say nice things to her."

Roger's frown deepened. "Like what?"

This time Terry's sigh was audible. "Tell her you love her. Tell her she's beautiful. Tell her that you like her dress. Tell her the dinner was good."

He paused, running out of ideas. No need to overwhelm at the beginning. "Oh, and if she asks, she never looks fat. In anything. Ever."

Roger nodded seriously. He understood. He could do these things. He was sure of it.

"Thanks," said Roger.

Terry had never heard Roger say thank you. "Don't mention it," said Terry. And he meant it.

"Fiona, I'm worried."

"What about?" asked Fiona as she talked with Elisabeth on the phone and fiddled idly with the pen on her kitchen counter. It was late afternoon, and although sun no longer flooded the room at this time of day, the smell of coffee and cinnamon made it comfortable and inviting. It seemed to Fiona that Elisabeth should be filled with newlywed bliss, not worrying about anything. Particularly not on a beautiful winter day like this one.

"It's Roger," continued Elisabeth. "He's acting strangely."

Fiona thought this was hardly surprising. Roger always acted strangely. It was what he did. She tried to come up with some diplomatic way of expressing these thoughts and failed.

"In what way?" she asked.

"He's taken up yoga."

Fiona did not answer for a moment. This was, indeed, surprising.

"Hmmm," she said, biding for time. "That is… unlikely, I have to admit. But it seems harmless enough."

"It's just that it's so out of character." Elisabeth paused. "And there's something else about it that I don't like."

Fiona stopped fidgeting with the pen. It was the tone of Elisabeth's voice that caught her attention.

"Oh?" she asked, casually.

"It's the teacher. The yoga instructor. Her name is Shay. And she looks exactly the way her name sounds." Elisabeth stopped talking and took a breath. "And she says Roger is gifted."

With effort Fiona controlled herself.

"Really." Fiona picked up the pen again as a distraction. "Well… maybe he is."

"Come on, Fiona. I'm being serious here."

Fiona was instantly contrite.

"I'm sorry. I know you are. But surely you don't think Roger is interested in Shay."

"Why else would he be taking yoga classes?"

"Now listen, Elisabeth. You can't make a big deal out of one yoga class."

"He's taking three. One is in Sturgeon Bay."

"Oh. Well," said Fiona lamely. "That is a lot of yoga."

"It would be a lot of yoga for anyone. But this is Roger. And you know how good-looking he is. Everywhere we went in Italy I saw women staring at him."

It occurred to Fiona that there were many reasons to stare at Roger that had nothing to do with his looks. But this was probably not the thing to say to his wife, no matter how close their friendship. Was Roger good-looking? Fiona thought about this. She supposed he was. He was so off-putting and strange that she had never noticed. Yes. Upon reflection, Roger really was extraordinarily handsome. "Huh," she thought to herself. This was an interesting revelation.

"How do you know what this teacher—Shay—looks like?"

"Facebook." Elisabeth stopped for a moment, recollecting her first glimpse of Shay. "She is a bit older, though."

"How much older?"

"Maybe… forty?"

"Forty?" Fiona was surprised.

"But a young forty. A beautiful forty. A young, blonde, lithe, and limber forty with a perfect figure."

Fiona felt she needed to gain control of this conversation. "Listen," she said. "You need to get a grip. You are a newly married woman. Roger is a newly married man. He's crazy about you. And Roger is not the kind of guy who goes around picking up women in yoga classes." And not by a long shot, she thought to herself. "I refuse to believe that there's a romantic reason for Roger taking a yoga class," she continued. "I can't for the life of me think of any reason for him to be taking a yoga class, but that is not the point. You are a beautiful woman. He loves you. Now just stop it."

Elisabeth sighed into the phone. "So you think I'm being silly?"

"You are not being silly. You're being an idiot." She paused, suddenly struck by a thought. "What," she wondered aloud, "does Roger wear to yoga class?"

"Sweats, I guess," said Elisabeth. "Why?"

"I don't know," said Fiona. "Just wondered."

That, at least, was a mental image she could live with. She couldn't quite countenance the thought of Roger in yoga pants.

Pali arrived home at dinner with his arms filled with packages from the mainland. He appeared jovial and smiling, as he kissed Nika and teased her about not looking in his closet. But she stopped him, her hands on his arms, and looked into his eyes. "What is it?"

He shook his head briefly, brushing her worries aside. "It's Christmas. It's a time to be happy."

Nika looked into his eyes for an instant longer, then smiled, holding his glance. Whatever it was, it could wait until he was ready. "Well, hurry and change. Tonight's Ben's school concert."

Elisabeth was not, by nature, a worrier. She was blessed by nature with a serene disposition that accepted life's vagaries with equanimity. Her calm demeanor had long been a primary factor in her friendship with Fiona, as a balance to Fiona's passionate intensity. It wasn't that Elisabeth didn't feel things deeply. But she had a deep inner calm that guided her path through life like a compass: steady and sure.

Roger's yoga practice, however, had knocked her off her course. The very notion that Roger—Roger!—had taken up yoga was suspect on every level. But that his classes should be centered on this woman—this... Shay—well, that could only have one explanation. All Fiona's reassurances to the contrary meant absolutely nothing. Elisabeth looked ahead to the holidays without her usual joy, her heart wreathed in anxiety.

When Roger came home that evening, Elisabeth thought he seemed to have something on his mind. He seemed to be engaged in some deep inner struggle. Elisabeth braced herself. Was he about to confess? Was he about to say something she desperately didn't want to know? Anxiously, she stood waiting, barely taking a breath, the chicken she had been sautéing ignored on the stove as it gradually darkened from golden brown to nearly black. Rocco, always nearby, and sensitive to every emotion, stood between them, looking from one face to another. He whined nervously and jumped to touch Elisabeth's face. This comforted him.

Roger paused, thinking hard. He looked at Elisabeth for a long time and with much concentration. At last he took a breath to speak. She felt as if her heart would stop.

"You don't look fat in that," he said finally. Hanging his jacket on the hook by the door, he went into the living room to sit with Rocco, feeling a deep sense of accomplishment.

Chapter Eighteen

On Christmas morning, Ben was awake before anyone else in the house. He lay on the floor and pulled his present for his parents out from under the bed. Jim had suggested that he wrap the birdfeeder before bringing it home, and had even supplied him with paper and a red stick-on bow. Ben had to admit to himself that the whole project had turned out pretty well. The paint to simulate birch wood made it look a lot less like PVC pipe, and it was sturdy and solidly made. It didn't hold all that much seed, but Ben knew enough to know that his mother, at least, wouldn't care. She would hang it outside the kitchen window with her other feeders, and fill it when she filled the rest.

Ben's biggest problem now that the feeder was finished was how to explain where he was going every day. But he would think about that later. Today was Christmas. Ben ran down the hall to his parents' room and jumped, with splendid accuracy, on his father's stomach.

Christmas week passed with its usual speed, and Fiona decided to celebrate New Year's Eve at her house by inviting a few guests. It was, she admitted to herself, a ploy to keep from thinking incessantly about Pete. The flaws in the relationship were made evident by her needing to spend so many holidays alone, and her frustration that night—coupled with anxiety about his safety—led her to drink just a bit too much champagne.

Among her guests were Nika and Pali. Although he was polite to others and attentive to Nika, Fiona could see that Pali was really not himself. He had often confided in her, but so far, in this, he had not.

"So, how's your writing going these days?" she asked him, when they met refilling their glasses. "It seems as if all anyone talks about lately is politics, and it's starting to make me crazy."

As she spoke she saw his face close, and she knew that she had brought up a subject he did not want to discuss.

"Too busy," he said, just a bit too casually. "Not a priority, really."

Fiona, who knew perfectly well how much of a priority Pali's poetry was to him, merely nodded and changed the subject. "Have you seen Stella's new car? It's one of those vintage designs that looks as if it's sneering at you."

Pali smiled. "An appropriate choice, then?"

Fiona smiled and was about to comment, when one of the other guests approached, and the conversation shifted in another direction.

Too much champagne made Fiona's sleep restless and shallow. She had hoped that somehow Pete would call to wish her a happy new year, but so far he had been silent.

"Joyful evenings make sad mornings," was one of Martin Luther's maxims. In this, at least, they could agree. Her head was pounding, and so far in the new year, there hadn't been that much joy to begin with. As she lay in bed, she pondered the absence of the chewing creature. Perhaps, he too was hungover. It was odd to lie there in silence, no sound of chewing in her ear. She hoped the creature—wherever it was—was all right.

Fiona had just returned from an afternoon of doing doors when the phone rang. It was Pali. Fiona was glad to hear from him. He had still seemed a little flat lately, a little down. Tonight he sounded more like his usual self.

"Dean Hillard is speaking tonight at St. Thor's. Want to go?"

Fiona, who had spent every night that week either doing doors or attending community events, gave a little cry of horror.

"Good God, no. The idea of spending time listening to that…" she searched her mind for a word that was not obscene "… windbag is an affront to all that's holy."

Pali laughed. "It's kind of hard to argue with that."

"Besides," she added. "I haven't had a decent night's sleep in a week. I'm going to take a long, hot, bath, read a book, and go to bed before it's dark. There may be scotch involved."

Pali nodded understandingly. He was tired, too.

"Okay. We'll check it out for you."

"Report back."

"You got it," he said.

With mutual expressions of goodwill, they hung up.

W isconsin State Assemblyman Dean Hillard stood in the basement of St. Thorlakur Lutheran Church with his arm around Stella, beaming at the crowd.

"I don't think you have to worry about State support for the harbor this time," he said. "Not with my aunt as your Chairman... errr... woman." He chuckled at his little joke. "In Madison, we like to see good leadership when we invest in a local project, and with my Aunt Stella, we know you'll be in good hands. I'll see that the bill is introduced, and we will make sure Washington Island gets the support it needs!"

The crowd applauded warily. The harbor dredging was essential, no doubt, but the prospect of Stella's leadership was a high price, indeed.

Pali and Jake, standing at the back of the group, exchanged glances.

"I was afraid this was coming," said Jake. "Soon as I heard she was bringing him in."

Pali nodded, grimly. Silently they stood watching the faces of the crowd, of Hillard kissing Stella, grinning, and shaking hands. The event was winding down, and Hillard was moving, with his aide, toward the exit. The crowd began to disperse.

"Come on," said Jake to Pali. "I'll buy you a beer."

At Nelsen's, the little group of Fiona's friends were quieter than usual, as Eddie lingered sympathetically at their end of the bar. He kept their glasses filled, slipping away only briefly to attend to his other customers, and then returning to listen in on the conversation.

"That guy's a scum bag," said Jake. "I don't know what it is about him, but for some reason I don't trust him."

"Well, one good reason is that he's related to Stella," pointed out Nika, reasonably.

"Think there's any chance we'd get the harbor funding without him?" Jim asked.

Pali shook his head glumly. "Nope. We've already been turned down once. We can't even get the State to acknowledge our school funding problems. How do you think we'd be able to get this kind of money for the harbor?"

"Are you going to tell her?" asked Nika.

"Of course we're going to tell her," said Pali with a brusqueness that was unusual for him.

"She isn't stupid," said Jim. "She'll figure it out herself anyway once she hears the news."

"What do you think she'll do?" asked Charlotte.

Nancy, who rarely came out for a drink, had been summoned for this conversation. "Well, she won't run home crying, we know that for sure. She's a lot tougher than you all think."

Pali looked at Nancy from down the bar. "It won't matter, though. It won't matter how tough she is, or how smart, or how hard she works on the campaign. The outcome will be the same."

They fell silent, contemplating the Island's future. Unless

Stella was elected, there would be no money for dredging, courtesy of Dean Hillard.

Without the dredging, the harbor could not continue to function. Without the harbor, the Island economy would die.

There was only one way to vote, and they all knew it.

For once, the Island grapevine had included Fiona, so she had already heard the news by the time Pali, who had been deputized to tell her, knocked on Fiona's door the next morning.

"Come on in," she said. "I just made coffee."

Pali followed her into the kitchen and accepted a mug. They sat at the kitchen table facing one another.

"So, it's hopeless, isn't it?" asked Fiona.

"Well," said Pali. "I like to think there's always hope. But I really don't know what we can do." He paused. "Unless you have a cousin in the legislature."

Fiona nodded silently and stared out the window. Stella's house next door showed no signs of life, and the sky had the deep blue-gray that meant snow was coming. There were no birds or squirrels in the yard. Everything had the stillness that comes before a storm.

Stella was going to win. She would find ways to make life on the Island impossible, and Fiona would have to sell up and leave. Maybe that would be a good thing. She could go somewhere to be closer to Pete. Or, at least, closer to him sometimes. But this, she knew, was against her instincts. She was not going to follow him around the globe. It was not her style.

Fiona remembered, like a movie playing in her head, specific instances of Stella's arrogance and malice, her sense of entitlement and selfishness. She felt her temper rising. Stella running the Island would be a nightmare, not just for Fiona, but for everyone. Why should they give in to this? Why should she assume that there was no other means of solving the Island's problem? No. She had come this far. She had knocked on all those doors. She had attended all those events. She had painted ceilings, wrangled bats and goats, survived a blizzard, and weathered a barn fire. She had spent her little nest egg on repairing the house. She would not give in. She would not simply back off and let Stella win. There had to be a way.

Fiona took a deep breath and looked back at Pali.

"We are not giving up. We are not going to lie down and let her win. I don't know how, yet, but we are going to find a way."

Pali looked at her with sympathy. "You're the boss," he said. He didn't think she had a chance, and they both knew it.

Shay could not help noticing that the attendance in her church basement yoga class was growing at a surprising rate. What had started with one California transplant—that incredibly beautiful man, Joshua—had grown to three men, then five, and was now an astonishing twelve. Every week some new man arrived, awkwardly attired, placing himself in the back of the room, among the others.

What was more remarkable was that Roger, who had not at first struck her as having any particular talent, was making up for it by being highly motivated. His practice—and attendance at her Sturgeon Bay class on Saturdays—were showing astonishing results. He was increasingly flexible, and his strength made it possible for him to achieve poses that for most of her students were the stuff of dreams. It was clear to her that he would soon outstrip her capabilities as a teacher.

But for now, what interested her most was how this man who spoke in monosyllables had managed to draw so many other men to her class.

One afternoon after the closing *"Namaste,"* Shay approached Roger as he was rolling up his mat. He was surrounded by his acolytes, men in various stages of awkwardness and badly fitting sweatpants, who seemed intent on doing whatever Roger did.

"I've been watching your progress, Roger," she began.

Roger stopped his preparations for departure and looked up, but he said nothing. The other men were busily pretending not to listen avidly.

"You must be practicing a great deal."

Roger frowned.

Shay, waiting for a response and finding none, forged bravely ahead.

"Are you? Practicing? I mean, you must be, I know, but I'm interested in learning more." Unconsciously she tossed back her wild blond locks as Terry, in his twenty-year-old sweats, ancient high school basketball t-shirt, and white socks, looked on, rapt.

Roger seemed to be composing a thoughtful response for a long moment. "Yes."

Shay was nothing if not determined.

"I'm interested, because I'd like to know how to advise beginning students. Most of them don't progress as quickly as you have. Have often do you practice?"

Roger's silence gave Terry an opening. He was neither shy nor unwilling to interact with this slim, blonde, yoga goddess. He was a happily married man, but, he told himself, he wasn't dead.

"We meet every morning at Ground Zero. Five o'clock." He paused for a moment, before adding hopefully, "You should come."

Shay looked for a moment at Roger, trying to understand his silence, then smiled dazzlingly, completely unaware of the effect on her students.

"I'd love to. I'll see you tomorrow, then."

She walked back to the front of the room.

Roger's icy look was lost on Terry, whose eyes were on Shay's every move as she bent to gather her things.

Fiona was not overjoyed to find herself in line behind Stella at the grocery store late one afternoon. Stella was in the midst of a conversation with the cashier when she noticed Fiona.

"As soon as I'm finished here, I'm driving to Madison to see my nephew, Dean," she said pointedly, and deliberately loud enough for Fiona to hear. "The Assemblyman," she added, in case they had missed the point. "He has a parade this weekend, and he wants the convertible." Her smile was an ugly grimace. "I figure he will be doing me some favors in the future, so I may as well do one for him." This time she shot a look at directly at Fiona. "I like to think it's for the good of the Island," she said smugly.

Fiona kept her face carefully neutral. She would not give Stella the pleasure of reacting, and she no longer made any effort whatever to attempt civilities with Stella. There was no point. She looked for something to divert her gaze and found herself drawn to a magazine displayed nearby. "205 Ways to Make Your Life Easier," shouted the cover.

"I could use at least 103," she thought.

She was pretty sure that number one would be not running into Stella.

E lisabeth was sitting by the fire when Roger came home. There was a bottle of wine on the table nearby, and an extra glass, her own already poured. Rocco bounded up to Roger, entwining himself around his legs. Roger bent to stroke the big dog's head, and spoke quietly to him. Elisabeth looked up at him as Roger poured his glass. If Roger noticed that her smile was absent, he did not make any indication. Subtleties were not among his talents.

"Fiona's coming tonight," Elisabeth said, without preamble, and even as she said it she observed herself as if from a distance. This was not how she wanted her marriage to be: business-like and impersonal, devoid of affection. It was not how it had begun only a few months ago, before Roger's yoga obsession. She could not fathom how that had started, but she felt fairly certain that she knew why. Annoyed with herself, however, she determined to start the evening again. She got up and went over to Roger, putting her arms around him.

Still holding his wine glass, he absently patted her on the shoulder. It occurred to Elisabeth that Rocco received more attention from Roger than she did.

True to her word, Shay arrived at Ground Zero a few minutes before five the next morning. Her normal pre-class chatter was subdued. She was not a morning person. Her hair was a trifle wilder than usual, and she yawned sleepily but good naturedly as she set up her mat among the morning group of men. Some members of the Lutheran contingent were a little uncomfortable at her presence, but they dutifully searched their consciences and could find no necessity of leaving on her account, or, for that matter, their own.

Roger, who had no grasp of the concepts of grace or hospitality, simply nodded in her direction and made a noise that might have been a greeting. It was left to Terry and The Angel Joshua to create an atmosphere of welcome. Shay had not come to any clear understanding of Roger's personality, but it was her practice to accept people as they were, so she settled comfortably into the little group. Laying out her mat near the back of the room, the better to observe, she began a gentle warm-up.

Fiona was gazing into Pete's face on the computer.
"Are you coming for the election?"

"I don't know that I can. But isn't April a peculiar time to have an election?"

"It's to fill a vacancy, and there are legal requirements about the timing. But the general theory about off-cycle elections is that they're scheduled to minimize the turnout."

"Why? To whose advantage?"

"I don't know. Depends, I guess. But reason doesn't always play a big role in conspiracy theories."

"True. Is it a conspiracy?"

"I don't know. I'm beginning to think everything is a conspiracy."

"Maybe everything is." He smiled his engaging smile, and changed the subject to something more interesting to them both.

After her first visit, Shay became a regular at Ground Zero's morning practice. She had found that rising early made a useful and pleasant extension to her day, and she was always happy to expand her practice. The men did not seem to mind her presence, and not being overly familiar with the workings of the male mind, it never occurred to her that anyone might be uncomfortable about her being there.

For Shay, the ability to sit and drink her morning coffee so comfortably and conveniently after practice was an added benefit she thoroughly enjoyed. A few of the group stayed on as well, and after the first few visits, their casual chats with her were a sign of their acceptance. The men would soon scatter to their various responsibilities, however, and a calm would descend on Ground Zero.

Beautiful Joshua occasionally lingered nearby, and his easy banter was a sharp contrast to Roger, who simply went about his business, occasionally filling her cup, though rarely speaking. Seeing him in his native environment, Shay now could see that this was who he was, and no longer worried about how and whether she was communicating with her star pupil. He learned in his own way, she could certainly see that, so she inwardly shrugged at the many varieties of human personality and stopped thinking about it. Roger was Roger—whoever Roger actually was. Shay was intrigued, and, she had to admit, somewhat attracted.

She had noticed the gold wedding band, and wondered about what kind of woman would make a match with this taciturn fellow. But Shay had noticed long ago that the attractions between people were mysterious. There was someone for everyone, she firmly believed. She would be interested at some point to meet his wife. "Not," she thought to herself, "that it would make any difference."

E mily woke with a start to the sound of screaming. She was learning to adapt to the cries of coyotes running nearby. It was an unnerving experience, but a fact of island life. Now, she tried to reassure herself, but this was not the usual cacophony of voices yipping and crying in the distance as they ran. It was one voice. It was nearby. And she was pretty sure it was human. Emily dug her elbow into her husband's ribs. "Jason! Wake up!"

"What?" asked Jason irritably, pulling a pillow from his head.

"Listen!"

Together they listened for a few seconds. The bloodcurdling sound of a woman screaming was coming from somewhere near the pasture. Jason was city born and bred, and rural life was new to him. He had been thinking about getting a gun, but so far he hadn't gotten around to it. He rolled over and grabbed the phone. "I'm not going out there."

He dialed 911.

Chapter Nineteen

"**D**o you ever listen to opera?" Eddie was polishing the bar where there were no spots. Pali looked at him with mild curiosity. "Not often. Why?"

"Well, I've been taking an audio course on it. One of those great ideas things. I'm really enjoying it." He was interrupted by a request for a refill, and disappeared down the bar for a moment. Returning, he picked up a clean bar rag and began polishing glasses.

"So anyway one of the operas is by Mozart. About the Don Juan legend."

"Don Giovanni," said Pali, surprising himself. "I saw that once in Chicago."

"So you know that scene at the end when the demons drag him down to Hell?"

Pali nodded, unable to see where this conversation was going.

"That's what I keep hoping for. That somehow, the demons will come for her, Stella will be dragged away, and the whole problem will be solved."

"Not for Stella."

"No. But I think you're missing my point."

Pali laughed. "No. No, I see your point."

"I don't think you do," said Eddie quietly. "What I am saying is that we need a political equivalent."

"A political equivalent to Hell? Isn't that kind of redundant?"

"We need her to be taken out of the equation."

"We should assassinate her?" asked Pali cheerfully. "She's not worth it. We'd all have to go to jail and she'd probably come back as a ghost. That woman has persistence."

Eddie laughed. "Well, it may come to that. But, no. What I'm saying is that we need—"

Suddenly a light dawned on Pali's face. "A *deus ex machina*," he said slowly.

Eddie looked at him with respect. "Exactly."

By the time the police arrived at Windsome Farm, the screaming had stopped. Emily and Jason Martin waited for Chief Yahr to get out of his car before venturing into the yard.

The Chief had a look of stoic resolve as he directed his team of officers and volunteers in the methodical grid search that was by now a familiar exercise. Jason joined with some reluctance, uncomfortable with the thought of what he might find, but with a sense of obligation that he was learning from local custom.

The eastern sky was pale when the volunteers returned to the kitchen yard. Emily had made coffee and served it in the Styrofoam cups she kept for Scout meetings. It was cold, and the visible breath of the little group, rising in the air, reminded Emily of her goat herds when she brought them out to pasture.

"Well," said the Chief, "Here we are again, and no better off."

He looked at the circle of grim faces around him. "If this is some-body's idea of a joke… " he paused, at a loss. "I suppose we should be grateful that we haven't found a body. We can reassure our neighbors about that much, at least: no bodies, and no victims."

He was silent again for a moment, thinking about whether to say what was on his mind. At last he spoke, looking at the expectant faces around him. "I'm starting to think that Lars is right: some crazy is living in the woods. We're going to have to find him… or her… sooner or later. No one can hide on the Island for very long." What he didn't say was the rest of his thought: that they needed to find whoever it was before he… or she… decided to do something more than scream. Chief Yahr was beginning to wonder whether he should issue a warning in the interest of public safety.

Emily and Jason expressed their thanks as the group dispersed, the sound of the volunteers' voices drifting back as they walked down the long driveway to the road where their trucks were parked.

Wearily returning to the house, Emily was grateful for her own particular blessing: the children had slept through the en-tire thing.

Elisabeth had been doing some soul-searching. She had ex-amined, in minute detail, her memories of her early rela-tionship with Roger—she couldn't call it courtship, exactly—and had come to a clearer understanding. Roger, she knew, had nev-er been demonstrative. Most people—she also knew—couldn't imagine why she had married him. But until recently, Elisabeth had always had an instinctive ability to empathize with Roger, to sense his moods, and she had known he loved her.

For Elisabeth, this had always been the key point. She was not a hearts and flowers kind of person, nor was she interested in fireworks. She wanted connection and intellectual companionship. Roger's ability to connect was flawed, of course, but the connection, once made, was deep. This Elisabeth could not doubt.

These reflections had brought her a new calm, and a resolution to address what wasn't working in her marriage. She recalled her mother's counsel: "Marriage is about building habits," she had often said. "Both the good and the bad. You must take care that the habits you build are good ones."

Her marriage was still new; this was the time. Elisabeth was determined to get it right.

Buoyed by this decision, Elisabeth recalled how many mornings she had used to spend sitting at the counter of Ground Zero—then still unnamed—basking in the presence of Roger. There was no reason, she realized, that she shouldn't continue to do so, and, in fact, she chided herself for having abandoned this rather core principle of their relationship. They had rarely spoken much, but they had been together, and this, she suddenly saw, was how he had known that she was interested in him. It was entirely possible, she thought, that he felt her absence there as neglect.

Elisabeth did not mention to Roger that she would be coming to Ground Zero that morning. She wanted to surprise him. So she kissed him goodbye at his pre-dawn departure, planning to arrive later, as she had always done in the past. Pleased with her plan, she spent extra time on her preparations as she dressed, humming happily to herself. Rocco, alert to a change in routine, lay on his bed in the corner, watching to ensure that she could not leave without him.

As she drove to Ephraim, Rocco happily ensconced in the back seat, Elisabeth felt a twinge of joyful nostalgia. It felt right to be returning to this old routine, to be going to sit at Ground Zero, to drink coffee and forget the outside world for a while.

The sun was barely up on this dark winter morning as she pulled into the parking lot, but it was nearly 7:30. She left the engine running while she gathered her things: her gloves, her bag, Rocco's leash. She mentally checked her list, and was about to switch off the car when she looked up.

In the winter dawn, Ground Zero was lit up like a stage, its interior fully visible to the outside. She could not, at first, tell what was going on, the activities being so unexpected. Suddenly she realized that what she was seeing was two bodies, entwined and moving on the floor in front of the counter. Her heart stopped. It was Roger. Roger bent on all fours, his legs straight, his... behind... up high. And there was a woman, clearly slim and fit, as she lay, her back to Roger's. Yes, she could see that the woman lay on top of him, a mass of blonde hair falling around them, falling around Roger's shoulders and face.

Fiona was mid-train of thought in her writing when the phone rang. Feeling slightly irritated, she answered in an unusually brusque tone.

"Hey," said Pete.

"Hey." Her tone changed instantly, and she leaned back in her chair with relief. "Where are you?"

"Guess."

Fiona sighed deliberately and for effect. "I can't imagine. Tell me."

"Nope. You have to guess."

"Is it someplace far away?"

"Depends on where you are."

"You know where I am. Is it someplace dangerous?"

"Quite possibly."

"Is it someplace that will worry me?"

"It may well be."

"Is it—"

Pete interrupted impatiently. "You know, for a reporter, you're really bad at asking questions."

Fiona laughed. "That's because I don't even want to try. You like teasing me too much."

Pete smiled to himself. "I do, actually. But you make it easy."

There was a long silence that Fiona was determined not to break. She could hear announcements in the background, and occasionally people talking.

"You're not going to ask?"

"No. I'm not playing."

"Well, okay, then. But don't be mad at me when your hair is messy, or you haven't got anything to drink in the house."

Fiona's heart stopped and started again. "How soon will you be here?"

"About five or six hours. I'm driving up from Chicago."

"You'll have to drive fast; the last ferry is at five. How long have you been in Chicago?"

"I just walked out of customs. I have to rent a car, and then I'll be on my way."

"I'd better go. I have a lot to do. I have an article to finish before you get here."

"Okay," said Pete. "Don't forget to brush your hair."

"You'll be lucky."

"In any case."

After they hung up she wondered briefly, how he had meant that last remark, and then shifted her focus to her work. She switched off her Internet connection and turned off the phone. There was just barely enough time, and she needed to block all distractions.

It was 5:43 when Fiona heard a car in the driveway. She watched him walk around to the porch, carrying a small overnight bag. She flung open the door, and he was there in the front hall, dropping the bag on the floor and kicking the door closed behind him. Their greeting lasted for some time before Fiona extricated herself.

"I didn't have time to get food. I only have a few slices of stale bread and some black bananas. I thought it was better to finish the article."

"Food is not on my list of priorities at the moment," said Pete, his lips on her neck.

"Nelsen's serves until nine."

"We'll see how it goes."

"I have scotch."

"Bring it along."

She went to the living room to get the scotch and returned. He took her hand and they went upstairs together.

Elisabeth spent the rest of her day driving aimlessly around the peninsula, occasionally stopping to walk in the cold with Rocco. She could not think, or eat, or speak. She didn't want to see anyone, and besides, there were not many places she could go with Rocco, and she didn't want to leave him in the car. Roger had called her numerous times, but she didn't feel like answering. She didn't want to talk to him, or know what she should say. He might be worrying, but, she asked herself, what was worry compared to what she was feeling?

If she had been able to reach Fiona, she would have gone there, but the ferry was on its winter schedule, and by the time she felt equal to it, it was too late. The last boat had gone.

"Too cold to swim," she told Rocco, and he looked at her with intelligent interest. He knew the word "swim," and he liked it. Very much. Cold was a matter of complete indifference to him. He expressed his feelings with as much enthusiasm as he could muster.

But Elisabeth was too absorbed in her thoughts to pay attention to Rocco's clear communications. She patted him absently on the head as she stared into the distance. She was not ready for a confrontation with Roger. She couldn't face it. But she would go home. She had to go home. She would say she wasn't well and go to bed early. In the guest room.

It was dark when Fiona woke. As she stirred, Pete pulled her back to him.

"How long can you stay?" she mumbled into his lips.

"I have to be in China on Tuesday."

"So you leave… "

"Saturday."

"I like China better than the other places lately."

"One of my colleagues was arrested there last year for espionage. But he was Taiwanese, so that probably was a contributing factor."

"Did he get out?"

"Not yet."

Fiona peered at him reprovingly through the darkness. "Do you want me to worry?"

Pete considered this for a moment. "Maybe I do, a little. But only a little."

"A little which?"

"A little want you to; a little worry."

"Hrmph."

There was no talking for a while.

Pete bestirred himself at last. "My priorities have suddenly shifted in the direction of food. What time is it? My watch is still on Dubai time."

Fiona twisted around to see the bedside clock. "7:11. Want to get up?"

"I need to keep my strength up."

Fiona smiled at him. "Yes, you do."

They lingered.

Some time later, Pete, having endeared himself to all and sundry on his past trips, was greeted at Nelsen's like an old friend. Fiona and Pete ordered burgers, ate ravenously, shot some pool, were treated to several rounds, and then excused themselves.

"Pete is still on Dubai time," said Fiona. This was perfectly true, but no one supposed his exhaustion was the reason for their early departure.

As they left, there were some glances exchanged between people who were not among Fiona's circle. Eddie noticed, but said nothing. Bartenders are used to knowing everything and saying only what they choose.

lisabeth woke in a calmer frame of mind, but not any clearer about a course of action. Roger had come in early before he left, stood for a few moments in the door as if to gauge whether she was awake, then tiptoed away. Elisabeth had pretended to sleep. She heard the door close, and his car start up and drive away. Rocco, who had followed him as far as the kitchen, now returned and leapt onto the bed, curling up at the foot and sighing deeply. Elisabeth sighed with him.

When she went into the kitchen she found a note from Roger on the table. For a moment she thought it might be something meaningful and loving. She picked it up eagerly. It said: Gone to work.

Basking in the sparkling brilliance of a winter morning's sun, Pete and Fiona sat at her kitchen table drinking coffee. "I'm afraid I have to attend a fundraiser while you're here," she said in a tone of great regret. She had already developed a healthy distaste for fundraising. "You can come, if you like."

"Is it a fundraiser for you, or for some Island cause?"

"I like to think that I am an Island cause."

"In that case, I'll come."

She looked out the window. Stella's red convertible was there in the driveway looking sinister. Fiona had a sudden, visceral memory of the day before the barn had burned down. She and Pete had been sitting here, just like this, and Robert had been there, in the barn.

She was shaken out of her reverie by Pete's voice. He had been watching her face as she looked out, seeing her moods clearly reflected there.

"I don't mean to be unduly pessimistic, but what will you do if you lose the election?"

Fiona shrugged. "Sell the house and leave, I suppose."

"That might be good for me."

Fiona eyed him skeptically. "It might. But I would become a shadow of my former self."

"Technically, wouldn't we be discussing a shadow of your present self?"

"Don't quibble."

"I like quibbling. It's fun."

"What do you want for breakfast?"

"How black are those bananas?"

"Actually, the black bananas are gone. They were getting runny, and I threw them out. Want to go somewhere?"

"I don't want to go anywhere, but it seems like days since that burger last night, and I don't think a slice of stale bread will suffice."

"You should have eaten your onion rings."

"Perhaps."

The telephone rang, and reluctantly, Fiona rose to answer it.

The island's affection for local events and its nearly universal sense of camaraderie meant that there was a big turnout for the Boy Scouts' presentations on animal husbandry, with a focus on goats. The community hall was buzzing on Wednesday night, filled with the intense anxiety of the boys and the cheerful anticipation of the crowd. The hall smelled of the coffee brewing in urns at the back of the room, the pitchers of fruit punch, and the assortment of homemade cookies, bars, and cakes that had been set out for the post-presentation festivities. There was also the pungent fragrance of goat cheese, provided as part of the refreshments by the proprietors of Windsome Farm Goats.

Emily had been lobbying intensively for the actual presence of goats at the presentations. "It will add such a lovely sense of the bonds between the boys and the animals," she had urged. But the idea had not been welcomed by the community hall's volunteer cleaning crew, and Emily was forced, with great reluctance, to abandon it. That rural people should be so adamantly opposed to a basic fact of rural life was shocking to Emily. In fact, "I'm just, frankly, shocked by the attitude," was her frequent and very public remark, and although her comments might have been considered insulting, islanders generally found in them another highly amusing reason to attend the presentation. "Who knows," they asked one another, "what she might say next?"

The group was called to order by the Scoutmaster, and then, in a gesture of modesty and hospitality to a newcomer, he turned the proceedings over to Emily Martin. She spoke rapidly and with great emphasis on the importance of the animal husbandry badge, and of her own generosity in sponsoring the boys at Windsome Hill Farm. It was, she told them, her husband's and her little way of serving the community, and she was so very happy to be able to do it, even though, with the new farm and all, they were so terribly, terribly busy. She then outlined the purposes of the badge and its requirements.

There were sidelong glances exchanged among the audience as Emily sat down. The first boy's name was called, and he stepped forward, carrying his poster to set up on the easel, and looking nervous.

The Animal Husbandry presentations, once they began, varied only in the artistic skill and color choices of the particular boys, their differing talents in public speaking, and the level of their parents' participation in their preparations.

The boys who had done all their own work might have appeared to have been at a disadvantage to those who had had assistance, but the depth and staying power of their knowledge would some day offer compensation, provided that knowledge of the composition of goats' milk was of any relevance to their futures. These delayed gratifications in life, of course, are of no comfort whatsoever in the present, particularly not to boys, but also not to their uncomfortable parents, who must watch their sons' struggles and worry whether they are bad parents, all while observing the smug gratification and superior smiles of the parents who had spent long evenings drawing their boys' posters while the boys themselves watched Netflix and chatted online.

By the time the seventh poster on the components and nutritional value of goat milk—along with various details about goat health and well-being had been presented—the polite crowd was beginning to stir with ineffectual attempts to stifle boredom. The lure of the refreshments had become nearly irresistible, and the longing for them was in disproportion to the actual hunger of the audience.

By the luck of the draw, the final presenter was Ben Palsson. Ben was one of the boys whose parents did not consider poster-making among their responsibilities, but his poster, though not stylized, was clear and well-thought-out, and his explanation poised. He had worked his way through the milk components, and was wrapping up his coverage of health and well-being. Emily Martin was standing impatiently at the side of the room, waiting for him to finish so that she could again take the stage.

"The gestation for goats varies from breed to breed," said Ben with childish earnestness. "But it averages 150 days, or five months. Based on this information, it seems likely that several of the does at Windsome Farm will give birth in May."

Emily gasped, and her eyes widened. The crowd chuckled with surprise at this youthful prognostication, and burst into applause, whether from relief, appreciation, or an enthusiasm for goats was difficult to determine. The jostle began to reach the cookies and coffee, and Emily moved with determination toward Ben, who was standing with his smiling parents.

"Why did you say that, Ben?" asked Emily as soon as she approached. "Why did you say that my does are due in May? You know that the ones we are breeding will give birth in April."

Ben looked from Emily to his father, to his mother. He didn't know what to say. He had been taught not to contradict adults, and he did not want to appear rude. But no matter what Mrs. Martin said, Ben was an observant boy. Unlike some of his fellow scouts, he had loved the animal husbandry badge, and he had paid attention when Mrs. Martin had given her little talk on the facts of life. He had seen the signs, and he recognized them from his observations of other animals. There were no fewer than a dozen does in Mrs. Martin's herd whose pregnancies were not part of her original plans.

The night of the fundraiser Fiona asked Pete to drive. It felt good to let go of this one simple task, and this realization made her aware of how exhausted she was.

As they drove up to the Martin's house, there were cars parked along both sides of the street and on the edges of the driveway leading up to the house. Although Pete offered to drop Fiona off, she preferred to arrive with him, so they walked together up the drive. As soon as they entered, Fiona was pulled toward various groups of people who wanted to talk with her. She looked regretfully back at him, but he smiled and waved her off.

Looking around the room, Pete spotted Pali and Eddie standing together and went over to them.

"Gentlemen," he said, in greeting.

"We were just talking about you," said Pali.

"Have I done something?"

"Not yet. We were hoping you had some brilliant solution for Fiona to win the election."

"This isn't exactly my territory." He paused for a moment. "And anyway, I'm not sure it's altogether in my interests for her to win."

"No," said Pali. "We realize that. But we're getting desperate."

"I don't know how much Fiona told you, but it looks as if Stella is a shoo-in," said Eddie. "She has a nephew in the State assembly who will pull strings to get the Island the millions it needs to dredge the harbor."

"I imagine the harbor is an important point on an island," commented Pete dryly.

"It is the important point."

"So, despite the fact that everyone hates her, everyone thinks they have to elect Stella for the Island's survival, is that it?"

Eddie and Pali nodded glumly.

"We've been racking our brains, and we're just about out of ideas," said Pali, glumly.

They were silent, contemplating the future of an island run by Stella.

Pete broke the silence after a few moments. "When you say 'just about out of ideas' do you mean that you are actually out of ideas or that there may be one more extremely unlikely one?"

Eddie and Pali looked at each other and smiled ruefully.

"Tell him about your opera theory, Eddie," said Pali.

Eddie told Pete about the demons dragging Don Giovanni down to Hell. "Do you know the part I mean?"

Pete nodded, a small smile of recognition on his face. "I know it well. The Commendatore scene. The statue of the murdered man comes to life and calls on the Don to repent, and when he refuses, the demons appear, and it all ends badly for him. There's usually some rather effective screaming." Pete began to look pensive. "Unfortunately, the demons are usually elderly chorus members who creep about the stage looking awkward in black cloaks. Not my idea of demons. I've always thought someone could do better. And on top of everything else, that scene ought to be the end, but Mozart makes a rare mistake— rare for him, I mean—and adds the 'I-told-you-so's' afterward."

Eddie got that look people get when someone says something they've been thinking all along. "I know! That last scene ruins the whole effect." And then he added, somewhat apologetically. "I think it was Da Ponte's libretto, so it wouldn't really be Mozart's fault."

Pete nodded absently. "Right. Not entirely, anyway. I saw it done once where the director cut that final ensemble. It was so much more satisfactory, and you got to imagine that Donna Anna ends up with what's-his-name in the end, which is better, somehow."

"Don Ottavio," said Eddie. "He's kind of wimp, though."

"True," said Pete. "I've never liked that character, myself. But even so, she clearly doesn't deserve him."

"But I don't like Donna Anna, either. I mean, I know she was a victim, but… "

Pali could see that the conversation was taking a wrong turn. "So the point is," he said firmly, "we need some kind of intervention."

Pete and Eddie looked at him, reluctant to abandon the thread of their conversation.

"It seems to me that you have your share of demons already," said Pete returning to the present problem. "What did you have in mind?"

"You're the *deus ex machina* guy around here," said Pali.

Pete grinned. "She told you that?"

Pali nodded apologetically. "Yes. Sorry."

"That's okay. I know what it's like. Probably the whole Island knows."

Pali nodded again. "Always possible."

Eddie, with a bartender's discretion, said nothing.

They were silent, thinking.

"So we need some local equivalent of demons."

"You could dress a bunch of old guys in black cloaks."

"Wouldn't have the desired effect."

"Never does."

Chapter Twenty-One ✤

Pete and Fiona were driving home in Pete's enormous rented SUV. After last winter's adventure, he wasn't taking any chances.

"Why didn't you tell me about the Dean Hillard event?" he asked.

"How did you even know about it?"

"Pali told me."

"I didn't think it was of interest."

"That's where you're wrong. I am extremely interested. Most extremely. Interested." He smiled, his eyes on the road.

Fiona rolled her eyes and smiled back.

"Well, okay, then. We can go. But don't say I didn't warn you. He's insufferable."

"My favorite kind of politician."

"The only kind."

"You are running for office. If elected, are you planning on becoming insufferable?"

"I think it's inevitable. Like ink-stained fingers for journalists. No, wait. I take it back. Lars Olafsen isn't insufferable. He's rather sweet, I find. I will be like him."

"You'll need less hair. Where is this event to be held?" asked Pete, with an admirable grasp of the conversation's thread.

"Nelsen's. He'll want to serve alcohol, and none of the

church basements permit it."

"Not even the Catholics?"

"The Catholics meet at the Lutheran Church."

"Interesting. But I always have a good time at Nelsen's. I'm becoming a regular. It's a fundraiser?"

"If it were, we wouldn't go. I wouldn't give a dime to Dean Hillard. It's a town hall meeting, I think he calls it. A chance to meet with his constituents and mingle with the common people." Fiona raised her eyebrows at him. "He is, as Jake likes to say, a slime bag."

"I can't wait to meet him." He pulled into Fiona's driveway and turned off the engine. "I am now finished discussing Dean Hillard."

"I'm always finished discussing him," said Fiona. "Let's go in."

"Hold on a minute," said Pete, leaning toward her.

The morning after having witnessed the scene at Ground Zero, Elisabeth wasted no time in calling Fiona. But the call had been deeply disappointing. Before Elisabeth had been able to tell her own story, Fiona had joyously revealed the news that Pete was there. Unwilling to intrude on her friend's happiness, Elisabeth had quickly extricated herself, and left her own troubles out of the conversation. She would have to cope on her own, she thought. Whatever that meant.

Shay was impressed by the rapidity of her star student's prog-ress. He was, she thought, proof of the value of consistent daily practice. Of course, she told herself, it didn't hurt that was in great shape to begin with. He had strength and fitness and dedication. All he really needed to reach the most advanced levels was flexibility. But she needed to do more for him. She needed to help him reach the next level.

She was thinking about this as the men's yoga group was packing up after their morning session. What should she sug-gest for Roger's advancement? Suddenly, an idea occurred to her that was so obvious that she was surprised at herself for not having thought of it sooner. Her yoga workshop! The group she was leading on the week-long retreat in Utah. It was the perfect solution. She was about to talk to Roger about it when she was waylaid by one of the members of the Lutheran Men's Prayer Group. He needed help with his triangle pose.

At the Hillard event, Fiona was once again pulled into con-versations. Unfazed, Pete made his way toward the bar and ordered a bourbon. Eddie was busy, but he gave Pete a quick nod, and managed to convey the message that he'd return shortly.

Pali came in, and seeing Pete, joined him at the bar.

"What'll you have?" asked Pete.

"A beer. Thanks."

Eddie knew Pali's preferences without asking and slid a beer glass down the bar as he passed.

"Cheers," said Pete.

"Skal," said Pali.

They drank.

"So tell me about this harbor dredging situation," said Pete, as he withdrew a dollar bill from his pocket to begin the process of folding it around a quarter and a thumbtack so that it could be flung to the ceiling, a local pastime he had learned on his last trip.

Pali launched into a lengthy technical explanation of water levels, ferry capacities, and Wisconsin politics.

They had attached a number of bills to the ceiling, and were in the process of ordering another round of drinks when Dean Hillard approached. He smiled an unctuous smile.

"I couldn't help hearing you talking about the harbor. You know that's a particular interest of mine." He turned to Pete.

"I don't think we've met."

"Peter Landry." He offered his hand.

A slow smile slid along Hillard's face. "I know who you are. You're the... friend of Fiona Campbell, who's running against my Aunt Stella for Town Chairman."

Pete's eyes sparkled, but he maintained a neutral demeanor. "That's true. We are... " he deliberately paused, as Hillard had. "... friends."

"I think we have some things to discuss," said Hillard. He turned to Pali. "Would you excuse us?"

Pali merely nodded, and watched as Pete allowed Hillard to

lead him away from the bar.

"Do you mind if we step outside?" asked Hillard. "What I have to say is private."

Pete shot a look at Pali, who nodded almost indiscernibly.

"Not at all," said Pete, and held the door for Assemblyman Hillard to precede him into the parking lot.

Pali and Eddie exchanged glances, and Pali settled down to watch the conversation taking place outside with all the intensity of Rocco on alert. It wasn't until Pete returned that Pali allowed himself to relax. Pete bought them all another round of drinks.

"I need a shower after talking with that guy. But I'll settle for a bourbon. Thanks, Eddie."

Elisabeth was not one for scenes. She did not like upheaval. She liked order, calm, and quiet good sense. The situation with Roger defied all her experience and resources. She simply didn't know what to do. Elisabeth had managed to avoid a confrontation with Roger by pleading a series of headaches, leaving dinner in the kitchen for him to find, and disappearing into the guest room before he arrived. There was a part of her that hoped that Roger would come to see her, to sit on the side of her bed and ask about how she felt. She hoped that somehow this would lead to the things that needed to be said.

But she began to realize that she had been playing a stupid game. Roger was who he was. She was trying to pretend that he was otherwise. If she wanted things to change, if she wanted a conversation, then she would have to take the initiative.

Elisabeth was ashamed of herself. She had been acting like a teenaged girl. Lying awake in the guest room, with Rocco snoring at her feet, she stared out the window at the stars. Tomorrow, she would change her methods.

Chapter Twenty-Two ❊

Fiona stepped into the living room carrying mugs of coffee. It was another cold, sparkling morning, and the sun streamed through the windows.

Pete had been staring into the distance, apparently lost in thought, but he roused himself as she entered, and made room for her on the couch before accepting one of the mugs.

"I have an old school friend in Chicago," he said as she settled in. "We should go visit him some time. You'd like him. Works for the federal government." He was silent for a moment, clearly distracted, and then turned his attention back to the present and smiled suddenly.

"Now, where were we?"

"Nowhere really, yet." She was silent as she drank her coffee.

"You are thinking rather loudly," observed Pete.

"I saw you talking with Dean Hillard last night. What was that about?"

"Jake is right. He's a slime bag."

"Actually, I think I led you astray. What Jake actually says is 'scum bag.'"

"They would both apply."

"Yes. So, what did he want?"

Pete put his cup down and turned to her. He cupped her face gently in his hands, and looked seriously into her eyes.

"There is no reason on earth that we should waste our precious time together discussing that slime-slash-scum bag. Life is short."

Fiona grinned. "Yes, it is. And Jake really has a way with words, hasn't he?"

"I like Jake," said Pete. "He promised to show me his technique for attaching dollar bills to the ceiling at Nelsen's." He looked at her, considering. "But on the whole, I think I'd rather stay in tonight."

After the morning group had dispersed, Shay was seated at the counter at Ground Zero sipping her coffee. The Angel Joshua was nearby, radiating peace and joy as he polished the coffee machine, while Roger took inventory of supplies.

"So, Roger, I've been thinking about you," began Shay.

Roger looked up from his task and gazed at her with a scientist's intensity. He said nothing.

Brimming with innocent enthusiasm, Shay continued. "You know. Thinking about how I can help you get to the next level. And, well, I'm leading a group on a yoga retreat to Utah. It's past the deadline to register, but I'm sure there's room. You should come."

"I am already registered," said Roger mechanically.

Joshua looked up, studied Roger for a moment, and silently went back to his polishing.

Shay was astonished. "You are?"

"Yes," said Roger. "I saw the flyer in Sturgeon Bay and contacted the travel agency that was listed."

"And you signed up when you saw I was leading?" Shay smiled modestly. "That's really sweet, Roger."

Roger's face registered no change, but he shook his head. "No."

Shay looked at him quizzically. "No?"

"I didn't know you were leading."

"You didn't?"

"No. I just thought it seemed like a good opportunity to improve my technique."

Shay shrugged good-naturedly, and beamed her sunny smile. "Well, that's what I call fate! I'm really glad you can make it. You'll love it."

Roger gazed at her without changing his expression.

"Yes," he said.

E lisabeth was in the kitchen when Roger got home that night. She was standing by the stove, stirring a pot au feu that had been her great grandmother's recipe. There was an open bottle of wine and two glasses on the table.

She had been waiting for him before pouring a glass for herself, a break in her usual habit, but she wanted to remain clear-headed for the conversation she had planned. They would have a glass together, they would have dinner, and she would not confront him. She would ask. She would ask him what had happened. He would tell her when she asked. Roger was not a liar, and she doubted whether he was even capable of minor dissembling.

Elisabeth knew what she had seen. But she needed to hear him tell it. She needed him to know she knew. More than anything, she needed this terrible weight on her chest to be lifted.

Roger walked into the kitchen, bringing the cold air with him. Rocco greeted him joyously, and Roger stooped to rub the big dog's ears.

"Hello, Roger," said Elisabeth calmly as he came to her and kissed her dutifully on the cheek. "Would you like some wine?"

"Yes," said Roger. And then, "Do you feel better?"

Elisabeth shrugged, "A bit. I thought we should have a nice dinner. We haven't had dinner together all week."

Roger nodded. "I want to tell you about my plans," he said seriously. "I have plans for the future."

Elisabeth, her heart softening, turned to face him.

"Oh? What plans?"

"I am going to go away for a week. I leave on Saturday."

Whatever Elisabeth had been expecting, it had not been this.

"That's a bit sudden. This is Thursday." Her outer calm did not reflect the turmoil within. "Where are you going?"

"To Shay's yoga workshop in Utah. She says it will help me make the next step."

Elisabeth's eyes narrowed dangerously. "And what step would that be?"

Roger looked puzzled. He knew that something was wrong. He searched his brain for some clue. He looked at his wife. She was wearing jeans and a heavy white sweater. Her hair was loose and falling around her shoulders. Her complexion was rosy from the warmth of the room. Suddenly he remembered, and looking at her with a profound sense of satisfaction he said, "You look nice. You look very nice in that."

Weeping with fury, Elisabeth fled the room.

B en was a faithful friend to the herd of deer that had learned to trust him. Almost every day after school, no matter the weather, Ben made his way to the watering place. Sometimes there would be nothing there but tracks, or it would be too cold or wet to wait, but he always left some food anyway. On other days, if he waited patiently, they would appear, one by one. He had learned to settle himself on a large rock nearby, and to listen for the sounds of their approach.

Soon it began to seem that the herd had learned to time their visits to meet him, and although there was only one member who easily approached him, the others had come to accept his presence. A sudden move or a sneeze would send them scattering, but otherwise, they grazed peacefully as he watched. When something startled them, they would stop to stare with their big brown eyes, nervously flicking their ears, and if they were not reassured by what their senses told them, they would make their sudden flight into the brush, their white tails high as they leapt and ran. Ben's particular friend would follow then, too, but clumsily, with his awkward gait.

It was The Angel Joshua, not Roger, who took it upon himself to make arrangements for the men's yoga group to continue their practice while Roger was away. Roger's indifference to the group's presence made him utterly unconscious of their being affected in any way by his absence. It did not even occur to him to mention that he would be away for a week.

At the end of the session on Friday morning Joshua asked Roger whether he should host the group while Roger was at the workshop with Shay the following week. All heads turned to hear this conversation.

Roger shrugged and went on with his work at the counter. Joshua turned his shining gaze upon the group. "I'll open up at the usual time, and we can just carry on while they're gone."

The men were far more interested in the details of the workshop and the trip that Roger was taking with Shay, and they asked many questions, most of them in low-voiced asides to Roger when they were certain that Shay would not hear. When she excused herself a bit earlier than usual, saying she had an appointment in Green Bay, the questions flew thick and fast.

"When are you leaving?"

"What's this workshop about?"

"Is Elisabeth going?"

"She's not?"

"Is she okay with it?

"I don't think my wife would go for me taking a trip with Shay."

Roger did not deign to answer most of these questions, finding it necessary merely to grumble that Elisabeth had gone to Madison to visit her brother. Meaningful looks were exchanged behind his back at this piece of information.

Terry, who had been silent during the conversation, looked at Roger, shaking his head in disbelief while he made a long slow whistle. His thoughts were a whirl of envy on the one hand, and sympathy for Elisabeth on the other.

"Man." He shook his head again before adding, "You better watch yourself."

Roger glared at him, but whether it was resentment or his usual expression, no one could tell.

After Pete's departure, Fiona had to mentally slap herself to keep from moping around the house. She had debate prep to do, and all the routine household things she had neglected while he had been there, not to mention some deadlines to meet, but she was having a hard time motivating herself to do any of it.

Once again, Pete had left with great expressions of tenderness, but no word about when he would return. Fiona knew that his work created for him an erratic schedule, and she also knew enough about him to know he would not make promises he could not keep. But none of this was any particular consolation.

On the one hand, she asked herself what the point might be of a relationship of this kind: more based on uncertainty than commitment. On the other, she knew that Pete had spoiled her for anyone else. Whether she liked it or not, waiting—or pretending not to—was the price of this relationship. So far, at least, she was choosing to pay it. But an indefinite future like this did not hold great appeal.

She was drinking her third cup of coffee and playing listlessly with a spoon on the table when it suddenly occurred to her that she knew exactly what she needed: Elisabeth. She would take the day off, and see if she could convince her friend to do the same. It had been ages since they had done anything fun together.

But Fiona's call to Elisabeth told her immediately that something was wrong. They had not spoken for a week, not since Elisabeth's call the morning after Pete had arrived, and Fiona, distracted, had not been attuned to any particular signals. But she could hear now the stress in Elisabeth's voice, even though Elisabeth was not forthcoming.

"Hey," said Fiona, casually. What's going on?"

"Oh," said Elisabeth, "nothing much." And then she added, "Roger's away for a few days, so I'm a bit at loose ends."

Fiona's attention was caught. Why would Roger go somewhere without Elisabeth?

"Oh, really? Where did he go."

"To a yoga workshop. In Utah."

"Ah," said Fiona, endeavoring to be neutral as she visualized increasingly unlikely scenarios. "Well, that sounds... interesting."

"With Shay," said Elisabeth quietly. Her words hung in the air as Fiona's startled mind raced through the implications.

"With Shay? Really? Are you sure?" This did not sound like Roger. Roger wouldn't do something like this.

"Of course I'm sure," snapped Elisabeth.

"But how? How are you sure?" Fiona could not get her head around this. Roger? Unfaithful? Never! It was not even plausible.

"Because he told me." Elisabeth's voice had begun to tremble.

Fiona went instantly into action. She could talk sense into Elisabeth later. First she needed to do some triage.

"Look," she said, brightly. "This is really great timing. I've got this debate coming up, and I could really use some help with my prep, not to mention some moral support. Why don't you pack up Rocco and come over? I can have a fantastic dinner ready by the time you get here."

"I'm in Madison," said Elisabeth. "At my brother's." Fiona could hear the catch in her voice.

"Where's Rocco?" she asked. Elisabeth's sister-in-law was not among Rocco's fans, Fiona knew.

"He's here," said Elisabeth. "Busily protecting the kids." She tried to laugh. It was a pathetic attempt.

"Look," said Fiona. "This must all be some kind of dreadful mistake. If I know one thing, it's that Roger loves you. Come home. Come to the Island. I haven't seen you or Rocco for weeks. We can talk. I could use your company."

She hoped that the appeal to Elisabeth's altruistic nature would do the trick.

Elisabeth took a deep breath. She loved her brother and his family, but in her present mood, she did not feel that she was an asset to their household, and besides, she was tired of avoiding questions. Fiona would be different. Fiona would understand.

"Well, all right. I suppose we can come. If you're really sure."

"Of course, I'm sure," said Fiona briskly. "Come as soon as you can. Tomorrow, maybe. And since you're in civilization, bring a case of something good to drink. Something South African, maybe."

"I don't think we need a case."

"Speak for yourself," said Fiona.

It was dark and the temperature was below zero, but Emily went straight to the barn after the animal husbandry presentations. Embarrassed and angered by that child, Ben's, remarks, she was determined to prove him wrong. But even as she considered this, the doubts swirled in her mind. She was remembering the open barn door, the loose latches, the excessive consumption of goat chow, and the random disappearance of things. Someone had been letting her goats mingle. Her first thoughts were on the carelessness of children. Those scouts! They must have been the ones who had been so careless as to leave the barn unsecured, and after she had been so generous, so giving of her time.

"No good deed goes unpunished," she thought bitterly.

But then another idea came into her head. She remembered the screaming, the open door, the missing rope, and the rumors that a stranger—and, no doubt, a crazy one—was living in the woods somewhere on the Island. Could someone have been in the barn? Could a stranger have left open a gate, taken the rope, allowed the animals to mingle?

Nervously, she looked behind her as she flipped on the barn lights and went to look into the does' stalls. She looked them over, one by one, and then she began to count. One… three… five… eight… twelve. A dozen pregnant does who should not be. Just as the boy had said.

Emily was annoyed, wondering how she could have been so oblivious as to have missed this. She had been busy, sure, but this was basic stuff, the kind of thing an experienced farmer should notice. That she was not all that experienced was something that would not occur to Emily. But to be shown up by a child! That was a difficult pill to take.

Emily was not one for self-doubt, however, and her mood swiftly changed. "Well, after all," she thought to herself. "The mind is a tricky thing. I wasn't looking for the signs, so I didn't see them." The more she thought of this, the more the idea grew on her, and the more it seemed absolutely true and perfectly understandable.

Now properly reassured, Emily's customary complacency returned and settled around her like a shield. She was not to blame. If anything, she, herself, was a victim. Although, whether of irresponsible children or of… something else… she couldn't be sure. And, of course, she reminded herself, she really had been terribly, terribly busy. True, she preferred to choose the mating pairs of her flock, but she could always sell the kids and make a tidy profit.

Telling herself all this, and resolving to have a strong word with that do-nothing police chief, she closed up the barn and bustled into the house.

After the phone call with Fiona, Elisabeth had announced her plans to her sister-in-law, kissed her nieces, and driven home from Madison that afternoon, stopping only to visit an exceptionally nice wine store on the way. She and Rocco had been the first car in line when the early ferry arrived at Northport the following morning.

Fiona greeted them with joy. The guest room was ready with fresh linens and flowers on the table; there was a pot of coffee brewing, warm banana bread made from the latest bunch of black bananas, and a box of treats for Rocco. Elisabeth's suitcase had been brought upstairs and her coat hung on the peg in the hall. Rocco's bed had been set in his favorite corner of the living room. The case of South African wine had been stored in the pantry, and the first two bottles extracted for chilling, ready for later.

After investigating the house to see what had happened in his absence, Rocco settled comfortably under the kitchen table, while Fiona and Elisabeth sat down to drink coffee. Fiona studied her friend's face with concern. She looked pale. Her eyes were swollen and heavily lined with dark circles.

"So, what's going on?" she asked matter-of-factly.

Elisabeth took a deep breath and poured out her tale.

After two days indoors talking and preparing for the debate, Elisabeth and Fiona were spent, and Fiona suggested a change of scene.

"It's too damp and cold to walk very far. Let's just take a drive around the Island. We can stop on the way back to pick up some milk for morning."

Rocco joyfully agreed that a ride would be welcome, and they piled into Fiona's car.

The sights in this miserable final phase of fading winter were not especially stirring, but they drove around the edges of the island, stopping here and there to look at the water and the great, floating slabs of ice that blew with the wind and currents. They had rounded the eastern edge of the island, and were driving northwest along Detroit Harbor when they came upon the historic Washington Hotel. The lovely restaurant there had been closed, and the shuttered windows conveyed a sense of desolation in the dreary weeks-old snow. A For Sale sign, with the name of the realtor who had sold Fiona her house, stood prominently at the roadside. Awash in a sense of nostalgia that had been augmented by Elisabeth's mood, Fiona pulled up so they could look.

"It's sad," said Elisabeth, gazing at the elegant old building with its venerable trees, expansive lawn, and broad porch. "We had such lovely dinners there."

"I'm afraid it's an indicator of health for the Island's economy. The fact that it's stood empty so long is a bad sign." Fiona sighed. "I wish I could buy it."

Elisabeth gave her a skeptical look. "Because you've done such a great job at restoring your current place. You still have vermin living in your walls."

"You say vermin as if it were plural. I think there's only one."

"Judging by the noise I heard last night, it could be fifty. You need to do something about it, Fiona. Your house is going to fall down around your ears."

"But he's my vermin," said Fiona complacently. "We understand one another. We read Martin Luther together."

Elisabeth rolled her eyes. "I don't know how you function on your own, I really don't." Her tone became brisk. "Look at the time. If we want to have milk with our coffee in the morning, we'd better get to Mann's before they close."

Obediently, Fiona put the car in gear, and they made their way back to Main Street.

They were well into the second bottle of wine that night, talking about what to do the next day.

"It's hard to plan when we don't know what the weather's going to be like. Let's see if we can find something on TV." Fiona reached for the remote, turned on the television, and began flipping through the channels. A rapid secession of programs passed before their eyes before Elisabeth suddenly called out. "Wait! Stop! Go back!"

With a quick sidelong look at her friend, Fiona obligingly reversed direction in her channel hopping.

"There." said Elisabeth. "Stop there."

They gazed at the screen.

It was a yoga class. A group of at least twenty students, men and women in varying sizes and shapes, were following the instruction of a lithe, though no longer young, woman with a Southern accent.

"The down dog," she was saying, "is among the most fundamental poses of your practice, but so many of us take its form for granted. Today we will work on building our down dog, so that it takes us through our practice like a faithful friend. Choose partners, everyone!"

She smiled wickedly. "And make sure it's someone you don't mind getting close to. This one's pretty up close and personal."

Fiona tried to gauge Elisabeth's reaction, and whether she should switch the channel, but Elisabeth was engrossed.

"Everybody's going to get a chance at this, so just decide which of you will be in the A group and which in the B."

The facility with which the group divided itself suggested to Fiona's skeptical mind that this was not a random process.

"A's on the floor into down dog," directed the teacher.

"Now. I will demonstrate the next move for the B's. It's important to work carefully, here, so that you don't drop your full weight onto your partner. Remember, this is an advanced move for advanced practitioners. The idea is to gently use your weight to help your partner move more deeply into the pose."

And here, she turned her back on her student partner, who was in downward dog. The student's hands and feet were on the floor, her legs straight, the top of her head pointing toward the ground, her body forming the shape of an inverted V. Backing up to her until they were touching, the teacher bent back until the backs of her legs were leaning against the backs of her student's legs, and then, gradually, she lowered herself backward so that their backs were against one another.

Elisabeth was watching intently. Slowly she turned her face to Fiona, her face alight with revelation.

"That's it," she said quietly. "That's what I saw."

Her eyes were shining, and at first Fiona thought she was about to cry.

"It wasn't infidelity that day at Ground Zero," said Elisabeth, her voice beginning to crack. "It was yoga."

For a split second, Fiona was afraid to look at Elisabeth, but their eyes met, and the absurdity of the situation struck them both in the same instant. They laughed until they were both breathless, and Rocco had to lick both their faces to ensure that all was well. He was kept busy going back and forth between them for quite some time.

"Poor Roger," said Fiona the next morning. "He probably doesn't have any idea what's been going on."

Elisabeth had regained her customary equanimity. "Poor Roger?" she enquired tartly. "Don't forget, he's still on that retreat with Shay."

Fiona shrugged and smiled. "After last night, I think you should give him the benefit of the doubt. You owe him at least that much."

Elisabeth almost smiled back. "I suppose you're right," she said reluctantly.

"I'm going home. He'll be back tomorrow." She twisted a piece of her hair around one finger as she gazed out the window. "We have a few things to discuss."

That afternoon, Fiona watched Elisabeth drive away, with

Rocco's big head leaning out into the cold wind, his ears up, his face turned to the scents that were flying by. With their departure, Fiona felt as if she were losing her last connection to sanity. The debate and the election loomed ahead of her, with no compensating pleasures or distractions in view.

Elisabeth and Rocco were waiting when Roger arrived home. They heard the car come up the drive, and while Rocco felt no need to contain his excitement, Elisabeth counseled herself to stay calm.

When Roger walked in Rocco exploded with joy, jumping and singing, and spinning in circles. He nearly knocked Roger over with his exuberance.

Elisabeth's greeting was less effusive. She watched Roger's reunion with Rocco like an outsider who didn't belong. Feeling awkward and unsure of what to say, she scanned the little pile of things Roger had dropped on the counter by the door, and picked up the cardboard folder on the top.

"What's this?"

"It's the group photo. Of the class."

"But," said Elisabeth confusedly, "A group photo—"

She looked into Roger's face. "I thought you were there alone. There. With—Shay," she finished, lamely.

Roger simply looked at her, puzzled. "No," he said. "Why would you think that?"

Elisabeth glanced at the smiling faces. There were no dazzling bodies in skimpy outfits, just a group of about twenty men and women in varying degrees of fitness, all clad in shapeless but comfortable clothing. They looked relaxed and calm, and behind them was the dramatic scenery of the Uinta Mountains.

The enormity of her misjudgment flooded over Elisabeth. Her lack of faith in him, her doubts in his integrity... in his love for her. She saw in a flash how her initial misinterpretation of what she had seen at the shop had led her down a path of jealousy, distrust, and false narrative. She felt small and stupid. "It would have helped, though," she told herself rebelliously, "if he had just told me what was going on."

She stared at him, uncertain of what to do or say next, but her roiling emotions began a rapid mutation from agitation to relief. It was okay. Everything was going to be okay. He was Roger. Just as he had always been: steady, constant, and, she realized, utterly dependable in all the ways that mattered. Elisabeth was enveloped in a cloud of joy.

Roger put his bag down and took off his coat.

Working to come to terms with this new state of things— with her old happiness—Elisabeth busied herself with getting a bottle of wine, opening it, and pouring them each a glass.

"So, how was it? What did you learn?" she asked as she handed him his glass.

Roger frowned, considering her question.

"My down dog is better, I think. And I feel more confident in my sun salutations." He sat down at the kitchen table, and unconsciously ran a hand through his hair. "And Joshua would say that it has been a success. At least," he looked up at her as she stood leaning against the kitchen counter, "I think he would."

Elisabeth looked puzzled. "A success at sun salutations?"

"No," said Roger, equally puzzled that she did not follow his meaning. "At getting in touch with my feminine side."

And with that, he rose from the table, walked to where she was standing, and kissed her.

Chapter Twenty-Three

S pring was the Island's annual time of frustration. Months of winter had led to general restlessness among the populace, and spring's virtues, celebrated elsewhere, were less obvious on the island.

The change in seasons did not begin with sunshine and balmy breezes. It began, instead, with temperatures that were warm enough to melt snow, but not warm enough to feel comfortable, and the moisture in the air from the melting snow seeped deep into the bones with a burrowing cold. If anything, the weather became less tolerable than the deep freezes and blizzards of winter.

Months of living indoors, the relentless necessity of shoveling snow, of driving on it, of worrying about ice underfoot and snow on the roof, of having to protect against cold, sleet, rain, ice and mud simultaneously, without ever knowing in which form it would appear, made for a more or less universal winter fatigue.

Even though everyone knew perfectly well that spring rarely appeared until late April or May, the general mood was, as someone once said of second marriages, the triumph of hope over experience. Daily expectations were disappointed. Tempers were short.

Fiona huddled indoors, drinking coffee and tea, writing, reading, and doing bad translations of Martin Luther. She made periodic forays into Island society out of the campaign's necessity, but otherwise kept to herself. She realized now how essential the obligations of caring for Robert had been to her state of mind last year. This year, being alone and thinking only of herself made her restless and anxious. Robert, she now knew, had been a key element of her survival through the island's hard winter. The realization was not a welcome one.

As the debate grew closer her anxiety grew with it, and Fiona found herself sleepless, restless, and spending more and more time in the company of the Midnight Chewer. She was beginning to feel that it was the best part of the day.

As Fiona was tossing and turning, the midnight creature began its nightly activities. "Maybe," she thought, just before she fell asleep, "the chewer is lonely, too." Lulled by familiarity—if not completely consoled—she drifted off to sleep, the sound of crunching in the wall continuing well into the night.

She woke to a dark and misty morning. A swirl of fog engulfed the island, and she could hear the drip of melting snow in the gutters. Deeply elated at this augury of spring, she lay back under the warmth of her comforter and listened.

The debate between candidates for town chairman had been looked forward to eagerly by the entire population of the Island. This was a community that—of necessity—was accustomed to making its own entertainment, and the prospect of any debate would have been highly anticipated. This particular debate, however, would be the highlight of the year. Maybe of a lifetime.

The date had been set for one week before election day. Fiona had done her best to prepare, with the help of Elisabeth, Pali, and, whether she liked it or not, Emily. Emily's little piece of advice about holding the pen made Fiona somewhat more inclined to pay attention to her counsel, but only somewhat.

She had earnestly studied the questions Elisabeth had prepared for her, practiced answering them in front of the bathroom mirror, tried to anticipate various manifestations of hostility that might throw her off her game, and planned to wear relatively sensible shoes—though still Italian—to reduce the prospect of tripping and falling on her walk to the lectern.

The debate was to be held at Nelsen's, the scene of many local events, and one which might induce more of the public to attend. Fiona felt as ready as she could reasonably expect to be.

Fiona arrived at Nelsen's exactly fifteen minutes before the debate was scheduled to begin. She had calculated what she believed was the least possible amount of time to be exposed to anyone's casually devastating remark, while allowing sufficient time to prevent anxiety about missing the beginning.

Elisabeth had expected to come, but at the last moment Fiona asked her not to.

"You've been great. And I really appreciate the support, but you will actually make me more nervous. I think I'll do better going by myself."

"Pali and the others will all be there."

Fiona noted guiltily that Elisabeth was a tiny bit hurt.

"True. But I can't ask them not to come. They live here. You are—speaking politically, of course—non-essential personnel."

Elisabeth laughed in spite of herself. "Fine. But I will remind you of this. Just you wait."

"You can come to my swearing-in ceremony."

"Try and keep me away. I have already purchased my outfit. And there's a hat."

"That will make you inconspicuous."

"I should hope not."

Just before the debate was to begin, the town clerk approached Fiona and asked her to join her on the podium. "It's time for the coin toss."

Dutifully, Fiona followed, and arrived at the same time as Stella.

Automatically, Fiona put out her hand, and Stella shook it reluctantly, as if worried about contracting some disease.

The coin was flipped, Stella called heads. "It's heads," announced the clerk. "Ms. DesRosiers wins the coin toss. Will you speak first or second?"

"First," said Stella smugly, betraying a lack of strategy that Fiona found surprising.

"We will begin shortly."

Fiona and Stella seated themselves at narrow, rather rickety folding tables on either side of the lectern, in uncomfortable and rather rickety folding metal chairs. Stella glared at the audience with eyes narrowed, her normal look. Fiona maintained a wholly false air of steady calm, her Emily-prescribed pen in hand as she made meaningless scribbles on the notepad before her.

Lars Olafsen, the outgoing chairman, climbed the platform and faced the audience.

"Welcome, Ladies and Gentlemen, to a debate between our two candidates for Chairman of the Town of Washington Board."

In a last gesture of public service, Lars had agreed to moderate the debate. He was perfectly at ease in this role, having been in the public eye for most of his adult life, and having accepted several offers of brandy before the event started.

"The rules," continued Lars, "are simple. Each candidate will make a brief, three-minute opening statement."

"As opposed," thought Fiona irreverently, "to a lengthy three-minute statement." She drew a picture of Stella's head exploding on her notepad, and quickly flipped the page before anyone might see it.

"Afterward, the moderator will read written questions from this basket, which have been collected from the community in advance, courtesy of the newspaper, *The Observer.* Each candidate will answer the same question.

"At the end of forty-five minutes, each candidate will have three minutes to make a final statement."

Lars paused looking around the room at his rapt audience, and then at the two candidates. "Ladies, are there any questions?"

Fiona smiled slightly and shook her head. Stella said "No" rather too loudly.

"Then let us begin. Ms. DesRosiers."

The audience applauded more out of enthusiasm for the event than for the candidate, but Stella chose to take it personally, nodding with her best impersonation of graciousness.

The graciousness, however, did not last long. Stella, apparently, had never heard advice about the effects of negative campaigning. She lost no time in launching into a long list of invective against her opponent, including the now nearly forgotten goat incidents, accusations of wild parties, and of immoral behavior that was vaguely, but breathlessly implied.

Fiona listened with increasing indignation, but she managed to keep an expression of calm indifference. She was fairly sure that this effort would have earned an Oscar had it been recorded on film.

When her turn came, Fiona did not respond to Stella's smears and sneers, choosing, instead, to focus on topics that were pertinent to the campaign. When her three minutes were up, she sat down, feeling emboldened.

The questions posed by Lars Olafsen were neither difficult nor hard-hitting, and although Fiona was relieved, the crowd, having expected something more exciting, was disappointed and grew restive. It was fortunate, Fiona thought, that the bar was just in the next room.

At last, it was time for the final three-minute speeches. Once more Stella allowed her bitterness toward Fiona to engulf her. She was just beginning to get into the meat of her subject—Fiona's arrogance; self-importance; and immorality—when the timer bell went off, and she had to be reminded twice by Lars Olafsen that she should stop.

Fiona now stood and, pen in hand, approached the lectern. She smiled a trifle nervously and began.

"I suppose I am fortunate that Ms. DesRosiers isn't in charge of my public relations."

The audience chuckled at this minor witticism, which served only to incite Stella's indignation. She glowered from the stage as if she held a personal grudge against everyone in the room, which was quite possibly the case.

Steering well clear of Stella's personality and her accusations, Fiona made her case for honesty, clarity, and simplicity.

"For the most part, as far as I can see, the Island has managed perfectly well without me for a long time, and I do not intend to impose myself on political life here. I expect to be—as I believe most of you would hope—as unobtrusive and as unnecessary as possible."

Fiona heard a sound that might have been a growl coming from Stella.

"But when we do need leadership, it's for the big things, like the harbor dredging. My research tells me that there are a number of organizations that make small harbor grants for precisely this kind of situation. There is no need to believe that we have to fight our way through this problem alone."

Fiona, now well launched, remembered Emily, and raised her pen for a carefully practiced gesture. She was feeling that things were going extraordinarily well, and thought she could sense the support of the room.

Moving inexorably toward her final summation, she continued. "If I am elected, I will put my experience in research and writing to make every effort into applying for and securing such a grant."

Now flowing with confidence, Fiona made an extravagant motion of the hand to emphasize her last word, and at its apex of speed and movement, the pen slipped from her fingers. It flew like an arrow, at great speed and in a spectacular arch, straight into the teased—and rather dated—hairdo of the Baptist minister's wife, about five rows back.

At the moment of impact, the lady gasped and jumped, her hands clutching her hair, unclear about exactly what had landed there. Was it a fly? A wasp? Her alarm grew from her uncertainty. There was a flurry of activity as the other women nearby came to her aid, and attempted—with little cries of alarm and sympathy—to console her and to extricate the pen, which was rather a nice one, from the hairdo. Fiona looked on in petrified horror from the dais.

One elderly gentleman, seated a row ahead of the ladies, turned around to add his assistance, and in his gallantry, knocked over his chair, beginning his own little hubbub of apologies, stumblings, and related activities, and the chaos grew as he, too, was assisted by his nearest neighbors.

The minister's wife's hair was by now in extraordinary disarray, as innumerable women plucked at it like hens around an anthill. Others joined in, or stood to see what was happening. This led to shouted instructions to sit down from those in the back, while others began milling around in search of a drink or conversation. It was a matter of moments before the room was engulfed in what an outside observer might have guessed was a minor riot.

The havoc was beyond the capabilities of even Lars Olafsen to restrain. He attempted valiantly to make his voice heard above the noise. "Thank you, Ladies and Gentlemen, and candidates, for attending this important part of our civic life… ." He looked on, bemused, at the furor before him. "And, er… good night."

Helplessly, he turned to Fiona and shrugged. She smiled wanly back. Feeling that it would be better to be in a less conspicuous location, she gathered her notes with the meaningless scribbles on them, and wandered off, penless, toward the bar. Stella, of course, was somewhere nearby, but Fiona was almost past caring. This election thing had been going on far too long for her taste, and she was heartily sick of it, and of Stella, too.

In the aftermath of the debate, the television in the bar was already playing again in the background, a feature of the establishment that Fiona never particularly enjoyed, although she had to admit that local news always afforded possibilities for entertainment. Endeavoring to forget what had just occurred, she was engaged in various conversations as people approached to discuss the election, when Pali suddenly called out.

"Hey, Eddie! Turn it up! It's Hillard! He's on TV!"

All eyes turned to the television set, the bar grew quiet, and the voice of the Green Bay anchorwoman filled the room.

"Local Assemblyman Dean Hillard was arrested in Madison today, on charges of prostitution and possession of illegal substances. Police say that the arrest was part of a sting operation that included a number of prominent public figures."

Fiona heard a gasp and the sounds of commotion from the back of the room, as a campaign photograph of Hillard accompanied the anchorwoman's story. But Fiona's full attention was riveted to the television screen. This was being treated as a major story.

The video shifted to a reporter on the scene, and continued with an interview of the spokesman from the local branch of the FBI, who described the seriousness of the charges. Then came the images of Dean Hillard being helped into the back of an official car, his head carefully protected from hitting the roof by the officers who held him by the arms.

A stunned silence fell over the crowd at Nelsen's. No one had ever known someone targeted in an FBI sting. It was as good as one of those big city crime shows. Eyes began to turn toward the back of the room where increasingly urgent whispers came from the small cluster of Stella's followers as they tried, unsuccessfully, to escort her from the room.

"I never liked that guy," said Jake in a carrying voice. "Always thought he was a scum bag."

Jake's sentiments were echoed—though more discreetly—throughout the room.

But the story was not yet over. There was a shift in the televised scene, and the camera cut to footage of a shiny, red, vintage car, shown abandoned in an official lot. Suddenly there was a shriek from the back of the room that momentarily stunned the crowd.

"MY CAR! THEY'VE GOT MY CAR!"

Stella had broken away from her assistants and began elbowing her way through the crowd toward the television set, as if somehow, being closer might enable her to reach into the screen.

"Look!" said someone. "It is! It's Stella's car!"

The news set the room into a furious buzz of excitement. There could be little doubt. The FBI agent was standing in front of a shiny, red, vintage convertible with a sneering grill. It certainly looked exactly like Stella's car, and since it had been in Hillard's possession, it must surely be hers. The agent was saying things like civil asset, and forfeiture, but the meaning was clear. The car, having been part of a crime, was now the property of law enforcement.

"They can't take it! It's mine! They can't take my car!"

Stella did not seem to care that she was being observed by her voting public. She was beside herself with rage, her face mangled by it. Fiona stole one look and turned away from the public display of such raw emotion. There was no reason she should feel even the smallest shred of sympathy for Stella, and yet, her anguish was painful to see. That Stella's feelings should be expressed for the car rather than the nephew was, Fiona thought, an interesting detail.

The crowd fell silent as they struggled to hear the rest of the story with the sound of Stella's howling in the background. A group of women—more out of consideration for others than compassion for Stella—escorted her outside to the relative privacy of the parking lot. Cries of "My car! My car! They have no right!" came floating into the building each time the door was opened. An unusual number of patrons found the need to go outside for a quick smoke or to retrieve some forgotten necessity from their cars, and only just happened to be able to witness the drama going on in the parking lot.

Inside, the volume in the room increased.

"They've impounded it!"

"What does that mean?"

"Will she get it back?"

Fiona sat still, slow to fully comprehend what had just happened. As the realization dawned, people began coming up to her, slapping her on the back, and offering to buy her drinks. The congratulations flowed as freely as if she had already won the election. Everyone, it seemed, had come to the same conclusion: Dean Hillard would no longer be a factor in Island politics.

Some hours later the crowd had diminished, but the excitement still seemed to hang in the air. Fiona had long since excused herself and gone home.

Pali leaned over the bar to talk with Eddie before heading out.

"Well," he said quietly, "that didn't play out in quite the way I'd imagined."

Eddie nodded thoughtfully. He was marveling over the workings of Fate.

"No," he said, his eyes sparkling. "It was way better."

He became suddenly serious, and lowered his voice.

"But we're not out of the woods yet. With Hillard out of the picture, Stella won't have the guarantee of state funding to dredge the harbor. But can we get the word out? There's only a week left."

Pali shrugged. "Well, half the damn Island was here tonight. If that's not getting the word out, I don't know what is." He paused, reflecting.

"Fiona made some good points, but the harbor problem isn't really resolved."

"No," said Eddie. "It's not."

He stopped, thinking it all through. "So somehow—and damned if I know how—we got our demons, even though they were played by federal agents instead of elderly choristers." He shook his head slowly as he contemplated the chain of events. "It's almost as if we made it come true by imagining it. Hardly seems possible."

Pali nodded, laughing. "Stella may not be the one who got

dragged away to Hell, but it works just as well." He took a last swallow of beer before heading out. "You're right, though. It's almost too good to be true." As he was about to head out the door he turned back, his face serious. "Let's just hope it's enough to win the election."

F iona woke to the sound of a Skype call coming in from her laptop. Only one person in the world used Skype to reach her, and she leaped from bed to her desk instantly awake.

The strange glunking sound—like an electronic frog—responded to her click, and there was Pete, his face slightly distorted by the camera.

"Hi," he said.

"Hi," said Fiona, trying without success to tame her sleep hair with one hand.

"Sorry to call in the middle of the night, but it was now or never."

"I like now."

"Me too."

"Where are you?"

"Tsingdao."

"Have you been arrested yet?"

"Don't even joke about it. Nothing in China is private, you know. Have you been elected yet?"

"Not yet. But there's been a development."

"You have my full attention."

Chapter Twenty-Four ❖

There were growing rumors about some strange goings-on at Ground Zero. At first the stories seemed so unlikely that they were brushed aside by local residents. But when the 7:00 am customers began arriving to a full parking lot, and when earlier arrivals happened to glance in the windows, all doubts were dispelled.

The growing yoga practice at Ground Zero had unforeseen consequences. The post-yoga coffee crowd had brought a significant increase in Ground Zero's bottom line, so much so that finding a seat on most mornings was nearly impossible from six until nine o'clock. Out of necessity—and against his principles—Roger began to stock to-go cups, lids, and disposable stirrers, and had to set up a separate table for milk, sugar, and cardboard sleeves, just to keep the flow of people from clogging the space around the counter.

Along with the general astonishment that Roger—of all people—might countenance this sort of group activity in his establishment, came the news that some of the area's most solid citizens were participating. Gerald Barker of the County Board, Larry Sommer, head of the Chamber of Commerce, and the entire men's prayer group of St. Johann's Lutheran Church had all been seen doing yoga at Ground Zero.

Doctor Sam Abramson was asked his views on the subject,

and he further astonished all within earshot by declaring it a damn good thing that might lower the mean blood pressure readings of the entire county. Not to mention making a few people less cranky. Not mentioning any names.

As the participants in Ground Zero's yoga practice increased, there began to arise a growing list of complaints from the community. There were too many cars; sweaty men in a restaurant were a health hazard; no license had been granted—or, for that matter, even existed—for such activity.

These complaints inspired visits from multiple government entities, but the results were not all that opponents might wish.

The City Inspector declared that the capacity of the building had not been exceeded. The practice of yoga, after all, required that each participant have a certain amount of space around him, so the size of the meetings was self-regulated. Those who didn't fit simply left, or lingered outside until someone else did.

The Health Department determined that there was no code violation, and unfortunately, in the inspector's opinion, sweat was not something that could be regulated. That the gentlemen had bare feet may have been undesirable in a place where food was served, but it was neither illegal, nor against code. Just a bit… icky. *Caveat Emptor.*

Meanwhile, news of the men's yoga group had been spreading beyond the peninsula. Men in search of yoga camaraderie were beginning to travel from Green Bay, and even Madison and Chicago. The resulting traffic and commerce—not to mention the increasing difficulty in getting a place to park at Ground Zero—were becoming a bit of a local headache.

Supporters of Ground Zero were quick to point out the boon

to the local economy that came from the growing celebrity of Ephraim's coffee shop and yoga gathering spot. For local restaurants and inns, business at this time of year had never been better. Some of them had opened early—long before the usual May beginning of the season—in order to accommodate demand.

A certain yogic theme began to emerge in local marketing, with emphasis on relaxation, organic foods, and a surfeit of lavender-scented everything. The impact of these extra weeks on the bottom line of Ephraim's businesses—and, as the popularity grew, on the entire area—could not be overstated.

Chapter Twenty-Five

Ben lay in his bed, waiting for his mother to call him to get up. From the moment he had awakened and seen the strange reflected light on his bedroom wall, he had been wreathed in the joy of a new snowfall. The world would be transformed for as long as the snow lasted. Ben could not have explained exactly why he loved this transformation, except to say that it was beautiful. The adults around him would grumble and complain about the long winter and the slow spring, but Ben loved the snow, no matter what time of year it was. He loved, too, that the snow gave him more obvious clues to the locations of his animals, and he was excited to see what they had been up to.

All of Ben's school day was colored by the presence of the snow outside the classroom windows. When at last the bell rang, he was like a homing device, purely focused on the preparations to mount his expedition. He gathered his things, made perfunctory farewells, and headed out.

An April snowstorm. Pali, who ordinarily loved winter weather, was finding he didn't have the heart for it lately. He was tired of the struggle: the shoveling, the ice, the heavy clothes, the boots, the hats, the gloves and the heating bills. This unusually late spring had left nearly intact the ice fields on the lake, and it made the crossings longer and more tedious, and for Pali now, all pleasure had gone out of his daily routine. Everything was dull, gray, and joyless. He knew what was bothering him wasn't the weather, but he tried not to think about it.

The snow had stopped, but there was a biting wind, and the clouds were heavy and blue, with the look of more to come. There had been quite a bit of chop on the lake today, too, and combined with the jolts from the ice, it would be easier for things to shift on the way over. The cold felt as if it went straight into a man's bones. Pali looked at his watch. Ten minutes to departure. He needed to double-check some fastenings before they headed out.

At precisely five p.m. the ferry began its slow turn away from Northport, toward the open water and home.

The strait between the tip of Door County and Washington Island is the notorious Death's Door Passage, so named for the long history of shipwrecks and maritime disasters dating at least as far back as to when Wisconsin was Indian country. The strait connects Green Bay to the southern part of Lake Michigan, and Door County's name derives from it. It has shallow shoals to catch at ships and a propensity for brewing sudden, violent storms. Pali knew all this, but Death's Door was home territory, and he traversed it many times a day. He had seen some rough waters, and he did not trivialize the storms that rolled up without warning. But he had good sense, experience, modern equipment, and a sailor's stoicism, enhanced by the Nordic calm of his forebears. He took stock of his instruments, the sky, and the waters, and judged that his ferry would be safe.

But he had lost the small surge of joy he had always felt see-ing the Island there on the horizon. Pali squared his shoulders and shifted his hands on the wheel. He would have to learn to find his path in this new gray existence. The wind and snow bat-tered the ferry all the way home.

Nika was not a worrier. She knew her son and his little ways, and, despite his recent secretiveness, they had an under-standing about his after-school wanderings. She did not take se-riously the rumors about some lunatic wandering the island, and although she was troubled by her husband's fears solely on his account, she refused to believe in evil spirits. Ten years without incident had, perhaps, given her a certain amount of compla-cency about her son's good sense, but despite the lack of human threats, Nika knew well enough that the island had its share of the other kind.

At this time of year, her biggest concern was ice. Even the most experienced outdoorsman could misjudge the soundness of ice over open water, and she had made a habit of reminding their intrepid boy of the need to avoid all water crossings until his father had investigated and given his approval.

Ben was well aware of his parents' strictures, and had al-ways respected their authority. He understood that icy water was deadly. Hypothermia and the prospect of being trapped beneath the ice were the topics of many dinner table conversations. The lake, in particular, was off-limits at this time of year. The lure of its beauty, however, with its ice floes and crackling waves, and the inviting appearance of solidity, with open space to walk where no one walked at any other time, was often hard for a boy to resist.

Ben's paths through the woods often took him along the bluffs above the shoreline. He liked this route, because it afforded him a view of the horizon to the north and west, while keeping him among the shelter of trees and the activities of the woods. He noticed birds, and admired the eagles, owls, and vultures, but mammals were his primary interest, and they, too, had the sense to avoid the lake in winter. He had once seen a fox playing with her kits near the waves, but that had been in the heat of August, not in winter, when the waves carried blocks of ice that could crush a living thing, or worse, push it beneath the water.

It was this path that Ben had chosen today. He guessed that the foxes would be out to play in the snow, and their trust in him—which had been hard-won with months of patience and offerings of food—meant that they would allow him near to watch. He was, of course, also looking for his friend.

In addition to the food for his friend, he had carefully saved the crusts of his peanut butter sandwich from lunch for the foxes, and had a reserve of dog biscuits he kept in his backpack for such occasions. His mother had discovered this recently, along with copious evidence of mice in their back hall. After a sigh, an affectionate shake of the head, and vast quantities of bleach, she had replaced his backpack and its contents. Now instead of a worn, mouse-eaten, plastic bag, Ben's supply of dog/fox biscuits were stored in a brand new green metal box with a tightly-fitted lid. It rattled a bit when he walked, but it gave Ben a great deal of secret satisfaction, knowing that he was prepared for a chance meeting. Along with his pocketknife, this was his most important tool. His mother's discovery had given him some anxiety, but she had not seemed to think anything was out of the ordinary.

The new-fallen snow had obliterated his footprints from the weeks before, but the path he had broken was clearly discernable. There were deer and turkey paths, too, which crossed his route, and they had already seen some use today. It was not cold for a Door County spring, only in the twenties, and Ben felt hot inside his down parka. He pushed the hood off so he could feel the air, and hear what was going on around him.

A woodpecker was busy in the tops of the trees, and a red squirrel chucked angrily from somewhere nearby—probably at Ben. He stopped and slowly turned in a circle, looking up. The woods were filled with movement. A slow wind circled overhead. Snow fell from trees, birds and squirrels chirped and pecked, and Ben listened to see if he could discern the short snorting breath of deer anywhere nearby. They had been studying Wisconsin history in school, and he had read of the tracking skills of the Potawatomi, the Ho-Chunk, and the Menominee Indians. He was trying to teach himself to pay attention to the little things in the woods as the Indians were said to have done. He wished he knew an Indian who could teach him. His father had told him that he had a friend who was Potawatomi. Maybe he would know. Ben made a mental note to ask.

It was as he was standing still in the woods, teaching himself to observe, that Ben heard a sound he had never heard before.

It was a cry of terror that chilled him to the core of his soul, and that continued, with rising panic, resonating even in the snow-deadened air. Without pausing to think, Ben turned and ran toward the sound, down the rough, snow-covered pine path, past the ravine where the creek ran, and over the short, rocky bluff, down the rocks toward the lake.

Chapter Twenty-Six ✣

Running, Ben followed the sound to the beach. The water seemed to be ice-covered, but the weather had been fluctuating between winter and spring, and Ben knew that the appearance of solidity was potentially deadly. There were mounds of ice thrown up against the beach like sand dunes, and black pools of open water surrounded by deadly ice—either thick or thin, no one knew until he was under. Some of the pools were springs feeding into the lake; the weakest ice, and the most dangerous.

The sound was coming from there.

Suddenly Ben knew that voice. He knew that it was perilous to go out by himself. He also knew that if he did not, the sound would subside forever beneath the water.

Ben knew his father's stern principle: "You don't sacrifice your life for an animal." But he did not heed. He could not. This animal was afraid, and it trusted him. He owed something to that trust, and if he betrayed it, he would be diminished under Heaven.

He opened his back pack and grabbed the rope he still carried, and scanned the beach for a slim, long log, which he found quickly. Speaking to the animal in the best combination he could manage of volume and comfort, he readied himself. He put the rope around his waist, and fastened it to a birch tree, which was the closest he could find to the water. His rope was not long, and it did not reach. Impatiently he ripped it away from himself and ran toward the water dragging his log.

With a steady hand, he pushed the log out, in as solid a fashion as he could, and slid out on his belly along the log. The frantic animal was kicking with its feet, and Ben feared that he would be injured by the flailing limbs. To his relief, the animal recognized him and when Ben put his two arms out to grasp its front feet, it stopped struggling and allowed him to pull it toward him. With all his strength Ben grasped and pulled, until, at last, the soaking, shivering creature lay panting next to him on the ice.

Soaking wet himself, and shaking, Ben threw his coat over the creature, and then his own sweatshirt. He spoke soothingly and gently pulled it in safety to the rocky beach. It was injured, he thought. Its rear leg.

It was after five o'clock, and Nika was worried. His habits had been shifting over the past few months, but Ben was always home before now, so long after dark on a cold afternoon. If nothing else, his ten-year-old appetite drove him home in time for supper. She knew that the spring snow would have drawn him to his favorite trails. But what could he see at this hour? And which trails had he chosen? With an outward calm she did not feel, she stood at the kitchen window in the last light, scanning the field from which Ben usually emerged, hoping to see his red jacket popping out against the snow. There was no sign of him.

It was too early to panic, or to ask for help, but something told her that things were not as they should be. Ben had never been late like this. Never. Something wasn't right.

As she scribbled a note and pulled on her down parka, their yellow lab, Sugar, eagerly rose from her place by the fire and stood by the door wagging her tail. Nika looked at the dog for a moment, hesitating, and then made her decision. "Do you want to come, Sugar? Do you want to come find Ben?" Sugar ran to the door and stood looking back at Nika and wagging her tail.

The dog would be company, and a comfort in her anxiety.

"Come on, then," said Nika. She zipped her cell phone carefully into an inner pocket, and opened the door to let the dog precede her. Taking a deep breath, she closed the door on the warm kitchen and headed out toward the woods.

Nika hadn't gone far when Sugar began to bark excitedly. Joyously, the dog ran ahead on the darkened path in the woods. Relief flooding through her, Nika followed as fast as she could, burdened with boots and nearly a foot of snow. Coming toward her, she could see the outline of her son in the dusk.

"Ben!" she shouted. "Ben! Are you all right?"

"Mom!" His voice sounded tearful and frightened. They met and she clutched him in her arms. His parka was missing, he was soaking wet and shivering violently, weeping with fear and relief.

"Come on," said Nika quickly. "Let's get you home right now. Sugar! Come on, we're going home."

She wished she could still carry him, but instead she stripped off the sodden shirt, pulled off her own parka, and stuffed him into it, zipping the collar up tight and pulling the hood over his face.

"Now run, Ben. As fast as you can go. Get into the house. I'll be right behind you."

"Mom," he said, reluctantly.

"Do as I say. NOW."

He ran raggedly the mile or so toward the house, Sugar leading the way. Nika followed clumsily, but swiftly, fueled by the adrenaline of fear and anger.

Once they were safely in the house, Nika sent Ben to soak in a hot bath, and went to her own room to change her clothes. She was shaking now, too, not from cold, but from adrenaline withdrawal. Wrapping herself in her warmest bathrobe, she went to the dining room and poured herself a sliver of brandy. She stood at the window, looking out at the moonlit fields as she held her glass. She was, she thought to herself, a lucky—no—an extremely lucky woman.

"Skal," she whispered to herself, and drank it all down.

Later that night, Nika and Pali lay in bed discussing Ben's adventure. "He says he got too near the creek bed, and slipped when he wasn't looking down."

Nika's voice was calm now, but she could not retell the story without a quiver of fear running through her.

"We don't have any reason to doubt him," said Pali. "He's a good boy, and accidents like these help to shape a young man. It will teach him that bad things can happen, and you have to be careful." Pali had a father's skill for remote analysis.

Nika nodded in the darkness.

"I was so scared, Ver." She rarely used his given name, calling him Pali, as everyone else did, except when she was being serious.

Her husband rolled over and put his arms around her.

"He's safe now, Nika. That's all that counts."

But Nika lay awake all night, running through the terrifying alternative scenarios over and over in her mind.

In his own room, Ben too was sleepless, and for his own reasons. Ben had never lied to his parents; never even felt a need to. The fairy tales he had been fed like mother's milk from the time he was very small had taught him the code of knights, and princes, shepherd boys, and honest miller's sons: tell the truth; do your duty; and be kind, because you never knew who was a fairy or elf in disguise. But when his mother, her face serious and sad, asked him to tell her where he had been and why he had disobeyed her rules about going near the water, Ben looked her in the eye, and without a moment of doubt or hesitation, had lied to her face.

He could not explain to himself why he had done it. Not exactly. Except that he felt a protective instinct he could not ignore. His conscience hurt him, and he saw, in his mind's eye, his mother's sad face. It wasn't that he had told the lie that hurt so much. It was that she had believed him.

And now that he had told it once, he was going to have to tell it again, and again, and again.

Chapter Twenty-Seven

F iona was standing in the ruins of an old barn on a hill-side with vistas across great expanses of rolling hills. The roof was gone, but the stone walls were still standing, and hanging along the walls was a collection of paintings by a great artist. She knew they were his, and yet she had never seen them before, and the style was a bold departure for him. She was gazing at them when suddenly she realized that the artist was standing beside her, and they were friends. Other people she knew vaguely were there too, and Pete. They wandered then, along the hills, and the group dispersed. It was sunset. She wanted to see the paintings again, when suddenly the artist appeared, inviting her to come to see some other paintings in a different place.

"Let's play!" he said, and suddenly he dropped to the ground and rolled down the hill and under a bush, and was leaping like an animal through the countryside toward, Fiona knew, another barn filled with his art. She followed him, leaping and rolling as he did, and Pete did, too. She realized then that the artist had become a fox, and they followed him gaily. All at once, there was an explosion and the sky filled with light. The artist fox pointed at the horizon. She knew that the fire was his paintings, and she stood, alone and unmoved, watching the red glow along the sky. She felt no fear of loss or remorse. She knew that the paintings would be unharmed.

Fiona awoke to the silence of the house. It was pre-dawn, and one bird sang rather tentatively. There was a cool breeze through the open window, but it was warm under the covers, and she didn't want to move. She lay listening to the bird as others joined him and light slowly crept along the edge of the sky. There was a change beginning in the birdsong. It was a difference in tone and quality, brought on by the addition of newly-migrated voices. Though cold, the breeze was sweet. Even after a heavy snowstorm, it almost seemed like spring.

But it was far too early for spring on the island, where April—and even May—snowstorms were not uncommon, and spring was a long season of mud and disappointment. Today was instead a small offering of hope after the fast-melting snow; an indication that winter would not last forever, and that, whatever else might change, the turn of the seasons would go on despite the shifts in human purpose.

Feeling this, but not as a conscious thought, Fiona urged herself from bed and padded barefoot down to the kitchen for some coffee. She was in a playful mood after her dream: relaxed and optimistic, until a sudden realization struck her with the thud of emotional force. Today was the election.

Fiona spent the day in a state of mixed agitation and resignation. She had done all she could. She had gone beyond what she had thought she could. Now it was out of her hands. It was up to the voters—her friends, neighbors, and otherwise—to determine whether she would stay on the Island, or leave, humiliated.

Even as she thought this, she questioned whether it were true. Supposing, for the moment, that she lost the election. Would she really allow herself to be driven from her home? Or would she stay and fight, only—she reminded herself—to meet an even more ignominious fate? Fiona thought through the specific and most likely ways that Stella could make her life a misery. It was a clear and vivid picture. She had to admit: there didn't seem to be much hope.

This mental turmoil began to take its toll, and late in the day, she had accomplished nothing except worry.

She would not be alone for the night's ordeal. Terry, his wife Anne, Mike, and his wife Ella were coming; and Elisabeth and Roger were arriving on the last ferry to offer moral support. The house was ready. She had already voted. There was no need to get to the town hall until the polls closed. Fiona still had hours of uncertainty left, and nothing to do.

Resolutely turning her mind from her troubles, she put on her warm sheepskin jacket to cut the wind, and struck off for the fields.

Fiona had chosen a different route from her usual one, hoping that the change would engage her mind a bit more. She walked, today, along the road, heading north through the interior of the Island. There was never much traffic to speak of, and here there were more open fields and sky to rest her soul. There was still snow piled along the sides of the roads, but it had melted on the fields, and they were a rich golden color, sharply contrasted against the blue of the sky.

She had reached the western edge of the Martins' place, and knowing she had their permission, she cut through toward the wooded trails she knew. She was looking down to avoid the worst of the mud when, to her surprise, she heard a voice.

"Ms. Campbell! Ms. Campbell! Over here!"

It was Nika and Pali's boy, Ben. Nika had often spoken of his wanderings with a mixture of affection, pride, and worry, but Fiona had never encountered him on one of her walks before. She waved and obligingly shifted her path in his direction.

Fiona couldn't know that Ben saw her in this moment as the answer to his many hurried prayers. For months now, he had been longing for an adult to ask, to confide in, and now he realized, all at once, that she was the perfect person. Ms. Campbell would be sympathetic and she wouldn't scold. He also knew instinctively that she wasn't like the other adults he knew, even if he couldn't exactly say why.

He ran to meet her, and after a brief exchange of greetings they stood gazing at one another with nothing much to say.

Ben looked up trustingly into Fiona's eyes, and she could see in him his father's steady warmth. Ben liked Fiona. He suddenly realized that one of the reasons she was different was that he could sense her respect for him, something few adults expressed toward a child.

"I have a secret," he said solemnly.

Fiona studied his face. He was a remarkable boy, and he would probably grow up to be a perfect Island man: steady, reliable, kind, capable, and just a tiny bit mystical. She felt a twinge of envy for the life he would have, and of how much he had left of it.

"Secrets are important things," she said, seriously.

"Would you come to see it?" His voice was insistent, and his eyes pleading.

Fiona hesitated. What kind of adventure would she be committing to?

It was getting late. The ferry would be arriving soon, and

she didn't have much time before she would be expected at the town hall. But the boy's trust in her and his urgency made her know she had to say yes.

She chose her words carefully. "I would. If you would like me to."

Without a pause, Ben began to trot off into the field. "We'd better hurry," he called over his shoulder. "It will be dark soon."

And shivering a little, Fiona shoved her hands into the pockets of her sheepskin jacket and followed him, jogging a bit unsteadily on the rough ground, the boy's figure only a shadow against the rutted yellow grass as the dusk came on.

At the town hall, members of the community were already gathering to witness the vote counting. Most people felt they had done their duty when they voted and were content to wake up in the morning and wander over to Mann's for the results. Those who showed up for the counting were the stalwarts and busy bodies, and possibly, thought Jake, people whose televisions weren't working. Jake stole a glance over at Stella, who was glowering, alone in the corner.

He shivered and whispered in Pali's ear. "Snakes," he said.

"What?" asked Pali, startled. He had been lost in thought.

"In her hair," said Jake. "Who was the witch who had snakes instead of hair?"

In spite of himself, Pali laughed silently. He tilted his head toward Jake and whispered, still laughing.

"Medusa," he said. "She wasn't a witch. She was a Gorgon. One look into her eyes turned men into stone."

"Close enough," said Jake.

F iona followed Ben on a path that led along the northern edge of the island, on a rock bluff that was sometimes thirty feet and sometimes only three or four feet above the water. It was an old path, possibly even an ancient one, and occasionally there were the ruins of old log cabins, long abandoned. Fiona did not know this part of the island well. She was fairly certain that it was private land, but this was not a moment to worry about details. Ben seemed skittish, and she didn't want to dissuade him from whatever he was embarked upon.

There had been silence for most of their journey, with Ben leading the way, and Fiona behind. It wasn't easy to hold a conversation this way, and Fiona was content with her own observations. She was worried about being late to the election festivities, but a part of her was relieved to be away from it all. This excursion with Ben felt like real life. The rest was just… she struggled for the right word and failed. But it was a waste of energy, whatever it was.

"We're almost there," Ben called back over his shoulder, and he broke into a trot. After fifty yards, or so, he suddenly turned and disappeared off the path into a clump of brush.

Fiona trailed behind, noting the path through the crusty spring snow. The boy had come here frequently through the winter, and probably even earlier today. The path led to the remains of a cabin. The roof was gone, and there wasn't much left of the walls, but there was some shelter from what was still there. It didn't look terribly safe to Fiona, but, gamely, she followed him in.

Immediately, Fiona was struck by a familiar smell. Ben was kneeling, bending over a filthy animal that had been covered with a red parka.

The animal's coat was matted with mud and burs. He lay in a pile of leaves and pine branches that had been hacked, rather than cut, from nearby trees. There was an old metal bucket with water, now frozen solid, and a blue plastic bowl with food, but both looked untouched. The red down parka, now quite dirty, was placed over his chest. The animal's yellow eyes were clouded, and his leg was splinted and bandaged, but it was at a frightening angle, and he must be in tremendous pain. He followed her movements with his eyes.

Fiona gasped, and knelt down next to Ben. "Robert!" she said. She reached her hand out to touch his nose, but he did not respond.

Fiona looked down at the injured animal and then at Ben. "Where did you find him?"

"He was in the lake. He almost drowned, but I heard him screaming, and I dragged him out."

"You dragged him out?" Fiona was amazed. "When was this?" she asked urgently. "When did this happen?"

Ben looked down. "Yesterday. After the snow."

"But why didn't you tell someone? Why didn't you get some help?"

Ben began to cry. "I thought they would shoot him. I thought they would make me kill him."

Fiona was silent for a moment. "What made you change your mind? What made you come to find me?"

"He isn't getting better. I think his leg really hurts. I couldn't fix it."

Fiona nodded and put her hand on the boy's shoulder.

Ben looked at the ground.

"I thought he was a deer and I was going to save him. I thought he had a broken leg. But then I saw him, and he liked me." Much of this story made no sense to Fiona, but she was silent, letting him get it out.

Ben was grief-stricken, and the tears poured down his face as he spilled out his confession. "He came and went wherever he wanted. But he always came back."

He looked up at Fiona. Ben didn't know how to explain what it had meant to have this secret, something that was entirely his own. He didn't know how to express the happiness it had given him. He couldn't explain even to himself how bad it felt now to realize he had done wrong. His heart felt split in his chest. It hurt desperately. The world was a different place.

"I first saw him in the fall. I didn't mean to do anything wrong."

Fiona looked into his troubled face. "You didn't do anything wrong, Ben."

Her answer didn't seem to comfort him. Now that he had begun, he couldn't stop telling his story. All the emotion of the long-kept secret poured out of him.

"I wasn't supposed to do it. I wasn't supposed to go into the lake alone. Not on the ice." He shuffled aimlessly at the dry leaves on the ground. "My mom and dad told me never to." Ben looked pleadingly into Fiona's face, then dropped his gaze again to the leaves.

Fiona took a breath and nodded.

"Well, we have to tell someone now. He is very sick." She looked at the stricken boy. "It's all right, Ben. You did a good thing in bringing me here."

Ben nodded, still staring at the ground. "I think his leg really hurts him," he said, softly, urgently.

Fiona patted him on the shoulder as she reached into her pocket for her cell phone. She hoped to God there would be a signal here, on the northern edge of the Island. As the ringing started, she knelt down and stroked Robert's dirty flank.

"Do you think he can walk on three legs?" she asked Ben over her shoulder, as she waited for the phone to be answered.

Ben shook his head slowly. "No. He's been lying here since yesterday. He won't get up."

Fiona nodded without speaking, and at this moment she heard a breathless voice answering the phone.

"Hello?"

"Jim? It's Fiona. Where are you? I need your help."

It took only a moment for Jim to figure out approximately where they were and agree to come. Fiona hung up and tucked the phone back into her pocket. She put both hands on the ragged, smelly snout and forehead, as the yellow eyes closed in acquiescence. Fiona sat in the filthy leaves, and stared down at the animal's face.

"It's okay, Robert," she said. "It's going to be okay." Two drops of water splashed onto his cheek, and as she reached to brush them away, Fiona realized that they were her tears. "This is a fine thing," she thought. "Why am I'm always crying over Robert?"

lisabeth and Roger and the others arrived at five-forty-five to find the house open, but no Fiona.

Elisabeth, who knew Fiona well, was unfazed. "She probably went for a walk to calm down. Let's just settle in and wait for her to get back."

She showed the guests to their rooms, and went to the kitchen where she knew she would find a bottle of wine to open.

t was nearly half an hour before Fiona and Ben heard the sound of an engine, and Jim's voice calling through the woods. It was getting dark.

"We're over here!" they both shouted in unison, and through a series of these communications, Jim was soon with them, driving along a parallel trail further back in the woods, in an official State All Terrain Vehicle. Jim wasted no time in entering the cabin, and he, too, knelt in the mud to peer at the injured animal. Fiona felt as if they were in some odd version of a nativity scene.

"He does not look good," said Jim after a moment, with a

professional's understatement.

"What do you think we can do?" asked Fiona, casting a quick look over at Ben's face.

"Not sure. He's got an infection, or pneumonia, maybe, or both. And if he won't walk with that leg... ." Jim frowned.

"He's in pain," Fiona said.

"You can tell that by looking at him," said Ben. "You can tell he doesn't feel right."

Jim nodded.

"Will he be okay?" asked Ben, voicing the question Fiona had avoided for fear of upsetting him.

Jim took a deep breath. He was an honest man, and did not believe in sugarcoating the truth, even for children. "He might not. If it's a bacterial infection it might have gotten too much hold of his system; he may not be able to fight it." Jim stood up briskly. "We don't have a lot of time to stand around. Let's get him out of here while we can still see." He looked at the serious boy standing beside him. "Ben, go get the backpack on my seat. We'll have to make a sling to lift him."

Jim and Fiona were silent looking down at the sick animal. There was no vet on the Island. The closest was Dr. Amy Wilson in Sister Bay, a ferry ride with another ten-mile drive. And there were no more ferries tonight.

Jim broke the silence. "This is not going to be easy," he said quietly. "But if you want me to, I can shoot him."

Fiona swallowed and nodded. "Thank you, Jim. I understand. But I want to try. I want to try to save him."

Jim looked down at her face and felt the surge of emotions he had been working so hard to repress these past months. He would do almost anything for her, but he would not allow an animal to suffer needlessly.

"This isn't about you," he said, at last. "You have to do what's right for the animal."

Fiona lifted her head and looked at him. She was serious and dry-eyed. "I promise you, Jim, this is not about me. But I believe—and I think you do, too—that animals have souls. We shouldn't waste a life."

Jim held her glance for a moment and nodded.

"All right. I'm in. Let's see if we can get him through the night."

Ben returned, and together the three of them gently rolled the animal in the blanket that Jim had unpacked, and wrapped him securely. Jim made sure that he was tied into the blanket so he couldn't wriggle loose and hurt himself further. Robert was too sick to resist. He simply lay wherever they placed him and closed his eyes.

Jim turned his attention to how to arrange transport. He pulled two life jackets from the storage compartment and arranged them into a bed across the back of the vehicle, using duct tape and bungee cords.

"Never go anywhere without duct tape, Ben," he said smiling for the first time. "You never know when it's going to come in handy."

Fiona smiled a little, too.

"My dad says that all the time," said Ben. "He keeps rolls of it in the pilot house."

"I'm going to see if I can get a little closer so we don't have to carry him so far."

Fiona and Ben stood back as he maneuvered the ATV into place.

"Okay," said Jim at last. "You're both going to have to help lift him. We'll put him sideways along the back, like this. See?" Fiona and Ben nodded.

"Now, he's going to be heavy. You two stand on that side, and I'll take this one. Are you ready? On three. One, two, three, lift!"

Robert was remarkably light, and they managed to get him gently onto the life jackets. Jim began to tie Robert into position so he couldn't fall.

"Okay, you two, better start running." Jim climbed onto the ATV and looked back at Fiona. "Where do you want to take him?"

"Call Nancy. Take him there. She has livestock. She'll know what to do."

"Okay. I'll meet you there."

He lifted his hand in farewell, but he didn't look back as he drove away, much more slowly and carefully than when he had arrived.

"Okay, Ben," said Fiona. "You heard the man. Let's go." And together they headed back down the path where they had come, Ben tearing off ahead, and Fiona jogging doggedly behind, trying to keep from stumbling in the dark.

The mood in the room was somber and tense as the town clerk began to tally the votes. Since there was only one precinct and fewer than 450 votes cast, this would not be a lengthy process.

Terry looked at Elisabeth. "Where is Fiona?" he whispered.

"I don't know," she whispered back. "I've called her cell phone half a dozen times and she's not answering."

"This is a little strange."

"I know," said Elisabeth. "I'm getting worried."

When Fiona finally reached Nancy's, Ben and Jim had already arrived. The ATV was parked in front of the barn, so she went directly there.

The barn smelled of healthy animals and hay. The door was open to the last stall, and Nancy, Jim, and Ben were there, with Robert on a bed of straw, still wrapped in the blanket.

"I keep antibiotics on hand, because you never know," said Nancy without greeting. "We already gave him a shot, so if infection is his problem, it should start working pretty quickly."

"What about his leg?" asked Fiona.

"Broken," said Nancy matter-of-factly. "I'll take a look at it when we've got him more settled, but antibiotics should work on that, too, in case it's infected."

"Is it serious?" asked Ben.

"Could be. Hard to say. I'm not a vet." Nancy looked at Ben for the first time.

"You say you found him?" Her blue eyes searched his face.

Fiona jumped in quickly. "Ben came to get me so we could decide what to do." She turned and smiled encouragingly at the boy, breaking uncharacteristically into ungrammatical speech. "He did good. Which reminds me, Ben. Your mom's going to be worried."

"That's okay. I already called her before you came. She's coming to pick me up." He looked up at Fiona. "Can I stay?"

Fiona looked at him, with the look of mild apology and doubt that adults give children about other people's rules. "That's up to your mom. It's okay with me."

Nancy was made of sterner stuff. "We'll be here all night, and you have to go to school in the morning. Go home with your mother." She saw his crestfallen face and took pity on him. "You stop by around three-thirty tomorrow afternoon," she said in a kinder voice. "We should have news for you by then." She turned and looked at Fiona.

"And shouldn't you be at the hall?"

"Oh my God!" cried Fiona. "The election!"

Chapter Twenty-Eight ❖

With all eyes on her, the town clerk continued the process of counting out loud. The assistant sat nearby keeping the tally.

"DesRosiers. DesRosiers. Campbell. Campbell. Campbell. DesRosiers. Campbell. DesRosiers. DesRosiers. Des-Rosiers. Campbell. Campbell. DesRosiers... ."

Pali sighed and looked at his watch. Less than an hour—if they were lucky—and the Island's future would be determined.

At this moment, Fiona burst into the room, bringing with her the smell of barn. Her boots and jeans muddy, her hair was wind-blown. All eyes but those of the two clerks turned to her. Pali couldn't help noticing that her wild appearance did not harm her looks. Stella's eyes narrowed into thin slits and she sniffed pointedly.

"Where have you been?" hissed Elisabeth. "I've been calling you all night. And by the way, you stink."

"Sorry. Long story. My phone battery died. What's happening?"Terry leaned over. "Final count nearly finished."

Fiona merely nodded and said nothing. She was wrung of emotion. Silently she sat next to Pali on one of the folding metal chairs arranged along the wall, her mind and heart elsewhere. The others, having been there now for hours, were restless and fidgety.

The clerk and her assistant began whispering together and comparing their tallies. The rest of the room drew a collective breath and waited to hear their announcement. Everyone, that is, except Stella.

"What are you whispering about?" she demanded. "This is public business. You have to tell us what is going on."

The clerk ignored her, and continued her conversation with the assistant. After a moment she turned to the rest of the room.

"We have reviewed the tallies," she announced with great dignity, "and believe we have a discrepancy. We will count again."

Jake groaned loudly, expressing the feelings of them all. Stella made a stage-whispered remark about incompetence.

And the counting began again.

Chapter Twenty-Nine

"Campbell, Campbell, DesRosiers, Campbell, Campbell, Campbell DesRosiers, DesRosiers… " The droning of the voices had a soporific effect, and Fiona found herself beginning to doze. Each time her head fell she was jerked awake, and embarrassed to think that someone might have seen. She looked furtively around the room, and saw that Jake, too, was falling asleep. Stella, wide awake, glared from across the room, her lips in a sneer that reminded Fiona of the impounded car. This thought, at least, she found cheering.

The clerk looked up at last from the numbers and turned to her assistant who was finishing his separate tally at the same time. They exchanged glances and then the clerk turned resignedly to her waiting audience.

"It's a tie," she said.

"That can't be right," said Stella immediately. "Count them again."

The clerk took a deep breath and stood. She was not a particularly brave woman, but she knew her job.

"We already have two counts," she said, with quiet authority. "We will need to count again, but not tonight. Tomorrow we will have a recount."

The room was silent. Even Stella said nothing.

Under all watchful eyes, the ballots were locked in the vault, and both the clerk and her deputy placed their seals on the door. This might be a small municipality, but its principals took their duties seriously.

After the seals were signed, the clerk turned to address the little group. Although she had never faced this situation before, formality, she knew, was the only way to keep order in this kind of circumstance. Even Stella, with her face of cold fury, was forced to bow to protocol. Here, in this room, and for this moment, the clerk ruled.

"We will meet here again tomorrow morning at nine a.m., at which point we will consult town ordinance on how to proceed. Good night, everyone."

The clerk said this firmly, dismissing the candidates and observers. It had been a long night, and she wanted to go home.

Respectfully silent as they left the room, everyone began talking once they hit the parking lot. Fiona's group stood around her to hear her story. Pali waited to listen, but afterward would not stay longer. He was anxious to get home and see Ben.

As they were walking toward the cars Fiona whispered to Elisabeth.

"Do I really stink?"

Elisabeth gave her a long-suffering glance. "You take a shower. I'll fix the drinks."

"I can't. I'm sorry to abandon you, but I want to get back to the barn. I'll come with you, though, to get my car."

"Do you want company?"

Fiona hesitated a moment. "No. But thanks. You go play hostess for me. You're better at it than I am, anyway."

As she entered the barn, Fiona found Jim still there with Nancy. Their patient lay motionless on a pile of straw. In his misery he looked like a warrior returning from the field. He had a red bandage around the splint on his leg, and a cone on his head to keep him from chewing off the bandage. He was still dirty and matted, since Nancy had deemed it unwise to add to his current distress with a bath. His eyes were closed and his breathing was slow.

"What's your news?" asked Nancy, her voice unusually low.

"It's a tie."

Nancy nodded, frowning. She was not an outwardly expressive person.

Jim studied Fiona's face. "You okay?"

Fiona smiled weakly. "I'm okay. It never occurred to me that election night events would leave me indifferent to the outcome."

Jim said nothing, but went to get her a wooden stool. She sat gratefully.

Nancy reached into the pocket of her battered barn jacket and withdrew a gleaming, silver flask. "It was my grandfather's," she said, when Jim commented. "These are his initials. I can

remember him on nights like this in the barn taking little nips."
She held up the flask. "I think we could all use a slug."

She took a long swallow and offered the flask to Fiona, who
shook her head.

"I'm sorry. I can't. I'm likely to fall asleep as it is."

Nancy passed the flask to Jim. He lifted it in tribute first to
Nancy, then to Fiona, took a drink, and handed it back to Nancy.

Nancy took another swallow of brandy. "Frankly," she said,
her blue eyes fixed on Fiona, "you look terrible. Why don't you
go home? I have a cot in the corner over there, for these sorts of
occasions, and I'll have a better night without you two hovering
around and whispering. Go on. I'll let you know if anything
changes."

Fiona hesitated.

"Go," said Nancy firmly.

"You'll call me?"

"You'll be the first to know."

Jim stood up. "Okay. We'll leave you to it."

He looked at Nancy. "You let me know if you need anything. I'll hear the phone. I'm a light sleeper."

She nodded, a small wry smile on her face. "Will do."

"Come on, Fiona," said Jim. "You look exhausted. I'll walk
you to your car."

Fiona took a long look at the sleeping animal and allowed
herself to be lead away, Jim's hand on her elbow.

Together they walked down the dirt drive. The moon was
half-full, and the sky was a deep, almost metallic blue. The toe
of Fiona's boot caught a rock and she stumbled. Jim's grip tight-
ened to keep her from falling.

"You sure you're okay to drive? You can't even walk straight." He was smiling.

"I'm fine." She smiled back, a weak, exhausted smile. "Don't worry about me." Even as she spoke she felt the tears begin to fall. She cursed herself. She hated crying. She rarely cried. And she knew instinctively that triggering Jim's sympathy was dangerous. She couldn't let him see. She extricated herself from his grip, and pretended to be looking for her car keys in her pocket. When they reached her car she wanted to make this quick and casual, but he stopped, and taking her arm, turned her to face him. He left his hands on her arms, looking down at her.

"Are you worrying about the election, or about what's going on back there?" he indicated the direction of the barn with his head.

"Both, I guess. But more the latter than the former."

"I can't speak to the outcome of the election," he said. "But I think he's going to be okay. You did the right thing. You made the right decision. You were right to try to save him."

One tear slid down her cheek.

"I couldn't have done it without you. Thank you, Jim. I can never really thank you." She caught herself before her voice broke.

He raised one finger to the tear, wiped it away, and looked into her eyes for a long moment. She saw him waver, then make a decision.

"It's okay," he said, and reaching for the handle of her car door, he opened it and watched her get in. "I'll be here tomorrow in case Nancy needs anything. I'll see you then."

"I have to report to the clerk's office in the morning."

"It doesn't matter, we'll take care of things here."

She started the engine.

"Good night, Jim."

"Good night. And good luck."

She watched him for a moment as he turned and walked back up the hill toward the ATV.

Chapter Thirty

T

he next morning at nine o'clock sharp, following the instructions of the town clerk, the two candidates and their representatives arrived for the recount. In addition to the clerk, Lars Olafsen, the retiring Chairman of the Town Board was there. His decades of steady leadership would lend an authoritative calm to the proceedings. Gradually the rest of the board members began to arrive as well.

Word of the tie had spread to every corner of the island, and as a result there were significantly more spectators than the night before. Folding chairs had been set up yesterday around the perimeters of the room, and when the chairs ran out, people leaned against the walls and doorframes.

The clerk's office was small, and although she had carefully consulted the law about her duties in these extraordinary circumstances, she had omitted to take into consideration the increased number of observers. After a brief conversation with Lars, it was agreed that the recount should be moved to the community room.

The seriousness of the situation did not drive the islanders to stand on ceremony, and in no time the assembled observers were busily setting up the chairs in the usual arrangement for town meetings. When the last chairs had been scraped noisily into position, the clerk, her assistant, and the rest of the Town

Board seated themselves at the long folding tables in the front. Stella and Fiona sat in the front row, but at opposite ends.

The clerk stood to explain the rules.

"Good morning," she began.

"An electoral tie is a rare occurrence. I have consulted the records, and to the best of my knowledge, it has never happened before in the history of the Island. Under Wisconsin law, if the totals are within point-five percent, a recount is automatically triggered. This begins with a canvassing of the precincts: a reporting of the ballot totals in each precinct. In a canvassing, the ballots are not re-counted."

A low buzz of surprise began.

"However," said the clerk loudly, silencing the crowd, "since the Town of Washington has only one precinct, and we have a tie, a re-count is necessary."

She eyed the group severely.

"This is a serious event, and it is incumbent upon us to do everything properly. I will therefore request that the conduct of the observers be serious and respectful. The observers' role is an important one: it is to safeguard the integrity of the process by bearing witness to all that is done."

A smattering of applause began, and the clerk looked over her glasses with disapproval.

"This is not a sporting event. I have the authority to dismiss from the room anyone who is disorderly." She watched to see the effect of her words on the crowd. They sat now in respectful silence.

"We will begin." Returning to her place at the table, she took her seat and opened the lone ballot bag. "DesRosiers, DesRosiers, Campbell, DesRosiers... ."

Elisabeth, holding a yellow legal pad with two columns, kept a careful tally of the votes as they were called out. Fiona, bored out of her suspense and distracted by wondering what was happening at the barn, tried not to slump in her seat.

When the counting finished, the clerk and her assistant tabulator spoke to one another in low voices. Elisabeth nudged Fiona and showed her the legal pad.

The clerk removed her glasses and stood.

"The results are: Stella DesRosiers, 222 votes. Fiona Campbell, 222 votes. We have a tie."

The crowd stirred and a low murmur began, but the clerk continued speaking.

"In such cases, the law calls for a coin toss."

Fiona and Elisabeth exchanged glances.

Stella stood up, outraged. "A coin toss? You can't be serious."

Lars stood up and stepped around to the front of the table. "I can assure you, this is quite proper, and according to law. As outgoing chairman, I will conduct the coin toss."

"That can't be correct," insisted Stella.

Chairman Olafsen looked at her with long-suffering patience. "Election law is available to everyone on the Internet. The point is quite clear. You can check it yourself. Later."

Subtly, but distinctly, he turned his attention away from her.

"We will use this quarter," he said, pulling a coin from his pocket, and turning it to demonstrate that it included both a head and a tail. "Will the candidates please come forward?"

Not quite muttering under her breath, Stella came forward, glowering. Fiona rose from her seat and followed, hoping that her now chattering nerves were not showing.

"Ms. DesRosiers will call. Heads or tails?" asked the chairman, politely.

"Tails—no—heads!" said Stella as Lars flipped the coin into the air, caught it neatly, and slapped it onto the back of his hand.

Irresistibly, Fiona and Stella both leaned in as the outgoing Chairman removed his covering hand to reveal the coin.

"It's tails," said Lars Olafsen, calmly. "Ms. Campbell wins."

The room erupted in cheers from Fiona's friends.

Fiona offered her hand to Stella, and it was refused. Surrounded by her supporters, Fiona left the hall in a wave of triumph.

Stella was conspicuously aloof from the people there who were her voters. Her shoulders were stiff and she seemed to emanate the resentment that was her normal state of being. For one brief moment, Fiona felt pity for her, but she quickly dismissed it. Had the results been different, Stella's ruthlessness would have been unbounded. If Stella had any capacity for pity—which Fiona thoroughly doubted—she would not have shown any.

Dismissing Stella from her thoughts, Fiona gratefully accepted the congratulations of all the observers.

Elisabeth managed to work her way through and gave Fiona a hug. "We're going to leave you to get on with it," she said, smiling. "Roger and I thought we'd go for a little drive before the ferry."

Fiona smiled back. "Things are good?"

"Yes," said Elisabeth simply. "They are."

S chool that day was a torment for Ben. Normally attentive in class, he had to be reprimanded three times by his favorite teacher, Ms. Larson.

He did not know the answer to a simple question about American History, he didn't finish a test in the time allotted, and he daydreamed through the explanation of a new concept in Math. By the end of the day, Ms. Larson was exasperated.

"Ben, if you don't put your head on straight, I'm going to have to ask you to stay after school."

"Sorry," said Ben, humbly. Staying was the last thing he wanted.

When at last the day was over, he burst from the school doors, and was shocked to see his mother's SUV waiting there.

"Mom," he said, in greeting. "What are you doing here?"

"I came to take you home," said Nika. "I think maybe we've been letting you run a little wild, young man."

Ben's heart fell. "But I can't!" he cried. "Mom! I have to go to the barn. I have to see if Robert's okay!"

Nika was silent, considering. They were reaching a cross-roads with Ben. She needed to be careful to keep him talking, and to make their restrictions sensible. There was no reason not to go to the barn. He had rescued the animal, after all. And besides, she was eager herself to find out more about what had happened. She smiled at Ben.

"Let's go together."

He knew better than to argue. Reluctantly, Ben got into the truck, and they headed up the road to Nancy's.

Fiona was there when they arrived. The vet had come. The goat was clean and newly bandaged, lying in fresh straw, and sleeping from the painkiller he had been given. Fiona was leaning over the stall, watching him when Nika and Ben arrived.

"Is he going to be okay?" Ben asked, without greeting.

Nika caught Fiona's eye, and they smiled at one another.

"I think so, Ben. The vet says he needs to sleep for a while and let his body fight the infection. But he should be all right."

She stepped back to make room for the boy to look into the stall.

"Congratulations," said Nika, quietly. "You won."

"Thanks. I've barely had a chance to think about it." "There's still time," said Nika. And then, "I'm glad you're staying."

"Me, too," said Fiona.

They chatted for a while, as Ben contented himself with watching the sleeping animal. After a half hour, Nika went over to him and put a hand on his shoulder. "We should go, Ben. I have things to do at home."

"Can't I stay?" he asked. "Please?"

Behind him, Fiona caught Nika's eye and nodded. Nika sighed with pretend exasperation.

"You will have to ask Ms. Campbell."

Ben turned pleading eyes to Fiona, and she smiled at him. "You can stay, Ben. I'll take you home."

"Thanks!"

"But I expect you home for dinner," said Nika sternly. "No later than six o'clock. You will set the table, and tonight's your night for dishes."

Ben would have agreed to anything. "Okay," he said, happily. And without a backward glance at his mother, he returned to his place at the stall.

Fiona walked with Nika to her truck.

"Thank you," said Nika. "This animal is all he can think of."

"He's good company," said Fiona. "I like having him here."

At a quarter to six, Fiona and Ben were in her car, driving to his house. The light had shifted, and the days were getting longer. Where only a month before the stars would already have been out, now daylight still remained. The spring snow lingered only in shady places along the edges of the roads where the plows had piled it. The rest of the land was clear, the fields of last year's grass golden in the late afternoon sun.

Fiona was imagining herself walking across them, her boots sinking into the spring mud. She lost herself in reverie, reliving the events of a few days before. She was more exhausted than she had ever been, both mentally and physically. Everything loomed large and bleak. She longed for Pete's comforting voice and his nonchalant approach to crises. Now that she had won the election, she was confronted with the perennial challenge of successful candidates: she had to do something, and she was damned if she knew what.

Ben, meanwhile, was lost in his own thoughts. There was something he needed to know, but he didn't quite know how to ask.

"Ms. Campbell," he began tentatively.

"What's up, Ben?" Fiona glanced at him sideways as she drove. His face was turned from her, looking out the window. She heard him take a deep breath.

"Are you going to tell?" he asked. "Are you going to tell my parents everything?"

Fiona was silent as she drove, thinking.

"I wasn't planning to, but to be honest, I haven't had time to think about it." She looked at him again, quickly. "What do you think I should do?"

He hadn't expected this question.

"I'm not sure." He hesitated, not wanting to ask for her silence, but desperately hoping for it.

Fiona looked in her rearview mirror, saw nothing coming, and pulled over to the side of the road. Surprised, Ben looked over at her, but as she began to speak, he broke the glance, and looked straight ahead.

"You know, Ben, everyone has things they don't tell anyone. Things they think, or feel, or do. Not because they are shameful, but because they are private." She watched his young face. He was listening earnestly, even though he wasn't looking at her.

"It's okay to have private things, Ben. It's part of what makes you human." She paused, unsure whether she should go on. "It's also part of what makes you grown-up."

He slowly turned his head to look at her.

"But," she said, and she waited until his eyes were on her face, "sharing our secrets with people we love is also something grown-ups do. It's not always easy, but it is one of the greatest bonds we have in life. The sharing and keeping of our deepest selves."

Ben frowned. Fiona couldn't tell whether he had understood what she meant, or whether it had made any difference. She needed to say one more thing.

"You're a young man, Ben. What you tell people is your decision. You have to decide what is right."

And with that, she pulled her car back onto the road and took him home.

That night, Elisabeth and Roger sat together on the porch, listening to the singing of the spring peepers. Rocco lay contentedly at their feet. It was a cool night, and breezy, but the fresh air was alluring and the house seemed stuffy by comparison. It was too nice to go in, so they sat together in companionable silence, a candle burning on the table between them.

Elisabeth, exhausted by the excitement of the election was about to suggest that they go in when Roger suddenly spoke.

"Listen," he said. "I have an idea. It's a plan. A plan for the future."

Elisabeth sat back in her chair and listened. After he finished speaking they were silent again. Elisabeth's mind was whirling with new ideas and possibilities, and she felt an intense awareness of her surroundings. The peepers seemed to be growing louder. "Possibly," Elisabeth thought, "there are more hatching every minute."

Roger cleared his throat and she looked at him. She hadn't realized she had been silent for so long. He would be expecting an answer of some kind.

"So," said Roger. "I also have a question. Something different from the other idea." He paused. "Would you like to come to yoga with me?"

Elisabeth smiled in the darkness. "I thought you'd never ask."

After she dropped Ben at home, Fiona contemplated stopping off at Nelsen's for some companionship, but she turned instead back toward Nancy's. When she pulled up, she saw Jim's truck parked in the drive. He was leaning over the stall when she came in, just as she had been doing so frequently the last twenty-four hours.

"I was worried about him," said Jim when he saw her. "I wanted to make sure he was okay. To see for myself."

Fiona smiled at him. "I've always said you have a soft heart for a ranger."

They stood together gazing at the sleeping animal. He already looked better, Fiona thought. It wasn't anything she could put her finger on, but he seemed whole, somehow, and healing, and different from the irascible creature she remembered. "Or maybe just clean. And quiet," she told herself wryly.

Jim broke into her thoughts. "Have you noticed anything strange?"

Fiona looked at him.

He was thinking carefully about his words. "He's not talking." He held her glance.

"Well, he's been sleeping a lot."

"Not all the time. You've seen him awake, haven't you?"

Fiona admitted that she had.

"Why do you think he's not?" she asked. "Speaking, I mean."

"Well, there are two possibilities. One: he's still not fully recovered... ."

He paused.

"And the other?" asked Fiona, puzzled.

"He isn't actually Robert."

That week, a review referring to a Men's Yoga Practice in Ephraim, Wisconsin, appeared in a well-known yoga magazine: "This drop-in practice is the perfect way to begin a day of relaxation. Set in a local coffee shop known as Ground Zero, the one-hour sequence is unguided. The Master, who does not speak, brilliantly allows his students to follow his example, internalizing, personalizing, and intensifying the path. What is most innovative is the Master's use of music to train the mind for the perfect state of relaxed awareness. The music presents a continual challenge to calm that improves balance, focus, and concentration. Afterward, there's always great coffee and conversation with fellow seekers. Don't miss this opportunity to start your vacation right."

It was late the next night when Fiona entered the barn and peered over the stall door. She had had a busy day of meetings, and had gone home to eat, planning to stay there. But she found herself unable to sleep, drawn to the barn and its mysterious inhabitant.

The Goat Formerly Known As Robert was lying in the center of a mound of straw. He looked toward her as Fiona approached with no sign of recognition. Fiona reached over the stall and touched his neck beneath the cone. He gazed at her dully.

"Hello, Robert," she said softly, testing his response.

He tried to turn his head away, but the cone prevented him.
"It's me. Fiona. Remember?"

She was hoping for a vocal response, but his eyes were glazed and he did not seem interested.

He sat sullenly, his head down. Fiona watched him for a long time, thinking. It was late when she finally left the barn and went out to her car.

The goat was still lying with his head down, facing the rear of his stall. Up the road she could hear the church bell ringing midnight.

Chapter Thirty-One

Fiona was on a train that was rolling slowly through a small village. Somewhere nearby was a voice from someone she couldn't see, that she couldn't associate with anyone in particular, but which was companionable and familiar.

As they passed places along the way the voice was saying to her, "See that old man dressed in rags on the corner? That's Lars. At the next little café look for the old woman, that will be Jake. The little girl nearby will be Ben. The man at the newsstand with the briefcase will be Eddie." And in each case, she would look, and below some deep and brilliant disguise she would recognize someone she knew, pretending to be someone completely different. It was not disquieting, merely fascinating, and she strained to identify who the actors were before the voice could identify them. In each case, she would catch some single quality: the slant of a profile, a hand gesture, or some indefinable aura of individuality that would help her to see through the disguise to the real person beneath. As they reached the far limits of the village, there was a bright light that suddenly shone into her face as from another train bearing down on her. She struggled ineffectually and without any particular alarm to get out of its path, but she could not get off the train she was on. She was running up and down the carriage of the train when she heard a strange pinging that sent an alarm into her being.

Wrestling herself awake, Fiona answered the phone at her bedside. It was Nancy's brusque voice, undiminished by the late hour. "I think you'd better come," she said.

Fear clutching her heart, Fiona stumbled to dress and find her keys.

There was a poignant stillness when she entered the barn a few minutes later. Nancy was sitting calmly in the venerable rocking chair she kept there. From the looks of it, the chair had born witness to generations of farmers' vigils. Nancy seemed unaware of any alarm Fiona may have felt.

"What's going on?" asked Fiona.

"Sit down," said Nancy, indicating a bench nearby. "Just wait."

Obediently, Fiona sat, her fear giving way to confusion.

The goat in the stall stirred. He was standing now, and he pivoted his body to be able to see the newcomer despite the cone on his head. His yellow eyes glittered. He eyed Fiona for a long time, seeming to be evaluating her by some standard known only to him. Returning the animal's gaze, she felt that it was likely she was coming up short.

Without warning, he opened his mouth and gave a piercing scream. Fiona jumped, her heart pounding. It sounded exactly the way Fiona imagined a man falling from a high place would sound. He screamed again, horrifyingly, for almost thirty seconds. Then again, and again, again, the screaming continued, sounding as if whole platoons of men were being murdered in Nancy's barn.

Recovering from her shock, Fiona looked over at Nancy, who, apart from occasionally wincing at the volume, sat composedly in her rocker, a small smile playing around the corners of her mouth.

"He woke up me doing this," she shouted above the noise. "About an hour ago. Rattled me so thoroughly I got my grand-dad's shotgun down off the wall before I came out here." She indicated the weapon leaning against a corner of the barn. "Fortunately I didn't need it. Couldn't for the life of me say when it was cleaned last."

Nancy did not appear rattled now. She rummaged in her pocket for her silver flask and offered it to Fiona, the screaming continuing all the while. "I'm taking this as a sign he's feeling better."

"Should we try to stop him?"

"I can't think how," said Nancy.

Fiona took the flask gratefully and drank. She felt admiration at the courage Nancy must have had to leave her house with the sound of screaming going on outside. The brandy burned going down, and Fiona felt its heat coursing through her limbs. The goat screamed on, its pitch rising from a man's scream to a woman's. It occurred to her that Robert's vocal idiosyncrasies had been nothing compared to this, or, if this goat was Robert, that he really had not been in need of any additional bad habits.

"Do you think anyone else can hear him?" shouted Fiona at last.

Nancy chuckled. "I guess we'll find out soon enough." She passed the silver flask again to Fiona. "Are you thinking what I'm thinking?"

Fiona wiped her mouth on her sleeve. "What are you thinking?"

"That this explains a lot of things. The tattered bicycle seats, all ripped to shreds. Piggy wouldn't eat leather. That's something a goat would do. And there was Bill Hanson's trampled orchard last fall." She paused reminiscently. "And don't forget those pregnant does at the Martin's place... ."

"Oh no." said Fiona in a small voice. "You don't think... ."

Nancy looked at her steadily.

"There was screaming at Windsome Farm. And Emily mentioned that she'd found the latches open several times. Goats are escape artists. Why shouldn't it work in reverse? It's certainly possible."

Fiona was digesting this information when they heard the sirens joining the cacophony of goat screaming.

Jim got there first, bursting into the barn, breathless from running up the drive. He looked first at the screaming goat, then at Nancy, then at Fiona, his face registering first surprise, then confusion, then dawning understanding.

The two women exchanged glances and suddenly began to laugh.

In moments there were more breathless men coming through the door, each bewildered: first separately; then together. Before long, there were ten would-be rescuers in the barn, all standing helplessly before the relentless screaming of an agitated goat and the convulsive laughter of Fiona and Nancy. Chief Bill Yahr looked on the scene with long-suffering patience.

"I suppose as long as you're all here," said Nancy at last, wiping her eyes, "You may as well have a drink." She opened the big bottom drawer of the desk in the corner, and pulled out a bottle she used to refill her flask, offering it first to the Chief. He took it, smiling tolerantly.

After the bottle had been passed around, the mood of the barn lifted, despite the screaming. Relief from months of worry over an inexplicable phenomenon now shifted into general hilarity. As the level in the bottle dwindled, several of the would-be rescuers began to join in, experimentally, with the screaming. Their companionable noisemaking was no match for the goat. Human voices tired more quickly, which was perhaps, thought Fiona, just as well.

Exhausted, she leaned her back against the wall and closed her eyes against the noise, noticing with surprise how one could become accustomed to anything. She felt someone sit next to her on the bench, and opened her eyes to see Jim. They exchanged a glance. Then he, too, leaned back against the wall, eyes closed, his legs stretched out in front of him.

Abruptly, without warning, the screaming stopped. The conversations that had been shouted over the racket were suddenly audible, and they quickly sputtered out.

Fiona looked over at the goat who might not be Robert. His eyes glittered in the warm light of the barn. If attention had been his goal, thought Fiona, he must be feeling extremely satisfied. As she watched, he turned his back on the crowd and began to rummage ravenously in his trough. It was the first time he had eaten since his rescue. Fiona looked over to see if Nancy had noticed. She caught Fiona's look, smiled, and nodded. Whoever he was, the goat was going to be okay. Fiona leaned back against the wall and nudged Jim with her elbow.

"We did it. He's going to be fine."

But Jim did not respond. He was sound asleep.

Chapter Thirty-Two ✤

The morning dawned with a sullen, gray light. Thick blue-black cumulus clouds covered the sky, signaling the shift of seasons. Spring would come soon, but it had not yet arrived. The water moved in heavy, unshining waves, striking the ferry with slow thuds. Nearly all the ice was gone, melted or blown north of Death's Door. There were only a few remaining white cliffs of ice shoved up against portions of the shorelines. A stiff wind kept the ferry crew moving quickly and without much conversation. Passengers stayed in their cars with the engines running and the heaters on.

On the second trip, before heading back, Pali stayed on deck as long as possible, dawdling with unnecessary tasks. Young Joe was in the pilot house. He had just passed his licensing test to be a captain. It was Pali's helm today, but Pali was giving him the space to garner a sense of being in command, not always an easy thing for a young man. At two minutes to the hour, Pali headed up the stairs to the wheelhouse, taking the steps two at a time, using the railings to balance himself. As he crossed the upper deck, Pali could see Young Joe through the windows, standing at the helm. He went quickly up the several steps, opened the door, and stepped into the warmth. It was a relief to be out of the wind. He hadn't realized how thoroughly chilled he was. He remembered suddenly, and with pleasure, the thermos of coffee he had tucked into a corner.

Young Joe looked up, and nodded.

"You can take her out," Pali said, as Joe began to step back for him.

The engines started their slow rumble, and Joe stood at the pilot's wheel looking ahead, his face alight with pride and pleasure. He had a beginner's sense of extra caution, and he was doing everything by the book, his whole body on alert like a young dog out hunting for the first time.

As they passed the shelter of the breakwater and headed into open water, suddenly Joe stiffened. Pali could see it happen.

"You all right, Joe?"

Joe did not answer. He seemed frozen at the wheel. Pali could see his face from the side. Joe's eyes were focused straight ahead, a look of shock or fear on his face.

"Joe," said Pali again. "You okay?" Pali stepped forward instinctively to take the helm, but Joe held fast to the wheel, and Pali, concerned about his young crewman, but with his duty always first in his mind, debated whether to push Joe aside and take over. The ship, though, was clearly in no danger, and although he stayed near and on alert, Pali did not force the situation.

After what seemed like forever Pali saw Young Joe's body relax. Joe's head went down for a moment, and then he looked up again, taking deep breaths.

"Joe," said Pali. "Are you sick? What's going on? You have to tell me."

"Joe! Answer me!"

Joe took a deep breath and spoke, his eyes still ahead. "I felt it, Captain," he said with an odd formality. "I felt it."

"You felt what?" Pali was beginning to be impatient. "Come on, Joe. Out with it! Talk some sense."

Joe turned his head and looked straight into Pali's eyes. "The ghost. I felt the ghost. I felt his hand on my shoulder. Just like you said."

Pali said nothing, unable to gather his thoughts. He did not ask any questions. He didn't know that he was silent, or that he was standing and staring. Joe was invisible to him in that moment, and he felt he was alone in the pilot house.

A change in the light made Pali shift his gaze. He saw a faint gleam ahead, and in one swift moment, a shaft of sunlight pierced the blue clouds and hit the water. The lake was alight with blue gleaming, changing the bleak landscape in an instant. In that moment, as if a switch had been flipped inside his brain, Pali felt an old insistent rhythm. In that flash of sun, the lines of his poems—not one or two, but all of them—formed in his mind with crystalline clarity and played their soft music in his head and heart. They were not lost. They were all there, one after another, spinning their lines unceasingly. Immersed in their music, Pali watched as the wind broke the clouds for one more moment of light. It glimmered in a straight golden line from the open sky to the water, and then, in the next second, it was gone.

Pali stood still. He felt his heart beating within him. He looked ahead at the shifting, blue-gray waters that a moment before had sparkled in the sun. The Island was ahead, serene in the soft light of a cloudy morning. He felt the slow diffusion of emotion in his chest, his arms, his body, and he knew in that moment that all was well. He was bathed in a tide of gratitude.

He put his hand on the shoulder of his helmsman.

"I'll take her, Joe," he said. The two men, no longer separated by age, looked into one another's eyes with mutual understanding. Joe stepped back to make room for his captain.

His mind resonant with the rhythms of his words, Pali took the ferry's wheel in his two hands and turned his eyes toward home.

The sound of the Skype ring woke Fiona from a deep sleep. She wasn't sure at first where she was until she realized she had fallen asleep on the couch. As she moved her head, she caught the faint smell of barn in her hair.

"Hey," said Pete. "Guess what?"

"What?" Fiona's voice croaked a bit.

"I'm taking some time off. I've been accumulating it for a while now."

"And you're coming here?"

"If you'll have me."

Fiona smiled sleepily. "I guess I will. Will you be here for my swearing in?"

"That depends. I'm flying out tomorrow. I'll be there in three days—depending on how you count."

"That gives me time to get some food in the house."

"And to throw away the black bananas."

It was after nine o'clock when Pali went in to say good night to his son. Ben was sitting up in bed with only a reading light on, his book face-down on the blankets, the new badge in animal husbandry proudly displayed above the desk nearby. He was wearing one of Pali's old t-shirts, still far too large for him, and a disreputable but beloved pair of sweatpants. The edges of his hair were wet from washing, and he smelled of soap and toothpaste. Pali felt again the sweep of gratitude he had felt that morning. He sat without speaking on the edge of his son's bed.

"Dad," said Ben, after a moment.

"Yes?"

"Dad, I've got to tell you something." Ben paused and shifted his position, gathering his courage.

Pali, aware that there was some struggle going on, waited, patiently, as he would if there were a wild animal he didn't want to frighten.

Ben took a deep breath, and turned his eyes on his father.

"You know how we take the oath in Boy Scouts? The oath to be morally straight?"

Pali nodded solemnly, but said nothing. He thought he had an inkling of what was coming.

"Dad, I've got to tell you something. And you've got to believe me. I swear I'm not making this up."

Pali frowned slightly. This was not going in the direction he had expected. He had expected some confession involving the other night's mishap. He knew most of the story already from

Jim, but he had been waiting to hear Ben tell it.

"The other night, on the lake... " Ben swallowed. He was about to jump off an emotional precipice, and he hesitated for long seconds as his father counseled himself to silence. "Rescuing the goat.... Something happened."

Pali turned his full attention to not showing any reaction. Whatever this was, he wanted Ben to know he could say it. He sat very still, trying not to deter this confession by showing his own feelings.

"There was someone there, Dad. Someone helping me. At least.... I think it was someone."

Pali felt his breath stop.

"I didn't see anyone. But I felt him. I felt a hand. I felt someone pulling me out of the water; helping me pull the goat out of the water."

Pali did not move or stir, his eyes fixed on his son's face. He noticed suddenly something he hadn't seen until now. The chubby sweetness was almost gone. The brow and cheekbones were gaining definition. It wasn't the face of child anymore.

"I didn't see him. I don't know who it was. But it was a feeling. I knew it. I knew he was there the whole time. He helped me find Ms. Campbell. He was with me the whole time."

There was a long silence as Pali tried to adjust his mind to what his son had just told him.

"Dad?" Ben's face was worried, fearful. "Do you believe me?"

At last Pali could breathe. He put his hands on Ben's shoulders, and looked into his son's eyes. "Yes, Ben," he said. "I believe you."

As with so much of life on the Island, any occasion was an event to be turned into a gathering of the entire community. Fiona was duly sworn in at the town hall, a ceremony that took place in front of the long folding tables where the ballots had been counted. The familiar smell of brewing coffee mingled with the scents of the various baked goods arrayed across the back of the room.

As the ceremony ended, Lars Olafsen came up to Fiona, took her hand and placed a quarter in it. "I have something for you," he said. His eyes twinkled. "It's the coin I tossed the day you won. I thought you might like it."

"Thank you," said Fiona. "I'm going to need some luck."

The outgoing chairman smiled knowingly, and patted her shoulder before drifting into the crowd. He was soon replaced by his fellow citizens, all eager to shake their new chairwoman's hand and begin to tell her their complaints.

Among the last to offer congratulations was Emily, who came up to Fiona in the parking lot outside the community room.

"You'll have your hands full, now," warned Emily, after she had shaken Fiona's hand. "But I want you to know that we are here as a resource for you. When you find yourself over your head—even if it's something as simple as advice on Island culture, you just give me a call." Fiona smiled rather weakly and made her thanks. "We'll see you later at Nelsen's, but first we need to get home to the chores. There's so much to do, you know!" With a final pat on Fiona's arm, she headed off.

As Emily pulled away, Fiona noticed that there was a new bumper sticker on the back of the gleaming, black SUV. It said: "If you think you are the solution to all the Island's problems, do us all a favor and go back where you came from." Watching her drive off, Fiona considered the wisdom of this advice.

As the festivities ended, people naturally gravitated to Nelsen's, and the usual group of Fiona's closest friends and supporters gathered at the bar. Fiona was swept around the room, moved from one group to the next. Pete, who had arrived only that afternoon, watched her passage for a moment before heading off to find some familiar faces.

There was a celebratory feeling in the air, assisted by the growing conviction that spring had finally arrived. The conversation was buoyant and filled with laughter. Eddie was at the ready, shelves of glasses and bottles filled with various elixirs sparkling behind him.

"Gentlemen," he said, in greeting, as Pali and Pete stepped up to the bar at the same time.

"Eddie," said Pali, with great good cheer. "It's been a good day. And all because you got your demons. Even though they were in blue uniforms rather than black cloaks."

Eddie grinned. "Blue uniforms and an orange jumpsuit. I couldn't have written a better libretto."

Pali turned to Pete. "I can't help having the feeling that you had something to do with the way things turned out. But I don't know how you did it."

Pete shrugged modestly.

"Let's just say that Representative Hillard made some remarks at his town hall event that suggested to me that he was not a model citizen. You remember. He asked me to step outside."

In response to a call from a customer further down the bar, Eddie held up his hand to acknowledge an order and leaned in to hear Pete's story. The bar was noisy, and Pete's voice was low.

"After he inquired about procuring some… paid companionship… I suggested to a friend of mine in law enforcement that he might be a person of interest. The good Assemblyman did the rest."

Pali looked puzzled.

"Paid companionship? What the Hell was that about?"

"Stella," said Eddie calmly. "She was spreading the story all over the island. Didn't you know?"

Pete took up the story. "Apparently, his loving aunt had informed him that Fiona and I were involved in an international prostitution ring, and he was interested in our services. That was why he wanted to talk to me that night."

Pali's face turned red with anger. "She was saying that?" He looked at Pete, furious. "I would have slugged the guy. And possibly Stella, too." He looked down at his glass. "Still might," he muttered under his breath.

Pete finished folding his bill around a tack and a quarter. There was a pause as he was visibly wrestling with some thought.

"Actually, not slugging that guy may have been the hardest thing I've ever done. What a slime-slash-scum bag he is."

Eddie smiled as he wiped the bar. "Jake sure called that one."

"So, what actually happened was perfect justice," said Pali, still musing. "It was Stella's own rumors that triggered the whole series of events leading to Hillard's felony charges and her car being impounded. That, I believe, is the very definition of karma."

"And the drugs," added Eddie, with satisfaction. "Don't forget the drugs."

Pete grinned. "Well, I couldn't have foreseen that one. But every once in a while the right thing happens. Fate just needs a little assistance now and then."

Pali nodded with ungrudging respect.

Eddie was thinking. "So you have a friend in law enforcement?" he asked.

Pete nodded. "An old friend in Chicago. We went to school together, and he's with the FBI. Hillard's questions made me think he might be interested in our Assemblyman's activities." He smiled reminiscently. "And he was. Fortunately, the good Assemblyman cooperated by being even worse than I suspected."

Pete flung the little bundle he had made at the ceiling with an artful flick of the wrist, and ducked to avoid the falling quarter.

Pali caught the coin in one hand, slapped it on the bar and started chuckling.

"What's the joke?" Eddie was mixing old-fashioneds at remarkable speed.

"He is," said Pali tipping his head toward Pete.

Pete looked at him inquiringly.

"You're the source of the whole thing," said Pali. "You really are the *deus ex machina.*"

Pete smiled modestly and shrugged.

Eddie looked at Pali over the bar and their eyes met in a moment of mutual satisfaction. They were both profoundly pleased with themselves.

Eddie stopped his work, put his hands on the bar emphatically, and looked at Pete.

"Commendatore," he said, almost hearing the music from the operatic finale in his head. "I salute you!" He slid the drinks he had been making across the bar to waiting hands, and turned his attention back to Pali and Pete. "What'll it be? It's on me."

"Brandy," said Pete. "Thanks." He turned to Pali. "And I'll buy one for you. What'll you have?"

"The same," said Pali.

Eddie put their glasses before them and poured one for himself. The three men looked at one another and raised their glasses.

"Skal!" said Pali.

"Skal!" said the others. And they drank.

Later that evening, Fiona and Pete were walking on the rocks along the shore where the goat rescue had occurred. The ice had almost gone, making its slow shifting shapes and eerie clunking sounds. It was a chilly spring evening, with a brisk wind coming from the water, but the frogs were singing, and the sky was clear. Fiona shivered, and shoved her hands deeper into her pockets.

Pete was absently skipping stones into the waves, in the open places where the ice chunks had drifted away. There was a waxing moon, and its light on the water was enough to see by.

"You know," said Fiona to Pete, "you can't go through life rescuing me from situations."

"I was about to tell you the same thing," said Pete, mischievously.

Fiona was indignant.

"I didn't ask for your help."

"True," said Pete, as he sent a stone skimming out, with two full skips.

"I didn't even know where you were or how to reach you."

"Also true."

"And even if I had known, I wouldn't have asked."

"As I suspected."

"So?"

"So?" he echoed.

"So you can hardly advance the theory that I was waiting to be rescued."

"No, actually that is not my theory." Pete was crouching on the beach, engrossed in sorting out the best stones for skipping. "My theory is that you needed to be rescued. A small, but vital difference." He stood up, and took aim. His stone sailed over the water with five skips.

"Maybe I could have won all by myself."

"Maybe," said Pete seriously. "Your turn."

Fiona accepted the stone he handed her, smooth and flat, and sent it off into the water. She got one skip, and shrugged, smiling.

Pete was bent down again, hunting for more stones. "Is it so hard for you to admit that you needed me?" he asked, looking up at her. "That I could be helpful to you?" He gathered a handful of carefully chosen stones and stuffed them into his pockets. "Is it so hard for you to understand that I might want to be needed? Or that I could enjoy helping you?"

Standing, he looked at her, his head tilted to one side, and tested the weight of one of the larger stones, tossing it up and down in his throwing hand. "Isn't that the whole point of being in love with someone? To need and to be needed?"

Fiona looked at him astonished. Pete seemed to her—as he had seemed from the very start—to be someone utterly complete and self-sufficient. Not someone who needed someone else.

"Are you saying that you need me?" she asked.

"I'm saying that I love you, silly ass," said Pete. He sent his last stone skimming over the water with one, two, three, four, five, six skips before it sank beneath the waves. "And I'm also saying that your throw is sloppy. You need to work on your wrist action. If you're going to live on an Island, you have to be able to skip stones. It's a known requirement." He brushed off his hands with an air of finality. "I win. Madame Chairman, you owe me a drink."

Fiona smiled at him, a slow, warm smile. "You're in luck. I have a flask in the car—a victory gift from Nancy. Is bourbon okay?"

"Perfection." He smiled back. "No ice."

Fiona was already on her way up the little hill to the car, and called over her shoulder. "Don't go away."

"I won't," said Pete. And turning his back to the water, he stood, hands in pockets, to watch her go.

ACKNOWLEDGMENTS

Novelists spend rather a lot of time in a room alone, making things up. That's all very well, but it's not enough, and this book would not have been possible without the help of many kind and talented people. To wit:

Bob Kalinoski, Mary Beth Sancomb-Moran, Dionne King, and Alicia Manning: friends, guinea pigs, and proof readers extraordinaire.

My friend, Jodie Tierney, who made me laugh out loud by myself for about fifteen minutes when she suggested the idea of Roger doing yoga.

Novelist and friend, Mike Nichols, for his honest critique and good counsel, which I took. Mostly.

My island hosts, Susan and George Ulm, who take good care of me and give delightful cocktail parties—which isn't always the same thing—and Bosun, who still finds Moses annoying, but will now occasionally deign to play.

Captain Bill, Captain Joel, and Captain Eric, for their camaraderie, gossip, and wisdom, and for filling my head with island lore.

My editor, Megan Trank; my publicist, Felicia Minerva; my production editor and artist, Michael Short; and my publisher, Eric Kampmann for their talent, patience, dedication, and sense of humor.

Pete and Moses, for keeping me company in my work and in my travels, for reminding me what matters, and most especially for their very effective assistance in procrastination, which is essential to all writing.

Roger Kimball for his infinite generosity, kindness, and guidance.

And of course, my unfailingly supportive, charming, and erudite husband, Charlie, who is my best and most appreciative critic.

My affection and gratitude are not enough, but it's all I have.

J.F. Riordan
April 2016

Excerpt From J.F. Riordan's new novel Robert's Rules,
Book Three in the North of the Tension Line series

ROBERT'S
RULES

If you have no trouble, buy a goat.

—PERSIAN PROVERB

PROLOGUE

My earliest memories are of fire.

I was lying in my crib in the dark, and my father woke me, wrapped me in my blankets, and carried me from the house. There were sirens coming closer. I remember the scratchy wool of his jacket on my cheek, its dusty smell in my nostrils, and the feel of the cool night air. Then the smoke was everywhere.

My mother and father and sister and brother were all there, with jackets over their night clothes. My father carried me in his arms as we all moved toward the fire down the street.

"The pig farm," my mother said.

I knew the pig farm. I knew the comfortable smell of well kept animals; the sight of the red barn on the hill, the pleasures of catching a glimpse of a a tractor, or better yet, a family of piglets, on an afternoon ride.

Instead, I could see the silhouettes of men against flames that reached into the sky, the yellow and orange fire that flickered and shot up; the black shadows of men in big coats, and boots, and helmets, carrying hoses and axes.

There was a low rumbling sound from the diesel engines of the fire trucks; the crackling static voices of the radios and walkie talkies.

My father hoisted me up on his shoulders, and I could look

down at the tangle of hoses, the gleaming puddles everywhere, with the circling red lights. I could hear more sirens in the distance, more fire companies arriving, the undulating shift of their sound changing as they moved.

"The poor animals," murmured my mother, watching the flames. There was another smell in the air that was not wood burning.

I was afraid, but I did not cry.

Maybe I slept on my father's head.

At last the men's voices changed from shouts to words, the brilliant, intoxicating light in the night was gone, leaving a gray dawn. The red lights of the trucks still turned, reflecting in the puddles of water as the firemen coiled the hoses. The voices on the radios still crackled, but with less frequency, as the fire men, weary, diminished their conversation.

I do not remember being tucked back into bed. But I remember the flames.

I always remember the flames.

It was after school on a warm June afternoon, and Ben Palsson was on his way to Schoolhouse Beach. The public entrance to the beach cut through the island cemetery, and graves from other centuries along with those from the recent past were on either side. It was a pretty cemetery, carefully maintained, surrounded by trees, and within the sound of the waves of Lake Michigan. The place held no fear for Ben, who at the age of ten was fully confident that death was for other people, never for him.

Ben always went for a ramble before heading home from school. These days his pattern had shifted a bit, in order to go first to visit the rescued goat living in Nancy Iverssen's barn. It was Ben who had found the animal while it was living in the wild, befriended it, and saved it from drowning when it had fallen through the ice. These experiences had formed a deep bond in Ben's young heart.

But now that spring had finally come to the island, the warm weather was so enticing that even his love of animals in general—and of this animal in particular—could not keep him from his walk. The visit today had been brief.

Ben was looking forward eagerly to the vast expanse of summer vacation stretching before him when he would have all the time in the world. Only one more day.

He leaped to try to touch the low-hanging branches of a hundred year old maple tree along the way. It was getting closer, but he still couldn't quite make it. Maybe in that far away time at the end of summer.

A small childlike tune was playing over and over in Fiona's head: "totally meaningless drivel, totally meaningless drivel." She instinctively liked the rhythm of it, with the two three-syllable words at the beginning, and the harder sounding two-syllable word at the end. Its rhythm reminded her of a cart rolling along a bumpy sidewalk. It played in her head in minor thirds, like a child's taunt. She thought suddenly of a Yeats poem she had learned as a child.

Us who are old, old and gay,
O so old!
Thousands of years, thousands of years,
If all were told.

"Songs made of words," she thought. She still loved those ancient rhythms that played like music in her head. She often found Yeats obtuse, filled with obscure references to Irish myth, as, in fact, was this. But she loved the music of this poem, and had memorized it the first time she heard it. Its rhythms, she reflected, were actually quite complex.

She was unaware that a vague drifting smile had come over her face as she sat fiddling mindlessly with her pen. Her yellow legal pad was covered with doodles: storm clouds, lightning bolts, flying cattle, and a rather loopy and bedraggled daisy. Fiona hated meetings.

Unfortunately, as the newly-elected Town Chairman of Washington Island, meetings were the one thing she had in abundance these days.

"Fiona? What do you think?"

This question, which she had dreaded, now burst through her awareness. She took a moment to look at the faces around the table, all looking to her with varying degrees of patience and condescension. By and large, her fellow members of the town board did not expect much from this newcomer—from Chicago, of all places—and even though most of them had voted for her, it had been more a case of voting against her opponent—the almost universally detested Stella DesRosiers— than an endorsement of Fiona's knowledge or experience. They were united, at least, in their conviction that she had neither. Lately Fiona herself was increasingly convinced that they were right.

She took a deep breath and changed her smile to one of rueful deference. Her chin was down as she raised her eyes and looked directly at each individual around the table, reading them one by one.

No matter what her fellow islanders might think, Fiona was no fool. She was fully aware that the triviality of the issue was inversely proportional to the rancor it could stir in the hearts of Islanders. Though she had discovered this insight into human behavior on the Island, it is a universal truth of small town life.

She smiled again. "This is a matter of precedent, and I think we should handle this exactly as it has been handled in the past. No one appreciates changes in tradition, and there's no good reason to upset everyone about this. As Lars Olafsen likes to say, "if it ain't broke, don't fix it."

This allusion to Fiona's beloved predecessor was greeted with solemn nods around the table. During his decades of leadership, Lars had used a steady hand and good sense to herd this particular group of the Island's notoriously unruly cats.

"I agree," said Mary Woldt, who was prone to agreeing with whatever had been said last. There were murmurs of agreement as heads nodded around the table.

Fiona sighed inwardly. Another example of committee work in action. One decisive voice could almost always determine the matter, but only after hours of wandering conversation. Totally meaningless drivel, sang the child's voice in her head.

"Well, that's enough for today, then," she said briskly. She started to rise. "Thank you, everyone."

"But what about the fire department question?" asked Tom Sumner. Fiona stopped, as did everyone else around the table.

"That's too important to take up as a secondary matter," said Fiona, feeling secretly proud of herself for her quickness. "And we need to give notice for it to be on the agenda. Let's address it first thing next time when we're all fresh." And with a grace and swiftness that would have made Lars Olafsen proud, Fiona gathered her doodle-filled notes and glided smoothly and smilingly from the room.

A small voice from her inner self observed disapprovingly. "You are starting to sound like a politician," it said. Fiona shoved this unpleasant thought aside and replaced it with anticipation of a well-earned glass of scotch.

On her way home from the meeting, Fiona stopped by, as always, at Nancy's farm to make a visit. Having fully recovered from his lake trauma, the Goat Formerly Known as Robert was there, in the field along the drive, industriously demolishing some small scrubby bushes along the fence.

Fiona's own barn had been destroyed in the fire that had supposedly also caused the demise of the original Robert, and Nancy had kindly offered to host for the time being.

Fiona was still unsure whether this goat was hers, or some other goat. He did not appear to recognize her, despite her regular visits, nor had he demonstrated any of Robert's uncanny vocal abilities. This goat, it appeared, merely made blood-curdling screams at unpredictable intervals. The first Robert's peculiar speaking abilities had been preferable, Fiona felt.

She leaned over the fence and spoke to the animal with a

mixture of acerbity and reluctant affection. If, in fact, he were Robert, he had been practically her sole companion during her first year on the Island. She had come to realize rather belatedly that the responsibility of his care had given her early days here a focus and purpose that had kept her going through a particularly bitter winter. It had not been an unmitigated good time, however, and their relationship—if that's what you'd call it, she thought drily to herself—had been a rocky one.

Robert was not a creature whose personality inspired devotion, and yet he seemed to fit well with Fiona's unacknowledged affinity for eccentric characters.

Leaning on the fence, Fiona mused over the dramatic and unpredictable shifts in her life during the course of less than two years. It had started when she had quit her highly stressful job as newspaper reporter in Chicago, and moved to Ephraim Wisconsin in hope of finding some tranquility. So far the tranquility had proven elusive.

Within a few months after her arrival in Door County, she had accepted a dare that she couldn't survive the winter on Washington Island, bought a house, acquired a goat as a gift, held on through a difficult winter which had included a campaign to publicly humiliate her and drive her from the Island, endured a barn fire in which Robert seemed to have perished—until he didn't, or possibly did—decided to run for Chairman of the Town Board, mounted a campaign against her vicious neighbor, Stella, won, and now was keeping body and soul together through a grim series of particularly dull and mind-numbing meetings.

There was, of course, one adventure that had more than

made up for the various trials of her Island life. Smiling to herself, she said goodbye to the indifferent animal and headed home, where, undoubtedly, Peter Landry was waiting. Even more undoubtedly, he had a scotch already poured.